HERE COMES the SUN

HERE

COMES

the

SUN

NICOLE DENNIS-BENN

ONEWORLD

A Oneworld Book

First published in Great Britain and Australia
by Oneworld Publications, 2017

ISBN 978-1-78607-124-8 (hardback)
ISBN 978-1-78607-125-5 (export paperback)
ISBN 978-1-78607-126-2 (eBook)

Printed and bound in Great Britain by Clays Ltd, St Ives plc

Oneworld Publications
10 Bloomsbury Street
London
WC1B 3SR
United Kingdom

For Addy and Jamaica

PART I
God Nuh Like Ugly

1

THE LONG HOURS MARGOT WORKS AT THE HOTEL ARE NEVER documented. Her real work is not in answering the telephones that ring off the hook, or writing up delinquent housekeepers for sleeping on the beds and watching TV when they're supposed to be cleaning. Her real work is after hours when everyone has bid their goodbyes and piled up in the white Corollas—robot taxis—at the massive gate of the resort, which will take them home to their shabby neighborhoods, away from the fantasy they help create about a country where they are as important as washed-up seaweed.

Margot has been employee of the month for several months in a row, because she was the first to arrive and the last to leave. And for good reason. Requests are called in, not in conversational tones but in code that only Margot knows in case anyone is listening on the line. "*Ackee*" means he wants to taste her down there. Foreign men love that. "*Banana*" means he wants her to suck him off. "*Sundae*" means he intends to be kinky—anything goes. Of course they know she's in business, because she makes sure to slip them a wink on the first day of their arrival. Flattered, they initiate conversation. Margot flirts, reading their stray glances, which almost always land and linger between her exposed cleavage. That is Margot's cue for a forward invitation. She goes to the employee restroom to freshen up, spray perfume between her breasts, and powder her face before sauntering to the client's room. She undresses for the client, whose main goal is usually to satisfy a deep curiosity that he never had the balls to satiate with the women in his own country. Like a black woman's breasts, for instance. Many of these men want to know the shape of them; the nipples, whether or not they are the same color as tar pressed on the heels of their leather shoes from the paved roads in Europe or America; or if black nipples have in them the richness of topsoil after a thorough rain shower. They want to touch. And she lets them. Their eyes widen like children ogling baby frogs for the first time, careful to hold them so they don't spring from their grasp. She doesn't see it as demeaning. She sees it as merely satisfying the curiosity of foreigners; foreigners who pay her good money to be their personal tour guide on the island of her body. Margot stashes the money in her purse when she's done and hurries home. By then the robot taxis are scarce, so she walks into town and waves for one there. She has long ago rid herself of any feelings of disgust. She used to stay back and shower in the clients' rooms, scrubbing every part of her until her skin was raw. These days she goes straight home and falls asleep with the smell of semen sunken in her pores. Replacing the disgust is a liquid hope that settles inside her chest and fills her with purpose. She rolls over in the bed she shares with her sister knowing that one day she won't have to do this. That one day Thandi will make everything better.

But until then, she must work.

On this night she looks both ways to see if the coast is clear. The hotel maids have all left, and so have management and most hotel staff. The concierge, Paul, is the only one working. Since it's almost midnight, the night front desk clerks, Abby and Joseph, take turns resting on the sofa in the office. Margot doesn't pass their desk when she exits the hotel. She exits from the side by the pool, surprised to see Paul outside smoking a cigarette.

"Good night, Margot," Paul says with a slight bow. He's always polite, so polite that Margot wonders what he knows. She wonders if he hides his contempt behind that poise. Does he whisper to the other concierges that he sees her leave the hotel late at night? Does he tell them that he has caught her on more than one occasion adjusting her blouse and skirt after coming out of a guest's room? Such occurrences would have helped the man to put two and two together, but then again, he's not so bright. And for this, Margot is grateful.

Outside, the night is cool. The stars are sprinkled across the sky like grains of salt. The chirps of crickets in the bougainvillea bushes follow behind her like gossip, their hissing sounds deafening. She walks to the street, thankful for the anonymity the darkness provides. In town, the regular taxi drivers are there: Maxi, Dexter, Potty, Alistair. Maxi jingles his keys first. It's a sign to the other drivers that he'll be the one to take her. "Whappen, sweetness?" Margot blows him a kiss. They grew up together and attended the same basic school, primary school, and secondary school. Maxi dropped out of secondary school, embraced Rastafarianism, and started referring to himself as "I an' I." He smokes ganja all day and by night he's a taxi driver and a dealer to the tourists who are adventurous enough to go looking for ganja in the town.

"Wha g'wan, Maxi?" She settles in the front seat of the taxi. The smell of peeled oranges and smoke greets her. She begins to wonder if the scent will stick. But then again, she has her own scent.

"Me deh yah." Maxi starts the ignition. His dreadlocks are a thick, matted pile on his head. He tells her about his two children, whom she always inquires about for the sake of conversation that doesn't involve flirtation. One of them just started primary school and the other one is just starting basic school. They're from two different mothers, women Margot also grew up with. Women she no longer associates with because of their small minds and quickness to judge. "*So she t'ink she is big shot now, eh, working in di hotel. Look pon har, nuh. Thirty years old an' no man, no children. Har pumpum mussi dry up. Can't even come down from har trone fi fuck right. She t'ink she too nice.*"

"When yuh g'wan get yuh own car, Margot?" Maxi asks. "Ah hear seh di hotel pay good, good money."

Margot leans back on the leather seat and breathes in the pungent smells. "Soon." She looks out the window. Although it's pitch-black, she can tell she's passing by the sea. For a moment she wants to give her thoughts freedom to roam in this dark, in this uncertainty.

"How soon?" Maxi asks.

"What? Yuh dat desperate to go out of business?" She smiles at him—it's a slow, easy smile; her first real one all day. Her job entails a conscious movement of the jaw, a curve of the mouth to reveal teeth, all teeth—a distraction from the eyes, which never hold the same enthusiasm, but are practiced all the same to maintain eye contact with guests. "*It's a wonderful day at Palm Star Resort, how may I help you?*" "*Good morning, sir.*" "*Yes, ma'am, let me get that for you.*" "*No, sir, we don't offer a direct shuttle to Kingston, but there's one to Ocho Rios.*" "*May I help you with anything else, ma'am?*" "*Your shuttle is outside waiting on you, sir.*" "*You have a good day, now. I'm here if you need anything. No problem.*"

"We jus' haffi stop meeting like this. Dat's all," Maxi says.

Margot returns her attention outside. "As soon as Thandi gets through school. Yuh know how dat goes."

Maxi chuckles softly. When she looks at him, she sees the flash of his teeth, which seem luminous in the dark. "*Yuh know how dat goes.*" He mimics her.

"What?"

"Nottin'."

"What's di mattah with you, Maxi?"

He uses one hand to smooth the mustache over his wide mouth. In school all her friends had crushes on him. They thought he looked like Bob Marley, with the naps in his head that grew longer and longer, his peanut-brown skin, and his rebel ways. Once he told a teacher that she was ignorant for believing Christopher Columbus discovered Jamaica. "*Wha' 'bout di indigenous people who were here first?*" He was always book-smart, using words no one had ever heard used in everyday conversations: *indigenous, inequality, uprising, revolution, mental slavery.* He skipped classes to read books about Marcus Garvey, telling anyone who would listen that real history was in those books. The principal, Mr. Rhone, a high yellow man from St. Elizabeth, grew concerned about Maxi's rebelliousness, fearing it might influence other students, and expelled him. Maxi hadn't been back to school since. Had he not filled his head with rubbish about freedom and Africa, he would've been a doctor, a lawyer, a politician, or some other big shot by now, since he had certainly been the smartest boy in school. Margot doesn't want the same thing to happen to her sister. Like Maxi, Thandi is book-smart. She has the potential to be somebody. Margot has to make sure that Thandi doesn't ruin it for herself.

"Yuh put too much pressure pon di poor chile. Why yuh don't focus on your own dreams?"

"My dream is for my sister to be successful."

"And what's her dream?"

"Same."

"Yuh eva ask har?"

"Maxi, what's with all dis talk?"

"Jus' saying if yuh eva ask yuh sista what is her dreams. Yuh so set on pushing her. One day di bottom aggo drop out."

"Max, stop wid dis foolishness. Unlike certain people I know, Thandi 'ave ambition."

"*Certain people.*" Maxi grimaces. Again he runs his hand over his faint mustache. "I an' I did know weh me want long ago. An' it didn't have nothing to do wid weh dem teach inna school. Dem creating robots outta our children, Margot. Is di white man's philosophy dem learning. What about our heritage and culture?" He kisses his teeth. "Ah Babylon business dem ah fill up di children's minds wid. Yuh sista, Thandi, is a sweet girl. She know har book. But as ah say, when pot boil too long di wata dry out an' di bottom aggo drop out."

Margot holds a hand to his face like a stop sign. "Ah t'ink we done wid dis convahsation."

They fall into the hum of the silence. Maxi begins to whistle as he concentrates on the dark road ahead of them. Only the white lines are visible, and Margot tries to count them to calm herself. Of course she has dreams. She has always had dreams. Her dream is to get away as far as possible from here. Maybe America, England, or someplace where she can reinvent herself. Become someone new and uninhibited; a place where she can indulge the desires she has resisted for so long. The hotel actually doesn't pay much, but this Margot cannot say to anyone. She dresses nicely to go to work, her dove-gray uniform carefully pressed, each pleat carefully aligned; her hair straightened and combed into a neat bun, not a strand out of place except for the baby hairs slicked down with gel around the edges to give the impression of good hair; and her makeup meticulously perfect, enough powder to make her seem lighter than she is; a glorified servant. Maybe that's how Alphonso—her white Jamaican boss—sees her. A glorified servant. As heir to his father's Wellington empire—which includes coffee farms, rum estates, and properties all over the island, from Portland to Westmoreland, including Palm Star Resort—he was nice enough to keep her aboard after firing everyone else that his father, the late Reginald Wellington Senior, had hired. At first she despised herself for letting him touch her. But then she despised herself for the pride that made her believe she had a choice. What she got from it (and continues to get from it) was better than scrubbing floors. She didn't want to lose this opportunity. All she wanted in the beginning was to be exposed to other worlds, anything that could take her out of this squalor and give her a chance to get away from Delores and the memory of what her mother had done to her.

Maxi nudges Margot on the elbow. "How yuh push up yuh mouth suh? Relax, man." He smirks and she looks away, trying to resist.

"Yuh so dedicated to yuh duties as big sistah," Maxi says. "Ah find it very honorable. Jah know." He reaches over and touches her knee with his hand. He leaves it there. She takes his hand and moves it. Fifteen years ago, when she briefly dated him in high school, this would've sent waves throughout her anatomy. Now it doesn't feel the same. No other touch feels the same.

When Maxi approaches the foot of the hill, Margot tells him to stop the car. "Ah can walk from here," she says. Maxi squints through the dark as though trying to see what's out there. "Yuh sure? Why yuh always mek me stop here? Me know weh yuh live. Why not just mek me drop yuh there?"

"Maxi, I'll be fine from here." She takes out the money and gives it to him. He reluctantly takes it from her, glancing once more at the pitch-black in front of them. Margot waits until his car drives off and his headlights disappear. The darkness claims her, encircles her with black walls that eventually open up into a path for her to walk through. She takes a few steps, aware of one foot in front of the other; of the strangeness creeping up her spine, wrapping itself around her belly, shooting up into her chest. The scent of the bougainvilleas that line the fence is like a sweet embrace. The darkness becomes a friendly accomplice. Yet, the familiar apprehension ambushes her: *Can she be seen?* She looks over her shoulder and contemplates the distance it would take for her to walk to her house from here. A good mile. She stands in front of the bright pink house that emerges from the shadows. It seems to glow in the dark. As though on cue, a woman appears on the veranda, wearing a white nightgown. The nightgown blows gently in the light breeze that rustles the leaves of the plants and trees in the yard, and carries a faint scent of patchouli toward Margot. From where she stands, the woman appears to be sailing toward her like an angel, the nightgown hugging her womanly curves. And Margot sails toward her, no longer cognizant of the steps taken over the cobblestone path or the fears hammering inside her chest. When she arrives at the foot of the steps, she looks up into the face of the woman; into those eyes that hold her gaze steady. She can never get them out of her mind, for they're the only ones that see her. Really *see* her—not her figure or the nakedness she so willingly offers to strangers, but something else—something fragile, raw, defenseless. The kind of bareness that makes her shiver under the woman's observation. Margot swallows the urge to tell her this. But not here. Not now. No words are exchanged between them. No words are needed. Verdene Moore lets her inside.

At Old Fort Craft Park, Delores links arms with the flush-faced men in floral shirts who are too polite to decline and the women in broad straw hats whose thin lips freeze in frightened smiles. Before the tourists pass Delores's stall, she listens to the prices the other hagglers quote them—prices that make the tourists politely decline and walk away. So by the time they get to Delores—the last stall in the market—she's ready to pounce, just like she does at Falmouth Market on Tuesdays as soon as the ship docks. The tourists hesitate, as they always do, probably startled by the big black woman with bulging eyes and flared nostrils. Her current victims are a middle-age couple.

"Me have nuff nuff nice t'ings fah you an' yuh husband. Come dis way, sweetie pie."

Delores pulls the woman's hand gently. The man follows behind his wife, both hands clutching the big camera around his neck as if he's afraid someone will snatch it.

To set them at ease, Delores confides in them: "Oh, lawd ah mercy," she says, fanning herself with an old *Jamaica Observer*. "Dis rhaatid heat is no joke. Yuh know I been standin' in it all day? Bwoy, t'ings haa'd."

She wipes the sweat that pours down her face, one eye on them. It's more nervousness than the heat, because things are slow and Delores needs the money. She observes the woman scrutinizing the jewelry—the drop earrings made of wood, the beaded necklaces, anklets, and bracelets—the only things in the stall that Delores makes. "Dat one would be nice wid yuh dress," Delores says when the woman picks up a necklace. But the woman only responds with a grimace, gently putting down the item, then moving on to the next. Delores continues to fan. Normally the Americans are chatty, gullible. Delores never usually has to work so hard with them, for their politeness makes them benevolent, apologetic to a fault. But this couple must be a different breed. Maybe Delores is wrong, maybe they're from somewhere else. But only the American tourists dress like they're going on a safari, especially the men, with their clogs, khaki apparel, and binocular-looking cameras.

"Hot flash and dis ungodly heat nuh 'gree a'tall," Delores says when the woman moves to the woven baskets. At this the woman smiles—a genuine smile that indicates her understanding—the recognition of a universal feminine condition. Only then does she finger her foreign bills as though unwilling to part with them. "How much are the necklaces?" she asks Delores in an American accent. She's pointing at one of the red, green, and yellow pendants made from glass beads. Delores had taken her time to string them.

"Twenty-five," Delores says.

"Sorry, that's too much," the woman says. She glances at her husband. "Isn't twenty-five a bit much for this, Harry?" She holds up the necklace like it's a piece of string and dangles it in front of her husband. The man touches the necklace like he's some kind of expert. "We're not paying more than five for this," he says in a voice of authority that reminds Delores of Reverend Cleve Grant, whose booming voice can be heard every noon offering a prayer for the nation on Radio Jamaica.

"It tek time fi mek, sah," Delores says. "Ah can guh down to twenty."

"Fifteen."

"All right, mi will geet to yuh for fifteen!" Delores says, suppressing her disappointment. As she counts the change to give back to the woman, she catches her eyeing the miniature Jamaican dolls. Delores imagines that those dolls, however exaggerated, might be the only images the woman sees of Jamaican people on a short one-day cruise stop. Her husband, who snaps pictures nonstop, surveys the table of the Rastas with their long, oversized penises, the smiling women with tar-black faces and basket of fruits on their heads, the grinning farmer carrying green bananas in his hands, the T-shirts with weed plants and a smoking Bob Marley with IRIE written in bold letters, the rag dolls wearing festival dresses that look like picnic tablecloths.

"If yuh buy three items yuh get a discounted price, all these t'ings are quality," Delores says, seizing the opportunity. "Yuh wouldn't get dem anyweh else but right yah so."

The man takes out his wallet and Delores's heart leaps in her throat. "Give me two of those in a large, the tank in a small." He points at the T-shirts. Once he makes his purchase, his wife, as though given permission to grab as many local souvenirs as possible, purchases a woven basket—"For your mom"—more bracelets with Rasta colors—"For Alan and Miranda"—and a couple of the rag dolls decked in festival dresses—"For the girls."

By the time they're done, they have bought half of what Delores had. Only Delores can sell this many souvenirs in a day, because, unlike the other hagglers, she knows she has a gold mine at home—a daughter she has to support—one who is going to be a doctor. She does it for Thandi. As she stuffs the foreign dollars, which will be saved inside the old mattress on the bed that she shares with her mother, inside her brassiere, Delores is convinced that someday all her sacrifices will be paid back. Tenfold.

Thandi wants more. She searches for it in Mr. Levy's Wholesale Shop, which is right across the street from Dino's Bar on River Bank Road—the only road that takes people in and out of River Bank, a former fishing village on the outskirts of Montego Bay where Thandi has lived all her life. Mr. Levy's Wholesale and Dino's are the only two businesses left since the seafood shacks closed down. The construction and the drought have not only driven the fishermen out of work, but out of River Bank, leaving behind a community with not much to live off besides the highly taxed groceries each month at Mr. Levy's.

Mr. Levy's Wholesale has been around since the beginning of time, it seems. The shop has fed generations of River Bank residents. Like the evolving population it serves, Mr. Levy's Wholesale has changed owners many times—the business being passed down from father to son to grandson to great-grandson to great-great-grandson. The current Mr. Levy looks just like his predecessors, squinting into the black faces that yell their orders—*"Missah Chin, Gimme a quarter poun' ah rice. Gimme a pound ah flour. Beg yuh a bag a sugah nuh, missah Chin? Me will pay yuh lata. Gimme a cake soap wid baby oil."* Though Mr. Levy's name is written on the outside of the store in bright red paint, people still refer to the owner as Mr. Chin by virtue of him being Chinese. Mr. Levy's wife is a stone-faced woman who silently fetches the orders in the back. His two sons sometimes work the register when he slips out with his wife to eat lunch or dinner behind the mesh door, where customers can see them devouring spoonfuls of steamed rice or noodles. The shop carries a small quantity of staple goods like rice, milk, cornmeal, Panadol for colds or flu, Foska Oats, tin mackerel, spices, bread, and butter. Once or twice Thandi has spotted something exotic. Like last month when she discovered a chocolate bar that she had never seen before—the purple wrapper emblazoned with gold letters. *Chocolat De L'amour.* She tried it. Savored the richness of it on her tongue, on the roof of her mouth. The shop is always hot and stuffy, the warm air constantly being blown by a large fan in a corner. People go in and out. There's nothing else they can do; if they lingered for too long they would faint from heat exhaustion or the smell of cat piss, courtesy of the big brown and white cat that sits by the counter and licks its paws. Thandi musters up the courage to raise her voice when Mr. Levy squints in her direction. "May I have a pound of rice and a bag of cornmeal, please?" She says this in perfect English, which attracts the stares of some people in the store. But the old *"Chiney"* man is unimpressed. He absently reaches for the items and shouts, "Five dolla!" without so much as a glance at her. His short fingers leaf through the *Observer* before him. Thandi wonders if he has ever seen her face. She wonders if he thinks she's like all the others. With his eyes half closed, all black faces probably look the same to him. Behind the counter, Thandi identifies the Queen of Pearl crème that Miss Ruby told her to get. Another exotic thing Mr. Levy carries.

She clears her throat. "Gimme Pearl too," she says, the patois sounding strange coming out of her mouth given that she's dressed in her Saint Emmanuel High school uniform, the pleated white skirt falling well below her knees, her white socks folded neatly at her ankles, her shoes polished to a shine. She gestures toward the crème with her chin, an action that she has seen the women in the shop do when they place their orders, their confidence evident in the way they stand, leaning with all their weight on the counter, one leg cotched on the back of the other. Thandi purchases the crème from Mr. Levy with the extra change from the groceries. She can tell her sister, Margot, that she bought a pack of pencils and an exercise book. Thandi has seen the effects of the crème on the women who use it, the lightness coming into their skin, and the darkness receding like a sinister shadow around their hairline. Take Miss Ruby, for instance. A woman who lives in one of the shacks not too far from the fishing boats. All over River Bank, people know about Miss Ruby and her new business. Because of her, women and girls who were nothing before have become something, their newly lightened faces rendering them less invisible and more beautiful, worthy of jobs as front desk clerks, bank tellers, models, head sales associates, and in some cases flight attendants.

It's her house Thandi heads to.

She walks along the Y-shaped river that cuts into the village. It separates and flows in opposite directions—one side runs into the wide expanse of the sea, while the other side runs in the direction of the hill that hovers over the town from the tail end of the fork. The water settles into a small cove shaded by bamboo and live oaks. The village got its name because if one were to look down from the top of the hill, the shacks would look like interspersed cardboard boxes on the land surrounding the river. A small fleet of fishermen's boats are anchored on the side where the river meets the sea. They've been there, floating on the water like sleeping whales, since last December before the drought. The area has been roped off for the construction workers—men marching up and down the shore with thick hard hats and heavy rubber boots, combing the sand with a sense of purpose as though searching for buried treasure.

When Thandi was a little girl she used to accompany her mother to buy fish from Miss Ruby out this way. She remembers standing in line outside Miss Ruby's shack, watching Miss Ruby scale the fish, effortlessly slitting them with a sharp knife that revealed the red lining under the belly. But Thandi's first visit to Miss Ruby by herself came only recently—long after Miss Ruby stopped selling fish. Thandi wanted to show her teachers and classmates how responsible she could be by running for form prefect, but she lost to Shelly McGregor, who, though average and unpopular, was voted favorite among the nuns and students. Thandi felt certain the loss had to do with her darker complexion, which she believes is the reason for the burdens that weigh as heavily as the textbooks she carries for subjects she has no interest in studying. But Thandi has one more chance to shine—Dana Johnson's sweet sixteen party, which is months from now. It's Thandi's first party and the last social event before the final exams in June. She imagines herself wearing the nice fuchsia dress she saw in the window of Tiki Boutique near her school in Montego Bay. Her lighter, brighter skin would look good in a color like that; and it will surely make her feel like she belongs.

Thandi sits naked inside Miss Ruby's old shack on a bench. The shack is made of zinc and wooden planks, the exposed nails rusted from the open air that enters from the sea. A leaning mango tree rests on the roof from Hurricane Gilbert, giving shade from the sunlight and protection from potential voyeurs. Black mangoes dangle inside, some of them rotting with dried seeds. Every so often the sea breeze whispers something against the zinc roof or the gaping windows, leaving behind a salty breath that Thandi can taste on her lips. It's mid-February, but the humidity and drought they've been experiencing make it feel like the dry, hot months of summer. Thandi's back is hunched and her shoulders rounded. Tiny ants crawl on the dusty ground, a few making their way up the bench. She crosses and uncrosses her legs, fearing they might crawl into the mouth of her vagina. Across from her, Miss Ruby combines creams together, squeezing them inside a big white jar that used to contain hair-straightening cream. The woman expertly mixes the concoction with the tail of a metal comb, her tongue stuck between her big pink lips as she furrows her eyebrows in deep concentration. She never breaks a sweat in the overbearing heat, though she wears a hooded sweatshirt that covers her forehead and arms to prevent burning from the sun. A pair of loose-fitting pants covers her legs.

"Yuh have the Queen of Pearl?" Miss Ruby asks. Thandi nods and hands it to her. "I don't want it now. Yuh should use it daily. Not dat it's any strongah than my concoction. But if yuh use dem together, yuh g'wan frighten fi see how it wuk miracle. Yuh mus' be careful same way," Miss Ruby says to Thandi. "How is school?"

"Fine," Thandi says in a voice as small as the ants crawling on the floor. She puts the Queen of Pearl crème back inside her schoolbag.

"Yuh ready fah the CXC?"

Thandi shrugs. "I guess so."

Thandi's entire high school career has been spent preparing for this one exam from the Caribbean Examination Council for nine subjects. All except one was chosen for her.

"You guess?" Miss Ruby puts her hands on her hips. "Yuh betta be. It's in four months, no? That's a big, big deal. My cousin in Kingston fail five subjects last year an' did haffi tek them ovah. Anothah girl end up dropping out an' going to vocational school fi learn a trade. You is yuh mother's only hope. Yuh know how hard she wuk fi send you to dat school?" It's true. Delores cheats tourists out of their money with cheap souvenirs she sells for triple the price in Falmouth Market, and Margot works long hours at the hotel. They do it for her.

Thandi swallows, looking down at her uniform piled on the floor like a rumpled sheet. It used to give her a sense of pride, but at this very moment, as she stares at it, she considers the other uses one could make of the white material that costs more than groceries for a month. Because of the expense, Thandi only owns two sets of uniforms, washing them by hand every evening after school, then ironing them for the next day.

She looks down at her brown thighs. They haven't changed a bit since her last visit. "Do you think I can get light in four months?" she asks Miss Ruby, thinking of the party and the boys who will be there.

"You took the plastic off," Miss Ruby says, a tinge of accusation in her voice.

"It was too hot," Thandi tells her. "I felt like I was going to pass out."

"I used to be black like you, but now look at me . . ." Miss Ruby turns her head from side to side for Thandi to see her salmon-colored skin, delicate with the texture of scalded milk. "See how bright my skin come? If yuh follow instructions yours will get this way quicker. Now dat yuh 'ave di Queen of Pearl, yuh might be lucky. If yuh want faster results, use it twice ah day."

She rubs the concoction up and down Thandi's neck, back, arms, and shoulders. She rubs everywhere but her butt crack. Miss Ruby is hardly tender. Thandi wonders if Miss Ruby's roughness is punishment for not having followed her earlier instructions. She imagines her blackness peeling off, the hydrogen peroxide Miss Ruby pours into the mixture acting like an abrasive, a medicine for her melancholy. She closes her eyes as the warm formula touches her skin. Miss Ruby works her way to Thandi's chest. The circular motion of a stranger's hands on her breasts makes Thandi blush. She has never been touched this way. She opens her eyes and searches for something—anything—that can take her mind off the sensation of this strange woman's fingers. She imagines herself as a fish Miss Ruby rubs down with salt and vinegar before frying. Her eyes find the ceiling. Had she been able to lift her arm, she would trace the things she sees projected from her mind.

"Luckily yuh 'ave good hair already," Miss Ruby says. "Good, coolie hair. Yuh daddy is a Indian?"

"I don't know," Thandi says, still staring up at the planks in the ceiling. "Never met him."

"*Tsk, tsk*. Well, God played a cruel joke on you. Because, chile, if yuh skin was as pretty as yuh hair, you'd be one gorgeous woman."

Miss Ruby isn't saying anything Thandi hasn't heard before. Her mother says the same thing, often shaking her head the way she does over burned food that has to go to waste. "*It's a pity yuh neva have skin like yuh daddy.*" Thandi is neither the nutmeg-brown that makes Margot an honorable mistress—a rung lower than a bright-skinned wife—nor is she black like Delores, whose skin makes people sympathetic when they see her. "*Who want to be black like dat in dis place?*" Miss Ruby once said to Thandi about her mother.

Miss Ruby gives Thandi the homemade mixture in the jar for her to apply as needed. "Only as needed," she stresses. "These are very strong chemicals that could kill yuh." She then reaches for the Saran Wrap and begins to wrap Thandi's arms and torso. A mummified Thandi sits and listens to Miss Ruby's instructions:

"If yuh waan come quicker, leave on the plastic. Don't wash. Don't go in the sun. If yuh haffi go in the sun fah whateva reason, mek sure seh yuh covah up at all times from head to toe. If yuh start to feel like yuh g'wan faint, jus' drink wata. It mek yuh sweat more. Whatevah yuh do, nuh tek off the plastic. An' remembah, stay outta that sun!"

Miss Ruby repeats these words like an ominous warning, her eyes pouring into Thandi's. Thandi listens and nods, though she wants to rip the Saran Wrap off and jump in the river. She imagines her skin boiling, becoming molten liquid underneath the plastic wrap.

"Do I have to wear this all the time?" Thandi asks.

"Heat an' sweat is yuh advantage. Jus' bear it," Miss Ruby says, stamping her with a look.

Thandi regrets saying anything, sensing her complaint might be interpreted as her wanting less out of life. Less opportunity. Less chance of attracting the type of boys her mother and sister want her to attract (the type who will be at the party for sure). Less chance of acceptance in school. Less chance to flunk school—the only ship on which black girls like her could float, given that their looks will never do it for them. Her mother tells her this too. "*Di only thing yuh have going for you is yuh education. Don't ruin it.*" Meanwhile, the unintelligent "brownins" in school end up with modeling contracts, or with boyfriends with money they can spend on them. The less attractive ones get good jobs in their family businesses. What else does she have to fall back on if she fails the exam, besides her drawings? But no one wants those. No one respects an artist. So when Thandi puts her clothes on, she pretends to ignore the crinkling of the plastic under her uniform and the nausea that comes over her.

Miss Ruby examines her skin, her eyes like a sharp razor raking over Thandi's body as though looking for areas she might have missed—dark patches that need to be rubbed, scrubbed down with the rigor of someone scouring the bottom of a burnt pot. Or the way she used to scale fish. Her dark eyes have in them a subtle hostility that reminds Thandi of the way the girls and nuns at school look at her. Can she tell Thandi doesn't belong? Can she sniff her deceit?

Perhaps in that moment Thandi reminds her of someone who did her wrong. Or of herself—the way she looked before she bleached her skin. How suddenly her mood changes once Thandi pays her the money.

"Remembah to stay outta the sun like ah tell yuh," Miss Ruby says. "'Cause you and I both know, God nuh like ugly."

When Thandi exits Miss Ruby's shack, she exhales. She hadn't realized she was holding her breath all that time to prevent herself from inhaling those chemicals that stank up the place. The pungent ammonia has replaced the fish smell.

On her way back, Thandi takes the shaded path, which happens to go past the pink house—one of the nicest houses in the entire River Bank community. In fact, it's one of only two houses in River Bank built with real cement and blocks and a shingle roof. It even has shutter windows and indoor plumbing.

The pink house is owned by Verdene Moore, who is watched closely because the whole community knows what she is capable of. There's no *Miss* before the woman's name—like there is for all the other older women Thandi has to address that way—for the same reason there's no *Mrs.* Not that the women in River Bank marry. Marriage is for people like the parents of the girls Thandi goes to school with. She thinks about the heavily made-up, well-dressed mothers accompanied by distinguished-looking fathers at school functions where Thandi's only parent in attendance is Delores. Her father, the last she heard, lives in Westmoreland. There are mostly common-law arrangements in River Bank, where the men live with the women, which is usually enough to seal a relationship. The thing about Verdene Moore that Thandi grew up hearing is that she lures little girls to her house with guineps so she can feel them up. Women have caught her in her yard smiling at them as they pass by with watermelons and icicles between their lips on those hot days when their skirts and dresses cling to their bodies like a second skin. It is known and has been known in River Bank's history that Verdene Moore is the Antichrist, the snake every mongoose should have hauled off the island and eaten alive; the witch who practices obscene things too ungodly to even think about.

Last August Mr. Joe, a stuttering nomad people hire to cut their weeds, found a dead dog in Verdene Moore's yard with what looked like teeth marks in the animal's bloodied side. He hollered and ran down the street, wielding his machete in the air as though slaying the wind. To this day people believe Verdene Moore killed the dog. A dried-up, bony mongrel. The type of animal that people kicked in the head or sides to move out of the way, the type of animal people fed bones and leftover meals and any rubbish they could find. The type of animal that attracted fleas and sniffed and licked its own rump. A detestable animal that became a poor, helpless animal overnight, because Verdene Moore killed it as a sacrifice in one of her rituals. People stay away from the woman, who keeps to herself anyway. No one even knows what *really* goes on in that pink house. Her mother, Miss Ella, had died and left it for her. Surely it's a beauty, with its shingle roof, big yard, French doors, and windows with shutters; but the darkness inside can be seen from the road through the open windows, where white curtains billow and fall like ghosts.

Thandi takes extra steps to hurry along, managing not to look at the beautiful garden in Verdene Moore's yard, with flowers of every color in the rainbow, or sniff the heavy scent of the bougain-villeas that line the fence, where hummingbirds hover, then zip out of sight. They are an anomaly, for the drought has made it hard for the flowers this year. Even the red hibiscuses hang from their stems like the tongues of thirsty dogs.

It's a big yard, so Thandi runs a little to cover the distance along the fence. She's sweating profusely in the heat, and her uniform clings to the plastic, macca thorns latching onto the hem of her skirt. She's aware of the weight of the bag with the rice, cornmeal, and crème of pearl, the only promising thing inside it. The uprooted stones press under her thinning soles, which slap her heels as she runs. She speeds up, pushing away shrubs and hanging limbs, her lungs filling with the fear of being caught.

By the time she gets to Miss Gracie's house, she's breathing heavily, holding her sides. She knows she's safe in front of Miss Gracie's house because, though Miss Gracie has a few demons of her own—which have to do with her permanent residency at Dino's Bar—Miss Gracie is a woman of God. She is inclined to have fits of the Holy Ghost in public, preaching in the square at the top of her voice while clutching a Bible.

A group of teenage boys sit on Miss Gracie's fence, gorging on fresh mangoes from the tree. They pause when they see Thandi, each of them lowering his hand from his mouth. She's the only girl in the neighborhood whose presence is likened to a figure of authority—a school principal, a teacher, a nun. When Thandi passes them, they are as silent as the caterpillars that rest on the leaves. All but one. Charles. Thandi walks with her head held straight, not because of the others, but because of *him*.

"Wha' g'wan, Thandi?" Charles asks, breaking the silence that serenades her. She nearly trips. Heat spreads from her neck to her face, though none of the boys let on that they saw what just happened. She nods and walks quickly past Charles, knowing that his eyes are following her as she walks. She knows they are watching the gentle sway of her hips. She knows that while his eyes trace the curves, his thoughts have already slipped under her skirt. And what might they find there? If only he wasn't a common boy, the kind Delores tells her to stay away from; the kind Margot would disapprove of because he's not one of those money-men with homes in Ironshore that even some of her classmates at Saint Emmanuel brag about dating. Besides, now that her skin will be lighter, she doesn't have to settle for a boy like Charles. And yet, a pulse stirs between her legs and she hurries down the path, holding it in like pee.

Thandi finally arrives home. It's the only shack in the open space next to a pasture where Mr. Melon, a soft-spoken farmer, ties up his nanny goat by the barren pear tree. Every day Mr. Melon walks the goat into the fields, to the only patch of land that has not turned into the rusted brown color of the trees around it. People think he treats the goat better than he treats his woman. Miss Francis and Miss Louise query Thandi with their eyes as she walks up the incline, passing the tenement yard that more than one family shares, their shacks joined like men leaning in a drunken embrace. The women use their hands as visors to shield their eyes from the sun. Though they don't immediately call out to Thandi, she hears them talking about her. "*Is Delores dawta dat? Look how she grow up nice. Mi hardly eva see her. Always in her books. But what ah beautiful sight.*" To their young daughters sitting between their legs on the veranda, whose nappy hair they rake wide-toothed combs through and whose scalps they grease with Blue Magic, they point. "*That's how yuh should be. Like Thandi. Now she's well on her way going to dat good school. See how neat her uniform is? Everyt'ing 'bout har jus' neat. An' she always pleasant. Not like har sistah, Margot, who g'wan like she can't mash ants wid har nose inna di air.*" They wave when Thandi looks their way.

Thandi greets them out of obligation. She manages to pass them by without lengthy conversations. "Good afternoon, Miss Louise. Good afternoon, Miss Francis. Oh, Grandma Merle is fine. Delores? Oh, yuh know, working as usual." She pauses, a steady lump in her throat, when they ask her about school. "Yes, I'm preparing for the CXCs. Studying really hard. Thanks for the prayers." And long after she walks away, she feels them watching her back.

When she opens her gate, Grandma Merle is sitting on the

veranda, staring at the sky. "Good afternoon, Grandma," Thandi says, though she knows there will never be a response. She often wonders if Grandma Merle is more conscious than she's letting on. They have not exchanged more than two words since Thandi was a baby. She's fifteen and has no recollection what it's like to hear her grandmother's voice. Grandma Merle fell silent after Thandi's Uncle Winston left for America. He was Grandma Merle's pride and joy. These days, the old woman stares at the blue sky as though she will see her son somewhere in the clouds sailing above the house, above all the trees and the sloping hills that swallow the sun in the evenings.

Little children are home from school, playing in the big open space where Mr. Melon ties his goat. Some are chasing the fowl in Thandi's yard that are let loose out of the coop. The squawk-ing birds fuss about the big yard, kicking up dust and startling the sleeping mongrel dogs that wag their tails to ward off flies. Thandi leaves Grandma Merle on the veranda and walks into the house. She puts the rice and cornmeal in their rightful places inside the cupboards, then fishes out the crème. She sits before the mirror and wipes the sweat off her face with the hem of her skirt. Twice a day after bathing, the instructions read. But Miss Ruby has warned her against taking showers.

Thandi holds the new crème jar in her hand, rereading every word of instruction. She wants it to work. It has been a month, yet her skin is still the same color. She has been doing everything she was told—wiping her armpits with a wet rag and washing her privates by squatting over a basin of soapy water to freshen up; wearing the long-sleeve sweatshirt over the Saran Wrap during the day to trap moisture and prevent sunburn; massaging Miss Ruby's concoction into her skin every other day. Queen of Pearl is her last resort for faster results. She is unable to wash her face at this time in the day when the water pressure is low. Her face looks clean enough. She touches it with her fingertips, traces the length of it, the smooth-ness. The longer she examines herself in the mirror, the more she begins to see what her mother and sister and the community see: Thandi the scholarship winner, Thandi the good girl, Thandi—a source of hope for her family, destined for riches and prestige. The shack falls away and so does that perpetual weight inside Thandi's chest as she stares at herself.

2

MARGOT BRAIDS THANDI'S HAIR WHILE DELORES STIRS RICE and peas inside a pot. Margot had brought home groceries—a dozen eggs, beef, cheese, mackerel, milk, oxtail, and chicken back, though the meats might go bad. JPS cut the electricity again. Thanks to Clover, the neighborhood handyman who disappeared but has recently returned, they are usually able to get electricity by stealing it from a nearby light pole, given that the shack isn't legally wired. The little vocational schooling Clover had at Herbert Morrison Technical High makes him River Bank's electrician, carpenter, and plumber. He helped to build half the shacks in River Bank, most on abandoned land. But tonight, there's nothing that can be done to restore the electricity. According to Radio Jamaica news, which Delores has turned up on the old battery-operated radio near the stove, several trees caught fire due to the drought and damaged a few main JPS wires. Half the country is without light.

The kerosene lamp glows in the shack. Delores switches off the radio and continues to stir the pot, one hand resting on her wide hip thrust forward atop sturdy brown legs. Her broad shoulders rise as though they themselves are a mounting wall of hard feelings— much like her clenched back, which seems to ward off conversation. Margot can tell that her mother is irritable. "All dis food going to waste in dis blasted heat," Delores says with her back still turned. "An' now di people dem telling we dat we not g'wan have no electricity for a while because ah dis drought. But yuh see me dying trial? How dat g'wan help we?" Delores sucks her teeth and leans over to taste the food. Margot imagines her face scrunching as she reaches for more salt. The smell of mackerel hangs in the heat.

Margot refocuses on Thandi's hair—the kinky curls that wrap around her finger like black silk when she stretches them. Thandi and Margot sit near the open window, taking in the cool breeze and mosquitoes that land on their flesh. They take turns squashing the fattened insects on their arms and legs, wiping off bloodied palms with old newspaper or tissue. They never know whose blood stains their palms; and rarely does it matter, considering that if it belongs to either one of them, then it's the same.

The thing Margot looks forward to the most whenever she's home is braiding her sister's hair. It's the only reason why she's here tonight and not at the hotel or at Verdene's, where there's a generator. She finds enjoyment in the softness of her sister's hair. Margot is older than Thandi by fifteen years, an age gap that makes Thandi regard Margot more as a second parent than an older sister. When her sister was a baby with a head full of curls, Margot discovered that in the braiding she found escape from various men's untying, unclasping, and unbuckling. It was in this soft, delicate texture that the roughness of the other touches faded. The braiding has been a ritual ever since.

"Ouch!" Thandi pulls Margot back to the present.

"What's di mattah?"

"You're pulling again!"

"I'm sorry," Margot says, feeling something greater slip from her fingers when her sister yanks her head away this time.

"Careful wid har hair!" Delores says, reeling from the stove with the dripping wooden spoon. "Yuh t'ink she's a playt'ing?"

Margot sucks her teeth while pulling balls of dark hair from the fine-toothed comb and wrapping them inside tissue so that she can burn them later.

"Yuh always in dat child's hair like yuh don't have yuh own."

"She has swimming lessons tomorrow," Margot says in defense, though there was a letter sent from the school concerning Thandi's lack of participation in swimming. According to the letter, her sister had to sit out swimming class eight times this term, saying she had her period. This became a concern for the school. Margot knows that Thandi hates water, save for taking showers. But she has always made sure that her sister learns how to swim, paying for the lessons anyway no matter how many times she fails to show up. It's also the one excuse Margot holds on to for braiding Thandi's hair.

"Then let me do it," Delores says.

Margot holds the comb as if it's a weapon. "You always think I'm hurting her."

Thandi is quiet. Delores steps back and dries her hands on the front of her dress. She wipes sweat from her upper lip, then goes back to stirring the pot. Without turning around she says, "Mr. Sterling increase di rent again."

"Again?" Margot asks, continuing to comb Thandi's hair. "But him increase it jus' two months ago."

"Yuh already know is so dat man stay," Delores says, stirring harder. "T'iefing culprit."

Margot looks down into the roots of her sister's hair. She brushes the curls, meticulously tames them, avoiding the weight of her mother's frustration on her shoulders. "I want to put down something for a house," she hears herself say. It sounds as if someone else is speaking—someone crouched inside the dark shadows in the corners of the shack. "I want to move us from dis rat hole. It don't mek no sense why we have to stay here an' keep paying dat man rent. We don't even have real electricity."

"Yuh sure 'bout dat?" Delores asks, pausing with the wooden spoon to look at Margot, her eyes hardening. "Yuh been working in dat hotel fah god knows how long, saying di same damn t'ing. If ah didn't know bettah ah woulda t'ink yuh spending it pon yuhself." Her eyes seem to have electricity running through them. The only source on the entire island. Their shadows clash in the dim light when Delores steps closer with the spoon. If it weren't for her sister pressing her head between her legs as if to allow her to carry on, Margot would have snatched the wooden spoon out of her mother's hand. Who knows what she would've done with it? Margot knows that Thandi gets uneasy with confrontations like these between her and Delores. She becomes anxious, watchful, acquiring the fidgetiness of a kitchen mouse and doing everything in her power to resolve the issue. Margot swallows the boiling-hot fury inside her for Thandi's sake. "Delores, yuh know very well dat everyt'ing I earn goes into Thandi's education. And into dis blasted place."

"We all know dat hotel work is good work," Delores charges. "Yet we can't see di fruits ah yuh labor. We ovah here barely holdin' on. Thandi 'ave har exam in June, di rent piling up, we haffi pay Clover money fah di electricity—"

"We owe Clover nothing," Margot says between clenched teeth. "Not one cent!"

"Well, is not like yuh stick aroun' at night to see dat we been using dis tired kerosene lamp even when is not a power cut. Poor Thandi haffi strain har eye undah dis dim light—" She gestures to the kerosene lamp. Inside it, the flame is dancing. Margot focuses on it. How weak it seems, trapped inside glass. This little flame that has the potential to destroy the whole house. Margot stares and stares, her own flame building on the inside, burning and burning until it's too hot to keep to herself. "I'll figure it out," she says in a low, tempered voice.

Delores is silent for a moment. The fire hisses under the pot. "How?" she asks. The liquid from the spoon is dripping onto the floor.

"I said." Margot lifts her head to meet her mother's gaze. "I'll figure it out. I always do."

Her mother lowers her spoon and her shoulders. Strangely, something flickers in her eyes—a sadness, or perhaps regret, more pronounced than Margot has ever seen it. It reaches out across the room, over Thandi's head, to confess that despite what she had done as a mother, despite the pain she had put Margot through, they are joined as mother and daughter. Her hand half lifts with the spoon—a gesture that Margot considers might be a first attempt at an apology. As she braces herself to receive it, Delores's voice strikes her like a cane. "Take care of what, Margot? Where di money g'wan come from if it not coming already?" Delores laughs, her eyes wheeling over the room as if in desperate search for the shadows. "Yuh see me dying trial? She say she will tek care of it as if money fall from sky. Or grow pon tree. Di chile done lose har mind!"

"I'll be up fah promotion any day now," Margot says.

"Promotion?"

"Yes. A promotion."

"To be what? Head servant?"

Delores's derisive laugh drives Margot back into Thandi's hair. But even her sister, in her stiff-backed silence, seems to be agreeing with their mother. Margot turns Thandi's head this way and that way like a rag doll.

"Ouch! Ouch! Margot!" Thandi yells. But Margot doesn't oblige. This time, as exquisite pain courses through her, propelled by her mother's disdain, Margot pulls at her sister's hair. The last thing she wants is to hurt Thandi. But Thandi's pain is different—the type that comes with relief like a balm over a scab, a needle drawing splinter from skin. Margot's stays. Delores's voice rushes at her, flogging her with its taunt: "Tek care of what? Bettah yuh go set up shop as a market vendor at craft market than tell people yuh work in a hotel."

They stare at her when she walks into school wearing the oversized sweatshirt, her hair newly straightened. Thandi ignores the attention, seeking the refuge of her desk in the back of the classroom. Heads turn as she makes her way down the row. Along with the speculation she hears her classmates whisper.

"Why is she wearing that dreadful sweatshirt? It's like she has AIDS or something."

"Or hiding a you-know-what!"

"No way!"

"Well, yuh know what they say. It's always the quiet ones. Even her hair change. They say when you swallow, it's extra protein. Good for the hair and skin."

"Says who?"

"I read it somewhere."

"But you think she has a man giving it to her on the regular?"

"Like I said, it's the ones you least expect."

Not since Kim Brady got slapped by her mother in front of the entire school for insulting one of the nuns has there been anything as gossip-worthy. Thandi keeps her head down during devotion in the hall where Sister Shirley, the headmistress, leads the school in worship. Sister Shirley's voice soars above the collective: "Hail Mary, full of grace, the Lord is with thee. Blessed art thou among women, and blessed is the fruit by thy womb, Jesus. Holy Mary, Mother of God, pray for us sinners now, and at the hour of our death. Amen."

Thandi makes the sign of the cross and focuses on her polished black shoes. The girls are ushered out of the hall under the direction of the prefects, older girls who have been given duties as disciplinarians. Before each class exits the hall in orderly lines arranged by height, the prefects march down the lines like army generals, holding notepads. They mark down the names of girls who have disobeyed some cardinal rule in attire—girls who aren't wearing slips underneath their uniform skirts, girls wearing hair clips that aren't black and inconspicuous, girls with any form of jewelry, girls wearing braids or any ethnic hairstyles outside of the accepted bun or neatly plaited ponytail, girls with ties that aren't tied properly around the collars of their blouses with the short end of the ties tucked away or pinned down, girls with skirts that are too short or socks that are too long, girls with heels that are over two inches, girls with the waistbands of their skirts not showing.

When Marie Pinta, the assigned prefect for Thandi's class (whose real name is Marie Wellington of the Wellington family in Jamaica, but who got her nickname because of her height), gets down the middle of the line to Thandi, she pauses. "Are you sick?"

"No." Thandi replies.

"Well, take that off. It's not allowed."

Thandi hesitates. Her homeroom teacher, Sister Atkins, did not complain before devotion. In fact, she marked Thandi present after seeing her wearing the sweatshirt. Marie Pinta's request is followed by a hushed silence in the corner of the devotion hall where Thandi's class is lined up. The watchfulness of Thandi's classmates makes her swallow a verbal plea. Instead she pleads with her eyes, hoping Marie Pinta will reconsider. Marie Pinta, whom Thandi has observed on many occasions during devotion wearily gazing out the window, her eyes focused on some elusive thing.

But Marie Pinta stands firmly next to Thandi. "I said to take it off."

Thandi's arms remain at her sides, her eyes trained on Marie Pinta's mouth. "Are you deaf?"

Thandi tugs at the base of her sweatshirt, aware of her classmates blinking rapidly as though gearing up for something to happen. Though fear pulls at her nerves, her body erupting in tremors she hopes aren't visible to their eyes, she lets her hands fall back to her sides. "I can't," she says, her whisper like a shout in the hushed hall. By this time the other classes have filed out of the hall, leaving only Thandi's class. They are being held back because of her. She knows that she's in deep trouble. She has never been singled out after devotion for not adhering to the uniform rules. Delores and Margot make sure that Thandi looks her best each day. They make sure that she doesn't look like she lives in a shack, worlds away from her classmates.

Marie Pinta glares at Thandi and then writes something down in her notepad. "I'm assigning you a demerit. Go to the principal's office. Now." Marie Pinta points directly at the door as though direction is needed. The other girls are giggling, cupping their hands to their mouths. Thandi's face grows warm. Marie Pinta whips around to face them. "Shut up!" There is a level of terror in Marie Pinta's voice that Thandi doesn't understand. She appears distraught, her small body shaking under the martial uniform the prefects wear—double-breasted blazers and pencil skirts.

Thandi gathers her belongings and walks out the door.

"Braeeeeeeee! Hee-haw, he-hawwwww." The sound starts as a single whisper, then builds into a low resonating force that pushes Thandi out the door faster. She almost runs to get away from the sound. She wishes she could unhear it, or, best, stand up to it. Tell her classmates that she's not a donkey. That her being from a rural area does not mean she should be associated with farm animals. But her inability to do this only fuels her anger.

3

MARGOT TAKES COMFORT IN HEARING THE CRUNCH OF HER feet on the dirt road, the chirping of birds from the crosshatch of branches, and the buzzing of wasps around the poinciana trees. There's a silence that seems to hold its breath at the sound of the gravel. Not unlike her coworkers, who seem to cease breathing and stop what they are doing when they see her approaching at work. And certainly not unlike Delores, whose whole body seems to halt at the sound of Margot's voice. All her life her presence has brought about pauses and silences louder than the white-hot sun and screaming crickets at the height of dusk. Even the sky, an arch of blue, seems to veer away from her with its distance.

It's strange how people always sense her. Before she approaches them, they look up and over their shoulders. It's as though she brings a change of weather in her dove-gray suit amid the languorous ease of a dry, hot day. Her gait and hotel uniform seem to reprimand the locals for their displays of idleness. Perhaps she serves as a reminder of their lost livelihoods as farmers and fishermen. Walking down River Bank Road, the heels of her pumps worn by dirt, Margot attracts the looks of men holed up inside Frenchies for a heavy breakfast of boiled yam, banana, ackee, and saltfish before going off to their various handy-man jobs in Montego Bay. She also draws the attention of women carrying buckets of water on their heads, their mouths curved with malice and necks stiff with resentment. There are some howdies and nods, but mostly stares. Some of the men holler, "'Ey, beautiful." But Margot has never slept with any of the men in River Bank. Though in her line of work she fucks anyone who can afford it, being with a man from her area is beneath her. Their fantasies alone have colored their lenses, easing their tension around her just a little. With her they become as unquestioning and generous as children, even protec-tive, her high, swaying backside and firm calves making them forget why they were annoyed that she—whom their women describe as *Miss High an' Mighty*—barely says hello to them and refuses to take their job applications with their crab-toe request for menial work at the hotel. She knows that mothers watch to see if she stops to open a palm full of sweeties for their children. And when she doesn't, they suck their teeth loud enough for her to hear them say, "*What a selfish 'ooman. Mean like star apple tree. Not even pickney 'im mek nyam outta 'im hand. No wondah why she barren.*" Margot doesn't have woman friends. She likes to think that maybe it's for her own sake and theirs. In the beauty parlor some of them greet Margot with reserved shy-ness, but in their hot heads under the hair dryers she can tell they have already marked her as a threat.

By the time she gets to the square, she has seen enough dropped gazes and begins a purposeful stride to the taxi stand. There too, breaths are drawn, as though the drivers are looking to see who she'll pick to carry her to the palace today. Mostly, they like to give her their information so that she can recommend their services to tourists who need rides. Some might even use the drive as an opportunity to pick her brain about job prospects as a kitchen boy, chef, server, housekeeper, maintenance man, concierge—anything that can get them through the door of the hotels, beating out the crowd of applicants. But Margot always goes with Maxi—if not for his indifference to working in the hotel, then for his ability to see her as just Margot. She never feels obligated to do him any favors. His smile eases the tension that has stiffened her back.

"How yuh doin' today, baby girl?" Maxi says, starting his ignition. Buju Banton's "Wanna Be Loved" plays on the car radio as Maxi backs out into the street. Margot fiddles with the pair of black, green, and gold boxing gloves on the rearview mirror.

"Been bettah. Dis heat is no joke. Can't wait to get some ice when I reach work."

"Yuh looking good. Look like is you producing all di heat." Maxi manually rolls down his side of the window with the knob and puts one hand out to catch the wind; the other one steers the car.

"Don't tell dat to yuh neighbors. Dem already 'ave me up fah wearing this uniform."

Maxi sucks his teeth. "Mek dem g'weh. Is jealous dem jealous."

"Can't wait to leave dis godforsaken place."

"Is it dat bad? We live by di sea. How much people can say dat? Give t'anks."

"Maxi, shut up wid yuh blessings nonsense. This is no paradise. At least, not for us."

"Yuh t'ink I don't know? Trus' me, I an' I see di struggles of di people every day. Dem look at people like you an' see where dem job went. Yuh can't blame dem. But yuh also can't say yuh not thankful fah what Jah give we."

"So River Bank is what God give we?" A bitter chuckle escapes Margot. "Stolen land?"

"Correction. We are di stolen people. Dis is our temporary land. Jah wouldn't give us what 'im didn't intend fah us to 'ave. Him soon move we again to a bettah place. Maybe back to Africa."

"Nonsense. We build our own destiny. Didn't nobody tell you? You once asked me what my dream was."

"Yuh say yuh want yuh sistah to mek it."

"An' I want to be in control of my own destiny."

"So let's start wid me, then. How about we get married?"

Margot smiles. "Stop romp wid me, Maxi." She opens the window on her side to catch the breeze. She almost closes her eyes as she tilts her head back. Finally, there's an exhale of transient whispers that brushes against her face.

"How come some man nuh own yuh yet?" Maxi asks.

Margot turns in time to catch his sliding gaze. "'Cause I don't want to be *owned*," she says.

"Yuh nuh want children?"

"No. River Bank full wid pickney already. Why would I want to add to the pile?"

"Lots ah woman me know want pickney. Jesus Christ, as soon as me pop off, another one say she pregnant."

"So now yuh believe in Jesus?"

Maxi sucks his teeth and shakes his head. "I an' I believe in one God."

"You should believe in condoms too."

"Yuh getting fresh. Anyway, ah was trying to say dat every warm-blooded woman me know want children."

"How yuh know dat is what dem want?" Margot asks. "Maybe is not by choice."

"Fi tek care ah dem when dem get old an' senile. Yuh don't want to end up old an' lonely wid no children."

"I will manage," she says, thinking about Verdene and the time they have been spending together. Just the other night they were in Verdene's living room and Margot noticed Verdene's slippers dangling off her feet when she rested her legs on the arm of the sofa. She imagined seeing those slippers parked next to hers on a welcome mat. Margot blinks away this memory in the beam of sunlight that spills onto the windshield when they exit the groves that flank the sides of the road.

"I nevah met a woman who like be by herself," Maxi is saying, almost to himself. "Yuh need a man."

"How yuh know what I need?"

"Yuh seem like a decent woman. I an' I still cyan wrap my head 'round how yuh still single. Dat's all."

"Ah jus' haven't found di right person," she says, thoughts of Verdene lingering like a faint smell of sun-ripe fruit.

It never feels wrong when she's with Verdene. But late at night when the whole world seems to pause around them, leaning in like the shadows of the mango trees and the moon against the window to observe two women spooning—one adrift in sleep and the other wide awake, her breathing rapid—paranoia keeps Margot up at night. Most times it moves her out of the bed and to the sofa in Verdene's living room. Two weeks ago it chased her from the house. She would listen to sounds outside—the chirping of crickets, the penetrating hiss of cicadas, the howling of a dog. The blackness of the unknown so stifling that Margot takes gulps of air every five seconds. Only when she's with Verdene does she experience such panic. Every night now she smells a faint scent of burning. It disappears when she jumps up to sniff out where it's coming from. It stays with her and she remembers the news that broke months before. It was not the main headline. Margot read it in the small section of the *Star* next the Dear Pastor column. Two women were burned inside their house when they were caught in bed together. Such murders aren't taken seriously, often shrugged off as crimes of passion committed by enraged lovers—more than likely of the same sex—who were wronged. No one mourned the loss of the women's lives, but instead rejoiced in the good judgments of karma. For what can women who refuse the loving of men expect? Verdene responded to Margot's nerves by pulling her close, as though she was prepared to throw her body over Margot's if she must, to protect her.

The taxi pulls up to the high iron gates of the hotel. Alan, the security guard, comes out of his little hut to open up for them. "Mawnin', mawnin'."

Once Maxi drives into the compound, the lobby is visible through the glass exterior. Already the concierges are busy pushing luggage on carts through the marbled interior, which boasts high ceilings and large chandeliers that glower above the champagne-colored lounge and the front desk. Gone is the rustic quality that Reginald Senior upheld until his death—a natural ambience created by vibrant colors, palm trees, and artwork by Jamaican artists. Under Alphonso's direction, tourists now have to leave the lobby and drive half a mile to be reminded where they are. Alphonso has also loaned a few abstract paintings—geometric shapes and swirling colors—from his personal collection to the lobby. The gift shop, manned by a young woman named Portia, is right across from the check-in desk and only sells picturesque views of the island; entry to the two main restaurants—Italian and French—are diagonal from one another. Margot gives Maxi a crisp bill and gets out of the car.

"If yuh evah wake up an' need a man, yuh know who to call." He winks at her.

"I won't ever need you, Maxi," she says, waving him goodbye and walking away with her fluid stride that emphasizes everything she knows his imagination has already seen.

"Not even on a rainy night?" he asks, driving off slowly.

Margot laughs, holding her stomach and stumbling merrily to the entrance of the hotel. "We in a drought, so keep wishing."

"See, if me mek yuh laugh dem way, then imagine what else me can do."

"Aw, lord, Maxi, yuh nuh easy. I will see you lata." She blows him a kiss.

Once Margot is on the property, the hush returns. She walks toward the front desk, holding her head as high as possible. The security guards, groundsmen, and concierges are not immune to her magic; but the housekeepers and other administrative staff, mostly women, are. Visitors seem to single her out to ask for directions or recommendations. She can also hold conversations with tourists longer than any other front desk clerks, who tend to be overly polite and too eager to smile, as though apologetic for their lack of knowledge. She's the best front desk clerk at Palm Star Resort. It's the only job that she has ever known. But soon this will change.

"Morning, Pearl," Margot says to one of the housekeepers who happens to be signing in. The older woman draws her lips together. The two younger housekeepers—Pearl's oldest daughter and youngest niece, respectively—nod at Margot, then look away as though embarrassed about something. Margot has an inkling that Garfield told everyone what he saw—Margot getting fucked by Alphonso in the conference room. Though this is old news—it's one of those pieces of gossip that could easily be a myth, given how smoothly Margot plays it off. Had it not been for the mysterious occurrence of Garfield's death shortly after—serves him right—then perhaps it would have been completely forgotten. Margot carries on with her business, greeting the lower staff whenever she has to assign them to clean vacant rooms. She makes direct eye contact that forces them to look away, ashamed for their filthy imaginations. She also dares them to retort with information they have bottled up and kept for when she writes them up. But this never happens. They keep the damning secrets among themselves. Occasionally these might slip out to new employees in the middle of spreading linen, folding towels, washing pillowcases, or emptying trash—tales of Margot's bare backside making their rounds among shoulder-jerking, tear-eyed laughter that is an amalgamation of envy and disgust—boisterous, as though the brutes think that they're alone and unobserved at work. But whenever she's around, the laughter drains like the last bit of water from a bottle.

"What oonuh laughing at?" Margot had asked Pearl's daughter and niece one day. They gasped when Margot appeared from a corner by the large ceramic vase where she had been watching them. Their heads immediately bowed. "A joke."

"What kind of joke sweet oonuh so?"

"Ahm . . . we was talkin' 'bout somebody we know."

"What did they do?"

The young housekeepers glanced at each other, damp-faced and shining under Margot's glare. When they couldn't answer, Margot knew. And because she slips easily and stealthily into occupied rooms at night and emerges looking as she did when she entered, a spy—be it a lone housekeeper catching up on the day's cleaning tasks or Neville, the room service attendant, knocking on people's doors with food—would think she was coming from a serious business meeting. Whereas they might speculate freely about her affair with Alphonso, her late evening deeds float under their noses. Besides the one or two run-ins on the property that she has had with staff that work late shifts, no one, as far as she knows, suspects anything.

Thandi makes her way to the nearest restroom by the upper school and locks herself inside one of the stalls. It's where she eats her lunch, enduring the pungent smell of urine and womanly excretions.

She takes out a pencil from her bag and draws on the whitewashed wall like she draws in the dust on furniture at home, or in mud after it rains. She pauses when she hears voices.

"Are you serious?"

"I'm dead serious. It happened aftah devotion yesterday morning."

"I missed it!"

"You're always late for school, that's why."

"What was she thinking?"

"I asked myself the same question."

"It's like she lives in her own world."

"She's just cuckoo."

"You notice how she's been looking more and more like Casper the Ghost?"

The girls' giggles follow them outside. After they leave, Thandi stays inside the stall. She stands back to look at her drawing, then scribbles all over it, turning it into a shapeless form—the eye of a hurricane spinning relentlessly out of control. Thandi adjusts the pin on her skirt where the button has fallen off (they have been falling off her blouses too, the meager threads giving way to the defiance of her newly fattened breasts) and exits the stall. She cuts across the lawn, making her way to the Vocational Block, where Brother Smith's office is located. It's another one of the modern buildings painted bright yellow. Brother Smith is gathering materials for class, his brown robe nearly swallowing his thin frame. When he sees Thandi, he closes the *Jamaica Gleaner* and puts it on his desk. "Damn politicians. This country has gone to the dogs. Did you know that we owe the World Bank billions of dollars?" Thandi shifts from one leg to the next, her backpack weighing heavily on her shoulders. Brother Smith must sense that something is wrong when he doesn't get at least a *Really, sir?* or *You don't say.*

"You don't look well," he says. "Come in and sit down."

Thandi does as he says, closing the door behind her, then removing a few cardboard collages off a chair by Brother Smith's desk, which is neat despite the disarray of his office. There are prints of paintings everywhere, some he had been meaning to hang on the already crowded walls. Van Gogh, Picasso, da Vinci, Botticelli. Artists he has discussed in Thandi's art class, assigning extensive readings about their life and work. Artists whose works Brother Smith says he has seen in Europe. Thandi wishes she could go to Europe too. To exist in those places, especially those paintings of the English countryside with wide-open fields, greener than the greenest grass in River Bank, and with flowers in the softest shades of lavender and yellow. Those images don't look at all like sunny days in River Bank, where weeds grow to your knees in the brown fields, itching around the ankles; and black boys hang from trees, foraging for ripe mangoes, their dangling, ashy, sore-ridden legs attracting as much flies as the rotten fruits.

Thandi sits and regards the frame on Brother Smith's desk that reads I CAN DO ALL THINGS THROUGH CHRIST WHO STRENGTHENS ME. She stares at it for a while. Surely she has been working hard, doing everything to please. Jesus Christ peers at her with sympathetic eyes that mirror the nuns' and those of the missionaries. She's supposed to want this. She's supposed to be grateful. *A girl like her* should excel at school, because it's the only way out—the only way to clamber up the ladder. *I'm supposed to want this.* Yet, year after year when she walks away with all A's on her school report, a nagging persists. Like she's running a race, panting on her way to a finish line that doesn't exist.

"Thandi, what's going on? Our class starts in thirty minutes," Brother Smith says. Though he's quite young, Brother Smith is prematurely balding. His bald spot shines in the natural light from outside like the silver plate he passes around during mass. He tries to cover it with four strands of brown hair combed to the side. He's small in stature, his fair skin interrupted by brown freckles covering his entire face like a dotted mask. But his kind, chestnut-colored eyes stand out like the languid strokes of a brush, capturing everything about a person, an object, or a setting. Currently they're steady on her face, as if trying to figure out a crossword puzzle. He leans forward to rub her arm in that paternal way she has gotten used to. He doesn't seem to hear the slight crinkling of the plastic underneath her sweatshirt. And if he does, he doesn't ask. It's here, inside Brother Smith's art class, that Thandi feels most free.

"Is it possible to be good at something even if you don't want to?"

"Yes, that's plausible. Why?"

Thandi shrugs, looking down at her hands. "I—I was thinking..." Her voice trails off. "I was thinking how much I love art. More than any other subject." Brother Smith takes his hand away and creates distance between them. A distance Thandi feels, which momentarily creates an ache within her. He's rubbing his chin as though suddenly aware of a burgeoning five o'clock shadow.

"My advice is for you to love all your subjects. The CXC is just around the corner."

"I know. And I am prepared to pass it. It's just . . ."

"Thandi, I teach art as a vocational subject."

His response puts a sinking feeling inside Thandi's chest like the melting of chipped ice. She looks around the room, her desires springing forth like vines across the white ceiling, coloring the beige walls. "Nothing else feels right."

"Thandi, you have a whole life ahead of you. It's too soon to be feeling this way."

Brother Smith clasps both his hands as if he's about to pray. "Think about your family, this school. People are rooting for you. You're a straight-A student who can do more with your life than be—"

"But you said I'm good."

"Yes, I did say that."

He reaches across a small stack of students' work on his desk and locates Thandi's sketchpad. The students had to turn in preliminary materials for the end-of-the-year project. He opens up Thandi's. "You have skills. It's obvious," he says. "But I'm afraid that—" He clears his throat. "I don't see a future for you there."

Brother Smith apparently picks up on her disappointment, because his face softens and his head tilts as though he's about to reason with a five-year-old.

"Here is the thing, Thandi. I favor landscapes and have to say that yours is my *favorite* by far of all the collection that I have! But this final project should give me a better understanding of you, the artist. I don't see that. I would like to challenge you to go deeper, reveal more of yourself," he says. "If I like what I see, I will nominate your work to be displayed in the Merridian. You can keep drawing, even if not professionally." He pushes her drawings that she did over the last few weeks to the edge of his desk.

The Merridian is the holy grail of artwork in the school. It was named after a white nun whose favorite pastime was painting workers in the fields whenever she came on missionary trips to the plantations. She would title her paintings *Negro Picking Corn*; *Negro Under Tree*; *Negro at Sunset*. Her paintings had gotten national acclaim.

"I'd like that, sir," Thandi says, almost falling out of her chair to rise with Brother Smith. They walk together to the studio, Thandi silently contemplating what she'll do for the final project as they pass the sewing room, where girls sit studiously behind Singer machines; the cooking hall, with its smell of cornmeal pudding; the typing lab, where keyboards take on the sound of pecking birds; and finally to the art studio. Brother Smith squeezes her shoulder firmly before they enter the class. As soon as she gets to her space around a large table that seats all six of her art classmates, Thandi pulls out her tools. Brother Smith instructs them to sketch for a few minutes, identifying objects in the room. Thandi angles the pencil in her right hand and concentrates deeply. She taps her pencil lightly on the sheet, the Merridian still on her mind. Brother Smith may say there's no future in art, but if he nominates her and she wins, who knows? But how can she reveal more of herself when she's so unsure of who that is? Her hand barely moves, though other images come into focus: the chipped ceramic vase with red roses that Brother Smith keeps at the front of the room for inspiration, the Virgin Mary figurine on the windowsill, a pair of slippers with the heels rubbed down on a side table, the defiance within the straight backs of the wooden chairs. Every object has character. Substance. A story about the people who made them, owned them.

Something slips inside Thandi, filling her with a familiar weight that presses down on her chest, holds her still, like the man's body that one time. It's a feeling of dread that causes her to pause, her pencil suspended in midair. Thandi's kept her terrible secret for years, and as time has gone on she has convinced herself that no one would believe her anyway. Like a bad dream, the pain of the experience lingers—the taste of licorice when she bit into the hand cupping her mouth, the roughness of the stones, pebbles, and sticks as her heels were dragged along the dusty path and into the bushes, the heavy weight on top of her that both blinded and numbed her. All she had was her hearing. "*If yuh tell ah soul, yuh dead!*" The words were like the blade of a knife by her temple, which she spent the days and nights after it happened trying hard to forget. Her imagination began to produce walls behind which she crouched in silence, closed off from the pain of the memory. She didn't have to leave this hiding place, for her imagination also produced its own food, water supply, and oxygen. After a while it became harder to piece the facts together. For example, how is it that she can remember the trees that she was looking at before it happened, and their names, the green of the water in the cove, but not the color of his shirt, what he had in his hand, or what his face looked like? Was he wearing red or black? Did he carry a knife or a broken bottle? Was he wearing a beard then? Or just a mustache? Something inside her collapses under the weight of the things she cannot remember. She sketches, knowingly and unknowingly turning the pointed pencil toward herself.

Thandi comes home and finds Margot counting money. She's in her work uniform, hunched over the table where the envelopes are piled and where a small flame burns from the kerosene lamp, though it's still early. She's so engrossed in what she's doing that she doesn't notice Thandi. Margot's mouth moves steadily with each bill she counts. The light from the flame caresses her face. By the pale green hue of the bills, Thandi can tell that they are U.S. dollars, not Jamaican. *Where does she get so much money? What does she do with it?* Margot stashes a few bills away in one pile. She then rolls the second pile, securing it with an elastic band. She doesn't take it to the old sweat-stained mattress with the exposed spring where she and Delores usually store money to pay bills. Instead, she puts it away inside her purse. When she looks up and sees Thandi, she jumps. "Have mercy pon me, dear God! Thandi, don't you scare me like dat!" She gets rid of the evidence, dropping her purse onto a nearby chair. "What yuh doing home so early?" Margot asks Thandi. "Yuh don't have extra lessons?" She's nervous, her eyes briefly scanning Thandi's face before returning to the now-empty table.

Thandi sits on the bed and takes out a book, aware of her sister fumbling around. "I don't have extra lessons today. Remember?" Thandi leafs through a math book, staring down at equations. "Where yuh get so much money from?" she asks her sister. She looks up in time to see Margot crossing her legs.

"Overtime," Margot explains. Thandi peeks at the purse on the chair, slumped like a black leather pillow.

"Are there any openings for summer?" Thandi asks Margot, who idly removes a clip from her straightened hair to let it fall around her shoulders. She uses both hands to fluff it. Something Thandi is learning how to do with hers, but, because of her hair's finer texture, she can never achieve.

"Wid your education, you can get bettah work than what I'm doing," Margot says, leaning back to ease her feet out of her high-heeled shoes. A fresh odor of sweat floats up to Thandi's nostrils from Margot's stockinged feet, and Thandi takes comfort in it. "Focus yuh energy on school. People should be working for you. Not the other way around," Margot says, pointing and flexing her toes—the sanguine nail polish she wears visible through the sheer stockings.

Thandi gets up and joins her at the table. Margot removes the purse from the chair so that Thandi can sit. Once she sits, Margot lifts both legs and rests them on Thandi's lap. "That hairstyle suits you," Margot says. It's the first she has ever commented on a hairstyle that Thandi did herself. All she did was a single French braid, the end secured by a black rubber band. Thandi massages her sister's feet, watching Margot's head roll back and eyes close. Margot sighs loudly as Thandi runs her hands up her calves, applying pressure. More than the velvety feel of the stockings, Thandi delights in the sturdiness of Margot's calves, conjuring up memories of her running track at the small secondary school she attended. Margot made it to girls' champs and could have gone further in track and field. But for some reason, she stopped training and fell off the path. When Thandi asked her why, Margot responded with a casual shrug. "*It wasn't worth it.*"

Margot's lips part, letting out a low guttural sound that reminds Thandi of a purring cat. "I wish I didn't have to go back to work so soon," Margot says, her eyes still closed. "I'd stay here just for this . . . You're good with your hands." Thandi decides that this would be a good time to ask for what she wants. "Can I have some money?"

"Money for what?" Margot asks, her eyes fluttering open.

Thandi shrugs, her fingers still working her sister's calves. "I have things I want to save up for . . ." She thinks about the party coming up and the fuchsia dress she wants to wear. The last time she checked, the price hadn't gone down. She also has to pay another visit to Miss Ruby.

"Name one t'ing," Margot says.

"A dress?" This comes out of Thandi's mouth sounding like a question.

"A dress for what?" Margot sits up.

"There's a party I was invited to by a classmate. A sweet sixteen party."

"A party before the exam? Yuh should be studying, trying to pass all nine subjects." Thandi's movement slows. Margot relieves her of her task, pulling her legs out of Thandi's lap. She's staring at Thandi as though focusing on the small pimple at the center of her forehead. "I just paid money for the subjects you'll be sitting in CXC. All nine of them wasn't cheap."

"What?" Thandi springs from the chair, which nearly topples over. "When?"

Margot is shaking her head. "I paid for them last week. Your education comes first, Thandi. You know that. How yuh going to go to a party before the exam, the exam I paid for?" Thandi swallows the solid mass that has resurfaced. "Nevah mind, then," Thandi says quietly. "I mean, all the girls in my class are going an' ah wanted to go too, but I don't have to."

Margot's eyes soften. "Jus' gimme my purse," she finally says. Thandi reaches it for her. Thandi knows that her sister can never say no to her. It's as though Margot fears Thandi might find some other alternative—another way of getting the things she asks for. And Thandi takes advantage, though her conscience reprimands her each time. "You really don't have to," Thandi says.

"Well, one day yuh g'wan pay me back tenfold. So, here." Margot peels off a couple bills. "I'm sure you'll put it to good use." Margot and Delores bank on Thandi as the one who will make it. Like the old mattress, Thandi is that source in which they plant their dreams and expectations. "*It's you who'll get us outta dis place*," they say to her. She hears Delores telling her friends this too when they come over to play dominoes. No one knows how crushing the weight of Thandi's guilt is when they excuse her from cooking, cleaning, and even church because of the importance they place on her studies.

Margot slowly gets up from the table and reluctantly slips back into her shoes. Thandi watches her touch up her makeup and spritz perfume behind each ear. In less than a minute her hair is back in a bun. She grabs her bag and heads out the door. That strange, officious perfume she has started to wear grips the air like a choke hold. "Don't tell Delores dat ah was here," she says to Thandi before disappearing. As though carried away by the wind.

4

MARGOT ROLLS OVER, HER LEGS STRADDLING HORACE. SHE pinches his pink flesh between her fingers and watches it turn white. Horace groans and smiles up at her through drooping eyelids. Had she been attracted to him, she would've kissed the place on his cheeks where his long lashes touch and placed her lips on top of his puckered ones. She would've even had the patience to lie beside him beforehand and run her fingers over the hairs on his enormous chest and belly. Instead, she mounts him and moves her hips steadily, rhythmically. His hands grip her thighs before moving to her breasts. In sex she finds a deep calm, a refuge in which she hides. She imagines herself as a vacuum, inhaling everything— every word, every thought, every glance, every tear. They'd all disappear out of sight, only to be emptied behind the hotel, maids throwing the balls of dust into big bins while humming their familiar sad songs that Margot used to hear her grandmother hum. As a little girl she knew the sorrows in those songs but felt immune to the pain in them. She knew already that helplessness is weak, and that there is no use in having faith in God. God is not the one to put food on the table or send her sister to school. And God is certainly not the one keeping the roof over their heads.

She sways high above Horace like a palm tree in a cool breeze as he whispers his gratitude, sometimes cursing her with expletives that cause her to throw her head back and pick up speed. His head is small and inconspicuous from where she sits. There are moments when another person comes to mind, feminine lips parting, hungry for more than Margot's body. The person's eyes are steady on hers. Margot knows these eyes. They plead with her, so she concentrates instead on the unremarkable man's head below her. She rocks and sways, aware of the creeping chaos, the sensation that spreads from her groin all the way to his curled toes as though her orgasm has possessed his body too. When it's all over, Margot spirals down and down, crashing like a big tree uprooted by nature's merciless ax. She lies next to Horace, postcoital disgust and a lurking disappointment coiling in her belly like days-old milk. She's human again. Horace reaches for her, touches her arm, and she flinches. She never wants to be touched in this state. A week in Jamaica's sun has turned him red. His dark hair falls into his face and he brushes it away. It falls back despite his effort. If he meant more to her, she would reach up and brush his hair aside so that she could stare into the blueness of his eyes. But she keeps seeing the eyes of someone else.

"I have to go," she tells him. She covers her breasts with the white sheet, something she never used to do. Margot is prone to prancing around naked. She used to revel in the lust she saw in her clients as they watched her move about the suite uninhibited. They expect that kind of behavior from an island woman.

"Go?" Horace says to her in his heavy German accent, which sounds to her like, "*Guh?*" "But ze night is still early."

Margot glances at the clock on the VCR. Palm Star Resort has yet to upgrade to DVD players like all the other five-star hotels on the strip. It's quarter after eleven. Where did the time go? Earlier in the evening Horace had ordered room service while Margot hid in the bathroom. They ate, and drank a bottle of wine between them. What did they talk about? Margot can't remember. Whatever their conversation, she was sure of only one thing: it ended the way it always ends.

Margot moves about the spacious room, picking up her stockings and uniform from off the floor. Horace is her oldest client. He comes to Jamaica just for her, always promising to take her back with him to Germany. And always, when he pulls out his wallet to pay her, she catches a glimpse of a smiling, yellow-haired family—a woman and two children, a boy and a girl. She wonders where he would put her if he followed through with his promise to take her with him. What would he tell the smiling woman and two children in the picture? Like Horace, all her clients promise the same thing, as though paying her isn't enough; as though somehow their fucking has given them a desire to "save" her. They need to justify their infidelity with an act of kindness, a generosity that Margot fights the urge to laughingly decline. If she says yes, it gives them power to know that there's a woman who depends on them, who needs them. It keeps them coming back.

"I have to meet someone—" Margot says, pushing her leg inside her sheer stocking. It rips and she cusses under her breath.

"Another man?" Horace asks. "Vat is he paying you? I can give more."

"No. It's not a man."

"Then who is more important than me?"

"My mother," she lies. "I have to meet her somewhere." She pulls up her skirt and hastily buttons her white shirt over her bra. Horace props himself up on an elbow and watches her. When she's dressed, she walks over to the bed and kisses him on the forehead. Horace puts his hand at the back of her head and brings her closer. Without warning, he kisses her on the mouth. Margot pulls away a little. "Yuh acting like yuh won't see me again, sweetness," she says, holding his hand.

"Okay," he says finally. "It's on ze table." He gestures toward the fat leather wallet sitting on the computer desk. "Take it all."

Margot hesitates. She counts three hundred. The Germans tend to exchange their money for U.S. dollars. It's the only currency accepted on the North Coast besides Jamaican dollars. Margot thanks him and hurries along, closing the door softly behind her.

The sight of Margot sleeping with her thumb in her mouth raises something intense inside Verdene. Margot stirs, her eyes barely fluttering awake, though it's noon. Her limbs are spread-eagled on the bed, sugar-brown skin on yellow sheets. St. Theresa's church bell rings in on the hill, and Verdene, instead of making a sign of the cross like she learned to do as girl when she went to mass, looks down on the woman she loves and studies her. An open face that wears its emotions. Wounded and sensitive.

She inhales deeply, the love swelling inside her lungs. Afraid she might combust, she exhales. She lowers the tray of breakfast food she cooked for Margot—fried dumplings, ackee, and saltfish, with a side of sliced pear—and glances at the wardrobe that holds two full-length mirrors. Verdene catches a reflection of herself holding the tray. At forty there are still glimpses of youth in the handsome face with sculpted features and eyes that blaze a startling black. She has gone gray early, a patch of silver surrounded by thick black curls. But since being with Margot she has regained a youthfulness that enables her to ease into laughter, fits of playfulness, and a sexuality that oozes from her without effort, without any fuss.

She adjusts the tray on the small night table and reaches for the Holy Bible (just for a little Sunday devotion like Ella taught her), which is kept there like a secret inside the drawer. But the sight of her mother's picture halts her movement. All the loveliness and life and breath seem to stop at the sight of Ella. *Oh, dear Mama.* Usually the picture is turned to face the wall when Margot sleeps over. Margot doesn't like the idea of Verdene's deceased mother staring at them in bed. Quite frankly, Verdene doesn't mind. Her whole life she has lived in secrecy. Why be ashamed at this point in her own house—the house her mother left her? Nevertheless, she complies.

Margot's eyelashes flutter, her eyes opening to glance up at the wide expanse of the room and the sheet falling below her waist. Verdene blushes, as ashamed as a little girl who has just walked in on her mother having sex.

"It's okay," Margot tells her, picking up the sheet to cover her breasts, suddenly self-conscious.

"Brought you something," Verdene says in the clipped British accent she adopted during her time living in London. It dances gaily with her Jamaican accent, so her intonations come out sounding proper—the kind of proper that makes people in River Bank just as curious as they are fearful of her. As a foreigner, or rather, a returning resident, she is untouchable.

Margot grins as Verdene places the tray on the bed. "You don't have to spoil me this way all the time, cooking breakfast and carrying it to the room."

"Are you saying you don't like it?" Verdene asks.

"I didn't say that." Margot laughs. Verdene laughs too, allowing her body to ripple with the effects of that pleasant itch in her belly. She pretends to turn away in defeat, but Margot leaps from the bed and pulls her back down, for a moment forgetting her nakedness. Verdene allows herself to fall, entangled between Margot's legs. They remain like this, trembling in a fit of giggles. When the giggles subside a minute later, their breaths rise in the pleasant silence of the room, contained within its four walls. Verdene moves away slightly, aware of how close they are—Margot with no clothes on and Verdene in a T-shirt and the wraparound skirt she always wears around the house that reveals the golden flesh of her thighs when it parts.

"I have to go back to the kitchen," Verdene says, untangling herself. "You must be hungry. Eat."

She pulls herself away and Margot lets her. Margot reaches for the cover again as if to hide. Verdene knows that she slept in the nude hoping Verdene would come into the room during the night and slip under the covers. But that didn't happen.

"Can't we just—"

"Not until you're ready," Verdene quips, sensing where the conversation is headed.

"Ready? I've been ready," Margot says.

Verdene looks down at her hand on the doorknob. She's squeezing it and letting it go. Her knuckles are shiny like marbles under her skin. "I don't want what happened last time to happen again," Verdene finally says in a whisper that comes off like a sigh. "I just can't—"

"I already apologized. What else yuh want me to do?" Margot grabs a pillow from the foot of the bed and puts it between her legs. It's another habit of hers, as persistent as the urge to bite her nails.

"Sweetheart," Verdene says, more softly. "I can't push you to do anything you don't want to do."

Margot moves the pillow and sheet away from her body and gets up from the bed. She moves closer and pushes Verdene against the door. It closes behind her. Up close her eyes are a pair of glistening onyx like the stone Margot gave her. Margot takes Verdene's hands into hers. "I'm ready."

Verdene fights the urge to follow her to the bed, for deep down she knows, for her, sex is a drug. She's tempted to let Margot do to her whatever she wants. But what happens afterward? It's the after that Verdene fears more than anything else. What if Margot's renewed willingness to be seduced is nothing but curiosity?

She remembers how Margot leapt off the bed in the middle of their lovemaking the first time, and wept. When they began seeing each other, Margot refused to do anything more than kiss and cuddle. She wanted to be courted first. So Verdene acquiesced, grateful for Margot's insistence that they should know and explore each other in other ways. But after six months of waiting, Verdene had enough. She made her move and Margot gave in, though reluctantly. She wept as if lamenting every wrong done to her in her life. She wept as though their intimacy were happening against her will. She stayed, but she wept. Verdene, stunned, asked if Margot was all right. Margot responded by shaking her head, her body trembling and shuddering. "*I've never felt this way with anyone*," Margot said.

"*It's okay, Margot. It's okay.*"

"*It's like that dream where I'm drowning.*"

"*You're not drowning, baby.*"

"*I have no control whatsoever.*"

"*Just let go.*"

But Margot wasn't ready to see herself this way, wasn't ready to give herself this label. She told Verdene that when she saw Verdene at the market after her years away, Margot began to understand something about herself. Margot described it in detail: How she gasped, because Verdene snatched her breath away. How she was transfixed by Verdene's smooth, peanut-butter skin against the sea-green dress. How she was taken by the dark unruly mass of hair with the patch of white in front. How the vision of her perfect silhouette convinced Margot she was in need of something else at the market—more cyan pepper, pimento seeds, more soursop, lime, and cauliflower, more ginger, cocoa, and yam. But the more Margot added to her already full basket, following Verdene down an aisle of vendors, the more she realized what she was really in need of.

Verdene herself remembered only the market vendors. How they watched her, turning to give her their full unfriendly stares. One by one they scrunched their noses as though the smells from the nearby fish market had finally gotten to them after thirty years of selling. Verdene, pretending to be untroubled by this, filled her basket with fruits, handed crisp bills to hesitant hands, and left. But once outside the market, she suddenly turned her head sharply to the right, meeting Margot's stare.

Months later Verdene was pulling a weeping Margot into her arms to comfort her. But Margot jumped up, got dressed, and fled as if Ella had stepped from the photo and chased her from the house. She ran all the way home in the pitch-blackness of the night.

Verdene leans in to kiss Margot on the base of her neck, then on her mouth.

"I'm ready," Margot repeats, her eyes caressing Verdene's face. They are a deeper brown than her skin, with the sun in their centers.

"No, Margot. Don't confuse desire for love. Maybe for you this is a—"

"I'm not confusing anything. I know what I want."

"Do you?"

Margot drops her gaze.

"Just as I thought," Verdene says softly, swallowing the edge in her voice. She gently pushes Margot off and cuffs her wrists with her hands. "I have something on the stove. I don't want it to burn. My mother left me that pot."

Verdene looks out the window of her kitchen and watches people go by dressed in their Sunday best—men wearing their good button-up shirts and shiny black pants ironed too many times. Women in their church hats and bright pastel colors, Bibles clutched in their hands like purses, each pausing to make a sign of the cross as they pass by the house. Verdene rolls her fists, her nails digging deeply inside her palms until the violent tremor rumbling inside her subsides. Sunday is the only day of the week that these people take the liberty to parade in front of her property, dressed in their holier-than-thou costumes. Verdene pauses in the stillness of the kitchen, turning on the faucet full blast to take her mind off them. But then she sees Miss Gracie, the old woman who lives next door. Her bearded chin is thrust forward, jutting from beneath the broad white hat that covers the rest of her face; her wilted body that once towered over men and women in River Bank is draped in an off-white dress with lace trimmings. A very handsome young man, whose face Verdene doesn't recognize, is walking next to her, supporting her weight as though the woman cannot walk herself. She too stops to make the sign of the cross as she passes by Verdene's house, instructing the reluctant young man to do the same. Had she been holding something other than her Bible, she would've flung it. Like that tree limb she wrapped in a bloodied cloth and threw in Verdene's yard last week.

"*The blood of Jesus is upon you!*" she had yelled with crazed eyes. It was as though she dared Verdene to say something. But Verdene remained on her veranda, stunned silent.

Before the tree limb it was a beheaded fowl that she left on Verdene's front steps. Verdene didn't see the woman do it, but she knew. Four Sundays ago Verdene found the body of a dead dog on her property. Since Verdene moved back from London there had been a total of four dead mongrel dogs found in her yard, their brown decaying bodies infested by flies. The incidents happened in spurts as though the perpetrator were operating on some kind of algorithm. The first time coincided with the first night Margot stayed over. A Saturday night. Verdene had woken up that Sunday morning to the slaughtered animal's blood trailing her walkway to the veranda. The blood was smeared across the doorposts and columns. And on the veranda grill and the gate. *The blood of Jesus be upon you!* was scrawled on the wall on both sides of the house.

Those were the same words the old woman had uttered just days before to Verdene. Verdene did not have it in her then to do anything about the incident. What could she have done? Her first instinct was to call the police. But they would hear her accent and want her to pay them something extra to track down the perpetrator. Her next instinct was to march next door, through the lush banana leaves that separated her house from the old woman's, but Miss Gracie might have gone off, drawing more unnecessary attention to Verdene. The old woman is senile, but it would still be her words against Verdene's. So Verdene cleaned up the mess herself. She fetched the shovel and silver bucket. She did so as quietly as possible, since she didn't want to wake Margot. The night before they had sipped tea and lounged in the living room—Margot on the sofa and Verdene on the floor mat—a good distance between them. It occurred to Verdene then, as she stood on the veranda with the pail and shovel, that while they talked that night, someone was violating her property. Someone who could have seen them.

That bloody morning she made her way toward the garden, though a steady stream of churchgoers were passing by. She waved at them, bowing her head reverently just like her mother had taught her to do. "*Always be nice and cordial . . .*" Ella used to quip, aware of the neighbors' eagle-eyes, especially the women's, when she returned with all her foreign dresses. And so, like her mother, Verdene waved, her arm a windshield wiper that smeared their frowning faces. She put on her best smile stretched across her face like a taut elastic band, barely touching her eyes. The churchgoers gathered speed, and once they passed, Verdene picked up the dead animal from the flower bed with the shovel. Margot appeared in the window, her face like a full moon, with the curtains hiding the rest of her body. Verdene lowered the shovel. She saw the terror in Margot's eyes and forced herself to keep digging a hole by the soursop tree. The same place she would put all the other carcasses.

"*Please*," Verdene had said, pushing Margot away gently when she came up behind Verdene inside the house that morning, "*give me a moment.*" She leaned against the kitchen sink, her back toward Margot. Following the huge silence between them, Verdene told Margot, "*It will always be like this. This life. With me.*" Verdene's back was still turned. As she awaited Margot's response, she closed her eyes to keep back the burning tears that had welled up. She sucked on her lips, almost tasting the kiss they had shared the night before. Their first. But Margot didn't respond. Not immediately. And though she held Verdene from behind, her body warming Verdene's, her face resting in the crook of Verdene's neck, Verdene sensed her reserve, felt her leave the room, the footsteps receding, a door closing softly.

It's ironic how she had wanted Margot out the picture when she first met her. During her second year at university, Verdene had come home to find a girl sitting on the sofa in her mother's living room. The girl was probably ten years old at the time, with long, skinny legs that were ashy with too many scratches. They were hanging off the couch, swaying back and forth. The girl's hair was uncombed and the pale dress she wore was soiled with dirt. Verdene wondered if her mother had rescued a stray. As a schoolteacher, Ella was inclined to take in neighborhood children and tutor them. When Verdene looked closer at the small brown face flanked by a mass of unruly hair like a sunflower, she realized the little girl was none other than Delores's daughter. Verdene didn't know the little girl's name then, but she had seen Delores with her a few times, the both of them walking to town with goods to sell. They lived in a small boarded-up house not too far from Verdene and her mother. Margot's Uncle Winston—an old classmate of Verdene's—was a street boy who gambled, smoked weed, and chased after young girls. He was the one who knocked-up Rose, Miss Gracie's daughter. Ella, out of the kindness of her heart, volunteered to look after Margot when her mother and grandmother weren't around.

Verdene was jealous of the girl at first. It had always been Verdene and Ella against the world, when Ella wasn't too busy working to be in her husband's good graces. But when he died, Ella grieved as though he were the best man to ever walk the earth. Sometimes the grieving turned to anger directed at Verdene for not respecting the man who helped to bring her into this world. Ella, who was probably lonely after the death of her husband and Verdene's departure to the university, did not mind Margot keeping her company. Verdene found Margot a little precocious. She followed Verdene around the house when Verdene came home on weekends from school (out of obligation) and asked about everything under the sun. And Verdene, who was then busy juggling exams, the pressures of being away at university and barely passing chemistry (her major), paid the girl no mind. Though Margot was bright, Verdene felt in her heart that she was Delores's problem. Why should Ella be in charge of this woman's child? Ella gave the girl extra lessons, since at ten years old she was only reading at a second-grade level.

"*Mama, it's not your duty to fix someone else's child,*" Verdene said to her mother. "*Let Delores tek care ah her own child.*"

But Ella wouldn't listen. She was taken with the child, calling her Little Margot. Ella gave Little Margot Verdene's old clothes to wear. They were nice dresses that Ella had to take in, stitching up the sides, adjusting the hems, adding extra buttonholes and buttons, whatever she could do to make the dresses fit Little Margot's tiny frame.

Then one day, Verdene saw Margot crouched in a corner, crying in front of Mr. Levy's shop. Verdene stopped to help her, imagining the girl had lost her money or fallen and bruised some part of her. "*What's the mattah?*" she asked. Little Margot sniffled and told her that some children in her school were calling her *Maggot* instead of *Margot*.

"*Dey say ah dirty an' smell bad.*" The little girl was shaking as she told Verdene this, her bony shoulders shuddering, her chest heaving. Verdene didn't know what to do. She rested her hand on the girl's shoulder, and Little Margot looked up into Verdene's face, her eyes large and watery, the pupils expanding into a well into which Verdene fell. Her fall was deep, endless; one that stirred her womb with a possessiveness, a feral instinct to hunt Little Margot's bullies down.

Every time Verdene had to leave for university, Margot cried. Ella would have to appease the girl with promises. "*She'll be back to see us next week, dear.*" Then, peering at Verdene, Ella's eyes would hold in them those very questions. "*Right, darling? You'll be back to see yuh dear mother next week, right?*"

Verdene turns her attention back inside the kitchen. She switches off the faucet, realizing water has overflowed, spilling to the floor. The dishes are piled in the sink from the breakfast she made Margot this morning—one pot full of her lopsided boiled dumplings and the other with chopped-up onions, tomatoes, and saltfish. Just an hour ago Verdene sang along to Ken Boothe, feeling hopeful, unaware of this mood that has befallen her. Unaware of the ambush of memory that awaited her. The mess in the kitchen repulses her. Verdene was never a tidy cook, or a cook at all. Everything is arranged in the cupboards the way her mother left it: plates stacked on top of each other, glasses and cups separated— the fancier ones with designs for visitors Verdene never has, and the ordinary, plain ones for everyday use. Since courting Margot, Verdene has been trying to cook more often, feeling domesticated for the first time at the age of forty. Before, when she lived in London, she would heat things up in microwaves or venture to a nearby restaurant for takeout. Such habits were possible in London, where there were restaurants everywhere. Indian, Chinese, Turkish, Caribbean, Pakistani.

Cooking is becoming a private joy Verdene works hard to maintain, delving into her mother's old recipes inside the kitchen drawers among the utensils. They were mostly cake recipes. For other food, Verdene draws from memory—those evenings when she used to watch her mother cook, throwing spices and sugar and flour inside pots without measuring. Ella only knew how something turned out by tasting it. Verdene has adopted this method. As she experiments, she finds herself tasting more and measuring less. The process softens something inside her, makes her hum tunes to little songs as she chops and stirs. One would never have known how much Verdene once resented her mother for doing the exact same thing for her father when he was alive and came home with his dirtied boots and soiled clothes from building the railway.

"*Why can't he ever cook his own food or set di table?*" Verdene would ask Ella, while observing her father recline on his favorite chair with the newspaper, smoking his cigarettes and taking swigs of white rum. He sought refuge in the clouds of smoke that surrounded him and the liquor that warmed his blood. Ella was mostly dismissive of Verdene's questions, fanning her away with, "*When yuh get to this stage you'll know why.*" Verdene never knew what that meant. In rebellion (she thinks), she had never been able to give of herself this way in relationships, fearing she would have to be some man's maid, or his personal servant. As abusive as Verdene's father was, Ella worshipped the ground he walked on.

In her first marriage, Verdene failed miserably. Not because she didn't love the man—a nice devout Catholic from Guyana her aunt handpicked for her—but because she could never pretend to be that kind of a woman. But here she is, in her mother's kitchen, finally understanding what her mother meant.

When Verdene reenters the bedroom, Margot is already dressed, ready to go.

"We have to talk," Verdene says, taking a deep, labored breath. Margot sits on the bed, her hands clasped. Verdene notices that the food remains uneaten. She also notices that Margot has been crying. Her eyes are red and the flesh around them is raw.

"What yuh want to talk about?" Margot asks. When she turns her face to the side, light catches it and Verdene is taken aback by her beauty. She walks over and sits next to the younger woman. She takes Margot's hand into hers and holds it. She lifts it to her lips, then presses it to her cheeks. Margot takes it away.

"Maybe you're right," she says.

Verdene lets her hand drop to her side. "Right about what?"

"That I'm not ready."

Margot sits frozen like a statue, her head held straight. The only hint that she is breathing is the slow rise and fall of her chest. Two buttons are open in the front of her blouse. Verdene catches a glimpse of the soft flesh underneath. Margot turns to look at her and repeats, "I'm not ready," as though to convince herself.

Verdene takes Margot's hand—in the same way she did the night before the discovery of the first dead dog. "We should try again," she says. "But I'll leave it up to you . . ." She takes a deep breath.

Margot visibly relaxes, as though she was expecting another response. Verdene feels an overwhelming urge to hold her, but she doesn't. They sit like this, both staring straight ahead, their hands in their laps. The words leave Verdene's mouth, floating above them in the bedroom, finally settling with the rise and fall of their pregnant sighs like a sheet flung over a bed.

"I only knew men," Margot whispers, still staring straight ahead. "I always had feelings for you." Margot is shaking her head as though she has gotten lost and is too overwhelmed with directions leading her to streets with no names. "But I'm not . . . I don't know if I . . ."

Verdene nods, but she says nothing. She focuses on the nails in the wooden floorboards, their round black heads appearing like dots. Margot rests her head on Verdene's shoulder. Her gesture seems to signal that they have stepped into an intimate circle and are joined together in this uncertainty. Breathing in deeply, Margot says, "I want you to teach me how to swim."

5

I T'S A COOL AND DAMP MORNING—THE WAY IT USUALLY IS before the sun makes its appearance, sucking all possibilities dry. Margot had gotten dressed at Verdene's house, entertaining the idea of them as a couple. It's not as though this has never occurred to her before—this seed that slipped into the cavity of her chest, settling itself inside her for the last few weeks. Something triggered its growth. Perhaps it was the way Verdene held her the night before, confirming for Margot that they fit together.

Margot begins to walk with clarity through the thinning fog, cradling this idea like a newborn baby. Her mind races ahead to the possibility of leaving River Bank for a nice beachfront villa in the quiet, gated community of Lagoons—a place far from River Bank where

Margot could give freely of herself, comforted by the cool indifference of wealthy expats from Europe and America. It would be like living in another country. Ever since Reginald Senior hosted a party years ago at a lavish villa in that neighborhood for a few of his friends and invited her, she has always wanted to live there. Margot was astonished by how the wealthy in Jamaica live; how for them, the island is really paradise—a woman who offers herself without guile, her back arched in the hills and mountains, belly toward the sun. For even in this drought her rivers run long and deep; her beaches, wide and tempting.

River Bank residents tend to bypass domestic positions in an area like Lagoons, going instead for the resorts. They are like ants, all of them, Margot thinks—latching on to the same bread as everyone else. *Well, let them keep nibbling away.* As far as Margot is concerned, she and Verdene will be a lot better off in a remote place without the neck strain from looking over their shoulders. Margot has it all planned out. Her promotion as general manager is in the works already. She is certain that she will get it; certain of Alphonso's feelings about her. She could use that money to live like a queen in her own country for once. Key-lime curtains and sweating glasses of lemonade in the sunroom. Grocery lists of imported goods and planting trees to complement the landscape.

As Margot moves through the expanse of her fantasy—padding lightly on the marble tiles of her dream house—she bumps into something solid on the ground. She looks down into the gutted carcass of a John-crow surrounded by flies, the rotting smell rising into Margot's open mouth. Margot pinches her nose and takes three steps backward. It has to be three—one for the Father, Son, and Holy Ghost. Grandma Merle would have told her to throw salt behind her too, to ward off bad luck.

"Holy Jesus!"

And just as she says this, three John-crows appear. They circle low, casting dark shadows in the face of the new sun. Their black wings are like sharp edges that seem capable of slitting trees in half. Margot feels the hair rise on the back of her neck when the John-crows descend. She watches in horror as they sink their beaks into the carcass—one that could have been a sibling, a spouse, a mother, a child. Margot will never forget this image—the sight of the crows feasting on their own, their Kumina dance celebrating death.

Back in the shack, she takes her time wiping the tips of her shoes with a wet cloth soaked with bleach. She'll be late to work today. She strips naked and puts her work clothes in a pan of water. She decides to take a shower, to scrub away any bad omen with pimento leaves. Never mind the flies and heat outside. She lathers herself with soap, grateful for the good water pressure. She never bathes outside this late in the morning after the fog lifts. But today she has no choice. She also does not feel like going back to Verdene's house this time of day, since the washers take that path to the river and may see her.

The water feels good in the heat. Without thinking, she tilts her head back to let it run through her hair, then remembers too late that she had just gotten it creamed. She makes a mental note to schedule another hair appointment. It has to be later today, since she cannot go to the hotel looking like a crazed woman. Margot busies herself with lathering.

"Look like is you g'wan drain di entire island of di likkle wata we 'ave lef'!"

Everything inside Margot halts at the sound of her mother's voice.

"Yuh nuh see dat we in a drought?" Delores asks. "Wah wrong wid yuh? Yuh look like a jackass, scrubbing like dat wid wata beating pon yuh head top."

"What yuh doing here?" Margot asks, shutting off the shower. "Ah thought you were at di market." She clumsily reaches for her towel to cover herself.

"Is suh yuh carry on when yuh t'ink nobody is here?" Delores asks. "Yuh run up di wata rate?"

"I was washing off."

"Yuh didn't 'ave di decency fi do dat earlier?"

"I wanted to change my clothes. I was on my way to work when I—" Margot fans away the rest of her words. She doesn't feel like going into details with Delores about the John-crow. Delores sucks her teeth. Margot thought her mother would leave her alone, but Delores just stands there as though waiting for more explanation.

"What else yuh want?" Margot asks.

Delores shakes her head. "Sometimes ah wondah 'bout you. If me neva come back here, you might ah been in dat wata all day. Shouldn't you be at work? Dat hotel yuh work at giving yuh di illusion dat we 'ave money fi dash weh? If yuh lose dat job, God help we! Washing off, my foot! Which sane person wash off inna broad daylight outside? Is want yuh want Likkle Richie an' any other Peeping Tom fi see yuh?"

"Would it make a difference?" Margot asks.

"Where did I go wrong?"

"Let me pass. I have to get to work. You said so yuhself."

Delores doesn't move. She regards Margot closely, like she used to do when Margot was a child—when she gave her the kind of baths that were meant to cleanse her of evil.

"What is it?" Margot asks. Her voice cracks under the weight of the memory.

"Yuh t'ink ah got di sense of a gnat?"

Margot chuckles lightly, though her knees buckle. "I don't have no time fah dis."

"You got time fah other t'ings. T'ink ah don't notice dat yuh don't sleep here no more? You is a sneak, an' God g'wan strike yuh dung."

Margot throws her head back and laughs out loud. "I am thirty years old. Ah can sleep anywhere ah please. An' besides, yuh soun' like ole Miss Gracie wid har drunk, crazy self." She is able to walk past Delores into the house. She doesn't let on that God was the first thing she thought about this morning when she stumbled upon death in her path.

"At di end ah di day, yuh can't seh ah neva try wid yuh," Delores says.

Margot is glad that she's not facing Delores; glad that she can focus on dressing herself, careful not to rip her stocking. The proof of her innocence—since she is always on trial—is in her calm, her ability to seem unaffected by anything Delores says. She tries hard in this moment not to seek comfort in the fantasy she had earlier of moving away with Verdene—a thought that skipped like a carefree child, shifting things around, making room. But try as she might, Margot cannot stop it from emerging. Neither can she protect it from Delores. Her best and safest bet is to kill it.

Margot watches Alphonso talking to the administrative staff in his office—the higher-ups who run his hotel resort when he's not around. Alphonso is pacing as he gives orders, looking like a boy balancing a crown on his head while walking a tight rope. Through the tilted louver windows with curtains that separate the front desk from the conference room, she can hear and see a few things— Dwight, the branch manager, clutching his pen in his tight fist as Alphonso paces before him; Simon, the activities coordinator, who is in charge of all the in-house entertainment at the hotel; Boris, the head of hotel security and a former police sergeant; Camille, Dwight's assistant, who struggles to write down every sentence coming out of the four gentlemen's mouths during the meeting; and Blacka, the accountant and Alphonso's right-hand man, looking like a pharaoh sitting with his arms folded and chest puffed, silently observing.

"Yuh t'ink I'm running a farm here? Yuh t'ink is chump-change people paying to stay at my resort?" Alphonso barks. "You are all incompetent!"

Dwight sits forward, dropping his pen. "Is who yuh t'ink yuh talking to dat way? If it wasn't fah all of us in here, this hotel wouldn't be open! Yuh father never intended fah you to take ovah . . . It was yuh brother. If Joseph never died in that car accident yuh wouldn't be no god dat you is now! He knew yuh was a disgrace! So don't you come in here now, telling us you're dissatisfied. We're not the fault why di hotel losing money!"

Alphonso pounces at Dwight and grabs him by the collar. Boris and Simon jump up to pull them apart. When he's free, Dwight fixes his tie and adjusts the collar of his pin-striped shirt as Alphonso calms himself. The other men, excluding Blacka, give Alphonso a look that reminds Margot of the way the other hotel employees look at her, when they whisper within earshot, "*Who does that Margot think she is? She act like she is some big s'maddy. Yuh see di way she walk around here like she own di place?*"

But Margot is somebody. She knows, for example, that she can do a better job than Dwight, who is a buffoon. Because of him the hotel isn't doing well. His fancy degree, expensive suits, and luxury cars don't hide the fact that he's incompetent. What makes Dwight favorable is the fact that he's Alphonso's second cousin and went to private school with him at Ridley College in Canada. Margot knows deep down that no hotel would've hired Dwight had it not been for his Wellington family name—Dwight, who shows up late, flashing his watch and telling others to be on time; Dwight, who overlooks complaints and any details having to do with the comfort of the guests; Dwight, who leaves the majority of the work to his assistant, Camille—who in Margot's opinion wastes her time every evening sitting on his lap. Poor girl chose the wrong Wellington to screw.

Margot returns to her seat at the front desk with Kensington. She can barely concentrate on checking people into the hotel.

"What yuh t'ink dey saying?" Kensington asks her. She's whispering.

"It's none of our business," Margot snaps.

"You an' him not friend?" Kensington asks.

"What's that supposed to mean?" Margot whips around to face a brazened Kensington. The girl shrugs. "You know . . . him laugh up, laugh up wid yuh sometimes. So I thought oonuh was friends."

The girl looks down at the surface of the desk in front of her, drawing heart-shaped patterns with her finger. She's rail-thin with a height on her, always fidgeting with the waistband of her uniform skirt, which is too wide, though it hangs well above her knees. Had it not been for her high color, Kensington wouldn't be considered beautiful. Or even be considered for the job. The girl was hired as a part-time secretary last summer after graduating from high school, but ended up staying longer. Now she thinks she has a right to make assessments about Margot and Alphonso's relationship.

"Just continue to do yuh work, Kensington," Margot says, in the authoritative voice she uses when wielding her seniority.

"How do you do it?" Kensington's tiny voice pierces the uncomfortable silence that follows Margot's order.

"How do I do what?" Margot asks.

Behind Kensington's head the palm trees blow wavelike in a breeze that brings the smell of the sea inside the open lobby. Margot is grateful for this breeze, for it cools her boiling blood as she watches Kensington stringing her words together.

"People are talking. Russ, Gretta, an' all ah dem."

Margot cuts her off before she can list every one of the lower staff—the maids, the cooks, the groundsmen—people who begrudge her because she sends Kensington to buy her patty and cocoa-bread at lunchtime from Stitch so that she doesn't have to pass by them and get into their idle gossip about management.

"Do me a favor, Kensington?" Margot says, her voice as bitter-sweet as molasses.

"What's that?" the girl asks, looking at Margot with hopeful eyes that incense Margot even more. She resists the urge to slap the girl. Instead, Margot issues a warning. Or more like a sound piece of advice. "If yuh want to stay here for a long time, then mind yuh own business," she says.

With that Margot cuts her eyes and turns to the window behind them. Alphonso is unpredictable, so she imagines the executive office watching him closely like a ticking bomb. Suddenly the door flies open and Alphonso marches out.

"Gimme that manila folder over there!" he demands, pointing to the hidden file cabinet where there are over a hundred manila folders—all of which are going to be entered into a secure computer system to keep records of the hotel finances and guest information. Murphy is bringing the computers in tomorrow. All five Gateway computers are being shipped from America. Kensington springs up to find the folder Alphonso is referring to. She hesitates when she sees that all of them are identical. Asking Alphonso to clarify would reveal her incompetence.

He's drumming his fingers on the counter and glances at his gold Rolex. His platinum wedding band glistens on his cream hand. "Am I going to wait here all day?"

Margot steps in seamlessly, subtly. It's she who moves to give Alphonso the folder. She has been fingering it all along, knowing he would need it in this meeting. It has all the budget information she helped him compile. As she gives Alphonso the folder, their hands touch. They pause, suspended like two birds holding the ends of the same worm. Margot clears her throat and takes her hand away. She smoothes her skirt over her thighs as though she has been caught with it inched up to her waist. Like the day they got caught in the conference room—the only time Margot has ever been inside it.

"You're welcome!" she says to Alphonso too loudly, though he says nothing. When he returns to the executive office, Margot rests her chin in her palm. Kensington clears her throat.

"What?" Margot asks.

"Nothing," Kensington says.

"Ah thought so."

6

O N HER WAY TO WORK, DELORES NOTICED THE BARREN FRUIT
trees, the wilting flowers, and the brown, brittle grass all
sucked dry. Dogs were lying on their sides with their tongues out,
goats leaned against the sides of buildings and fences, and cows
moved about with exposed rib cages, gnawing on sparse land.
Children crowded around standpipes to bathe or drink from the
little water that trickled out; the younger ones sat inside houses on
cardboard boxes, sucking ice and oranges, while some accompanied their mothers to the river with big buckets. Meanwhile, idle
men hugged trees for shade, or took up residence at Dino's, pressing
flasks of rum to their faces. *God is coming after all*, Delores thought.

But while the God-fearing people become intent on staking

their claim in heaven, crying, "Jesas 'ave mercy!," Delores prepares for another day of work. For money has to be made. With the sun comes that heat. They go hand in hand like John Mare and his old donkey, Belle. Delores fans herself with an old *Jamaica Observer*. Her bright orange blouse is soaked with sweat, like someone threw water and drenched her under the armpits, across the belly, all the way down to her sides. Two other vendors couldn't take the heat, so they packed up their things and went back home. The rest, including Delores, sucked their teeth: "Dem really aggo give up a day's work because ah di heat? Ah nuh Jamaica dem born an' grow? Wah dem expec'?"

Delores wipes the sweat off her face with a rag she tucks inside her bosom. She prepares for business as usual. Mavis, who has the stall next to Delores, is fully covered from head to toe. She reminds Delores of one of those Muslim women she sees sometimes—on very rare occasions—walking in the square with their faces covered.

"Di heat is good fi yuh skin. Mek it come quicker," Mavis says, adjusting the broad hat on her head. Delores fans away the woman, who has been trying different skin-lightening remedies since Delores has known her. Delores has already dismissed the woman as off. Like Ruby, who used to sell fish and is currently selling delusions to young girls who want more than apron jobs. Poor souls think a little skin-lightening will make the hoity-toity class see them as more than just shadows, slipping through cracks under their imported leather shoes.

"Why yuh nuh try drink poison while yuh at it?" Delores asks the woman.

Mavis rolls her eyes. "If me was as black as you, Delores, me woulda invest me money inna bleaching cream. Who want to be black in dis place? A true nobody nuh tell yuh how black yuh is."

"Kiss me ass, gyal! An' g'weh wid yuh mad self!" Delores throws down the old newspaper.

Just then John-John—the young dread whom Delores has known since he was a boy who helped his mother sell goods at the market—stops by with a box of the birds he carves out of wood. He was always creative—ever since Delores has known him—making keepsakes from scraps to occupy his time, since he didn't go to school. Because he and Margot were playmates, Delores has treated him more like a son. Now a grown man supporting children of his own, he makes birds, which he gives Delores to sell for him and collects half of what she makes from the sales. He sees the women arguing, sees his opportunity, and seizes it by defending Delores. "Ah, wah Mavis do to you, Mama Delores? Here, let me handle it. G'weh, Mavis, an' leave Mama Delores alone. Yuh nuh have bettah t'ings fi do? Like count out di ten cents yuh get fi yuh cheap t'ings dem? Yuh son sen' yuh money from America, an' yet yuh stuck inna dis place?"

Mavis whips around to face him like a player caught in the middle of a dandy-shandy game. "A an' B having ah convahsation. Guh suck yuh mumma, yuh ole crusty, mop-head b'woy!"

But John-John puts down his boxes of birds, a grin on his face as though he's enjoying this exchange. "Every Tom, Joe, an' Mary know dat yuh don't get no barrel from America. A lie yuh ah tell. When people get barrel from America dem come moggle in dem new clothes." He struts in the little space between them to mimic models on a runway. "But yuh still dress like a mad'ooman, an' yuh look like one too wid dat mask 'pon yuh face!"

The other vendors in the arcade erupt in boisterous laughter, their hands cupped over their mouths, shoulders shuddering, and eyes damp with tears. Mavis adjusts her hat, and touches her screwed-up face with the bleaching cream lathered all over it like the white masks obeah women wear. "A true yuh nuh know me," she says, her mouth long and bottom lip trembling. "My son send me barrel from foreign all di time. Ah bad-mind oonuh bad-mind!"

"Nobody nah grudge yuh, Mavis," Delores says. "John-John jus' saying dat it nuh mek sense if di clothes dat yuh son sen' from America look like di ugly, wash-out clothes yuh sell. American clothes not suppose to look suh cheap. There's a discrepancy in what's what!" The other vendors' laughter soars above the stalls, flooding through the narrow aisles where the sun marches like a soldier during a curfew. Delores continues, "Is not like yuh t'ings sell either. Usually di tourist dem tek one look, see di cheap, wash-out, threadbare shirt dem then move on. Not even yuh bleach-out skin coulda hol' dem!"

"G'weh!" Mavis says. "Yuh only picking on me because yuh pickney dem don't like yuh!" Satisfied after delivering the final blow, Mavis retreats into her stall with a smirk Delores wishes she could slap away. But she can't move fast enough; John-John is already holding her back. Her hands are frantically moving over John-John's shoulder, wanting to catch the woman's face and rip it to shreds. That smirk holds the weight of scorn, of judgment. She should never have told Mavis that morning that her birthday came and went without a card from either Thandi or Margot. Well, she didn't expect a card from Margot, but Thandi should've remembered. Every year Thandi gives her something—last year it was a necklace made of small cowrie shells; the previous year were petals from dried flowers used to decorate the inside of a card; the year before that was a bracelet with coral beads strung by yarn. And this year, nothing. Setting up her items took longer than usual at the beginning of the week. She's always the first to have everything presented well enough for the tourists to come by, but this week she struggled with the simplest task of covering the wooden table with the green and yellow cloth. One of the figurines had fallen, breaking in half during setup. Delores felt off. The thought of spending the entire day selling made her feel like she was carrying an empty glass and pretending to have liquid in it. She confided this to Mavis, because she wanted someone to talk to at the time. How she has been selling for years and has never felt this way. How Margot, and most recently Thandi, couldn't care less if she dies in this heat a pauper. And in the heat of this very moment, Mavis has called her out. Mavis—with her crazy, lying, bleaching self—knows that Delores's children hate her. Mavis—the woman with nothing good to sell and who can never get one customer to give her the time of day—knows Delores's weakness. That smirk Delores itches to slap off her face says it all; and even if Delores succeeds in slapping the black off the woman (more than the bleach ever could), it won't erase the fact that Mavis probably has a better relationship with her son than Delores will ever have with her daughters.

John-John releases Delores. "Yuh mek har know who is in charge, Mama Delores! A good fi har," he says. "Nuh let har get to yuh dat way." Delores ignores him and plops down hard on her stool. She fans herself with the *Jamaica Observer* again as John-John surveys her table, checking to see if she sold any of his carved animals since the last time she saw him.

"Notin' at'all?" he asks when she tells him. He sits down on the old padded stool in Delores's stall and runs one hand through his dreadlocks, visibly puzzled. Delores is the best haggler out here.

"Yuh see people come in yah from mawnin?" she asks John-John in defense. "Sun too hot." She doesn't tell him that she hasn't been in the mood to do the regular routine—linking hands with tourists, courting them the way men court women, complimenting them, sweet-talking them, showing them all the goods, waiting with bated breath for them to fall in love, hoping they take a leap of faith and fish into their wallets.

John-John shakes his head, his eyes looking straight ahead. "We cyan mek di heat do we like dis, Delores. No customers mean nuh money," John-John says. His jaundiced eyes swim all over Delores's face. "Wah we aggo do, Mama Delores?"

"What yuh mean, what we g'wan do? Ah look like ah know?"

Delores fans herself harder, almost ripping the newspaper filled with the smiling faces of politicians and well-to-do socialites. She wants John-John to leave her alone to her own thoughts and feelings. But the boy can talk off your ears. He would sit there on the stool and talk all day if she lets him. Sometimes this interrupts Delores's work, because tourists see him in the stall and politely walk away, thinking they were interrupting something between mother and son. "Well, Jah know weh him ah do. Hopefully him will sen' rain soon," John-John says.

"Believe you me," she says to John-John, who squats to diligently paint one of his wooden birds. "Tomorrow g'wan be a new day. Yuh watch an' see. Ah g'wan sell every damn t'ing me have."

"Yes, Mama Delores. Just trus' an' Jah will provide fah all ah we," John-John says. The pink of his tongue shows as he works on perfecting the bird's feathers. He has been working on that one bird since last week. Usually it takes him only a few hours. When he finishes the bird, he separates it from the rest, which he wraps one by one in old newspaper to place inside the box. Delores picks up the bird he's just finished. It's more extravagant than all the others, with blue and green wings skillfully outlined with black paint, a red and yellow underbelly, and a red beak. The eyes are sharp, the whites in them defined with the small black pupils. It looks like it will be a popular item, expensive. Delores already prices it in her head. She guesses fifty U.S. dollars.

As Delores examines this new bird she thinks of the parrot she once saw at Devon House in Kingston—a colonial mansion with a beautiful garden that had just opened up to the public. The year was 1968. It was her first trip to Kingston and she was eighteen years old. She left four-year-old Margot with Mama Merle and rode on the country bus to town all by herself. Initially she went to look for temporary work as a helper; but on a whim, she decided to visit the new attraction. Delores wanted to see it so that she could brag. So she wandered from Half Way Tree, where the country bus dropped her off, all the way up the busy Constant Spring Road. With a few wrong turns and stops to ask for directions (*"Beg yuh please tell weh me can fine Dev-an House?"*), she made it. It took a while for the nice Kingstonians she asked to understand her heavy patois and point her in the right direction. The mansion was just as beautiful in real life as it was in the papers—white paint glowing in the sun, big columns and winding staircases, a water fountain. But more amazing than the house were the parrots. They seemed suited for their habitat—flying from tree to tree with colored wings through a lush garden with so many different trees and flowers, Delores saw many she hadn't known existed. She followed the birds until she got to the courtyard, where genteel Kingstonians sat enjoying the outdoors under the shade of fancy umbrellas and broad-brimmed hats. As if caught in a limelight onstage, Delores fidgeted with her Sunday dress—bright yellow with lace and puffed-up sleeves. She felt like Queen Elizabeth in that dress, especially because she had a pair of frilly green socks to match and a shiny pair of flats with buckles on the sides that never showed any specks of red dirt. The only things missing were a pair of gloves.

And the Kingstonians must have thought so too, for a hundred pairs of eyes followed her when she walked by, frowning pale faces transforming into amusement. They covered their mouths as though to suppress a laugh or a sneeze. Slowly, Delores backed away. She didn't notice the pile of dog mess. She stepped right in it, and in her shock, stumbled into the path of a group of Catholic school girls on a school trip, who were gliding in a straight line across the courtyard like swans being led by their mother—a nun who walked with her head tilted confidently to the sky. The girls gasped when Delores stumbled in their path, immediately corking their small noses with delicate pale hands. The way they snickered as their eyes scanned Delores's dress made it seem as if the dog mess were smeared across it. Right then Delores hated her dress. But it was her shoes and socks that caused the most laughter. And then the nun, as polite as she thought she was, smiled at Delores, her pinkish face glowing like a heart. "You must be lost. Are you here with the group from the country? They're by the picnic tables." How did she know Delores was from the country? That morning Delores thought she did a good job putting her outfit together in preparation for a day in the big city. But the girls were all snickering, shoulders hunched and pretty ponytails in white ribbons jerking back and forth. Delores should have listened to her mother. "*If me was suh big an' black, me woulda neva mek scarecrow come catch me inna dat color. Yuh bettah hope di people inna Kingston nuh laugh yuh backside back ah country.*" Mama Merle was right. Maybe bright colors weren't for her. The girls' laughter followed Delores all the way back through the gate like the smell of dog mess she never stopped to get rid of. The humiliation was worse than the swarm of flies.

It was as though a veil had lifted from her eyes. When she looked down, all she saw was her black skin and how it clashed with the dress. With her surroundings. With everything. It had collided with the order and propriety of the colonial mansion that day, and the uniform line of those high-color Catholic schoolgirls. Something about that trip changed her, and on the bus ride back her home looked different: the sea-green of the nauseating sea, the sneering sun in the wide expanse of a pale sky, the indecisive Y-shaped river that once swallowed her childhood, and even the red dirt from the bauxite mines caked under her worn heels, seemed like a wide-open wound that bled and bled between the rural parishes.

Delores looks at this bird John-John has created—a creature of the wild that he too had probably seen and fallen in love with. Delores frowns. John-John looks up and sees her staring at the bird. He gives her one of his clownish grins, his front teeth lapping over each other like the badly aligned picket fences around Miss Gracie's pigpen. "Ah see yuh admiring me work, Mama Delores." He's only a boy, Delores decides. In time he will begin to see the ugly.

He raises the bird to Delores and she takes it. "Yuh didn't have to," she says, her heart pressed against her rib cage. She always wondered if she'd ever see anything like those parrots again.

"Is fah Margot," he says. "Tell har is a gift from me. Ah made it 'specially fah her. It's the prettiest one in di lot."

Delores's hand shakes and the bird slips from her fingers and drops with an impact that breaks its beak. She's not sure if it slipped or if she heard Margot's name and flung it. The grin fades from John-John's face. He says nothing. He only sits there, his shirt open, his hands on his knees, with his legs wide. He looks down at the de-beaked bird on the ground.

"Me nevah mean fi bruk it," Delores says. She bends to pick it up, but John-John stops her.

"Is okay, Mama Delores. Nuh worry 'bout it. I an' I can mek anothah one." But the shadow hasn't left his face, and his eyes barely meet hers. She knows he has been working on this one for a while. She knows it probably took him a long time to choose the colors.

"Ah can always mek anothah one," John-John says again after a while, his eyes focusing intently on something in front of him. "Maybe if ah start now ah can give it to you tomorrow."

Delores is silent. She knows if she agrees it would give him too much hope. Delores lifts her tongue and tastes the dry roof of her mouth. She takes a sip of water from the plastic cup that has grown warm sitting on the table. A wave of exhaustion comes over her. Like all other things that slow her down, she thinks this too will pass. Only this time she's not certain what exactly she hopes will pass first—the drought, the fatigue, or that dark, looming thing that has been present inside her since the trip to Kingston and has recently risen to the surface. She has held on to her anger all these years, knowing very well what she would say to those girls if she ever saw them again.

"She can come collec' it herself," Delores finally says to John-John. "Ah can't speak for Margot. Margot is a big 'ooman. She know what she like an' what she nuh like. If yuh want my humble opinion, not a bone in dat girl's body is deserving of anything yuh can sell fah good money."

7

MARGOT COMES HOME LATER THAT EVENING AND SEES HER sister curled on the couch. She's in a faded housedress with balls of paper scattered around her. Margot doesn't wake her. She wonders how long Thandi has been lying there like this on her side with her dress hiked up, hands between her thighs. And those damn drawings. It's four o' clock; shouldn't she just be getting home from extra lessons? Margot hardly knows her sister's schedule anymore, since she's never around much. Thandi's education means more to her than her own well-being. Just last week Margot had to march down to the school to beg that condescending nun to change Thandi's demerit status. Though her sister shouldn't be wearing a sweatshirt to school, Margot still argued on her behalf. Margot remembers herself at that age—how she had to be pried open like a lobster, though she had no choice.

At the school, Margot had flashed the Wellington name like a badge, her association with Alphonso her best asset. If she's good enough to sleep with, then why not exercise the little bit of clout it gives her? The nun didn't have to know that she's only his mistress and hotel employee. "Either you erase it from her record or else," Margot said. This *or else* carried a lot of weight. The Wellington family donates a lot of money to the school. It's their wealth that built the hall in which the students worship, the new gymnasium—the only one on the island to have an indoor pool—and even the vocational block that houses all the typewriters, an art studio, and Singer ovens for baking classes. When Thandi got into the school and couldn't afford to pay, Margot got Alphonso to write a check for her tuition under the guise of a scholarship. This carefully cultivated relationship pays her tuition each year, and Margot will never let this opportunity slip away for Thandi.

The innocence of her sister's face holds Margot in place. Margot wonders what she's dreaming. Maybe she's running through a field of marigolds, the sky arched above her like a billowing blue sheet hanging from a clothesline—stretching from the beginning to the end of time. Margot knows she should cover her up with a sheet, but instead she sits and watches. Her sister is turning into a woman. Her breasts have swollen as though pumped with air from her breathing. And her hips have formed, filling out the dress. She's even getting lighter, the mild discoloration evident around her nose and mouth. Maybe she'll be the same café au lait shade as her father—a coolie Indian with nice hair and just enough pocket change for Delores to bring him to the house one day and introduce him to Margot. People called him Jacques. Margot was fourteen when Delores met him. He liked to give Margot sweets—gizzadas, tamarind balls, coconut drops, plantain tarts, icy-mints. As an adult, Margot gags at the smell of those sweets.

Margot's virginity was plucked like a blossoming hibiscus before its time. But this won't be Thandi's fate. Margot chants this to herself over and over again under her breath, the only prayer she has ever uttered.

Just then Thandi's eyelids flutter open as if something tells her she's being watched. She raises herself on one elbow and rubs her eyes. "Why are you watching me like that?" she asks Margot, her voice gravel-like with sleep, but with that formal diction that irks Margot. Since attending Saint Emmanuel High, her sister speaks as though she comes from money. (Her speech is even more formal, more modulated than the diction Margot uses with Alphonso and the visitors to the hotel.)

"Good evening to you too," Margot says. She looks away to give her sister privacy as she pulls her dress over her knees.

"What time is it?" Thandi asks.

"Yuh feeling sick?" Margot asks her sister.

Thandi swings her legs off the couch to give Margot space to sit beside her. Thandi rubs her eyes again, suppressing a yawn. "Just tired. All the studying, you know . . ." Her voice trails off.

Margot looks down at the papers around them. "Right. The CXC is jus' around di corner. You're on yuh way to getting nine ones, ah hope."

Thandi nods. She glimpses Margot's overnight bag at her feet. "You sleeping out again?" she asks Margot.

"What's it to you?"

"Who's the new man?" Thandi asks with a smirk. "You've been staying out a lot lately."

"No one special. Don't change the subject, Thandi. I got you out of a demerit fah wearing dat stupid sweatshirt."

"For *a nobody*, he's surely keeping you out the house." Thandi says this in a tongue-in-cheek kind of way that surprises Margot. She attributes such an innuendo to the older women in River Bank with knowing gleams in their eyes.

"It's none ah yuh business," Margot says, suppressing a laugh.

"Is it that Maxi guy? Yuh know he checks for you."

"It's not him. He's jus' ah taxi drivah. And ah Rasta."

"What's wrong with dat?" Thandi asks.

It's the most they have ever spoken this way. It's a side of Thandi that Margot rarely sees, if ever. The trees are barren this year because of the drought, but Thandi has blossomed.

"If yuh ever come home saying yuh deh wid a taxi man or a Rasta man, ah g'wan bruk yuh neck," Margot jokes. This makes Thandi laugh, throwing her head so far back that Margot worries her neck might snap.

When Thandi sobers, she says, "Can people really choose who dey fall in love with? That's ludicrous."

"Ludicrous?"

"You know. Like foolish."

"Yuh calling me foolish?"

"No, no!" Thandi gestures with her hands. "I was jus' saying that the concept of choosing who yuh love is . . ." Her voice trails off. "Forget it." The razor cuts across Margot's belly when Thandi says this. *Forget it.* The way Thandi says it makes Margot more aware that they aren't on the same level at all. But isn't that what Margot wanted? At this very moment Margot's ignorance seems like a fly her sister merely fans away.

"Yuh not thinking about boys, are you?" Margot asks her sister.

Thandi wraps her finger with a loose thread in her dress.

"No."

"Yuh not lying?"

"Margot!"

"Margot, what?"

"I don't have a boyfriend, if it's dat yuh asking."

"Good. Yuh books should come first," Margot says, sounding like Delores. And Thandi, as though she hears Delores's voice too, shuts down completely like the mimosa plants in the cove that wilt when touched. The darkness Margot is used to seeing in her sister's eyes as of late returns.

"Now is not di time for you to be thinking 'bout boys or nuh love. Yuh hear?"

"Yes."

"Yuh promise me?" Margot asks, softening a bit.

"Yes."

"Good."

There is a ditch between them on the two-cushioned couch—the very first thing she ever bought with her salary from the hotel, an asset that Delores, brimming with excitement and the fussiness that comes with big purchases like this one, had Margot wrap in plastic. Between Margot and Thandi are holes in the plastic, and the fading of what used to be beautiful upholstery fabric underneath.

"A penny for your thoughts?" Verdene says to Margot. They had set the table together. Margot helped with the placement of the mats, plates, and silverware, and Verdene carried the serving bowls. A candle glows at the center of the table.

"Just thinking how I like being here," Margot says. "With you."

Verdene lowers her fork and reaches across the table, and Margot lets Verdene's hand rest on hers. Margot recognizes in Verdene the older girl she fell in love with—the teenager she once knew, with a worldliness that used to make her blush. A girl who, to Margot, was as mysterious as the force that altered the weather. At ten years old she felt her stomach jump the first time Verdene called her pretty. Come to think of it now, Verdene Moore must have been called pretty all her life. She had that good hair that touched her back and that peanut-butter skin—some would call it golden—the shade that could get her a job in those days as a bank clerk or flight attendant, or a crown on her head as Miss Jamaica. Nevertheless, when Margot gave Verdene this compliment, she smiled as though Margot's comment were a surprise. A generous gift.

If it had been up to Margot, she never would have let Verdene out of her sight. She clung to her like macca bush, which latches onto skin and fabric. When Verdene read books to her, Margot would inhale deeply the sweet air from her mouth. She would ask the older girl to read more stories about a sleeping beauty, children lost in the woods, and cursed princesses, just to buy more time curled up next to her. Margot could not bear being away from her. She rushed through chores on weekends just so she could see Verdene when she came home from university. The day Verdene left for England, a part of Margot left with her. Verdene has brought color back into her life. Before, everything was black-and-white: Make money or die trying. Feel pain or feel nothing at all.

After dinner they clear the table and move the dishes to the sink. Verdene washes the plates and Margot dries them. They settle in each other's company, pleasantly full and mindful of their tasks. "I'll get that," Verdene says when Margot picks up a small Dutch pot—the one that was used to cook the potatoes.

Margot continues to dry the inside of it like she has been doing to the others. Verdene almost grabs the dish towel. "Just leave it. It dries on its own."

"It's just a pot," Margot says.

"Not just any pot. My mother left me that pot. Margot, please. Respect my wishes."

"Are you choosing her over me?" Margot asks, startled.

"This is not about choosing. This is about accepting certain things about me. If you care about me like I care about you, then you respect my wishes."

Margot picks up the towel that Verdene had taken from her

and begins to dry the utensils. She doesn't say anything for a while. Verdene senses her resentment and pulls her close. "When I returned to Jamaica, I didn't know what I would do. I didn't even know why I agreed to come back. All those years that I was in London, I hardly spoke to my mother, fearing the disappointment in her voice. I felt guilty when she passed. I felt I owed it to her to be here. But then I got here, and there you were. The universe was trying to tell me that love lives here."

Margot rests her weight on Verdene, who leans against the kitchen sink, each soothed by the beating of the other woman's heart. Suddenly Margot cannot bear to go another night resisting her impulses. She lifts her face and holds Verdene's gaze, hoping her eyes have a look that confesses that her body is warm and impatient under her dress. They kiss deeply, fervidly, as though it is the one thing they have been denied. Verdene carefully undoes Margot's dress as if any swift movement might change Margot's mind and send her running again. But Margot surprises Verdene by gently holding her hands, lowering them, and shaking her head. Without a word, she undresses Verdene, untying the bows on the front of her nightgown. One of the bows knots, and they smile as Margot uses her nails to meticulously unknot it. The nightgown slides to Verdene's feet in a lilac pool. Margot then peels Verdene's underwear down her hips and it joins her nightgown around her ankles. When they are both naked, Margot steps out of the circle of her dress and stands back. Verdene—with her hands at her sides, the small risings of her breasts, the faint ripple of flesh on her stomach, and the trimmed triangular crease between her legs—is beautiful and desirable just standing there. In all the years Margot has seduced others, she has never been fully aware, fully invested in savoring every moment of intimacy. Before Verdene looks away, flushed as though anticipating Margot's refusal, Margot pulls her close. Verdene opens her mouth wider to receive Margot's tongue.

They walk to the bedroom, their mouths together still and hips joined. Margot glances at the window—at the black patch of night, at Miss Ella's turned picture frame. A flit of panic nearly stops her in her tracks and almost prompts her to reach for the light switch. But with Verdene's slow, controlled caress, a current of pure pleasure washes over Margot and she collapses onto the bed, on top of Verdene. Margot quickly forgets about the window and Miss Ella and the lights, and shudders when Verdene, rolling her over, one by one takes her breasts into her mouth, which eventually wanders to the meeting of her hips. Margot pulls Verdene between her impatient thighs and arches her back to receive not only the thrill of Verdene's body, but a deeper understanding of what it means to feel connected to a whole person. She lets out a joyous cry, surprised by this new, alien feeling—one that has surpassed the ripple of pleasure that comes from Verdene's deliberate, measured strokes; and plunges her into the molten depths of possession.

Verdene is lying on her back next to Margot, her head turned to the window, where she can see the shadows of the waving branches of the mango tree. She thinks of other firsts—the first time she ever flew a kite, the first time she dove into the river, headfirst; the first time she'd ever been free and open, reveling in her girlfriend's ecstatic moans in their dorm room when Verdene made love to her. Not since Akua has Verdene felt so optimistic, so invested in new beginnings. At the university in Kingston on a chemistry scholarship Verdene had been free from her nitpicking mother, who was far more concerned with how well she could balance a book on her head, iron a pleat or a collar, chew with her mouth closed, and speak without raising her voice. On campus she was encouraged to have an opinion and form relationships outside her family's claustrophobic circle. The girls on the university's campus were highly affectionate. They walked around holding hands. In the dorms they combed each other's hair, lay in each other's beds, hugged up on each other during lunchtime and between classes, and sat in each other's laps. More than schoolmates, they were sisters. Verdene was closest to Akua, her roommate. Akua had a wide face, though her features were too small for it, and slow-moving eyes that could make people cry; all she had to do was blink those heavy eyelids once and they would remember how she suffered. Her almost bald head—with a reddish tint to her hair, most of which had fallen off with the chemo—was there to remind them too. The cooks gave her extra servings of meat and mashed potatoes, and the janitor, Mr. Irving, let her walk on recently mopped floors. "*Dat poor chile!*" She wore a headband to accessorize; but it was her smile—a dizzying white—that stole all the attention. An ember that glowed from within. Whenever Verdene felt sad or angry, Akua's positive attitude and constant jokes were there to remind her that all battles can be won.

"*You're only four hours away. You always used to have time for me. I need you here too,*" Ella would say, begging Verdene to visit more. And Verdene would feel guilty about how much she preferred to be at school.

Akua would bolster Verdene's resolve. "*Listen, she's yuh mother. She'll understand if yuh can't go home this weekend.*"

"*But she needs me.*"

"*What she needs is to get used to the fact that you have yuh own life now.*"

Verdene wanted to be around Akua more and more. As an only child, Verdene had no reference for true sisterhood, but she had observed her aunt and her mother. They were close like the girls at school, cackling about this and that over the phone, sharing everything with each other, down to the intonations in their voices and the expressions on their faces. But Verdene learned that there was a thin line between sisterhood and something else she had no name for. She and Akua ended up crossing the line numerous times, taking things further than the other girls. Their hugs became kisses, and their gentle brushes became direct touches. Not to mention the fights. They were messy, each girl's tongue sharply edged, capable of puncturing the ego. They knew which buttons to push. Likewise, they knew which string to tug to reel the other back.

To Verdene, their act was natural, a physical expression of how they felt about each other: the scorching love and cooling hate, the abysmal highs and outrageous lows. But to the university, and to the residence hall director Miss Raynor, who discovered them one late afternoon in the dorm, they were no different from witches warranting public execution. Seeing them in their loving embrace, Miss Raynor's face caved in as though a sinkhole were embedded at its center.

Verdene was disgraced, her poor mother shamed. The news spread like a cane-field fire and made its way to River Bank. It hovered like dark soot for days, months, years. Ella never again left the house after she found out. Verdene thinks to this day that her mother's cancer started then. It was a slow, painful death brought on by heartbreak. More than the heartbreak and shame was Ella's guilt and loss. After Verdene's explusion, Ella had to send away her only child. She did it to save her life. Back in River Bank, Verdene could've been raped or killed. If she were a man caught with another man, she would've been arrested, maimed, mutilated, and buried. So she was sent to live with her aunt Gertrude in London, where she finished school. Verdene had boarded the plane with only her two long hands. No luggage. She wore a deep purple wool dress, the only clothing Ella thought appropriate for England's brisk winter. In her hand, Verdene held on to the smooth black river stone Little Margot had given her. "*To remembah me by,*" the little girl had said.

She had snuck out of her house and run up to Verdene as Verdene got into the taxi to the airport. Verdene took the stone and thanked her, and for years she kept it. She never told Margot this, but once in a while she would pick it up and sit with it until it warmed in her palm. Other times she would resist the urge to go to a nearby lake in London and fling the stone as far out in the water as possible; for it held inside it the memory of the bitterness that settled inside her, and solidified.

When Akua went home to Forrester, a town five miles from the university, she was beaten and gang-raped. Her body was found in the bushes, mauled and naked. She was barely breathing, but because of the shame she endured, she begged the Good Samaritan to leave her there and let her die. He refused and rushed her to the hospital. In a letter to Verdene many years later, Akua included photographs of her four beautiful children and the policeman she married in the same church where she was an honorable member on the usher board and the women's ministry. She ended the letter with: "*May God be with you, always. He works miracles.*" Verdene crushed it inside her fist. For many years, she could not bring herself to return to Jamaica to visit, too ashamed to show her face until she had to. When Verdene came back to River Bank with a lifetime of regrets and a small suitcase, Margot was the first person at her doorstep.

Verdene resists the temptation to kiss Margot, settling for just listening to her breathing next to her. Carefully, Verdene leaves the bed. Standing in the living room where she usually goes to meditate, Verdene realizes why Margot would think she's choosing Ella. Everywhere Verdene looks, there is a picture of Ella. The walls of the room are covered; so is the wooden whatnot that holds figurines of the Virgin Mary rested atop crocheted doilies, and a small television, which Verdene never watches. Ella smiles without parting her lips in each photo: a demure bride posing next to a Volkswagen Beetle; a new mother cradling a small baby, sitting stiffly before the dark, serious man behind her; a carefree sibling laughing with her sister—the only time Ella shows flashes of teeth—both women identical with Audrey Hepburn updos and light skin that glows almost white in these black-and-white photos; and finally, a picture of a modest, older woman whose face shows hints of the former blushing bride, but rounder and devoid of life—a vacant, colorless room.

Verdene runs her fingers through her hair. How strange she had not realized—the way Margot did—Ella's dominating presence inside the house. There is something wrong with this. It's as though Verdene doesn't exist—never existed—of her own free will. Here she is in her mother's house, surrounded by her mother's things, and her mother's inspection. Verdene had already missed a good part of her youth doing what was considered by Ella to be the right thing. Perhaps she was oblivious to this loss because she was too busy trying to bury memories of the past, using their brittle bones to construct a future.

One by one Verdene takes down her mother's pictures. Carefully, she lays them on the sofa and wraps them in newspapers and plastic she has kept from the market. She searches for a box to place them in, but when she cannot find one, she puts them inside the small suitcase she brought home. The room appears empty without the pictures, but now there is space for Margot.

8

ALPHONSO TELLS MARGOT TO MEET HIM FOR LUNCH AT A restaurant far from the hotel. He drives his Mercedes-Benz while she opts to take a taxi, arriving five minutes later. He doesn't get up when she approaches the table. There's chatter around them—a few European tourists eating fried fish and bami for lunch, their backs, shoulders, and faces red from sunburn, their tour buses parked out front, where the drivers smoke cigarettes and kick pebbles in the sand. Third World plays on the sound system: "96 Degrees in the Shade" fills the small, open space like the smell of fried escovitch fish and the salt-tinged breeze from the sea. Alphonso appraises Margot with his eyes as she sits across from him. She had applied another layer of red lipstick before leaving the hotel. She also brushed her hair down with more gel so that every strand stays in place.

"You look better every time I see you," he says, ogling her. She smiles with her lips. She has never been out with him or any of her clients this way. A black woman dining with a white man, though Alphonso is just as Jamaican as her, is viewed with suspicion. It might appear as though she's propositioning him. Margot crosses her legs and leans back in her chair, creating distance. She's aware of the people around them, especially the staff. She catches the eyes of the man behind the bar serving drinks and sizing her up.

"Why are we here?" she asks Alphonso.

"Where else would we meet?"

"Your villa?"

"Raquel is there. She and the twins leave later this evening."

"Oh." The sound of his wife's name makes Margot's eyes twitch, as though Alphonso has just reached over and plucked one of her eyelashes. Ever since his twins were born, Alphonso seems more distant, intent on getting work done in the office. Lately he sends Blacka, his assistant, to visit the hotel while he and his wife spend their vacations somewhere exotic like Greece. Margot thinks of all the time she has spent with him. Not once has his wife ever called to see where he was late at night. With all the money he spends on her, why would she dare complain or question him, even if she knows? Alphonso reaches for Margot's hand, but Margot pulls away. "Not here."

It's Alphonso's turn to lean back in his chair. He pats his chest for a pack of cigarettes and puts one in his mouth out of habit. Margot watches him let out a pillow of smoke that creates a thin veil between them. She wants to ask him the question that has been on her mind lately. The one he planted inside her head and left to sprout wildly like the creeping stems of Running Marys on a rosebush. She has to be sure. The last time she and Alphonso were together, the

L-word had slipped off his tongue and landed in Margot's hair when he lay on top of her. She needs to know how he feels about her and what this means for her prospects at the hotel.

"I want to ask you something," she says.

Alphonso takes another long drag of his cigarette. He exhales. "If it's about the new hire, it's a done deal."

Margot frowns. "What new hire?"

"I fired Dwight today. Just hired a more competent person to take his place. Miss Novia Scott-Henry."

Margot is sick with shock. She wants to hurl something, anything, at Alphonso's head. "Did she suck your dick?" she blurts out. Alphonso scans the menu in front of them.

"The steamed fish and okra looks delicious," he says, ignoring her outburst. But Margot cannot bring herself to focus on anything. She was only seventeen and fresh out of school when she met Reginald Senior, a wealthy white Jamaican whose people visited Jamaica once for vacation from Canada, fell in love with the country, and stayed. They bought hundreds of acres of land that his father, Alphonso's grandfather, turned into an all-inclusive resort. Margot was introduced to the hotelier by one of her clients, a man whose name Margot has long forgotten—a business type who liked to brag about his connections. True to his word, the man took Margot to an invitation-only gathering at Reginald Wellington Senior's colonial mansion on the hill. The property used to be an old plantation, its beauty rivaling Rose Hall Great House. The whole time she had her eyes on the older Wellington, unable to concentrate on her date. Margot made sure to be seen by the man who ran Jamaica, though he was never officially elected as Prime Minister. Margot stayed back after the party was over and waited. When he finally noticed her, Reginald Senior saw the ambition that burned in her eyes—a flame that other men often mistook for lust. He hired her to work at his hotel and taught her everything she needed to know about running it. Everything she's done since that day, every bitter compromise, every buried regret, was to lead to this point. That job should be hers.

"Come on, Margot," Alphonso says, lowering the menu. "Your time will come."

"When?"

The waiter comes up to their table. A young man with skin as smooth as the blackboard where the lunch special is written in chalk. His eyes scan Margot's face briefly and she looks down, her hand fluttering to her hair to smooth strands that lifted from the light sea breeze. It's Alphonso the waiter speaks to, as though he's the only one at the table. "Can I get you a drink, sah?"

"A Red Stripe for me. What do you want, Margot?" Alphonso asks, bringing her into the conversation.

"A promotion," Margot replies, too loudly.

Alphonso stares at her with his penny-colored eyes. He then fans away the visibly perplexed young waiter. "That'll be all for now. Just get the lady a glass of water." The waiter bows and leaves the table. Alphonso leans in as though he wants to climb over the table and smack Margot across the face. "I said, your time will come."

Margot laughs. "I've been hearing that for years now, Alphonso. I've seen other people get promoted. I've seen Dwight parade around the place like a jackass, pretending to be in charge. I'm tired of lying in bed with you feeding you ideas that you use without giving me credit. Or listening to you talk about how hard it is to run a hotel that your father still controls from the grave."

The waiter comes back with Alphonso's beer. He only takes Alphonso's lunch order, since Margot has lost her appetite. She folds her arms across her chest, staring out at the deep blue waves in the farthest distance of the ocean. She should've known this would happen. She's the one with the blinders on. Why would Alphonso give her the position to manage his hotel, and not someone else with connections? Isn't that what this is about? How many connections you have? Your family name? The reality stirs inside her belly, bellowing like the hunger pangs she refuses to assuage. She excuses herself from the table just as the waiter comes back with Alphonso's food. "I have to leave," she says.

"Was there something you wanted to ask me?" Alphonso says.

"I forgot." Margot gets up and pushes her chair under the table.

"Well, I want to see you tonight."

"Alphonso, you know I—"

"Please. I promise you'll like the deal I have in store for you." He winks at her as he puts a forkful of fish into his mouth and chews. Margot stands there for a moment longer, staring at his mouth. Had they been more than they were, she would've made a public display of dabbing the oil residues from each side.

Margot needs a distraction. She wheels into the street, blind to moving cars and deaf to their horns. She walks in a zigzag pattern, turning the heads of passersby. If they look any closer they might see the knife rammed in her back, its blade deep inside her chest. She stops under a tree to catch her breath and hide from the sun. As air slowly fills her lungs, so does the sharp pain of the moment Alphonso snatched it. "*I love you, Margot.*" She had heard him right. *So what happened?* Who is this bitch he has given Margot's job to?

Eight years ago Alphonso put himself in charge of his father's hotel empire. When word got around that the son of Reginald Senior and heir to his hotel empire would be on the property, everyone scattered, fixing what didn't need fixing, straightening uniforms and hair and papers on desks. The front desk clerks assumed postures. The concierges stood erect like police officers during a Jamaica House event, the housekeepers dusted places that were already glistening with shine. And the gardeners watered flowers and the manicured hedges that were already watered. Alphonso exited from a chauffeured vehicle and Paul, the concierge, gave a slight bow when Alphonso approached the door. *"Good day, sah,"* he said. But Alphonso didn't respond.

Alphonso didn't take off his dark shades inside the building. He stepped silently past the workers on the compound, who stood around holding on to things in their hands more for comfort than necessity—handkerchiefs, smooth stones for luck, papers soiled by sweaty palms. To them, he was God himself. Like his father—the one who granted them jobs that put food on their dinner tables. But to Alphonso, these people were mud crusted under his heels. At any point he could get rid of them, wipe them clean from the property.

He fascinated Margot. The hotel staff came to know him as the exact opposite of their beloved boss. He took over the hotel while Reginald Senior was still on his deathbed, fighting prostate cancer. This angered the employees. (*"Him couldn't even wait till him daddy get put dung inna di grave."*) It was feared that he would be the one to destroy everything his father and grandfather ever built. They were right. Alphonso immediately fired old staff without an ounce of remorse. He even fired the Jamaican chefs and hired foreign ones. (*"Tourists want to eat their own food on the island. They don't come to eat Jamaican food wid all dat spice."*) New boys were hired from other parts of the island, as far as Portland, to work in the kitchen under chefs that came from Europe.

When he saw her that first day, he lifted his shades, appraising her. *"And who are you?"*

"Margot."

"Margot," Alphonso repeated. He put his hands inside his pockets as he played with her name on his tongue, rolling the *r*. She spotted a flash of the pink flesh, and a perfect set of white teeth closing together as he swallowed the *t*. *"Marrrrgot."* He took her hand and squeezed it. *"My pleasure."* His eyes held a reflection of her face. *"You're very pretty, Margot."* Margot looked away, hoping that he would drop his

gaze. By twenty-two, Margot knew what that look meant. She knew how to smell lust rising from men's pores, enveloping her like the thick musk of sweat from the heat. She smelled it the way women at the market knew how to smell the ripeness of fruits even if they were green on the outside. But a man like Alphonso was a different breed. A different smell. Unlike the men she had been with, including his father, Alphonso was young, green, only a couple years older than her. He reeked of youthful privilege—a privilege that made him unaccustomed to ambition, sacrifice, hunger, hustle. His palms were too soft, teeth too white, nails too polished. She could smell his mother's milk on his breath. He wasn't ripened in a way older men were ripened—creased and blemished with old habits that thicken their skin like leather, blunt their edge. This man's skin was smooth. The girls in River Bank would have loved to catch the attention of a young man like that. Visions of light-skinned, pretty-haired babies would certainly dance in their imaginations. Add cubits to their height among other downtrodden women who could only choose from "ole neggars" who gave them nothing, except picky-head "pickneys" and swollen black eyes. Alphonso was a catch. The type Margot saw in movies with bow ties and tuxedos, plotting murders while seducing unaware damsels caught up by their charm. "*Yuh should be grateful fah a man like dat to show interest in yuh,*" Delores had said to her years ago when the stranger at the market brought her back to Delores's stall. *A man like that.* That was what Alphonso was—*a man like that.*

Margot was thinking all this when Alphonso said to her, "*Why don't you come by later, and show me what you're good at?*"

And so, when the sun went down and the staff went home, he led her to the conference room—the only time she had ever seen the inside of it. She opened the folder in which she kept all her ideas for the hotel. Her hands shook a little as she showed him how she had designed the small surveys so that management could know what guests were responding to. But Alphonso wasn't interested in that. Instead, he watched her. She

felt his eyes on her the whole time. When she finally gathered the courage to look at him, he leaned in and whispered, "*I didn't mean for you to
show me all that about the hotel. I wanted you to show me what you're good
at.*" Her first instinct was to slap him across the face and walk out the
office; but Margot thought of Delores. The thought held her in place as
Alphonso's hands traveled the width of her hips, pressing her into him.
There, his lust grew forceful. He bent her over and she let him. *It's fah di
bettah.* As he entered her, Alphonso breathed into the back of her neck.
"*Now I know why he kept you around.*"

Margot responded by moving his hands to her breasts. The folder
full of her ideas slipped from the desk and fell, papers sailing every
which way. After a few minutes Alphonso came. He stood up and
wiped himself clean with the handkerchief he carried in his left
breast pocket. He tossed it in the bin with the condom. "*Jus' keep
this between me and you,*" he said.

But Garfield—the security guard who probably heard movement
in the conference room after hours, and who worked for forty years to
prove himself in his old age as a noble guardsman who didn't deserve
to be laid off without a pension—busted through the door holding a
flashlight and a baton, only to behold the sight of Alphonso zipping
up his pants and Margot leaning over the desk, her ass exposed. In
exchange for silence, Garfield was given job security. A month later
he died of a stroke. The secret didn't die with him.

In time she has pushed aside the things about Alphonso that make
her cautious. His volcanic explosions when people dare question his
authenticity as a Wellington, given his tendency to squander money,
unlike his scrupulous predecessors. Already he has squandered the
revenue from the coffee farms and rum estates, and has had to sell
them. And since his family is currently threatening to take the hotels
out his hands, he seeks to pull from every vault his father painstakingly hid from him before he died. When Alphonso came up empty-
handed after being denied privilege to any more of his father's estate,

he combusted: "*The bastard cared for his three w's. His wealth, his whores, and his whiskey.*" He was drunk. He smashed a rum bottle on the wall and splattered the expensive Persian rug in his villa with the brown liquid. He kept on looking at the wall as though he saw his father's shadow there, though it was his own.

Margot's distracted memories carry her from under the tree to the crafts market in town. She just needs a scrap of kindess before she can recover, formulate her next move. Though Delores is hardly compassionate, Margot looks for her inside the arcade. The instant reprieve from the heat, though small, is something she's grateful for. She hasn't visited the stall in a long time. John-John is sitting there hee-hawing about something, and Margot has a feeling that she's interrupting. Delores lifts her head and notices Margot, and something comes over her face. When John-John sees Margot, he too stops talking and suddenly becomes shy, lowering his head and regarding her through the lashes of his downcast eyes. "Hello, Margot," he says boyishly.

"Wha'ppen John-John?"

"Nutten nah g'wan enuh," John-John says, bringing Margot's focus back. He seems glad for the opportunity to talk to her. "Same ole, same ole . . . how about you? Yuh looking good."

"Thanks, John-John," Margot says in a noncommittal voice. She focuses on Delores and the impenetrable veil over her face.

John-John must sense this, because he picks up his box of crafts and heads to the exit, apologetic when he says to Margot, "I'll leave you ladies alone." He bows slightly. "Likkle more, Mama Delores."

"Likkle more," Delores replies.

John-John stops at the exit as though he has forgotten something. He digs into his box and hands Margot a sculpted doctor bird. "Me did mek dis special fi you."

"Thanks, John-John," Margot says, holding on to the wooden bird as he hurries away.

Delores is chuckling to herself. "Him always did like yuh," she says. "Only a idiot in love would give up something fah free when him can sell it to mek good money." She sucks her teeth and fans herself with an old yellowing newspaper. "Lawd Jesas, what ah buffoon, eh?"

"I know." Margot examines the beautiful bird. She traces the contours with her fingers, every ridge meticulously carved. "Poor t'ing."

"Poor t'ing is right," Delores says. "Remember how him used to bring yuh flowers he pick from s'maddy else yard?" Margot chuckles when she remembers this—John-John stealing flowers to give to her. "Both of oonuh was so young," Delores continues, with the memory glistening in her eyes. "Him used to sit here an' wait on me, jus' so he could geet to yuh." But the humor quickly disappears from Delores's face, wiped clean by a scowl. "If only he knew."

"I guess you'd rather put me wid a man who was into fondling and fucking likkle girls?" Margot says, her voice conversational. She's been friendly with her mother, but the day's disappointment has her raw, prodding the wounds of her past. This painful fact has solidified into a rock she throws at her mother when it becomes too big, too heavy to carry alone.

Delores stops fanning. After a long pause, she braces herself into the chair, which creaks under her weight. "Why are you here?" Delores asks. "To tell me how me is a bad mother?" Delores's spit flies on Margot's face. Delores continues. "What should I have done, eh? Tell me!" Her eyes are bulging. "Didn't it put food on the table? Didn't it feed yuh? If yuh t'ink yuh bettah than dat—now dat you is Miss High 'an Mighty—then g'weh! G'long!"

Margot doesn't budge. She can't. "Ah want to talk to you," she says. Her voice drops, giving in to a slight tremor.

Delores's eyes gleam like the edges of swords, her mouth twisted to the right side of her face. "'Bout what?"

"Ah don't know where to start."

"Start somweh. Yuh wasting me time." Delores starts fanning herself again, but before Margot can gather her thoughts, three tourists enter the stall. Delores's attitude changes. Margot steps aside and waits until her mother is done with them. Suddenly she's a pleasant woman, the type of woman Margot would've liked to get to know, or wanted as a mother—not the mother she grew up with, who was quick to anger and even quicker to trample Margot's self-esteem. Margot always wondered what it was about her that made her mother so angry. She wished she could make her mother happy the way these tourists do. The way Thandi does. "Yes, sweetie, ah can give yuh dat for a discounted price," Delores says to the young American teen.

When the tourists leave, Delores goes back to being Delores. "So talk," she says. "More people soon come an' me need fi sell."

Margot treads lightly. "I'm seeing someone." She clears her throat, feeling an overwhelming need to specify, if not for herself, then for Delores, whose eyes hold in them the question that Margot can never avoid. "A man." It rolls off her tongue so easily, so naturally, so necessary. *A man.* Her mother's facial expression remains neutral, though Margot imagines the smirk behind the dark emotionless face.

"He's in di hotel business," Margot continues. "A Wellington."

"A Wellington?" Delores asks, her eyes wide. "What yuh doing wid ah Wellington?" she asks. "Since when those people commune wid di help? Don't you work fah dem?"

"He said he loves me," Margot says, defensive. All she hopes for is Delores's grudging approval. "He's willing to leave his wife. And he's serious about it."

"Oh?" Delores sits up straight and puts down the rolled-up newspaper she was using to fan with, a gleam finally creeping into her eyes, filling Margot with hope.

"So yuh get yuhself a *big* man."

"Yes."

"How yuh so ch'upid, gyal?"

Delores leans forward, her big arms flopping over her knees. Margot realizes that it wasn't pride she has seen in her mother's eyes, it was a sneer. A sneer that reveals the wide gap in her mother's teeth as she says, "My question to you, *Miss High an' Mighty*, is how ah man like dat can leave him pretty wife fi *s'maddy* like you? Yuh t'ink dem man deh want a black gyal pon dem arm in public? Dey like yuh to fuck. Not to marry. So know yuh place."

Margot feels the sting of tears, but she narrows her eyes. She doesn't even want Alphonso. All Margot wants—now more than ever—is to prove her mother wrong.

Margot bursts through Verdene's bedroom door and puts her palms against the woman's cheeks. Her lips trail Verdene's neck, her breasts. Verdene gasps in surprise, but slows Margot's fingers.

"Calm down, now. Why don't you sit down?"

Margot relents, resting her head against Verdene's before slumping onto the bed. "I wish things were different," she says. Verdene is watching her, watching the storm of unknown origin rage across her face. "Don't you just wish things were different?" she asks.

"Many times," Verdene says.

They peer at each other in the mirror.

"I don't think I can go on living like this," Margot says.

"What are you saying?" Verdene sits up against the headboard. Margot studies her face to see if the answer she hopes to find is there. But all she sees is concern and confusion just above Verdene's eyebrows.

"If you love me, then why haven't you offered to sell this house so that we can have a fresh start? You know. In an area where we can—"

Verdene cuts her off. "It's not that simple, Margot."

"Why not? What do you have to lose by selling this house? It's not like you have anything left here. We can build something together."

"It's all I have left of my mother." Verdene looks at the picture of her mother that sits on the small table, facing the wall—the only picture she kept out. She reaches over and turns the picture around.

"So I'm best kept as a secret?" Margot asks quietly, turning away from the smiling Miss Ella.

Verdene allows the question to fall between them before she says, "You're fooling yourself if you think things would be any different in another neighborhood. It's still Jamaica."

"Then why don't you take me with you to London so that we could have a life outside of this?"

"You've never been willing to leave River Bank." Verdene moves to the edge of the bed. "You're the one always talking about your sister and how you have to be here for her."

Margot walks to the rocking chair for her bag. Verdene has a point. Thandi needs her. But that was not what she wanted to hear. Alphonso would never choose her, and maybe she can never choose Verdene. She has been wasting time vacillating between two secret lives. She wonders if what she feels—and has always felt—for Verdene is nothing more than a spell, something temporarily debilitating like a gigantic wave in the ocean. She has to break the water's surface. Swim back to shore. She cannot afford to be controlled.

"I have to go," Margot says. She kisses Verdene goodbye on the mouth.

"When will I see you again?" Verdene asks.

"I don't know."

9

T HANDI GOES OUTSIDE TO THE BACKYARD WITH HER SKETCH-
pad. The grass is knee-high, neglected. The sun peers through
the branches of the trees. Two roosters that escaped the neighbor's
yard high-step toward the side of the shack. The old tire tied to
the tree where Little Richie likes to sit swings by itself as though
a ghost is pushing it. Thandi tries to sketch whatever she sees, but
every time an image appears on the page, she rips it out and balls it
inside her fists. Nothing looks or feels right. By the time she's halfway through ripping page after page out of her book, she's ready to
scream into the open air. Her frustration threatens to break free
and shatter to pieces the image she has struggled so hard to uphold.
But this backyard is too small. The web of branches above her head

might contain her frustrated scream. The sleeping dogs might holler at it. The chickens will halt, one leg suspended like the breaths
of the nearby washerwomen, who might wonder about the commotion and come running.

Finally, she decides that her growing discomfort might have to do
with the plastic that Miss Ruby meticulously wrapped around her
limbs and torso. She makes her way back inside, takes it off, and
slips a modest yellow dress over a tank top and a pair of shorts—
since she has to wash her slip. She grabs her sketchpad and leaves,
passing Grandma Merle, who is sitting stiff-necked on the wooden
chair; and Miss Francis and Miss Louise, who wave. The hum of
their voices washes her back. *"Is where she going in di hot sun dressed
like dat? Shouldn't she be in school?"*

She hurries along to the river, passing by the bathers who have
their clothes spread out on the rocks. She makes her way to where
the boats are tied up. The construction workers with their tools
aren't on site today. There is a sign that reads NO TRESPASSING on
the beach right where Thandi used to play as a child, which was
once an extension of River Bank. The hotels are building along the
coastlines. Slowly but surely they are coming, like a dark sea. Little
Bay, which used to be two towns over from River Bank, was the
first to go. Just five years ago the people of Little Bay left in droves,
forced out of their homes and into the streets. It was all over the
news when it happened, since the people—out of anger—ended up
blocking roads with planks and tires and burning them. In the past,
developers would wait for landslides and other natural disasters to
do their dirty work. But when tourism became the bread and butter
for the island's economy, the developers and the government alike
became ravenous, indifferent. In retaliation, people stole concrete
blocks and cement and zinc from the new developments to rebuild
homes in other places, but their pilfering brought soldiers with rifles
and tear gas. The developers won the fight, and the people scattered

like roaches. Some came to River Bank begging to be taken in, some fled to other parishes. Those who could not bear the stress of uprooting all their belongings to start a new life roamed the streets and mumbled to themselves. It was as though their own land had turned on them—swallowed up their homes and livestock and produce and spat out the remains. By the time the workmen arrived in River Bank, Little Bay had been long forgotten.

There is no sound out here. Just the gentle lull of the sea and her heart beating in her eardrums when she sees Charles, sitting in his father's fishing boat. He's looking at the tranquil water where the river meets the ocean. He looks like he belongs in a painting, contemplating the blue of the water and the sky. Just above them, the coconut trees rustle in the wind, their fronds wavelike. Thandi looks up at the sky between the palm branches through which the sun plays a game of hide-and-seek. She sits on an abandoned crate underneath one of the trees and sketches Charles with his head tilted back in the face of the sun, careful with each line, her fingers wrapped around the pencil. His back is an elegant stretch of muscle. It takes her longer than usual to get it right, erasing shadows and drawing them over. Charles turns and catches her staring. "What yuh doing out here?" he asks above the gentle roar of the sea.

Embarrassed, Thandi fumbles to cover the drawing with her hands as if he can see them from where he sits. He gets up out of his father's boat and walks over to her, his bare feet making footprints in the white sand. He's wearing a pair of khaki trousers cut off at the knees, a faded green shirt slung over his right shoulder. Thandi inches closer to the tree as if it can hide her. She crosses and uncrosses her legs, pressing her sketchpad to her chest as she watches him look around for a crate to sit on. She sits up straight, unsure what posture she should assume. She's afraid she might look too rigid this way. Too schoolgirlish. So she curves her back. Just a little. What would Margot do? Too many times Delores says to Thandi that she's nothing like Margot. "*Nothing like yuh sistah a'tall.*" Thandi wonders if this is good or bad.

When Thandi was younger she used to observe her sister. Under the appraisal of men's stares was the mysterious force that swayed Margot's wide hips atop sturdy bow legs. When she passed them by, they would turn their heads, their eyes trained on those hips, their hands stroking their chins as though contemplating a plate of oxtail stew. "*Wh'appen, sugah?*" *Brown sugar*, or *brownin'* for short. Margot never seemed uncomfortable, unlike Thandi, who shies away from such attention; Margot touched men frequently as she talked, her hand casually stroking their arm or chest. And when they said something, anything, Margot used to throw her head back and laugh a soft, titillating laugh that rippled through the air above the sounds of Gregory Isaacs, Beres Hammond, or Dennis Brown coming from the boom box at Dino's. This caused the men to pause and observe the skin of her neck, the length of her lashes that swept her full cheeks as her eyes squinted with delight; lust filling their own eyes, like smoke from a ganja spliff. In Margot's presence, a man would shout to his contenders amid the shuffling of dominoes, slamming his hand or his beer hard on the wooden table, "*Anotha roun'!*" Then, to Margot, "*Watch me win nuh, sugah?*" And Margot, gracious as she is, would decline, stroking the man's arm. "*Maybe next time, love.*" The man would proceed to play his hand, smiling to himself as though he had already won.

When Charles approaches Thandi with a crate he's found inside another abandoned boat, he's grinning from ear to ear. He plops down in front of her, smelling like the salty air. Their knees touch but she doesn't move hers away.

"So why yuh not in school?" he asks, his eyes gentle like the water with flecks of gold from the sun. She shrugs. She wonders what to tell him. What role should she play? Charles might like rude girls. Girls not afraid to raise their voices in the street. Girls who spar with grown men in the square, whom they let lift their skirts, slip their fingers inside. "Dis is a nice surprise," he continues.

"What's so surprising?" Thandi counters, immediately regretting that she forgot to mangle her words, chew them up, and spit them out in patois. She's afraid she sounds too proper. But Charles doesn't seem to mind.

"You neva strike me as a girl who would be out here jus' like dat," he says, regarding her face the way Brother Smith regards her paintings—with studied observation. "Yuh always to yuhself."

"You don't know me."

"Yuh neva gimme a chance to."

"So how would you know what I'm like?"

"I watch you. Like ah watch di sky."

Thandi blushes.

"So tell me," he says, cocking his head to one side. "What's in dat book of yours?" he asks. "Don't tell me is jus' me yuh draw in it." He's leaning closer, his lips parted, his thick eyebrows raised. Behind him the water seems to rise, mounting the rocks.

Thandi squeezes her legs together. "You're really full of yuhself to assume you're my subject."

"Ah wouldn't say it if ah didn't notice you staring wid it open on yuh lap." Charles twists his mouth to the side like he's sucking something from his teeth or trying not to laugh.

"I draw anything I feel. Don't have to have meaning. I mean, I can't really seem to capture what I really want to capture," Thandi responds, searching for a reaction in his face. But she can't tell what she sees. Charles listens to her with the intentness of a wizened old man, watching her gestures, affirming her ambivalence. She wonders how old he really is. She's afraid that she has revealed too much too soon. "I don't know why I even care. This might sound stupid, but I just want to win this art competition at school." Her nervousness makes her talk too much. Very rarely does she say this much to anyone about what she wants, much less to a common boy she barely knows.

"If it is dat important to you, then why would you t'ink it's stupid?" he asks.

Thandi shrugs her shoulders.

Charles reaches for her hand and holds it as though he has done this many times before. "Somehow ah get di feeling dis is more important to you than winning."

Unlike her sweaty ones, Charles's palms are dry and surprisingly warm, like sun-warmed stones. She doesn't pull away, though a girl like her—a Saint Emmanuel High School girl—should have rebuked such audacity. A series of thoughts chastises her: Who does he think he is? Since she's getting lighter, shouldn't she be looking elsewhere—at the boys in Ironshore, with big houses and cars? What now? But sitting here with her hand in Charles's feels oddly natural. Their brown skin seems connected; and a lump of uncertainty over her cream rises in Thandi's throat. Her inhibitions melt like candle wax under his heat. She imagines this is how girls with boyfriends feel. Thandi leans into Charles, closing her eyes. But Charles pulls back, his sudden motion rustling the sticks at their feet, snapping them in half.

"Yuh all right?" he asks.

"Sorry."

Thandi picks up the sketchpad, which had slipped from her lap. Charles puts his hand on her shoulder. She cannot read his expression.

"You'll figure it out," Charles says, moving away. She wishes she were still wrapped in plastic, for it might have worked to keep her broken heart intact. If this is a test, then she has failed miserably. She gets up and flees in the direction of the water.

"Where yuh going?" he asks.

"For a swim," she says, hoping to sound casual, though in fact she cannot swim. She takes off her shoes, and dips her toes into the water. The sand is warm and the water isn't cold at all. She takes off her dress, leaving her shorts and tank top like the local bathers do. She knows Charles is watching, waiting to see what she will do. Behind her is the skeleton of a majestic castle—one of the resorts emerging right here in her backyard. No one is in sight, but in months the white sands will be populated by the sunburned bodies of white tourists. From a plane flying overhead they might look like seals, their heads tilted toward the rays, bodies open for as much exposure as possible, basking in luxury. The castle fades away like a mirage as Thandi drifts and drifts farther away from shore. She moves forward as though going toward the middle of the sea—a dare she soon realizes was not a dare, but an impulse.

Charles hasn't followed. The disappointment disorients her, but it is quickly replaced by fear, which creeps up on her with each wave that rises like a giant blue wall. They tumble toward her, each one bigger than the other. Thandi loses her footing and goes under. She tries to float as long as she can, her eyes on the sky, angry at herself for acting a fool. Her hands flail against the avalanche of waves as she tries to swim. She's not sure which direction she's turned. The undercurrent pulls her with possessive force. She remembers why the fishermen call this area Pregnant Heidi—for the waves are majestic, rising like the concave belly of a woman with child. The tale dates back to the days of slavery, when a slave girl named Heidi flung herself into the sea after finding out that she was pregnant with her master's baby. Her body was never found. At night Pregnant Heidi gives birth in a surge of waves rushing to the sand, her screams carried in the swift breeze that whistles against every window of every shack. By day she seeks a victim to drown. Just when Thandi thinks she will be propelled to the ocean's floor into the crease of Pregnant Heidi's bosom, someone grabs her by the waist and pulls her. Through the water and terror, she sees the head of the person pulling her with impressive strength and dexterity. She might have imagined it, but he cuts through the water like a fish.

"Hold on!" he says, his voice riding steady above the roar of the waves. "Jus' hold on!" And Thandi obeys, holding Charles tightly as he snatches her from Pregnant Heidi's grasp and carries her back to shore.

Thandi feels exposed, walking next to a boy this way, with her dress clinging to her. She's soaked from head to toe. But there's something comforting in being led. Following one step behind Charles, she observes the back of his heels, crusted with dirt. He carries his shoes in one hand and Thandi's shoes and sketchpad in the other, whistling lightly as he walks. Occasionally he looks back at her. Thandi bows her head shyly. Had it not been for Charles, she would have drowned. "Thank you." She peers up at him when she says this, emboldened by gratitude.

"Let's get you a towel," he responds. He leads her inside his yard, where two big hogs are walking around inside a pen. By the fence there is a chicken coop where the cackling fowls are squared away, high-stepping over each other and digging holes in the ground with their beaks. Thandi is familiar with this yard, her childhood memories rich with adventures with Charles's younger sister, Jullette. While Miss Violet and Delores swapped ingredients from their kitchen ("*Beg yuh a cup ah salt. Gimme jus' a throw ah rice. Fill dis up wid some syrup. Yes, yes, dat will do. Likkle more.*") Thandi and Jullette would climb the soursop tree that once hovered above the chicken coop, pretending to be leaders of the squawking birds. What remains of the tree is a stump. Through the wire fence Thandi sees the ocean in which she nearly drowned. Miss Ruby's shack is not too far away. Like Miss Ruby, Charles and Jullette's father made money selling fish. Asafa was a fisherman who used to walk around River Bank with lobsters and crabs. He used to scare all the children by reaching into a white plastic pail and holding up the creatures with their scissor claws and antennas poised for attack. The children screamed. Dread would send their little feet running, some tripping over stones and gashing knees and elbows in search of safety behind their mothers' skirts. Though this was a terrifying event, every child in River Bank looked forward to Asafa cutting across the lanes with his bucket. They eagerly anticipated it like they anticipated Christmas market and the Junkanoo parade in the square. Asafa was the only fisherman who went beyond Pregnant Heidi to catch fish, his thick dreadlocks knotted on top of his head and shorts hiked up his long, skinny legs. Every morning he would be out at sea, patiently sitting with his rod or snorkeling, his bright yellow, green, and red boat docked in the bluest part of the water. The last time Thandi saw him was eight years ago, before he met a woman who bought a lobster, took him back to her villa, and invited him to go with her to America. He never returned.

Thandi remembers Delores offering Charles and his siblings some of her chicken-back soup with lots of boiled yam, boiled bananas, and dumplings on Saturday evenings the year Asafa left. Jullette went to live with relatives, since Miss Violet could not afford to feed all her children and send them to school. It was easier for Miss Violet with the boys, since boys can survive on their own. Charles, the oldest, was hired by neighbors to wash fences, move stones, haul fallen branches, cut grass, carry bags, and push vehicles that got stuck in the potholes up the steep incline on River Bank Road. But Charles couldn't feed his mother and his three brothers with the little money he made, so Delores and Miss Gracie offered to help. Charles would be the one sent to collect the food, his eyes lowered to his bare feet, his broad shoulders raised like a protective wall against the many whispers and the shaking of heads. Of course, they must have blurred in the periphery of his vision as he carried the pot of food the way pallbearers carry a coffin. He used to mumble his gratitude to Delores as though he expected such generosity and resented it at the same time.

Four dogs roam the yard, two of which follow Charles and Thandi. Charles shoos them away, picking up two sticks to throw. "Fetch dis!" He throws each stick as far as he can and the dogs limp and wobble after them. "That's Cain and Abel." Charles points to the dogs.

"You name yuh dogs?" Thandi asks.

"Yeh, man." Charles looks at his dogs, scratching the tip of his nose. "That one there wid the chain 'roun him neck is Cain," Charles says, pointing to a spotted white dog. "An' di brown one is Abel." He points to the other dog. He then turns to the hogs in the pen. "That's Mary wid di titties, and that's Joseph wid one eye." Thandi looks at each hog, paying close attention to Mary, the fat one with taut nipples who wobbles around. "We sell her babies last summer," Charles explains. "But she breeding again."

"Yuh talk about them like people," Thandi says.

"Of course!" His enthusiasm elevates one side of his face and spreads to his eyes. "Dey jus' as smart, if not smarter than us."

The outhouse is a few feet away from the shack, which is built on stilts like many of the other shacks. The planks are still painted in that same red and blue paint that Asafa layered before he left. Under the dense shade of trees, a zinc shack stands away from the main shack. "This is where ah sleep," Charles says.

"You don't live in the house too?" Thandi asks.

"Me is a big man. I get my own place," Charles says defiantly.

He opens the door to the small shack. It's cozy, with a mattress on a spring box made from four planks hammered together. The mattress is covered halfway by a white floral sheet, soiled with that yellowing hue of old sweat. A kerosene lamp rests on a wooden table next to the mattress. Her eyes climb the walls to the window through which a gentle breeze blows the banana leaves. Thandi wonders how he sleeps at night with no curtains. Standing in the shack next to Charles, Thandi feels exposed. She hugs herself and watches Charles put down the two pairs of shoes on the basket-woven welcome mat that's frayed at the edges. He then searches around the place for something, opening and closing the wooden chest by the bed. When he finds it he lets out a whistle.

"Take this." Charles hands Thandi a big bath towel. Thandi doesn't know how long it has been sitting at the bottom of that chest. She dabs her face. It smells like shampoo.

"It used to belong to my father."

He takes the towel from Thandi and covers her shoulders. Very gently he sits her down on a wooden chair. He sits on the makeshift bed, his long legs jutting up like the legs of a praying mantis. Thandi tucks a lock of her hair behind her ears and looks down at the space between her legs.

"How is Jullette?" she asks, breaking the uncomfortable silence. She sits back against the hardness of the chair.

"Last ah heard, she's doing fine," Charles says.

"Where is she now?"

"Still in Mobay. She's a housekeepah fi one ah di big hotel dem. Half Moon, ah t'ink."

"She not in school?"

"Nah, sah." He rubs the back of his head. "Jullette drop outta school longtime."

"Oh."

"She doing good fi herself, making har own-ah money. Good money too."

"As a maid?"

"It gi' har nuff independence. She ah handle har business."

"Good for her. Tell her I say hello."

Charles tilts his head and regards her sideways. "Yuh can tell her that yuhself."

This is followed by another silence that leaves Thandi empty of words. Perhaps Charles is torturing her. That he knows she hasn't even spoken to Jullette in, what? Five years? But this is not something Thandi or Jullette would ever acknowledge, for their separation is unspoken. She's embarrassed about the beating of her heart, which punches with the force of gloved hands inside her rib cage. "I—I have to leave," she says evenly, using every muscle, every ounce of willpower, to appear collected. "It's getting late."

"I can walk yuh back," Charles says, lowering his knees.

"No. No need." Thandi springs up from the chair. She can hardly bear to imagine what would happen if word got back to Delores that she was hanging out with Charles this late. Charles leans back on his elbows, watching her through long, thick eyelashes.

"Yuh really did intend fi swim?" he asks.

Thandi shrugs, her shoulders tensing under the weight of his question. "No." She moves with his towel, not offering to give it back. And he doesn't ask.

"And before dat, when I saw you?"

"I just wanted to be inspired."

"You're pretty good," he says.

"Who told you could look in my book?"

"You left it. Di breeze blow it open."

She lowers her eyes, embarrassed by what he probably saw. She touches the nape of her neck, feels her skin dissolve under the warm caress of his gaze. "Thanks," she says.

She walks out of the shack and all the way home with his towel draped around her shoulders, a smirk hinged on her face; and, under the gossip of watchful women, ignoble.

"Did you go swimming?" Margot is sitting on the sofa, her legs crossed. Thandi takes off Charles's towel and folds it. Each crease traps bits and pieces of her secret that she will unfold in private. "Yes," she replies with her back turned to her sister.

"You hate swimming."

"I was hot."

"Thandi, look at me when I'm talking to you."

Margot's face is illuminated by the light of the kerosene lamp. Thandi never sees her during the day. She forgets what she looks like in daylight. Tonight her eyes and lips are dark, and in this lighting, her glare is ferocious, the charcoal she draws above and under her eyes making her look like a dog with rabies.

"Sit."

"You okay?" Thandi asks, concerned. Her sister looks as though she has been crying.

"Don't ask me anything. I said sit."

Margot gestures to the chair at the table. Thandi hesitates. Her clothes are still wet and she needs to take them off. She sits anyway. Margot's eyes fall to Thandi's dark nipples. They stand erect through the thin material of the dress. She covers herself by folding her arms across her chest.

"Who were you with?" Margot asks.

"No one."

"Thandi, look at me."

Thandi raises her eyes. Margot appears to swallow something small, the base of her neck pulsing. "What's going on, Thandi?"

"Nothing."

"Nothing?"

Margot walks to the kitchen and fishes several balls of paper out of the trash. The crumpled papers with the sketches that Thandi had ripped from her sketchpad.

"Can you explain this to me?" Margot asks, pushing them forward.

"What were you doing in the trash?" Thandi asks.

"Never mind that. Answer me. What is this?"

"An art project."

"Thandi, all these years we've been sending you to school, and you're wasting time and paper on ah lousy art project and disappearing to do god knows what? Do you know how much ah sacrifice!"

Thandi clamps her hands over her ears and shakes her head. "Just stop! I don't want to hear this speech."

Margot reaches over the table as if to smack her, but instead pulls Thandi's hands from her ears and holds her wrists so tight that Thandi yelps. "You listen to me, an' you listen to me good." Margot lowers her voice into a hiss. "You have no idea what I do to make this happen. No idea." She's talking through her teeth, the words like strings being pulled through the tiny gaps. Thandi has never seen this glint in her sister's eyes. It burns into her with more force than her sister uses to squeeze her wrists. "Do you know the sacrifices I've made so that you don't end up . . ." Her voice trails off, but not before Thandi hears the tremor in it. She blinks it away, then releases Thandi's hands.

"What has gotten into you, eh? What is all dis?" Margot scatters the crumpled papers with Thandi's drawings on the table. They bounce off each other like balls on a pool table, some falling to the floor. "I thought yuh dropped art last term to focus on science for the CXC. Is dis what I've been paying for?"

"None of your business," Thandi says, using one hand to massage a wrist.

Margot slaps her across the face. The slap echoes inside the empty house, reverberating against the walls, the ceiling, out to the veranda, where Grandma Merle sits, mystified by the night sky. "If it was Delores who found this . . ." Margot rattles one of the papers for emphasis, without apology. "You'd be dead. You have no idea what that woman is capable of. None whatsoever! Yuh don't feel pain yet."

Thandi clutches her cheek and runs out the back door, into the darkness. She sits on one of the steps with her knees drawn to her chest and her head resting on them as she cries softly. How could she have gone from the most exhilarating thing that has ever happened in her life to a moment filled with pure humiliation? She tries to conjure up the light that skipped in her veins earlier when Charles held her. But it only fades in the familiar darkness.

A few minutes pass and Thandi hears Margot's footsteps approaching her from behind. She looks away when she feels the warmth of Margot's body next to her, the jelly of Margot's hips pressed to her bony ones. Margot has brought the kerosene lamp outside. They sit in silence, Thandi's sniffles being the only sound. Margot finally speaks. "In the real world, drawing cannot get yuh anywhere." She puts one hand on Thandi's shoulder, then very gently cups her chin so that she meets her soft gaze. "I still have that heart you gave me. Remember it? It was the first an' only time that someone ever gave me a heart." She chuckles softly. "You know, by the time I was your age I was working? I started at fourteen years old. Had no time to think about what I like and didn't like. I jus' had to work. I learned the value of making money. Is our only way to survive. An' even though money can't buy everyt'ing like class an' common sense, it can buy acceptance. That's when people pay attention to yuh, accept yuh as you are. Yuh could be half ah donkey or ugly as a mus-mus, but every man, woman, and child would show yuh respect wid a likkle money in yuh wallet. When yuh work hard, something good would come of it." The sides of her lips twitch, forming a smile or a scowl, Thandi doesn't know which. She looks up at her sister in the faint light as she continues to speak. "But if yuh not careful, yuh lose yuh own shadow. Yuh sense ah purpose. So that day when you gave me that heart I folded it up and kept it. Because ah remembered why I work so hard doing what ah do. You gave me something I never knew could come from a person without strings attached to it. I didn't have to do anything for it."

Margot straightens one of the crumpled papers, the sound of the paper crackling in the dark shadows like sparks from a flame. She stares at it for a while. "You draw this?" she finally asks.

"Yes," Thandi says. It's a sketch of clouds moving across the sky at dusk in the form of a woman. The woman appears to be leaping or running as the sun sets in the background. Below is the sea that stirs with her movement; and the hills and mountains that fade behind her. Margot studies it, her face opening up all kinds of ways. When she looks at Thandi again, her eyes slide lovingly over Thandi's face. "You're really good," she says. But then she folds the drawing and tucks it away inside her blouse. "School comes first. Leave this behind an' focus." Margot pats the left side of her chest where the paper is folded. "First thing in the morning I'm going to Sister Shirley and I'm going to tell her that I'm not paying for art. You're doing only science subjects in that exam. Ah g'wan see to this. Delores doesn't have to know anything."

Thandi turns away from her, her body shaking.

"Look at me, Thandi," Margot says, forcing her face back. The charcoal Margot wears has made its way into the pits of her eyes. "You're only going to focus on schoolwork. No art. No boys."

Thandi doesn't respond to this. She thinks of Charles carrying her back to shore, telling her to hold on. Him lifting her up and out of the water, their bodies wet and touching.

"Is it really true?" Thandi asks, thinking of Charles and the trust he bestowed upon her like a cherished gift.

"Is it true about what?" Margot asks.

"That I was the only person to ever give you a heart."

"Yes."

"I wish I didn't."

Margot's mouth opens and closes as though she has lost her ability to speak. She presses her hands and lips together. Then very firmly she says, "Go change off before Delores come home an' see yuh looking like something a dog dragged in."

10

THE LARGE BLACK AND GOLD GATES OF ALPHONSO'S VILLA
open for Margot to enter, and she takes confident strides down
the walkway, through the courtyard. The sound of laughter floats
toward her and swirls into the pitch-black sky. Margot runs her hands
down the length of her form-fitting green dress before she enters. The
door is always open when Alphonso is inside. During the day one
can look straight through the front door to the back patio, where the
turquoise sea is spread like a welcome mat at the end of the hallway.

Margot enters the villa, where the coral walls are decorated with
Caribbean artwork. Alphonso likes to collect. The furniture is sparse,
arranged to accentuate the airiness in all five rooms, where mahogany sculptures stand in corners (women with enhanced African fea-

tures carrying children or baskets, couples bent in shapes that aren't humanly possible, beheaded humans with sizable breasts and penises). Terra-cotta pots hold green plants with large leaves. The rustic Spanish tiles have a waxy shine, with strategically placed woven mats. When he's not hosting parties, Alphonso rents the villa to tourists—those who would prefer its relaxed atmosphere to the fenced-in, all-inclusive hotels like Palm Star. Alphonso profits either way.

Margot moves toward the music—a bluesy, jazzy woman's voice, singing something she has never heard. Four men are seated on the patio, smoking cigars and looking out at the pool that shimmers before them with floating tea lights. The sinuous smoke from the men's cigars forms a translucent veil. Each man has a girl or two—local brown girls wearing talcum powder on their necks, large gold earrings, and tight-fitting clothes that look to Margot like they found them in the arcade deep inside the secondhand barrels. Their coifed hairstyles are caked in place with gel Margot sees smeared at their temples. Margot feels she could stand there by the doorway and listen to the singer's voice for hours with her eyes closed, but one of the girls spots her, her face transforming with surprise. She regards Margot closely, perhaps trying to place her, perhaps hoping she doesn't know a relative. She looks familiar, though Margot could have seen her anywhere. She could have been one of the hundreds of faces Margot passes by daily in Sam Sharpe Square on her way to work. A girl like that might be one of the young vendors in the arcade, selling cosmetics or clothes.

"Margot!"

Alphonso floats toward her and kisses her on both cheeks before pausing at her lips. "I knew you wouldn't stay mad at me for long." She pulls back when she sees he's high, his pupils large. He rests one hand on the small of her back. "You look stunning . . ." he whispers.

"Thank you."

"Here, come join us."

He leads her to the group of men. She greets them with a slight nod of her head. "Good evening, gentlemen," she says. They respond in a tenor chorus. "Evening!" They have the accents of moneyed Jamaicans, their English with the right edge of patois to sharpen their innuendos and help them appeal to the common men they exploit. Alphonso leans back on his chair, his leg up, a cigar in his mouth. He converses animatedly with the other men. He openly caresses Margot's shoulders, rubs her back, and she leans into him without hesitation. The phone rings, and one man teases Alphonso that it's his wife who is calling. Alphonso runs to take the call, disappearing into one of the five empty bedrooms for privacy. When he returns, the men laugh. "See! Ah tell yuh it was di wife!"

That's when Margot gets up to pour herself a drink. The men were mid-discussion when she stood up—something about the monkeys in Parliament who are allowing P. J. Patterson to run the country into ruins since his win last year, and making sure Seaga takes the '97 election in three years. The girls sit around the men like decorative flowers, pretending to listen to the conversation as the men absently stroke their bony thighs. Poor things, Margot thinks, watching them hold glasses of liquor to their mouths, sipping it like medicine. Suddenly Margot feels maternal. The girl who noticed her earlier catches her eye again. She gets up from the sofa and comes over to Margot at the bar.

"Margot?"

"Yes?"

Margot cannot help but try to place her. "Do I know you?" she asks.

"Are you Thandi's sister?" the girl asks.

Margot mentally wipes clean the purple eye shadow; the red rouge on the girl's high cheekbones that goes all the way up to her temples; the beige mask that doesn't quite fit her deep mocha complexion, making her look like a ghost.

"I'm Jullette," the girl says, not waiting for Margot to piece it together. "Ah used to live in Rivah Bank. Me and Thandi went to primary school together. Ah remembah you."

Margot isn't sure how to respond. *Jullette. Jullette? Jullette!* Jullette from the river fork. Miss Violet's daughter. Last Margot heard of the girl, she was sent away after the father left the family. No one knew what happened to him, but since he left, his children scattered all over the place and Miss Violet locked herself in the house.

"How is Thandi?" Jullette asks.

Margot takes a sip of her drink. Before she can begin to imagine what she can say to this girl that won't threaten to reveal too much about her secret life, Alphonso comes up behind Margot. "Thought you went to the sugarcane plantation to make the drinks." He encircles Margot's waist with his arms, and wheels her off. Margot gives a surprised chuckle, grateful to be rescued from the conversation with Jullette.

"It was nice meeting you . . ." Margot says.

"Sweetness. They call me Sweetness. Nice meeting you too," Jullette says in a faraway voice like a pendant lost at sea. How little the splash; how great the effect. Margot leaves the girl standing by the bar.

In Alphonso's bedroom, Margot cannot stop thinking about Jullette. Had she been doing this all along? Who introduced her to it? She thinks about Thandi again, fear mounting in her throat. She swallows and slips out of her dress. When she turns around to face Alphonso, his head is already lowered to the night table, where he snorts three white lines. He pauses on the second and offers her some. "You seem a little fidgety. You should loosen up a bit."

She shakes her head. "You're my only drug," she says, smiling at him, though her mind is still on Thandi.

"Ah, you came ready," Alphonso says.

"Always."

"Then what are you waiting for, standing there like a statue?"

"I want to ask you something first."

"Why not after?"

"I want to know now, before—"

"Margot, for godsakes, I waited all day for this."

"Do you—"

"What? What!"

"Do you love me?"

Alphonso sits up in the bed. "Do I what?" He looks down at himself, then back at her. "You see this? If this doesn't say it all, I don't know what will."

"But you said—"

"Margot, you know you make a grown man say shit when yuh do what yuh do in bed."

"So yuh didn't mean it, then."

"I love your company. I love how you make me feel when we fuck . . . That's probably what ah meant."

"And me?"

He scratches his head, the dark hair falling into his face to cover his eyes.

"Where is all this coming from, Margot?" He gives a nervous chuckle. "Are you catching feelings? You know I'm a married man. And you open yuh legs every which way for a handout. Because of you my hotel is in good business."

Margot cocks her head to the side. And before she can say anything, Alphonso laughs. "Don't worry about who told me. I have my sources. Do I mind? No. Ah think yuh can do something for me."

Margot hugs herself in the middle of the master bedroom like an adulteress about to be stoned in Babylon. Who told him? Was it Paul? She knew that prick was an informer. Or was it Blacka? The way that midget looks at her is as if he wants Alphonso for himself. Or could it be Kensington? But the girl always leaves at four o'clock in the afternoon, two hours before Margot does her rounds. Margot could either leave, defeated; or she could stay and secure what she came for.

"What do you want?"

"Must I spell it out?" He reclines on the bed. Margot slowly climbs beside him. "Good girl. The two of us can profit from this. You give me fifty percent of your profit and I make you into a wealthy woman."

"How exactly will that make me rich?"

"Simple. You know how some hotels sell weed on their property?" Margot nods. "It's good business. More foreign money. We'll sell sex. Lots of it. We can make enough to supply millions to the new resort, the one I'll put you in charge of." There's a big grin on his face. "Our clients would be big investors."

"And I'll screw them all?" Margot is surprised by the sarcasm in her voice. Alphonso is serious.

"You will recruit and train girls you see fit for the business. You'll be the boss lady in charge."

She almost says no. What if Verdene finally takes her up on her offer to build a new life together? What would she say if she found out what Margot did when they were apart? But the money. "I'll do it," is what she says. Alphonso reaches for her and brings her ear close to his lips. "Now let's fuck." That night Margot fucks Alphonso with renewed drive. She marvels at the way he throws his head back, exposing his jugular vein, vulnerable and pulsating. He grits his teeth, clutches the sheet, and swallows hard—his Adam's apple slides up and down his neck like a ping-pong ball. For only then, while looking down on him from the height where she sits, rocking like a queen being carried on a bamboo raft across a river, can she feel her power over him. And she's sure he feels it too.

Maxi pulls into the driveway, his old white Toyota taxi shabby amid the manicured hedges and high, sturdy gates flanked by bushes of bougainvillea and red hibiscus. She told him earlier to pick her up by midnight. "Yuh went to a party up here?" Maxi asks as soon as Margot gets inside his car, smelling of cigars and whiskey. She ignores Maxi's eyes clocking the thigh-high slit in her dress and her exposed cleavage. She winds the window down on her side. "Jus' drive," she tells him.

Maxi drives them to River Bank, the sound of the breeze comforting Margot. Maxi must sense her need for silence, because he says nothing. She knows well how he feels about her breaking her back for foreign money, what it takes from her.

"Remembah when yuh asked me what my dream is?" she asks.

He nods, his eyes on the road as though he's trying not to look at her.

"I gave it more thought," she says, toying with her seat belt.

"Yuh did?" he asks with one eyebrow arched.

"I want to own my own hotel. Bettah yet, ah want to be in charge of tourism. And it g'wan happen sooner than ah think." The words seem to fill out her cheeks, and she surprises herself with a light chuckle. She hopes he can't see the uncertainty in her eyes. The guilt.

Maxi laughs. His laughter is like a faint cough.

PART II
Chicken Merry Hawk Deh Near

11

MARGOT WANTS MORE. THERE'S NOTHING SATISFYING ABOUT leading cattle—a herd of fifteen girls between the ages of sixteen and twenty-five. Even as she watches them graze, she's still hungry. She takes the girls under her wing, feeds them, dresses them, teaches them how to carry themselves among moneyed men. Men who have invested a lot of money in the hotel business. Men who come to the country for the sex and weed; and the sex, like the weed, has to be "*high-grade*." Which is why Margot spent four weeks scouting the girls. Some came highly recommended. Others she had to go out and find. She patrolled the Hip Strip at nights, skirted her way inside the dark, dingy hallways of brothels. Observed how the girls carried themselves, how they hustled. She followed the ones who struck her fancy—ones with sharp tongues and sharper minds, not afraid to tell the men they're short a dollar or two, pretty ones capable of fulfilling fantasies, the darker the better. She eavesdropped on their conversations, even in bathrooms at local clubs, their laughter penetrating Margot's stall like the baby-scented talcum powder they reapplied to their necks and cleavages. She knows who has been on the streets for years as well as who just started two days ago, who has a man and who shares one. Who has the John who can't get it up and who has had to fight one off. The one who sells herself for the love of her children as well as for the love of sex. The girls' conversations were unfiltered in these stalls, their confessionals.

When Margot approached the ones she wanted—the ones she knew the men would want—they gave her queer looks. She handed them cards with her number. "I want you to work for me."

And they would inch away a little, folding arms across bare chests as though just realizing that they were scantily dressed. "Me nuh inna di sodomite t'ing." Margot then assured them that her only interest in them was what they could do for her new business.

They called. Their voices quavered with uncertainty, unsure about the strange woman who had cornered them in the restroom. Margot brought them to Alphonso's villa for an orientation. They wore regular clothes since it was daytime, and Margot was able to see their faces without makeup, how they lit up like little girls when they admired portraits of the cream-at-the-top-of-Horlicks faces of the Wellington dynasty. Alphonso made sure Margot had the villa to herself that weekend, sending home the housekeeper. Margot was grateful for this, since the woman was too nosy anyway. She handed the girls contracts she drafted.

"Dis is a contract of secrecy."

"Secrecy?"

"Yes. Dis is not something yuh tell yuh friends. Under dis contract yuh must not, and I repeat, must not let anyone know about dis. Not even yuh mother. If you know a girl that might be eligible, mek me screen her first before yuh invite her."

"How much yuh g'wan pay us?"

"I will get to dat in a moment."

"More than we already getting by we-self, ah hope."

"Mek me finish, please."

"Me cyan sekkle fi chump change, boss lady. Me too hungry. Ah have meself an' me pickney fi feed."

"Shush, nuh! Let har finish!"

"The clients pay me and I pay you. Understood?"

"Wait, so how we know what we getting?"

"Yuh get what yuh put out. There's a set rate. And if di customer is pleased, him can add twenty percent tip, which you keep."

"Wha kin'a answer dat? We want to know how much we getting."

"Yuh want to know what yuh getting? More than yuh will evah get working by yuhself, patrolling fah men who can barely afford a trip from Mobay to Portland, much less a fifty-dollah fuck. Yuh getting the big-man dem. Moneyman. Man who can at least feed yuh while yuh at it. Yuh getting wined and dined at expensive restaurants dat none ah yuh put together could afford. Yuh getting nice clothes, ah makeovah, an' a place fi sleep. An' is not just anywhere you'll sleep, Palm Star Resort is yuh bedroom. Every sexual favor haffi tek place in rooms dat we reserve for yuh clients. Yuh getting exposure—an opportunity dat yuh can't get from di run-down holes yuh crawl from. Dat answer yuh question?"

There was silence as each girl contemplated her fate, their minds trying to reconcile the uncertainty of what was being offered to them. They looked at each other because, of course, there was no real reason to back away. Margot waited for thirty long seconds. In the arrested silence, the howling wind rattled the French doors of the villa, flung them open to reveal a glimpse of the Blue Mountains and the sea twinkling in the sunlight. Gradually the girls began to chat and bicker, thickening the balmy atmosphere: *Mama can use ah stove. The boys need school shoes—lawd, dem cyan guh barefoot nuh longah. Nuh food nuh deh inna cupboard. The landlord aggo kick we out if we nuh pay next month rent.* Margot heard each thought, saw them etched on the young dark faces before her. She knew they wouldn't turn this offer down, for there was nothing left in their exhausted lungs, which heaved and sighed.

"It answer mine."

"Mine too."

"Ah thought so. Now I'll go on," Margot said. "Do not accept clients without me knowing about it. I call the shots. If ah don't think you're the right girl for the job, then I won't use you. Because these aren't just tourists we dealing wid. Like ah said, they are also the men we want to invest in our hotel. Our clients will be able to request their favorites on a regular basis. But it's mostly my discretion. Lastly, yuh duty is to serve. So yuh have to be willing to do anything that the client asks. Anything. Even if is to lick di dirt off him shoes. I don't want to hear any complaints from them about stubborn girls. Remembah you're disposable. One slipup an' yuh gone. Yuh must be able to satisfy di clients an' walk away in good standing."

All fifteen recruits signed the contract, and it was this cohort that Margot introduced to Alphonso and the potential investors of his hotel empire. On the night of this private gathering, she paraded the girls like virgins through Babylon, having them walk out in veils and long cloaks with nothing underneath. Margot turned to Alphonso and his guests. "Gentlemen, I present to you our queens of the night." One by one the girls dropped their cloaks and lifted their veils. The men were visibly pleased. Privately, Margot admired them, content. She told them what Alphonso told her: *"Mek me proud."*

And just like that Margot became a boss lady. A boss lady can be counted on. Does the dirty work. The men dig into their wallets for pleasures pure and deep. Margot's girls can't be rivaled. Their customers exit the hotel with long, conquering strides, whistling softly through the lobby. Days later they might return for another round, another hour with an island girl who has them biting their pillows, curling their toes, and swallowing moans that rise from their throats. They're baffled by their own helplessness when Margot tells them that a particular girl they requested isn't available. No one has ever made them feel so dependent—not barmaids, not servants, not assistants or secretaries, not tailors of fine suits, not expensive bottles of scotch, not their wives' silences, not even God.

But even with all the money coming in, Margot isn't satisfied. Something about her new role feels fake. Though she has been selling herself since high school, there is something dirty about selling other broken women, especially girls as young as her sister. She hardens her heart again. If she can succeed with this—between the money it brings and the secrets she'll know—Alphonso will have to give her the manager job at last. She's lived with regret before. Delores once made her break a chicken's neck so that she could cook it for dinner. She will never forget the screaming bird, the drops of blood on dirt, the dangling tendon. Yet, they were all satisfied that night.

Margot watches Miss Novia Scott-Henry, the new general manager, closely: The way she floats around the property, barging into people's conversations and telling them to work: "*Leave idle chatter for later . . . we have a hotel to run, people to attend to. Chop, chop!*" Even the way she unpacks her salads at lunch (who eats only salad as a meal?), wielding a silver fork and chewing contemplatively, her eyes trained on a document before her. Once in a while a piece of leaf or a bit of salad dressing would fall on the way to her mouth and she would pick it up with a napkin or brush it away. She's not a clean eater, this woman. Sometimes she hands Margot documents with coffee stains on them.

Miss Scott-Henry leaves her office door open at all times. Margot knows the woman takes frequent bathroom breaks because of all the water she drinks. She also sucks her teeth when in deep concentration and likes to take the bottom of a pen to her mouth and chew. Margot even listens in on the woman's phone calls; hears her friendly chatter to a business associate or someone from the *Jamaica Gleaner* or *Observer* calling to interview her as the former Miss Jamaica Universe winner, "*the new face of the tourism industry.*" Margot rolls her eyes at this, because she believes Alphonso hired the woman for that very reason, to bring publicity to his hotel. Just put a high-profile beauty queen in charge—one who shaved her head of beautiful locks to donate all her hair to cancer patients and who left the modeling industry to pursue a business degree—and people will flock to the property, though Margot believes foreigners couldn't care less about that.

There are other surprising things about Miss Novia Scott-Henry. In the two weeks since she started, she has learned everyone's names. "*How yuh doing, Brenda? Take care, Faye. Don't work too hard, Rudy. Let me see dat hose, Floyd. Nice hairstyle, Patsy.*" She converses with the lower staff as though they are all the same rank as her—another trait Margot regards with mild suspicion. Margot became skeptical the minute the woman arrived on the scene with her turquoise blue cowrie-shell glasses, her closely cropped hair (all that's left of the long hair that once cascaded in waves down her back, which was seen on all the 1980s calendars), and her sharply tailored pantsuits. Her beauty is indisputable, and she's as sweet as she is tall. So sweet that she leaves a bitter taste on Margot's tongue. Something sinister lurks behind her bright beauty-queen shine, the "Good mornings" and "Good evenings" she gives so freely, and the openness of her face. It's the custard-pudding face of someone who will never have to work hard for anything; someone who enters a room and knows all the men's eyes will be on her, yet plays it off by complimenting other women, no matter how frumpy. It's the face of a snake who will accept a plate of food or a glass of water at your house and, when you turn your back, throw it all away. Margot wants to know what she's hiding and what's behind her power over Alphonso.

"How long yuh think she'll last?" Margot asks Kensington.

"Longer than Dwight, fah sure," Kensington says while stapling some receipts together. "An' definitely longer than dis drought! Is like we ah roas' in hell."

Margot looks in Miss Novia Scott-Henry's direction. She's outside, talking to Beryl, the voluptuous female security guard who never smiles. Their heads are lowered in conversation, sneaking furtive glances around the property as though whoever they speak of might ambush them. Margot wonders if they're talking about the girls who've been coming around as of late. Beryl prevented one of them from entering the premises last week because she didn't have proper ID. This infuriated Margot, because the girl couldn't get to her client on time. Beryl has complained to Boris, the head of hotel security, about the young girls, but Boris already knows about Alphonso's scheme. He promptly removed Beryl from front gate duty and put her in charge of the parking lot. Since then, Beryl has been more miserable than ever. Margot worries she's a threat to their business. She watches Beryl and Miss Novia Scott-Henry huddled together. They are laughing about something, both throwing their hands up as though in surrender to the joke rippling through them. Margot is surprised to see flashes of Beryl's teeth.

"Something is fishy 'bout her, that's all," Margot says.

"Fishy?" Kensington asks, lowering the stapler. "Is dat why yuh haven't been doing work all week? 'Caw yuh jus' waan watch fi see if she slip? She's really nice. Bettah than that crow we had for ah boss. Alphonso did good by firing Dwight an' hiring her. An' besides, ah still have her old calendar. I want her to sign it. She did mek Jamaica proud di year she won Miss Universe."

A ball of fire rises in Margot's belly. She turns to Kensington. "Yuh is a good Christian woman, right?"

Kensington nods so hard that Margot fears her neck might snap. Margot often rolls her eyes whenever the girl comes to work in the morning with her stomach growling, explaining to Margot that she's fasting yet again for her sins and therefore would not eat for the rest of the day.

"So can I ask you a question?" Margot says, scooting closer.

"What?"

"How is it dat yuh tolerate her?"

Kensington shakes her head. "I'm not following."

"When Alphonso introduced us the first time, she held my hand an' stroke it."

Kensington jumps out her chair. "Yuh lie!"

"Yuh calling me a liar? Look at her. The way she dresses, the way she wears her hair—what self-respecting woman wear har hair cut so close to har head without di decency to put on a wig? An' yuh really t'ink any woman wid nice hair would shave it off like dat?"

"Is fah the cancer patients."

"Cancer patients, my rear end. Something else is behind it. Yuh notice that we've never seen her in a dress? Look how mannish she is. A far ways from her days as a beauty queen." As she says this with authority and a conviction that she never knew existed within her, a shock of excitement runs through Margot's veins, taking hold of her tongue. "Plenty people know about di rumors."

"What rumors?"

"That she's a undah-cover."

Kensington is silent. A moment passes before she speaks.

"But she was a beauty queen. Those girls too pretty fah dat. And dey 'ave morals."

"That was jus' fah show. If yuh don't believe me, jus' ask around. Better yet, watch her."

Kensington studies Miss Novia Scott-Henry in this new light—the way she talks with her hands, touching Beryl often on the elbow. A dark soot fills Kensington's eyes, obscuring the whiteness. Perspiration beads form above her mouth from the humidity.

"How yuh know fah sure that she's *funny*?"

"Jus' look at her," Margot says. "She flaunts it."

Kensington makes a sign of the cross. And just like that, Margot knows she has planted a seed, perhaps the only one that has the potential to thrive in this drought.

The next few days are more bearable in the office for Margot—not because the hotel has installed new air-conditioning to ward off the unbearable heat, but because of Kensington. Kensington's budding suspicion of Miss Novia Scott-Henry keeps her so occupied that she's not able to focus on anything else—like the reservations being made to certain rooms on the sixteenth floor under fake names, the local businessmen who check in, then check out hours later, the girls who prance solo in a diagonal line across the marbled lobby straight to the elevator.

When Miss Novia Scott-Henry comes to the front desk to request the receipts and vouchers, Margot pretends to be busy with reservations, so she directs her question to Kensington. "I'm not sure what is going on here. Can you please explain what these 'special services' are on some of the bills? And why there are astronomical charges to rooms that were only reserved for two hours?"

Kensington has a genuine look of confusion on her face. She's mouthing words that aren't coming out.

"Am I speaking to myself here?" Miss Novia Scott-Henry asks.

Margot thinks fast. "We—well—Kensington and I are still working on the other vouchers. There might have been a slight mix-up in booking. But when we're done sorting things out we'll get to you right away." She is a bit concerned that Alphonso hasn't shared his underground business with his hotel general manager. Shouldn't she be the first to know what's really happening and where the extra revenue's coming from? This just proves her incompetence. Or is it Blacka who is feeding her these figures, forgetting to eliminate the miscellaneous profits? Alphonso should fire that pompous pest of an accountant. But when Margot clicks on an unopened file, she realizes that it was her error. She gave the woman the wrong file. What if she calls them to inquire about the charges? What if she finds out and reports it to the authorities?

"Please have everything to me by the end of the day," Miss Novia Scott-Henry says. She glances at Kensington, who is sitting stiff and mute at the desk. "Is everything all right, Kensington?"

The girl nods, her eyes sliding into her lap, where Margot notices a small Bible tucked discreetly between her palms.

"She's jus' a likkle undah the weather," Margot says.

"I see."

Miss Novia Scott-Henry glances at Kensington. "You may go home, if that's the case. Wouldn't want our guests to get sick on their vacation. Margot, has a Mr. Georgio McCarthy checked in as yet? We have a meeting at four." Margot pulls up her reservations files on the new computer, though she doesn't have to. "Yes, checked him in at two."

"Perfect. Also, can you please remind the guests not to leave towels that they only used once for laundry. Remind them that we're in a drought and our goal is to conserve water."

"I sure will."

When Miss Novia Scott-Henry walks away, Margot waits until the woman is out of earshot before she turns to Kensington. "What's di mattah with you? You lost yuh tongue?"

"No." Kensington begins to put her Bible away. "But if yuh say she is what she is, then it's a sin. An abomination. I don't want to be around it."

"So what yuh g'wan do? Quit? Because she'll be here fah a very long time. You said so yuhself."

"Maybe ah should mention it to him," Kensington says, her eyes getting big.

"Who?" Margot asks.

"Alphonso."

Kensington's eyes are crazed like old Miss Gracie's whenever she preaches on her soapbox in the square. Or when she stops people to give them a prophecy. (*"Yuh g'wan conceive t'day in di name of Jeezas!" "Yuh g'wan win di lotto!" "Yuh g'wan haffi prepare fah di third funeral tomorrow."*)

Margot leans forward in her chair. "You don't have access to the owner of the hotel like dat. None of us do. And besides, the man is very busy."

Kensington stares at her for a while, blinking rapidly like she's trying to regain focus, one hand clutching the strap of her handbag. "Him need fi know what going on undah him nose. Yuh nuh notice anyt'ing else funny 'roun here?" Kensington asks.

"No. What yuh talkin' 'bout?"

"Di girl dem."

"What girls?" Margot shifts her attention to the computer.

"Di young, naked one dem prancing in an' out like dem own di place. And not ah soul seh one t'ing to dem. Dat neva use to happen before. Dat woman bringing in some bad energy. Alphonso need fi know 'bout it."

Just as Kensington says this, a call comes in from room 1601, the penthouse suite. Margot picks up, her eyes on Kensington's back.

"Guest services, how may I help you?"

"Yes, I'd like to get a sundae."

Click.

She smells money as soon as she walks into Georgio's room, where the shutters are open to a picturesque view of the sunset. It leaves a trail of red and violet in the sky; and a half-moon sits a couple feet away, patiently waiting its turn.

"Smoke?" Georgio offers Margot. He's a man of a few words. She met him at the last gathering held at Alphonso's villa.

"Shame on you for asking. Yuh know why I'm here."

Though fresh from his meeting with Miss Novia Scott-Henry, he's already dressed down in a white Palm Star Resort terry-cloth robe that swallows his small, sickly frame. He looks like a skeleton with flesh—his green eyes peering at Margot from dark hollow holes, so powerful they seem to burn away the lashes. She imagines the old naked body underneath that awaits her strokes and kneading; the flaccid penis that hangs between his legs. She didn't send one of her other girls because Georgio is the biggest fish in the pond. It's his money that Alphonso needs to close the deal on the new resort. She undresses.

"Turn around," Georgio tells her as soon as she's naked. He places his cigar inside a simple ashtray by the desk. She does as she's told, bending over right there by the swivel chair. She imagines the last sliver of the sunlight casting them in gold—Margot bent over with her legs spread, and Georgio behind her. She closes her eyes and thinks of Verdene. The weeks she has let slip by without calling her. She has told Kensington to screen Verdene's calls at the hotel.

"Who is she to you?"

"No one."

"Suh why she calling yuh like every othah minute? It ah drive me crazy. Ah have t'ings to do, yuh nuh."

"Just keep telling her I'm not here."

A slight breeze embraces her, reminding her of her nakedness in this stranger's room. Margot bites her lips and sucks in her breath as she awaits Georgio's initial thrust. He's taking a mighty long time. She hears him cussing at himself.

"Is something wrong?" she asks him, turning her head slightly. She catches a glimpse of the old man sitting slumped on the bed, looking like a boy who has lost his best friend.

"Sorry," he says, not looking up at her.

"What you mean by 'sorry'?" Margot asks. She knows exactly what he means. She watches with annoyance and pity as the man gestures to his soft front. Georgio is shaking his head and pouring himself a drink from an expensive-looking bottle he keeps on the nightstand. Margot resists the urge to ask him to pour her some. She remains standing. She doesn't get dressed; and he doesn't instruct her to do so. She stands there for what feels like a long time. Long enough for the sun to disappear completely and the moon to spread across the night sky. She gets down on all fours. The new moon floods Georgio's room. Margot is down on both knees in front of him and takes the cigar out his mouth. She can make out the stricken look in his face when she does this. "Is there anything I can do?" she asks, taking his flaccid penis in her hand. She tugs it, gently at first. Then more vigorously. For what she knows—and has always known—is how to milk desire. Georgio stirs, tilting his pelvis as his penis hardens in her hand. Would there ever be a time, she wonders, when she will not have to do this? Only with Verdene did she begin to experience pleasure on her own terms, and not responsible solely for someone else's. She tries to shut this out by focusing on Georgio's grunts, but the thought is persistent, a nagging that has been long subdued like dark secrets she has held in her belly. It is here, while sitting in a moonlit puddle in the penthouse suite with her fist clenched around another man, that the gigantic organism she imagines her secrets to be uncoils and pushes from her navel. She doesn't take her hand away from Georgio but feels, for the first time, the sadness she ought to. It floods the room and pulls her back into the night sea. She's afraid she might drown. She remembers—too late—that Verdene had promised to teach her how to swim.

12

THANDI SITS IN MISS RUBY'S SHACK, FEELING THE COARSENESS OF Miss Ruby's palms on her skin. "Yuh coming along fine." Miss Ruby hums while she rubs Thandi. She is in a rare good mood. "In no time yuh g'wan be as white as snow white," Miss Ruby promises.

"You mean light brown?"

"Same difference." She touches Thandi's face. "Trus' me when I say this. Yuh g'wan see the doors open up so wide." Thandi relaxes under the woman's hands. This is exactly what she needs. More than promises of lightness in her skin is someone's touch. Though it is far from gentle, it is just enough for Thandi. She lifts her arms above her head for Miss Ruby to get under her arms and sides. Thandi closes her eyes when Miss Ruby gets to her breasts. This circular motion reminds her of other touches. Whenever she pulls out the neatly folded towel from under her pillow at nights and rests her head on it, her fantasies turn to Charles. His light brown eyes pull her gently in a dare. Her restless fingers seek comfort inside her cotton underwear. Her own wetness surprises and shames her. Since the attack on her as a child, she hasn't touched herself this way, not even to idly put her hand there while bathing. It became a separate entity from her body, an organ with its own blood supply, something mangled and left behind. But it's not *him* who comes to mind anymore. Some nights, before Margot comes home and well after Delores and Grandma Merle fall asleep, she floats outside of her body to the ceiling. She curls up next to a pillow of guilt, afraid she has conjured the devil; but more afraid of the possibility of Delores's eyes opening, the whites of them flashing. She hears Charles. *Come*, he says. And Thandi reaches toward him, her fingers growing and growing to close the distance between them.

Miss Ruby stops her rubbing and frowns. "Yuh all right?" she asks. Thandi hugs herself and crosses her legs. A wave of shame washes over her.

"Uhm. I'm fine," Thandi utters in a small voice, avoiding Miss Ruby's eyes. "Why?"

"Yuh jus' made a noise."

"It wasn't me."

Miss Ruby begins to wrap the plastic around Thandi's chest. But she still has a look of concern when she pauses again to study Thandi. Just then something shatters outside, and she hears her name: "Thandi!" Miss Ruby stops what she's doing, leaving the plastic dangling. Thandi leaps to the other side of the room to seek cover and Miss Ruby grabs a knife—one she once used to cut the heads off fish she sold—and opens the door of her shack. The door bangs on the zinc. She looks from left to right; then, up in the quivering branches of the mango tree, she sees Charles. "Hey, dutty, stinkin' bwoy! Don't mek me cut yuh backside t'day! If me eva catch yuh, me will kill yuh!" she screams.

"What yuh doing to yuhself, Thandi?" Charles shouts. Thandi can see a part of him in the mango tree just outside the window. She gasps. "How dare you! Yuh have no decency, to be spying on me this way!"

"Yuh beautiful jus' the way yuh is! Nuh mek di witch fool yuh!"

Thandi clutches her clothes to her chest. "Go away!"

"Ah not g'wan mek yuh do this to yuhself," Charles says.

"I said go away! It's my skin."

Just then Charles loses his balance and falls out of the tree. Thandi rushes to the window, afraid he has broken some part of himself, but he springs up like a cat and sprints through the yard, with Miss Ruby chasing him with the knife.

"Yuh damn pervert! Yuh is a shame to yuh parents! Yuh too out of order."

Garbage cans overturn, spilling garbage. Fowl scatter around the yard like they lost their heads. The one sleeping dog scampers from its rest spot near the standpipe.

"Bomboclaaaat!"

Charles's curse triggers a surge of terror inside Thandi. Miss Ruby must have caught him. She fumbles with the zipper on her dress and leaves the money for Miss Ruby on her bench. She runs out the door and into the backyard. Too embarrassed to use the front gate, she squeezes through a small fence that was once an entrance to the sea. Thandi struggles along the seashore toward the rocky incline that will lead her to the bank of the river. This is a longer way home, but she takes it. The castle rises into view. Though unfinished, it is several stories high already, the steel foundation glistening with promise, its shadow closing in on the beach that spreads before it. She hurries along, trying hard to dodge the sun. Everything else is wilting in the drought, but the sun is getting bigger and plumper by the day.

At home, the Queen of Pearl jar is sitting before Thandi, unopened. She touches her face, where the shade is uneven, especially the areas around her eyes and mouth. But what about the rest? When will she be fair like that goddess in the painting? The one that rises out of the oyster shell? Thandi had seen the painting for the first time hanging on the wall inside Brother Smith's office, to the left of *The Last Supper.* "*She was so beautiful that Botticelli used her as his muse for a very long time,*" Brother Smith said when he caught Thandi staring at the painting. She was in awe of the woman's long orange mane and delicate cornmeal skin. She can only imagine that if you touch skin like that, it melts. To Thandi, that soft pink skin had been part of an already long to-do list: to pass the Caribbean Examination Council subjects, go to university, become a doctor, marry well. Each night she's been pushing her sketchpad aside, studying hard, falling asleep with her head in her books; pushing away Charles, her pencils, the sea.

She swallows and dips her hand inside the Queen of Pearl cream jar and lathers her face with it.

"Thandi!"

She's pulled out of her fantasy by the sound of her name.

"Thandi, it's me!" someone wails outside the shack. She goes to the window and parts the curtains, fingering the embroidered flowers that Grandma Merle sewed decades before she became mute. Charles is standing in the tall grass where Mr. Melon ties his goat to the dying pear tree and where Little Richie sits and plays with himself inside the old tire. Charles's khaki shirt is open like a cape and his pants bulge at the pockets where he probably stole mangoes from somebody's yard. His bare feet are crusted with dirt from his swim in the river. His sandy brown hair has grass in it, like he has been rolling around in the bushes too. There's no blood on him, so Miss Ruby must have missed.

"Ah know yuh in di house." Thandi plays with the hem of her

dress, winding her finger in the thread that has come undone. How can she face him after what he has seen at Miss Ruby's shack? She hugs herself as though she were still naked and his look could tear down the walls at any moment. "I know yuh can hear me," he says.

Thandi busies herself. She dusts the furniture, sweeps the floor, fluffs the pillows on the bed that she and Margot share. When she's overheated from all the movement, she fans herself with a piece of cardboard, grateful that Miss Ruby did not have time to wrap her with the plastic, and relieved to feel just a tingle of cool air. A girlish giggle escapes her as she recalls what Charles called out to her earlier at Miss Ruby's shack. *"Yuh beautiful jus' the way yuh is! Nuh mek di witch fool yuh!"* No one has ever called her beautiful. It is a word she associates with the evening sun when it's thick and red-orange at the bottom of the sky, the blushing stars at night, the goddesses in the paintings at school. A word that brings to mind a billowing sheer curtain that rests like a fainting damsel on the back of an armchair—serene, graceful, elegant. She turns to the mirror again to look at her half bleached face.

Later in the week Thandi stops at Mr. Levy's Wholesale to pick up a few things for Delores. She stays by the fan that blows hot air and the smell of cat piss into the store. She itches to wriggle out of the plastic hidden beneath the uniform. But she won't give up so easily.

"Wh'appen, sweet girl?" Thandi stiffens when she hears his voice. It's as though electric wires are coursing through her in this moment, her fingers spread wide, mouth agape. She turns around to meet the jaundiced eyes of Clover, Delores's old handyman. After he hurt her he gradually came around less and less, until he slunk out of town and disappeared for years. By the looks of things he's a worse drunk than ever, though still a young man. He sneers at Thandi with the only two crooked teeth in his mouth. His skin is an ashen black that makes it look like it has been dried in the sun. With his knuckles he raps on the counter. "Missah Chin, ah wah tek so long? Gimme a pack ah cigarette!" He shoves a dollar under the opening and leers at Thandi. There is no way for her to move away from him in this small space. She hopes he will get the message and let her be if she doesn't acknowledge that he's there. But Clover reaches out and touches her on the shoulder. Always, at this very instant of physical contact, she would wake with a scream. But this is not a dream.

"Why yuh acting so?" He tilts his head like they are lovers having a harmless disagreement.

Thandi swallows, hoping her jumbled words will be measured when she utters them, standing there in her Saint Emmanuel High uniform. "Leave. Me. Alone." She hopes the fire in her eyes is enough to scorch him, burn him up in the flames.

But Clover's jaundiced eyes become watery as the sneer broadens on his face. "Ah love a 'ooman who got some fight in har." He grabs himself and moves closer. "Turn me on . . ."

Thandi steps away. This causes Clover to laugh, flinging his head back.

Distracted by a dream, Thandi had wandered off onto a remote path shaded by trees—mahogany, live oaks, wild lime. She was on her way home from school, thinking about sketching the marvelous arches of the trees, the extensive roots of the mahogany, the small green clusters in the lime trees. The stillness of the green water in the cove. Clover cupped her mouth and hauled her off into the bushes. At nine years old she knew what "*bombohole*" meant because the man kept whispering how much he wanted hers, splaying her legs to take it. When he was done he told her not to tell or else he would break her neck. Thandi wondered then which was worse, dying or lying there hurting between her legs. Thandi kept her ugly secret even as Clover came over—less and less—to help Delores hoist up a fence, string electric wires, hammer exposed nails in their shack; or to play dominoes with the other neighborhood men whose breath always stank with white rum and whose clammy hands were always cupping Delores's rump.

Clover takes the pack of cigarettes Mr. Levy shoves through the opening of the mesh door with those same blackened hands she remembers. Thandi watches him from the side of her eyes as he opens the pack and puts one cigarette behind his ear. The rest he slips inside his pocket. He leans on the counter with his ankles crossed, watching her as though expecting a comment. When she says nothing, he tells her, "Ran into Delores, she ask me to come by the house on Sat'day. Looking forward to seeing yuh cute face." Clover touches her chin and she slaps his hand away, stamping out of the store.

13

VERDENE SCRUBS THE BLOOD OFF THE SIDES OF HER HOUSE with a wet green rag. She concentrates deeply on the smudges and stains so she does not have to feel the rage, does not have to pause long enough to touch the collar of her housedress to her face to wipe the tears. So she rubs and rubs, muttering underneath her breath, "Damn ignorant imbeciles!" The rag dries in her hand and she dips it into the mixture of bleach and water. Since the water pressure is low, there is no way she can refill the bucket. "Goddammit!" The tears begin to fall faster than she can catch them. The fact that the culprits could be hiding in the bushes, laughing so hard that their guts pain them, makes Verdene angrier. "You think this is funny?" she asks the bushes and flowers. Something seems to brace in the yard, halting every sound except the murmuring of the big black flies around her. A family of vultures are perched on a coconut tree nearby.

"Answer me, you cowards!" Verdene stands up, her knees stiff from being on them all morning. She throws the rag inside the bucket and clenches both fists. She's spinning around and around, trying to pinpoint where the person could be hiding. "You get a kick out of this, don't you?" she yells. She's getting dizzy circling like that. Almost out of breath, she stops. The dead dog in the yard appears to be breathing, its moving ribs gilded by sunlight through the ackee tree branches. Verdene steps closer and stands over it. She brings her hands to her mouth, unable to believe that someone could be capable of such a barbaric act. They took great care to make a vertical cut down the animal's belly and another cut across its throat. Verdene mourns the poor dog that was sacrificed because of her. How many more does she have to deal with? *How many?*

She goes inside for the shovel. When she returns she attempts to dig yet another hole in the ground but stops, the shovel suspended in her hands, her attention on the lush banana leaves that separate her yard from Miss Gracie's. She lowers the shovel and marches over there. She will take care of this once and for all, she decides. She hasn't been in the old woman's yard since she was a little girl led by curiosity to the garden filled with rows of Scotch Bonnet peppers, which she thought were oddly shaped cherries. She bit into one of them and instantly choked. Her eyes watered so much that she could barely see to go back home to quell the fire inside her six-year-old mouth. One side of her tongue was numb for a whole week. And so were her buttocks after Ella walloped her with a rubber switch.

Verdene remembers when the yard had a scarecrow. Miss Gracie planted the peppers years ago, instead of flowers like everyone else. She used to make homemade pepper sauce and sell it in jars at the market. Fish vendors used to buy up the sauce to sprinkle on their fish when they realized that people liked it. Miss Gracie made a lot of money. Even Ella bought the sauce in bulk, because Verdene's father would never touch anything without it. When the fishing business died down, so did the demand for Miss Gracie's sauce. There was no indication that a young girl named Rose lived there—Miss Gracie's daughter, who was only two years younger than Verdene. A simple girl who read her Bible instead of school-books and who used to follow her mother around from door to door to preach before she got pregnant and ran away.

"*Do—do you know—Je—Jesus Christ?*" the girl stuttered to Verdene once when they were teenagers. Verdene had opened the door to see Rose and Miss Gracie standing on the steps of her veranda.

"*I'm busy. Come back later,*" Verdene had replied.

"*Yuh not too young fi hear di good word, sweetheart,*" Miss Gracie said when she stepped in front of Rose. Her eyes roved inside Verdene's house. "*Ella surely live like ah queen in dis place. Mind if we come in?*" This seemed to embarrass Rose, who always looked shrunken in her mother's indomitable shadow. "*My parents are not home,*" was all Verdene could come up with before excusing herself and closing the door. The last she remembered of Rose were her awkward waves at the front gate, which seemed more like pleas for friendship than eagerness to talk about sin and salvation.

Up and down the rows, from the fence to the house, the Scotch Bonnet peppers are dying. The smell permeates the air, making Verdene's eyes water. She makes her way across the yard with the shovel and picks up a stone to bang on the bars on Miss Gracie's veranda. There's no answer. Verdene bangs again, determined. Her tongue coils inside her mouth with an ammunition of choice words. She will tell Miss Gracie to bury the dog her damn self. That she has had it with cleaning up dead animals and bloodstains. She thinks she hears murmuring and steps toward it. Someone is working in the yard, on the other side of the house that leads to an open field of fountain grass. He's crouched, peacefully uprooting weeds by a post.

"Excuse me," Verdene says to the young man. He stops what he's doing at the sound of her voice and turns his head. When he sees her, he straightens himself, squares his shoulders. The muscles of his face tighten, the blood seeming to drain from it when he recognizes her.

"What is it yuh want, miss?" he asks.

He hasn't let go of the machete that he's using to cut the weeds. Verdene is taken by the title *miss*. "Please, call me Verdene."

The young man stands to his feet. "What yuh doing ovah here?" he asks.

Verdene licks her lips, realizing how dry they are. She knows that there is no way she can count on this young man to offer her a glass of water. She gets straight to the point. "I'm here for Miss Gracie. Is she here?"

"Why yuh want to know?"

"I want her to pick up the dead animal she left in my yard last night and clean up my walkway."

"Miss Gracie is ah ole 'ooman. An' from what ah hear, you kill those dogs yuhself."

"Look here . . ." She pauses. "What's your name?"

"Charles."

"Look here, Charles, you don't know me. You know nothing about me. So don't you dare tell me what I do and don't do in my own house. Now please call that old hag out here or else I will smash her windows with this shovel." She lifts the shovel for effect, though she no longer feels strong enough to deliver on her threat.

"She's not here."

"When will she be back?"

He wipes sweat off his forehead with the back of his free hand. "I don't know. I'm jus' here helping out 'round di yard."

"Then I'll wait. I need to get to the bottom of this."

"Miss Gracie can't even lift ah grocery bag, much less kill ah dog an' put inna yuh yard. So gwaan 'bout yuh business."

Verdene finally recognizes him as the young man she has seen escorting Miss Gracie to church. "Who are your people?" she asks, trying to place him. "I know Miss Gracie doesn't have a son. And I'm certain that she isn't deserving of a bodyguard. Why do you waste your time?"

"Why should it mattah to you?"

"It's you, isn't it? It's you who is helping her with this childish prank!"

The young man wrinkles his face. There's a youthful innocence there buried under the theatrical performance of disgust—the type toddlers display when they discern adults' disapproval of them eating dirt or sniffing their poop. He's just a boy, trying to be a man, she thinks. She has the sinking feeling that she has wrongly accused him. Something in his gentle manner gives this away. He's not at all threatening with the machete in his hand. Suddenly she's aware of the weight of the shovel hanging from her fingertips, her housedress soaked with perspiration, her wild hair. Surely she has given him more reason to fear her than vice versa. She watches him to see if he hesitates out of fear. A light sheen breaks out on his forehead. Verdene realizes that they have been standing in the blazing sun.

"Miss, ah t'ink yuh bettah leave Miss Gracie alone," he says finally. "She can't tek no trouble."

"Can you help me, then?" Her voice is calm and reasonable, as though she didn't just accuse him of putting a dead dog in her yard. "I need help cleaning my walkway and burying this dog."

"Why should I help you?"

"Because it's the only way I'll leave. I want this mess out of my yard. I want to live in peace. I want to be treated like a human being. I want—" The tears she had shed earlier are rolling back heavy down to her chin, wetting her collar. The young man relaxes and stoops to lay down his machete. All the frustration Verdene has been holding back comes spewing out in this young man's presence. She has never done this with Margot—not since the first incident—because she fears it might scare her away. And maybe it already has, since Margot hasn't been to visit in weeks. Hasn't even called. The young man raises his hand and rests it on Verdene's shoulder—a gesture Verdene did not expect or even think she needed. But she does.

"All right," he says.

Later, she waits up in the dark kitchen for Margot. She doesn't turn the lights on. Maybe she can catch the perpetrators if they dare step foot inside her yard again. And besides, she likes the dark. It's cooler, quieter, and more peaceful, the chirpings of crickets like a nocturnal lullaby. The red digits on the small digital clock on the counter, which Verdene sometimes uses as a timer when baking, is blinking 11 PM. It has been like this for the last four weeks. Waiting by the telephone. Pacing. Cooking to help take her mind off things. Setting the table, laying out meals she knows that only she will eat.

Verdene calls the hotel again.

"What you mean, she already left?" she asks the girl who answers. The girl sounds like she has a clothespin clipped on the bridge of her nose.

"Did you even check? The least you can do is check!"

"Ma'am, she signed out."

"But you said that yesterday too. How many breaks can one person take?"

Then she composes herself, taking a deep breath, allowing her question to take form. "Did she . . ." She pauses and looks at her fist on the counter by the telephone. "Did she leave with anyone?" As soon as Verdene asks this question she feels ashamed. Before the girl can respond, Verdene tells her never mind and hangs up. She thinks about all the reasons Margot could be unavailable. After all, she still has obligations as a working woman. But not even a phone call to say so herself?

Verdene clutches the blue ceramic mug in front of her on the table. She had poured some rum in her tea, hoping it would make her go to sleep quicker. She used to see her mother do the same on those nights after she had been beaten badly and needed something stronger than medicine to numb the pain, which Verdene suspected, even then, wasn't just physical.

So here she is, unable to close her eyes as she suffers from a different pain, its impact just as powerful as a kick in the belly or a clenched fist to the chin. Margot is avoiding her. She notices the shadows from the trees outside that dance in the breeze; they're faint like the dreaded dawning of intuition. Earlier she had taken a bath to freshen up. Just in case. In the mirror Verdene studied herself naked, regarding the love handles she had comfortably acquired around her hips and belly. For the first time in a long while, she frowned at them, conscious of the softness of her shape. Who is she? What has she become? She grabbed the fat around her hips and held it, disgust rising in her throat, settling on her tongue.

Tonight she cooked a nice meal and set the table. The candle is still resting in the center of the table like a mockery of her efforts. In the silence of waiting, Verdene sighs deeply, hoping the rush of air into her lungs and the rum warming her blood will steady her. Clear her head. In front of her, the plate of rice rises like a snow-covered mountain, its peak threatening to touch the ceiling when she looks up. The steam has cooled, but the sight of the starchy white grains promises to assuage her. She takes a spoonful with the serving spoon. One, then two, then three spoonfuls, until she loses count. She eats the plate of plantains too. And the plate of codfish fritters. Every time she swallows she feels nothing. Nothing at all. When she's emptied the plates she jumps up from the table, accidentally knocking her chair over and bumping into things on her way to the bathroom. It's here that she finds her reprieve, the calm that settles over her like a damp towel pressed against her forehead in the heat as the smell of stomach acid rises. Stays. She remains kneeling on the floor, too weak to move. Too tired to feel bad about what she just did.

Finally, Verdene presses her palms on the cold concrete and pushes herself up. As she stands, her vision is invaded by black polka dots. She balances herself by holding on to the sink, then the doorframe, then eventually to the walls as she makes her way down the dark corridor toward the kitchen. She moves closer to the table and clutches the mug that holds her tea mixed with rum. She lifts it to her mouth and drinks. When she's done, she reaches for the bottle of rum and drinks from that. She squints and grimaces as the liquid burns her throat. She slams the bottle down on the table. *But how could Margot not call? How could she not call?* Had she been religious, this would've been a prayer, a litany of pleas and questions.

Verdene tilts her head back and laughs at the notion of Jesus listening to her harp over a woman. *Haven't I learned my lesson?* Verdene has always been the one to push women away with her aggressive need for them to fulfill her, to pour their souls into the gaping hole inside her—a cavity with no bottom; she chased them and backed them into corners with her yearnings, her dependency on them to make her feel whole—the way Aunt Gertrude said Jesus is supposed to. On bended knees, a seventeen-year-old Verdene had bowed her head as Aunt Gertrude's priest anointed her. Aunt Gertrude had told him about the incident with Akua at the university. The priest placed his holy hand on Verdene's head, his grasp like a skullcap as he prayed away Verdene's sin. The same priest married her and her husband four years later. A firm squeeze on Verdene's right shoulder during her wedding reception was the priest's way of saying he approved of her salvation—that God had intervened and *healed* her. Made her *whole.* Those laughs she and her husband shared, the discussions that ebbed and flowed well into the nights, the comfortable silence that breathed with them after dinner when they each settled into their own readings, sailing into disparate worlds. But a woman has other needs too. The need to be connected to something greater—a cause, a passion. Unlike the other women, who offered an escape from the lies Verdene told herself and the people whose opinions once mattered, Margot offers countenance. But then there's that pain she senses in Margot—the kind of pain that makes other pains seem minute, insignificant in comparison. Even when Margot was a girl, Verdene sensed this pain. Saw it in her eyes. It was stifling enough to choke her if she wasn't careful to look away.

Verdene makes her way to bed. She haphazardly pulls the sheet back. This much she's able to do, though her limbs feel heavy like they do in dreams in which she's trying to execute some kind of a critical task, like tying a shoelace. In bed Verdene closes her eyes and sinks farther underneath the sheets, not wanting to believe it possible that Margot could have someone else. The crickets sound like they're inside the house, trapped under the wooden floors, or in the corners, behind furniture. Everywhere. A sliver of moonlight slips through the window. If karma is real—a payback, perhaps, for walking out on her husband one foggy Sunday morning, a year before her mother's death, leaving nothing but a letter confessing her extramarital affairs with women and her need for a divorce— Verdene knows deep down that she has already lost.

14

MARGOT SITS INSIDE RUPERT'S BOX LUNCH AND VARIETY RES-
taurant, waiting. She glances at her watch and then again at
the round clock on the wall that overlooks the small square tables. On
top of the tables are a salt-and-pepper rack, a bottle of ketchup, and
hot pepper. Flies pitch from one empty table to the other as though
playing musical chairs. The restaurant might not remind the tourists
who accidentally stumble into it of the nicer restaurants along the
hotel chain in Montego Bay or even the ones they're used to at home,
but it suits the habits of the natives: the way the cook prepares the
food without worrying about using too much spice; the way the tables
are close together because privacy isn't as important as hunger; the
way the dining area is resistant to light, because all you really need is

two senses while you eat—smell and taste. Margot has been coming to Rupert's for years—Rupert serves the best oxtail in Montego Bay. The old toothless man is like a grandfather to Margot, always asking how she is, and giving her extra servings of gravy on her plate.

Just as Margot is about to put a forkful of gravy rice in her mouth, the girl appears at the doorway, leggy and self-confident. She parts the beaded curtains and pauses to look around the dark restaurant as if Margot isn't the only customer in the place. The girl runs her hands down her dress to smooth the hem that only reaches mid-thigh. Margot doesn't greet her until she's standing directly across from her, smelling like camphor balls and something sweet.

"Hello, Margot."

"It's 'boss lady.'"

"Right. Boss lady."

"You're late. Have a seat."

The girl pulls out a chair.

Margot watches her get comfortable in her seat. She fixes the pink flower in her hair that matches her dress, under which smooth, velvety dark skin beckons more attention. Margot licks the gravy off her lips. "How yuh doing?" Margot asks.

"Good, good, cyan complain."

"Glad to hear."

"Suh yuh request to see me?"

"You were highly recommended by Bobbett. She said you get the most loyal customers, because, of all di girls, you're di only one willing to try anything. Is that true?"

"Yes." The girl smiles sweetly, revealing a gap in her front teeth.

"What name do you go by out here again?"

"Dey call me Sweetness, but since we go way back, yuh can call me whateva yuh want."

"I'll call you Sweetness, then. And not a word to anyone about our conversation. Understand?"

The girl nods.

"Now, Sweetness, if you want to work for me, yuh have to show me what yuh can do. Prove to me why you're the number one girl out here. Ah can't let any an' anybody into my camp."

"How yuh want me to prove it to you?"

"I have an assignment for you. Yuh first."

"So I'm hired?"

"If you do what I ask."

"What is dat?"

"I want you to seduce a woman."

"What?"

"Just for a night. I want you to seduce her. I'll pay you double what yuh making now."

The girl laughs. "Dis is a joke?" she asks.

Margot glances at the clock over the girl's head. She has to be back at work in half an hour. "Can you do it or not?"

"Me nuh go dat way."

"For two hundred dollars. U.S., not Jamaican."

"I—I don't know."

"Is just one time. Yuh don't have to think 'bout it aftah yuh do it."

"Why yuh want me to do this?"

"If yuh g'wan work fah me, then don't ask questions."

"Okay, how 'bout t'ree hundred?"

"Don't bargain wid me either. Take it or leave it."

"Who is di 'ooman?"

"Is that a yes?"

The girl pauses. She pushes herself away from the table. "Yuh t'ink I need yuh dirty money dat badly? What mek yuh t'ink I'd do such a t'ing? Yuh treating me like me is some kinda hungry mongrel who'd sniff rump fi food. What kinda person yuh t'ink I am?"

"There're not many girls like you out here. From what I hear, you is di kinkiest of dem all. Like dat story 'bout di two college students on spring break. The couple who yuh mek—"

"How yuh know 'bout dat?"

"Ah do my research before ah do interviews."

"Suh yuh t'ink if yuh sweet-talk or blackmail me, ah g'wan jus' agree fi yuh flimsy offer? Me is not no fool, boss lady."

"I know. You're a very smart girl."

"Suh now yuh acknowledge me as smart? Yuh g'wan like yuh neva know me before."

"Look, I'm not asking you to go to bed wid the woman. I just want you to tease a likkle an' see if she responds."

"Yuh trying to frame har?"

"What me tell yuh 'bout the questions?"

"She has something yuh want?"

"You're obviously not understanding me."

"Wid all due respec', why yuh don't ask some nasty woman like yuhself to do it?"

"Because I think you'd be better at it, wid all di nastiness you've done. Remember you're doing a job. It's not a reflection of who you are as a person. I'm sure yuh screw men and, according to those rumors, women too."

"It was only di one time."

"But yuh go home to yuh boyfriend."

"I don't have a boyfriend."

"Then to whoever yuh go home to."

"I live alone."

"Point is, you're good at what you do because you're able to sep-arate yuhself from it. What I'm offering you is better than what you're used to. After this, you'll work for me and never have to want fah anyt'ing again."

"When yuh want me do di t'ing?"

"As soon as tonight."

"Tonight?"

"Yes. Yuh have plans?"

"No. It's jus' . . ."

"One night. Is all I'm asking."

"If my mother know, she'd kill me."

Margot rolls her eyes at this. She glances at the clock again. Fifteen minutes left.

"Ah hope is not anyone from Rivah Bank. Suppose dey know me an' my family?"

"She doesn't."

"But you do."

"Why would I tell anyone? You're working for me. This is between us. Understood?"

"Suppose di woman tell people?"

"She won't."

"Suppose she want to sleep wid me fah more than a night?"

"Then do it. Your pay would double. No, triple."

"What?"

"Yuh heard me."

"It's asking too much of me."

"Tell me something. How many times yuh come across six hundred dollars from yuh nightly strolls? Six hundred dollars. Tell me if something is wrong wid earning six hundred easy dollars."

The girl shakes her head. "God wrong wid it."

"So that's the new thing now? Hookers who clutch dem pearls an' dem Bible ah talk 'bout God? When since yuh tun Miss Gracie? Any other night yuh willing to bend ovah, skin up, an' get dung pon all fours, an' now yuh ah talk 'bout God? Yuh even go as far as have a threesome."

"I jus' did the man."

"Nonsense."

"I'm not dat way."

"If that's the case, then I'll take my offer elsewhere." Margot gets up from the table. "Thanks for your time." She walks out the door, leaving the girl sitting there at the table.

"Wait!"

Margot slows. When she turns, she's face-to-face with the girl, who is standing a good three inches taller than Margot in heels, her eyes brimming with determination and something else Margot tries to pinpoint.

"I'll do it."

"All right. Tonight at Lux Bar and Grill." Margot eyeballs the girl's outfit. "I'll have something nicer for you to wear." Margot walks quickly toward the exit and the girl catches up with her again, holding on to her elbow. "Margot! Ah mean, boss lady?"

"Yes?"

"Me is not like dat. Not because me agree mean dat me go dat way." Her eyes are burning into Margot, their radius expanding, pleading, a blue streak of terror inside each iris. "Me is not like dat a'tall."

"Nothing wrong if you are," Margot says, meeting the girl's frightened stare, identifying what exactly she sees beyond the dread. "The more versatile, the bettah." And with that, she walks away.

15

"WHEN WILL THIS DROUGHT END?" THANDI ASKS CHARLES, her head tilted to the strips of white clouds in the sky. The sun hangs low to the water, searing the sand on the beach, and bearing down on Thandi and Charles until they must slow down, unable to carry such weight.

"Dunno," Charles says, wiping perspiration off his face with his hand. "It bettah be sooner than lata. The soil is bad fah di produce dis year. Ah saw couple farmers crying in di field wah day ovah dem yam, sweet potatoes, dasheen, an' corn. Even the passion fruit decay pon di vines before time."

Charles hasn't said anything about seeing her naked in Miss Ruby's shack, so neither has Thandi. She knows, in a remote corner of her mind, that he hasn't forgotten. Small talk about the drought relieves them of the intimate pressure. So she plays along, pretending that it never happened. Though that damp warmth that courses through her body lingers as long as the drought. They are walking along the beach barefoot toward the castle. Up close Thandi can see where the rooms might be. Once they're inside it, they exhale from escaping the sun. As soon as he catches his breath, Charles surprises Thandi by twirling her around in the empty space like they're a couple dancing to slow music. The area is spacious, with massive cylindrical columns. "Maybe it's going to be a dance hall," Charles says in a whisper, as though anyone might be around to hear. Their voices echo. "Men will dance in their tuxedos wid their women like this—" He dips Thandi, holding her back so that she won't fall. Thandi squeals and giggles in his arms. She lifts one leg up like the ladies do in movies. For a second they stare at each other, Thandi unsure if he'll kiss her and Charles looking like he's deciding whether it's the right time. They pull away as if simultaneously arriving at a consensus to wait at least until the sun sets. Charles's eyes drift to an empty pool. It's carved out like someone took a big ice-cream scoop to it. Around them are tools the construction workers use—wheelbarrows and pipes and planks. Outside there are several bulldozers parked. Thandi inhales the smell of cement as they stand inside the empty place. She imagines that she's in the mouth of a whale, looking up into the roof of its mouth—the crisscrossing of the bone structure and teeth—feeling small. Insignificant. She follows Charles to another area where she can see the sun slowly disappearing, its death march across the sky finally coming to an end. It's here that they settle. Charles spreads his towel for her to sit. He sits facing her.

"When do you think they'll be done?" she asks.

"By Christmas, maybe. Definitely by high season. More tourists come then."

"How long ago did they start?"

Charles shrugs his shoulders. "'Bout March, thereabout."

Where Thandi lives—the part farthest from the fork along the Y-shaped river—there is no construction activity going on. There's also no indication that what happened to Little Bay will happen to River Bank too. After all, River Bank is scrunched under the nose of a hill and the river overflows when it rains. It's not exactly a tourist attraction like Martha Brae, Black River, or Rio Bueno. Also, the beach won't be ideal for amateur swimmers, since one can easily drown if not aware of Pregnant Heidi's wrath.

"They been coming around, giving out papers," he says.

She's sitting Indian-style with her hands on her knees, her uniform skirt falling between them, and her head turned. She fixes her eyes on the arches above her head.

"Papers?" she asks.

Charles shrugs again. "I guess for the bulldozing noise. Mama can't get rest wid all di banging and drilling."

"We don't hear that from where we are," Thandi says, feeling panic for the first time. She thinks back to the workmen she has noticed whenever she's over by Miss Ruby and Charles's side of the river, which is closer to the sea and fishing boats. It never occurred to her that the men were building so close. They always seemed so far. "Do you ever think they'll kick us out?" she hears herself ask.

"That won't work," Charles says, his voice laced with something that makes Thandi suspect he has given it thought. "That wouldn't happen. We'll burn dem out first. What right do dey have fi kick people outta dem own place? Me tired of di government an' how dem mek we country open to foreigners wid money. Wah 'bout di people? If dey evah try fi get rid ah we, me will show dem who dem dealing wid."

He focuses on her. "Yuh not hot?" He asks. "Why yuh wear dat long sweatah every day?"

Thandi looks down at her sweatshirt as though noticing it for the first time.

"Take it off," Charles says. "It's all right, di sun not g'wan bite yuh in here."

Very hesitantly, Thandi peels the sweatshirt over her head. She feels Charles watching her. He watches her lower the sweatshirt to the floor. "Yuh can't tek that off too?" he asks, eyeing the plastic wrapping that is still on her arms under her white uniform blouse.

"I'm not supposed to."

"Says who?"

"Miss Ruby."

"Why?"

"It makes my skin come faster."

Charles sucks his teeth. "Yuh how I feel 'bout dat already." He studies her. "I told yuh dat you're beautiful."

She wishes that there were some kind of a distraction, but there isn't anything other than the transparent veil of silence, until he says, "My ole man was a artist. Ah eva tell yuh dat? Him use to paint everything him could get him hands on. People used to commission him to paint designs on buildings. But when him was by himself, he painted the river. Dat's all him use to paint. Dat river." Charles looks across the yards of sand where their footprints still are, tracing them back to the river. "See how it shape? Like a Y? He would tek him pencil an' draw suh." He moves his hand in the air to imitate the movement of drawing. "Then him would go street an' get equipment an' come back. The river was his muse. Mama always used to seh dat di river was him woman." Charles laughs at this, and Thandi laughs with him. "When him go fish, sometimes he stay out there an' just paint pon cardboard box or paper. Then when him p'dung the paper, him would just stare out into the sea as if waiting for freedom to come." He looks at Thandi. "If yuh ask me weh all him painting is now, I wouldn't know."

Thandi lets the waves do the talking. She knows the story. All of River Bank knows. On the canvases of people's minds they have already painted Asafa as a selfish man who left his family behind; their wagging tongues have colored him red in the imaginations of those who never met him.

"Dat's all right, though," Charles says. "He taught me a lot."

The next day they spend time together inside Charles's shack. Thandi, having told Delores she needs to study outside the house for the day, needs a change. Her books rest untouched on the floor. Charles sits beside Thandi on the mattress, looking at her sketchpad. Thandi shifts uncomfortably as he studies each portrait she has painstakingly drawn for her project. He laughs when he recognizes the drawings: a drawing of Miss Gracie clutching her Bible; Mr. Melon walking his goat; Little Richie in the old tire swing; Macka sitting on the steps of Dino's, watching a game of dominoes with a bottle in his hand; the women with the buckets on their heads on their way to the river; Miss Francis and Miss Louise combing their daughters' hair on the veranda; Mr. Levy locking up his shop; Margot hunched over stacks of envelopes on the dining table with her hands clasped and head bowed like she's praying. She blushes when he gets to a drawing of himself by the river. When he finishes, in his best British accent he says, "I am truly honored, madam, for having this pleasure of seeing your genius." He gives her a slight bow and she laughs, finally at ease. More seriously, he says, "Yuh is di real deal."

"Yuh think so?"

"One hundred percent," he says. "I like di drawings of di people. Ah like how yuh mek dem look real."

"They are real."

"Yeah, but you give us more. I don't know if ah making any sense. What's di fancy word yuh use fah when yuh can see inside ah person an' know dem life story?"

Thandi shrugs.

"You'll definitely win dat school prize," Charles says, tugging her arm. When he says it, the words stroke something inside her. Charles closes the book between them.

"You didn't mind me drawing you without notice?" Thandi asks.

"Mind?" Charles guffaws.

After their night at the construction site she forced herself to study the words in her textbook, but all she could think about was Charles. Over dinner she pined for him. Her appetite for her favorite meal, tin mackerel and boiled bananas, vanished. The untouched food agitated Delores, who looked at Thandi as though she had taken sick at the table. Thandi finally fell into bed, exhausted from fantasies and unable to smell his smell in the towel she kept under her pillow.

"Yuh really passionate about dis drawing t'ing," he says.

"It's not a thing."

"Yuh know what ah mean." Then, after a pause, he says, "When yuh g'wan tell yuh mother an' sister the truth?"

Thandi shrugs, his question gripping her in a way she didn't expect. "Margot is going to kill me if I tell her I'm considering art school. She was upset that I didn't drop art."

"Give har time," he says, his teeth parting to reveal the pink flesh of his tongue.

"She already put her foot down," Thandi says. "Everything for her is about sacrifice." She rolls her eyes. "I think she enjoys telling me what I should do with my life, as if she's trying to live it for me. Meanwhile, she's at the hotel, where all the jobs in this country are. I'm supposed to be the one to go to medical school and come out a distinguished pauper, while she makes all the money from tourism."

"Is that why yuh rebelling?"

Thandi looks up. "Who says I'm rebelling? I'm not your little sister's friend anymore. I'm a woman now." Charles raises his brow.

There is something urgent building inside her. She doesn't know where it rises from—this occasional burst of fire inside her chest. She goes over to where Charles sits and stoops before him. Charles remains silent as though he knows her mission and has agreed to be her accomplice. To leap into the fire. She brings her face to his and their lips touch.

She unbuttons her shirt for him. One by one the buttons slide from the holes. The bleached turpentine hue of her chest, smooth with the elevated roundness of her breasts, which are small and full, tapering off at nipples the shade of tamarind pods. Charles stares at her breasts wrapped like HTB Easter Buns in the Saran Wrap plastic. He regards them for what seems like a long time, as though trying to convince himself of something. He's blinking rapidly. She waits for him to do something, anything. To rip the plastic off so that she can finally breathe, to put his mouth to the small opening in her nipples where she hopes milk will flow someday for a child. All she needs is release. But it's his silence that grows, shaming her. He contemplates her with the compassion of a priest. She feels herself shrinking under his assessment of her.

"Put yuh clothes back on," he says.

"Why?"

"Jus' put it back on."

Charles raises himself up from the bed as though to get away from her as quickly as possible. He's no longer looking at her. She blinks back tears. She sits on the edge of the mattress, listening to the grunting hogs in the yard and the barking dogs and Old Man Basil selling brooms and cleaning brushes made of dried coconut husks. *"Broom! Broom!"* Every sound exacerbates the awkward silence inside the shack, where Thandi buttons her blouse, her back to Charles; and the flame glows inside her still.

16

MARGOT FOLLOWS MISS NOVIA SCOTT-HENRY TO ONE OF THE on-site restaurants where the woman often dines alone. She knows this because it's the fourth time she has trailed Miss Novia Scott-Henry here. Margot pretends to have things to finish up at work so she can be the last one to see the woman leave, the click of her keys sounding in the whole lobby. It's one of the best restaurants in the hotel—one that requires guests to make reservations days in advance. It's a fancy place with white tablecloths, sterling silver utensils wrapped in red cloth napkins, and violin music playing "Redemption Song" in the background. But Miss Novia Scott-Henry doesn't need reservations to dine in the company of visitors, mostly couples. Alphonso has promised to take Margot here, but that promise—like the other promise he has made—has never come to pass.

Here, the waiters are graceful, carrying trays on upturned palms, necks dutifully elongated, chins jutted upward, and smiles pasted to their faces like ivory-colored masking tape. Miss Novia Scott-Henry is led to a booth in the back. Tonight the patrons are dressed down, but still regal—men in nice light-colored shirts and women in long maxi dresses with floral patterns. Miss Novia Scott-Henry is dressed as though she's going to a business function, in a severely tailored red pantsuit. She is tall, a hibiscus in a weed garden. The waiters fuss over her, and other diners look to see what all the fuss is about. They are excited to see up close for the first time the big hazel eyes that light up the tourism billboard ads, and the golden-honey-toned skin on every moisturizing commercial, including Queen of Pearl crème, which is all the rage. Some of Margot's girls use the crème, against her advice. Why would anyone want to permanently damage their skin to look like a beauty queen who was born that way?

Margot sits by the bar with Sweetness, and they observe Miss Novia Scott-Henry together. "She's beautiful, isn't she?" Margot says to Sweetness, who has kept her eyes down.

Miss Novia Scott-Henry looks very much alone sitting there by herself while everyone else has a partner, their cheery voices carrying to the front of the restaurant. The waitstaff busy themselves pouring water into glasses, placing on the tables baskets of bread and saucers with butter. Each waiter has a task, a specific routine. Like a well-rehearsed performance made up of a cast of country boys groomed to be British gentlemen with bow ties, tuxedos, and plain accents with British inflections. *"How yuh do, madame? How is yuh meal, sah? May I get you h-anything else? H-anotherrr drink, perhaps?"* Margot cringes on the inside as she listens to them. For she's sure they don't speak this way at home.

"Yuh need anyt'ing fi drink, Margot?" Foot, the bartender, asks.

They call him Foot because he has only one leg, the other one a rounded stump that he favors. Nobody knows what happened to his other leg, but rumor is that it blew off in the Gulf War. This doesn't slow him down. He mixes drinks at the bar, delivering them with ease—from Bloody Marys to rum punch to just opening a bottle of ice-cold Red Stripe beer.

"A glass of water will do," Margot tells him. But she orders a drink for Sweetness, something strong, because Sweetness has been jittery since her arrival.

"Why yuh didn't tell me dat it's her?" Sweetness finally speaks, her eyes darting nervously around the restaurant, her voice a sharp whisper. "Yuh putting me in a real bad situation. She was ah beauty queen. People love har!"

"Jus' drink," Margot says.

She returns her attention to Miss Novia Scott-Henry, who takes her napkin from the table and places it on her lap. Another waiter comes to the table with a bottle of wine. He opens the bottle, spinning a metal opener into the cork, which gives a small pop when it's released. Miss Novia Scott-Henry lifts her glass, swirls it, puts it to her nose, then sips. She takes another sip. And another, smiling as though the wine is making her reflect on a shower of pink cherry blossom petals kissing her shoulders. *So this is how she dines*, Margot thinks—*three-course meals and wine every night*. Margot considers the wine list. The cost of a bottle could be Thandi's lunch money for a week. A month, even. Clearly Miss Novia Scott-Henry makes a lot of money and spends it on herself. No children. No word of a husband. The glass in Sweetness's hand is almost empty.

"Foot, gi har anotha one!" Margot orders.

Foot works his magic, hobbling from one end of the bar to the next on his crutch, pouring various hard liquors from the shelf into a silver mixer. He shakes it like a musician in a mento band and pours the drink into a tall glass. He slides it to Sweetness with a wink.

"Dis will mek yuh nice-nice."

Meanwhile, Roy, Miss Novia Scott-Henry's waiter, takes her order. He dutifully writes down everything like he's supposed to, nodding politely and making suggestions. He makes eye contact with Margot, who nods. When he enters the kitchen she can see right inside: the chaos of men dressed in white hovering over pots under which blue and yellow flames blaze, and yelling in patois over crates of food. "G'long wid di food before it tun col'!" "Rattry, annuh your ordah dis? Why di food come back?" "Tek yuh time wid di oil, 'less yuh waan gi di people dem heart attack!"

She hears all this when she gets up and follows Roy, pretending to be on her way to the bathroom. He's by the corridor waiting when she gets there. A young boy from May Pen with a beautiful face and an ugly past. He sneaks furtive glances over his shoulder as he whispers to her.

"Di food soon come. Me will sprinkle it jus' a likkle, since me nuh want to overdo it. Me can't afford fi go back ah prison."

"No one will know seh is you. Pour everything." Margot takes money from her purse and hands it to him. "Dis is half ah yuh pay. Yuh get di othah half after yuh empty di whole bottle."

Just then the chef calls the order. Serge, the assistant chef, emerges from the heat and manages to blow a kiss Margot's way. Margot returns it and waves.

"Ah haven't gotten any samples in a while," she says to Serge.

His face lights up like the kitchen flames behind him. "All yuh haffi do is ask, beautiful," he says, taking the time to lean against the wall with one arm over Margot's head, his ankle crossed over the other, appraising her. Margot strokes his chest with a finger.

"My feelings get hurt when ah don't get nuh special taste. Is like yuh done wid me."

Meanwhile, Roy doctors up the order, sprinkling every last bit of powder on to the food. Serge, too caught up in Margot fingering his collar, doesn't hurry him along. He leans closer to Margot. "Ah promise I'll mek yuh taste di chef special tomorrow, 'bout noon?"

"Sounds delicious," she says, waving him back to work.

"It done," Roy says after Serge returns to the kitchen, holding up the empty glass bottle for Margot to see. Margot pulls out the other half of the cash and gives it to him. She watches as Roy goes out with Miss Novia Scott-Henry's entrée. He places the food in front of her with a slight bow. Before the woman can take a bite of her meal, someone passes by and she pauses, lowering her fork. The woman engages Miss Novia Scott-Henry in light conversation, pushing a calendar and a pen to her face. Miss Novia Scott-Henry graciously signs it, and the woman leaves. Margot waits for Miss Novia Scott-Henry to take a bite of her food. She leans forward to watch her eat, watch her chew and swallow. Every muscle in her tenses as hope rushes in. A mento band begins to play the Wailers' "Simmer Down," replacing the violin music. *Simma down, Margot*, she tells herself, thinking of the promotion Alphonso will have to give her, the tragic loss of a beauty queen to scandal, the cheery faces of admiration turning to disdain. Margot makes her way back to the bar as Sweetness lifts her glass to take another sip of drink. Margot stops her.

"Tek it easy. Yuh don't want to be completely drunk fah dis."

Sweetness takes a deep breath to calm herself and grips the edge of the counter. "Me nuh sure me can do dis," she says. "Me nuh ready yet." This Margot hears loud and clear above the mento band. The molecules from Sweetness's rum breath sail toward her, assaulting her. Margot reaches for the girl's hand. But Sweetness is too fast. She grabs her purse and gets up from the bar.

"Where yuh t'ink yuh going?" Margot calls after her.

But Sweetness doesn't stop. As she nears the door, a wave of vertigo hits Margot as though she's the one who has been drugged. The buzzing inside the restaurant gets louder—the clinking of utensils

on plates, the Wailers' words via the mento band reminding her "*an'
when him deh near / yuh mus' beware*"—the warning clashing with
the joyous collision of conversations filled with foreign accents. She
blindly hurries toward the door, narrowly avoiding bumping into
guests.

"Sweetness!"

But the girl doesn't turn around.

"Sweetness!"

Margot walks quickly outside. Paul is standing by the door to
let people in and out, but Sweetness doesn't slow her pace for him
to open the door. She pushes it open herself. That's when Margot
decides to use her last bit of ammunition:

"Miss Violet can surely use some help wid everyt'ing going on
wid her head!"

Sweetness stops, or rather halts by the rosebushes like a race-
horse that has approached an insurmountable hurdle. Her back is
still turned and head bent. When Margot approaches her, she sees
that the girl is crying. "What's the matter with you?" She takes the
girl by the hand and leads her behind the rosebushes, where she
begins to massage her shoulders. "Why yuh want to ruin dis now?
If yuh didn't want to do it yuh shoulda say something before. Why
fight it? I'm giving you permission now to act on it. It not g'wan jus'
go away if yuh ignore it."

Sweetness sniffles but says nothing as Margot massages this into
her shoulder; the girl's muscles relax under the pressure of Margot's
fingertips, her head lolling. "You're ready . . ." Margot says to the
girl's upturned face. She kisses her gently on the lips. Sweetness's
eyes are still closed. Margot kisses her again, this time cradling
Sweetness's face with both hands. The girl tilts her head to receive
her tongue. Just then Margot hears footsteps and whispering voices.
A woman's high heels. A man telling her to call a taxi. Margot pulls
away from Sweetness and peers above the bushes. Paul is steadying

Miss Novia Scott-Henry, who appears light-headed and filled with lively chatter.

"I can go home on my own, Paul. No need, no need at all. Oops, was that thunder?"

"No, that's jus' di band setting up."

"Oh, my, I need my keys. What have I done with my car keys? You took my keys!"

Margot turns to Sweetness. "Follow me."

She walks toward Paul and Miss Novia Scott-Henry, Sweetness trailing a few steps behind.

"Margot? Margot, is that you?" Miss Novia Scott-Henry says, steadying herself. "Did you hear the thunder? It's going to pour!"

"I wish," Margot says.

"What are you doing here so late?"

"I should ask you the same question," Margot replies, scanning the woman's face. Her eyes are wide like a drunken person determined to display cognition. But she fails miserably, tripping over some invisible thing on the ground. Paul has to hold her up again. "I'm on my way home," she says. "I want to beat the storm."

"I don't think you should drive like this," Margot says.

"No, no. I feel great. Just need to get to my caaa . . ."

Miss Novia Scott-Henry stumbles again and Margot springs into action, breaking the woman's fall. She shoos Paul away. "I got this."

One week of lying awake at night, sweating through her pillow as the plan grows, white-knuckling the chair in the office every time she sat and watched the woman. So this act of kindness has become a part of the masquerade; so much so that it's hard to distinguish what's rehearsed from what's authentic. She instructs Sweetness to help her carry Miss Novia Scott-Henry to the penthouse suite upstairs. Margot fidgets with her clutch, not knowing at first where to put it. She lifts the woman's free arm over her neck and carries her to the room. Sweetness balances her weight on the other side.

"Where yuh taking me?" Miss Novia Scott-Henry asks.

"To a room upstairs," Margot says. "You're in no position to drive."

"I'm fine."

"You'll stay here for the night. I promise, Sweetness will take good care of you."

Upstairs, Margot opens the door to the suite and switches on the light. The burgundy drapes are drawn, and there, inside the closet next to the bathroom, is the recorder. They put the woman on the bed, lowering her gently. She's half awake and half asleep. Margot backs away to pour the woman a glass of water. She slips the rest of the drug into the glass and stirs in case the previous dose wears off too early. "Just make yourself comfortable," Margot says to Miss Novia Scott-Henry when she watches her take a sip of the water. She watches her lips pucker and the soft rise and fall of her throat as she drinks.

"Thanks a lot, Margot," the woman says, lying back down on the bed, her arms spread.

Margot instructs Sweetness to undress and climb onto the bed next to Miss Novia Scott-Henry. For a moment the girl hesitates. Margot dares her with her eyes. The girl obeys, slipping out of her dress like a child. Margot retreats into the closet to hide and fishes for the disposable camera she carried. She watches as Sweetness leans forward and undoes the woman's buttons. The woman stirs, but only a little. Sweetness rises to the challenge. She takes charge, looking like a lioness perched on all fours, her back arched, her magnificent rear swooping up from her spine, and her hands like paws. Miss Novia Scott-Henry inches closer to Sweetness once the coolness from the air conditioner tickles her nakedness. She scoots closer to the warmth Sweetness's body offers, and matches her pulse. But that illusion is the drug's secret drive—the control it tricks her into believing is hers, the excitement, the promise, the rubbed-down edge of fear. Her mind is no longer able to outsmart her body, for her body knows by instinct what it ought to do. Every single muscle of her body seems to be trembling, quivering, twitching. They are magnificent, the both of them, moving like silkworms. Margot misses Verdene this way, lowering the camera after capturing enough pictures of Miss Novia Scott-Henry and Sweetness. She is forced to turn away from the sight of them, her own hunger—her own primal want—begging to be assuaged. Margot takes her things, the recorder, and, for good measure, Sweetness's clothes, shoes, and handbag too. She tiptoes out the door, leaving it open for this private dream to become public.

17

DELORES COMES HOME FROM THE MARKET AND IMMEDIATELY begins to cook dinner, her stocky frame pouring over the small stove. She wipes her face with the collar of her blouse and stirs the cowfoot soup, mindlessly dashing into it salt and pepper and pimento seeds, talking to herself about the day's sales.

"Ah told di man twenty dollah. Jus' twenty dollah. Him so cheap that him pull out a ten. Say him want me to go down in price. But see here, now, massah. What can ten dollah do?" She laughs and leans over to taste the soup, her face scrunching as always as she reaches for more salt. "Eh, eh!"

"Mama, I have something to show yuh," Thandi says, taking small steps toward Delores, clutching the sketchpad filled with her drawings. The fire is high under the pot, and the house smells of all the spices. "What is it now?" her mother says. "Have you seen yuh sistah since mawnin'?"

"No, Mama."

"Where the hell is that girl?" Delores turns to Thandi, her eyes big and wide like a ferocious animal. "Ah tell yuh, yuh sistah is siding wid the devil. Several nights in a row she coming home in di wee hours. Is which man she sleeping wid now, eh?"

"I don't know. She neva tell me anything."

Delores laughs, throwing her head back so that her braids touch the back of her neck. She seeks the counsel of the shadows in the kitchen, the ones that lurk from the steady flame of the kerosene lamp. "Yuh see mi dying trial?" she says to the shadows. "Now she keeping secrets from me." She turns back to Thandi. "You tell yuh sistah that if she have a man, him mus' be able to help pay Mr. Sterling our rent. Our rent was due two days ago. Two days! And Margot deh 'bout, playing hooky wid god knows who. Or what."

Thandi remains silent, hugging the sketchpad to her chest. It steadies her. She considers her mother's back, the broad shoulders, the cotton blouse soaked with perspiration, the strong arms that look as though they could still carry her, the wide hips, the swollen feet shoved inside a pair of old men's slippers. She listens to her mother talk to the shadows crouched in every corner of their shack. Thandi looks away from each of them, her eyes finding her mother's back again. "I want to draw," she says out loud. Delores stops moving. She turns around to face Thandi.

"So why don't you sit and draw?" Delores asks. "See di table dere. Draw."

"I mean I want to do it for a living. I want to—"

"Hold on a second." Delores puts both hands on her hips, her big chest lifting as though filling with all the wind and words she would eventually let out to crush Thandi's dreams. "Yuh not making any sense right now. Yuh not making no sense a'tall, a'tall."

"I am really good at it," Thandi says. Her fingers tremble as she turns each page, showing her mother sketch after sketch. Her mother takes the book from her and examines a drawing of a half-naked woman standing in front of a mirror. Thandi is certain she recognizes the mirror. It's the one on the vanity. Thandi holds her breath as her mother studies the image. Brother Smith says she's good. *"You're a natural, Thandi."* All she has to do is strengthen her portfolio. Thandi looks at the page her mother is looking at, wishing that she had been more precise with parts of the sketch that seem amateur under her mother's scrutiny. She balances her weight on both legs, wringing her hands, then putting them to her sides, since she doesn't know what else to do with them. Delores is silent for a long time. Too long. "What yuh think?" Thandi finally asks. "I was working on it for Mother's Day, but it took longer than I thought."

But Delores is shaking her head. "Yuh draw dis?" she asks Thandi without taking her eyes off the woman on the paper.

"Yes," Thandi responds. "It's for you. A belated Mother's Day gift." But Delores returns the book to Thandi without saying a word. She resumes cooking, stirring the pot of cowfoot soup.

"I want to be an artist. Maybe yuh can start to sell my drawings to yuh customers." Thandi continues to talk as though talking to herself. "I'm really good at it. Brother Smith says I'm really talented. He nominated me to compete for an art prize at school. He even said I could go to a school for art."

Delores stirs and stirs the pot, Thandi's words seeming to drown in the bubbling soup.

"Mama, yuh listening?" Thandi touches Delores's arm. "Mama, yuh hear me? I want to go to art school and I only need five subjects."

"I'm busy," is all Delores says. "I'm sending you to school to learn. So yuh g'wan be something good in life. Nothing less. Don't come to me wid dis again, yuh hear? Yuh is no damn artist. We too poor for that. Yuh g'wan be a doctor. People can't mek a living being no ch'upid artist. Do you see the Rastas selling in di market making money wid dem art?"

Thandi shakes her head, her eyes on the floor. "But there are different types of artists, Mama."

"Different types of artist, mi backside! G'wan go learn yuh books, yuh hear? The CXC is jus' around di corner. Why yuh entering a blasted prize fah? Why yuh not studying? Yuh need all nine subjects to be the doctor yuh want to be. Not a ch'upid prize."

"*You* want me to be a doctor." Thandi puts the sketchpad down on the dining table.

Delores peers at her. "Thandi, what yuh saying to me?"

Thandi cowers under the weight of her mother's glare, her heartbeat echoing in her eardrums, her face hot. "Nothing," she replies.

"Is who filling up yuh head with all this, eh?" Delores asks.

"I have a mind of my own, you know," Thandi says. She walks outside into the darkness that consumes her, leaving the back door open.

"Where yuh going? Dinner will be ready soon!" Delores calls after her. But Thandi doesn't respond. She's too tired. She leans against the back of the house and slides down to her buttocks.

When Thandi disappears outside into the darkness, she takes all of Delores's breath with her. The girl must be smelling her ripeness, Delores thinks. Not her Thandi. She's supposed to be the good one, different from her sister. Had Thandi not been such a good girl all this time, Delores would've knocked her in the head with the spoon she uses to stir the soup. Thandi's eyes held in them the same glint of that thing Delores saw in Margot's eyes years ago; the same glint that made Delores look away in case it struck her down like lightning.

She cannot get the sketch of the half-naked woman standing in front of a mirror from her mind. The resemblance between Delores and the woman is uncanny, almost like a picture taken of her—same face, same eyes, same mouth, same sagging breasts resting atop the high bulge of her belly. The earnestness in her daughter's eyes when she looked at her and the hopeful grin that spread across the girl's face—one Delores hasn't seen in a long time, Thandi always being so serious. In the sketch Delores saw everything she thought she had hidden so well, tucked away in the folds of years, heaped upon each other like steps that she takes one at a time. In her daughter's drawing, she saw the lines in her face, her double chin. She saw an ugly woman—an ugly black woman with bulging eyes too wide to be peered into before looking away, and nose too flat on the broad face. In this sketch she was not human, but a creature. This is how her daughter sees her—bull-faced and miserable. All Delores's secrets and insecurities are exposed in the gaze of this child.

Margot was barely fourteen at the time. In the summers when Margot was out of school she would help Delores carry things to Falmouth and spread them out so that Delores could sell. While Delores sold items to tourists, Margot would help count the change and wrap the fragile items in newspaper. One day a tall, dark-haired man walked into Delores's stall. He was wearing sunglasses, like most tourists. He had a presence about him, an air Delores associated with important people—white people. Like the ones who just bought out her stall. Except the man wasn't white. A mixture, maybe. A mulatto kind. He wore a button-down shirt that revealed the dark hairs on his chest. When Delores peered up at him, she saw he was peering down at Margot. He turned to Delores, his eyes hidden behind the shades. "How much?" he asked in a voice that sounded to Delores like thunder.

"Di dolls are twenty, sah. Oh, an' di figurines guh for fifteen

U.S., but ah can give yuh fah ten. An' di T-shirts! They're unique, sah. One of ah kind! Only fifteen dollah."

"No," the man said, returning his focus to Margot. "I'm talking about her." He used his pointy chin to gesture to a skinny Margot, who, at the time, had barely started menstruating or growing breasts. Delores looked from her daughter to the tall stranger wearing the sunglasses. "She's not on sale, sah."

The man pulled out a wad of cash and began to count it in front of Delores. Delores watched him count six hundred-dollar bills. She had never seen so much money in her life. The crispness of the bills and the scent of newness, which Delores thought was what wealth must smell like—the possibility of moving her family out of River Bank, affording her daughter's school fee, books, and uniforms, buying a telephone and a landline for her to call people whenever she liked instead of waiting to use the neighbor's phone—all these possibilities were too much to swallow all at once. "Sah—but she—she's only fourteen."

"I'm staying right down there." He gestured to the large cruise ship, which was in plain sight. "I'll have her back before dinner." The man placed the bills in front of Delores. She tore her eyes away from the stack to look into the terrified eyes of her daughter. Margot was shaking her head slowly, mouthing, No, but Delores had made up her mind the minute the scent of the bills hit her. Her eyes pleaded with her daughter's, and also held in them an apology. *Please undah-stand. Do it now and you'll tank me lata*, Delores hoped her eyes communicated. She nodded to the man when Margot looked away, defeated. The man took Margot somewhere—Delores didn't ask where. It was in the direction of the ship that had docked for the day. The girl followed behind him, her steps uncertain. She never looked back to see the tears in Delores's eyes.

When the man returned Margot later that evening, she refused to speak to Delores. Delores had left the market that day with six hundred dollars plus a tip that the man had added. "*She's a natural, this one,*" he said to Delores with a wink. Delores stuffed the money in her brassiere. At home she hid it inside the mattress where she hid all her money. She hid it so well that she never noticed when the money disappeared. It wasn't until her brother, Winston, who was living with them at the time, announced months later that he got a visa and a one-way ticket to America that Delores wondered where he got the money. Immediately after Winston's announcement Delores ripped the sheets off the bed and stuck her hand inside the hole underneath the sponge layer. Nothing came up in her desperate fingers. The realization burned her stomach and spread across the width of her belly like the pressure of a child about to be born. For Thandi had just started to kick then. Delores almost collapsed, not with the fury and raging anger she harbored for her brother, but for the loss of her daughter's innocence, which, she realized too late, was worth more than the money she lost and all the money she would ever gain.

Though she doesn't know the story, Thandi has captured all of this pian. All Delores is to her is this ugly, dark woman capable of nothing but fits of rage and cruelty. Who knew that both her daughters would come to view her this way? Delores sinks into the chair around the dining table. Thandi, like Margot, hates her. And so does Mama Merle, sitting outside on that rocking chair. The old bat will spend another day wishing her beloved, good-for-nothing son home; while Delores will continue breaking her back to provide for the family, doing what she does best: survive.

18

ALPHONSO HIMSELF ANNOUNCED THE NEWS THAT MISS NOVIA Scott-Henry had decided to step down. But by the time the announcement was made, it had already been emptied of any potential shock. Certainly Margot could have gone to the woman with the pictures and given her an ultimatum: *You step down or I leak these to the press.* But there was no need, since what took place afterward was more epic in the unraveling. It began with a scream. A howl that startled the entire sixteenth floor when the maids discovered the two naked women in the penthouse suite. The maids' screaming drew other maids from other floors who had just slipped into their uniforms and comfortable shoes, still humming songs from last night's church revival.

Sweetness did not handle it well, crippled with guilt. Margot feared that she might come forward with some damning information about what really had taken place, so she decided to set her free, handing her severance pay.

"Yuh firing me?" the girl asked. "But ah did what yuh ask."

"You did what I asked. Now you can go."

"But ah thought yuh was g'wan hire me."

"Not when yuh mope around like yuh mother jus' dead."

"Ah was jus' feeling guilty, like a normal person wid ah heart. Now what g'wan happen to di 'ooman?"

"Nuh worry 'bout dat. It's done."

"Ah couldn't stomach it. Not even fah myself. To be ousted dat way. Why yuh did such a t'ing if you is—"

"Here is yuh money. Tek it or leave it."

But Sweetness let the padded white envelope fall between them. Margot was the one to pick it up off the floor and brush it off. "So yuh g'wan act like yuh neva earn it?" she asked the girl. "Fine, go back to where yuh come from. I'll put this money to good use. There are ah hundred more girls out there." Sweetness looked on as Margot placed the envelope back inside her purse. She swallowed. "I didn't say ah want to stop working fah you," she said.

"Well, if yuh want to continue working for me, then stop talking about what happened." Margot stepped closer. She used one hand to clutch the girl by the chin. "Look at me. It's done. The woman stepped down. Whateva happen to her aftah-wards is not your business or your concern. She's going to be all right. Those people don't suffer. They don't even know di meaning of dat word. We have biggah fish to fry. So yuh either swim or yuh drown."

The girl nodded. "Me is a very good swimmer."

That same day after it was announced that Miss Novia Scott-

Henry would step down, Margot attended her first board meeting. As senior clerk she had to help Alphonso with damage control. When she opened the door to the restroom where she'd gone to freshen up before her entrance, Miss Novia Scott-Henry was bent over the sink, both hands spanning the width. Her body was heaving and shuddering. Their eyes met in the mirror. That was when Margot saw her tears; the long streaks down her face. Like scars.

19

CHARLES HAS AGREED TO RETURN TO HELP OUT AROUND THE yard, uprooting weeds and washing the discolored walls and walkway. All morning long he has been working. He never pauses for a break, and declines Verdene's offers for food and water. Finally she convinces him to come inside for tea.

"Don't worry, it's not poison." Verdene lowers a tray with the teacups and saucers her mother once reserved for special guests. Charles watches her pour the peppermint tea. Her hand shakes a little as the liquid fills his cup, a plume of steam rising from its surface. He doesn't drink until she puts her cup to her mouth.

"You're not a talker," she says, sitting across from him at the dining table.

"Not when I'm working." He lowers his cup into the saucer. She notices that he doesn't look anywhere else like people tend to do when they are inside a place for the first time.

"So you're a hard worker." She regrets this statement as soon as she says it. She sounds pompous, condescending. She wishes she could take it back.

"I get di job done," he says. "My father always used to seh dat how ah man work is ah reflection of his character."

"Who is your father? If you don't mind me asking."

"Asafa."

"Lobsterman?" Verdene asks, remembering the fisherman. How could she not have known that this is his son? They look exactly alike—same sepia-colored eyes, same nose, same chin with the slight dimple. Asafa was just a youth when Verdene left. A youth her age who, like his father before him—a man people called One Eye Barry—started fishing from an early age. "Lobsterman is your father." This is a statement, a declaration, as the image of Asafa appears across from her like a blueprint. "You say used to? Where is your father now?"

Charles puts the cup to his face again, completely burying his nose. She watches the rhythm of his throat as he swallows. When he wipes his mouth with the back of his hand he says, "Gone."

Verdene plays with the rim of her cup. "I'm sorry."

Charles shrugs. "It is what it is."

Verdene picks up her cup and holds it to warm her hands.

"I'm still getting over my mother passing. So I can just imagine how you feel."

"He didn't die. He left."

"Oh."

A slick of blue sky frames his head. Usually when Verdene sits at the table this time of day she sees nothing but the sky. This only makes her want to do everything in her power to keep him there, her first real company besides Margot. "More tea?" she asks, hoping to change the mood. He nods. She pours more tea into his cup and rests the teapot at the center of the table. Charles inspects it. "Dis remind me of something I would see at Buckingham Palace," he says.

Verdene chuckles. "Have you ever been?"

"No, but dat's di kinda teapot ah imagine di queen would have in har cupboard."

"It was a gift my aunt sent my mother when she first moved to London."

"What is it like ovah dere?"

Verdene pauses. Her time in Brixton is a period she doesn't talk about.

"It was all right," she says.

"Jus' all right?"

"I didn't exactly move there by choice."

"Did you evah meet di queen?"

"No. In fact, I didn't go out much. Just work, home, and church. Every now and again I'd go dancing. My job as an editorial assistant for my uncle's small press was too demanding anyway."

Charles's eyes widen. "Yuh went to church?"

"Why is that surprising?"

"Well . . ." His voice trails off.

"I'm not a heathen. I'm just like you."

"You're nothing like me." He says this too quickly. Verdene must have looked hurt, because he corrects himself with, "Ah don't do church."

"Do you go to school?" she asks, glad to change the subject. "You seem smart."

"Don't do that either. Not since my ole man left. Ah had to take care of my mother."

"That's very responsible of you."

"If ah continued school ah woulda be ah architect. Yuh know, design buildings an' big hotels like di ones here on di North Coast. Ah woulda mek sure not to move people outta dem homes."

"It's not too late, you know."

Charles shakes his head. "For me it is. People like me can't afford all dat schooling."

"There are scholarships. I can help you apply."

"Wid all due respec', miss, me is not yuh charity. Me come here fi work. Chop yuh grass an' wash yuh walkway. I've always made my own way wid nobody to help me."

"Fine. All I'm saying is you can do so much. You're still very young. You wouldn't want to wake up one day and realize that you've wasted your whole life. It's not a good feeling, trust me."

"Yuh t'ink yuh waste yuh life?" he asks, cocking his head to one side.

"There are many things I would've done differently."

"Gimme one t'ing you woulda done different."

"I wouldn't have gotten married so young."

"Yuh married?"

"Yes. For five years."

"To a man?"

"No. A woman."

There is movement under his skin as his muscles give, slackening his jaws. That's when Verdene bursts out laughing and says, "Yes, silly. A man." He laughs too, but only a little, looking both relieved and confused.

"So is it true?"

"What?"

"What people seh 'bout yuh."

"They don't know me."

She gets up and lifts the teapot. "Let me warm more water. This is getting cold."

Charles leans back in his chair. He spins his saucer around but doesn't say anything—as though the questions that Verdene sees brewing in his mind are too much to ask all at once. The tea and small talk are good enough for today. Though Charles has proven himself to be more open-minded than other young men in River Bank, Verdene is unsure of what he can take and what he cannot.

"What made you help me that day?"

Charles shrugs. "'Cause ah know what it's like to be scorned. To be di talk ah di town. To feel like di whole world turn dem nose up at you 'cause dem t'ink dem bettah than you."

"Your mother raised a good son," Verdene says, almost reaching her free hand to touch his, but deciding against it.

20

SKETCHES OF THE NEW HOTEL ARE SPREAD OUT ON ALPHONSO'S dining table. It will be bigger and grander than Palm Star Resort, with butler service, a Jacuzzi in every room, a spa and wellness center with a range of different massages from hot stone to erotic, a sports bar, a poolside restaurant, and a gigantic ballroom. Margot studies the sketches and realizes that River Bank will be completely taken over. The Y-shaped river will be used for rafting or water sports, and the white sand beach will be transformed into a nude beach. Margot doesn't say anything in the midst of the excitement around her.

"Not sure what we'll call it yet, but whatever we call it has to have a good ring to it," Alphonso says to a group of private investors. "The brand is as important as the features."

"I agree," one investor says. He has an oddly shaped mustache.

"We have until August to figure it out. Right now we should be more concerned with the development. We're losing money with this government contract. NEPA hasn't given us the go-ahead yet." Alphonso's voice booms like thunder. He has been drinking scotch and his face is flushed.

"Why do we even need their approval?" one investor asks. He's the most serious, only pouring himself water despite all the liquor offered. "We can do it the easy way. Get property owners to sign off on it. If we get their blessings, we'd be good to go."

"Yes, I hear what you're saying, Virgil," Alphonso replies. "But even with property owners giving us permission, it would cost us. Don't we have to give them something? It's been hard getting people off the land. We need a government contract to protect us."

"That's complicated, waiting on those snails in Parliament to give us their signature," says Virgil. "While we wait, our materials are wasting away in the elements. That's a lot of money down the drain. More money than it would cost to give those property owners a small compensation and get the others out by force."

"Force?" Margot asks, speaking up for the first time since the gathering. "They lived there all their lives. Don't you think they deserve the decency of a warning?"

The men halt their bickering and look at Alphonso because, of course, only he can explain why she's there and why her opinions matter to their thirty-plus years of mergers, annihilations, forceful displacements, monopolies, and extortions. There is enough room to back away. But she stays.

"Don't worry 'bout that." Alphonso puts one arm around her waist. "You'll be taken care of." He kisses her neck.

But Margot stiffens. "What about the others? What about my . . ." She pauses to catch her breath. "My family lives there."

The other men avert their eyes, shaking their heads.

"Don't worry yourself," Alphonso repeats. He chuckles with the men in the room. Alphonso still hasn't made his offer to promote her. Yesterday in the boardroom he only spoke to the administrative staff about working overtime to pick up where Miss Novia Scott-Henry left off until he hires someone new. She should keep her mouth shut if she wants him to choose her to run the new property. She always wanted to leave River Bank anyway. With the new promotion she can send Thandi to sixth form in Kingston and then to university. She can buy that house she has been dreaming about in Lagoons and convince Verdene to come and live with her as a housemate. They can be together without anyone questioning them. She might find a golden-age home for Grandma Merle. And Delores? Delores will just have to fend for herself.

But maybe it's too late.

Alphonso doesn't let his hand linger on the small of her back like usual. He ignores her the rest of the evening as she slowly sips the glass of wine she poured herself.

"I haven't yet figured out who will manage the new resort," she hears him say to one of the gentlemen who is sitting on his right. Margot, who is sitting on his left, leans forward, nearly slamming her wine glass down on the coffee table. When the night winds down, she waits patiently as the men shake hands. They make their way to their luxury vehicles with bright faces flushed. Behind them, Alphonso is bowing his head as each man pats him on the back. "Good doing business with you." Meanwhile, Margot folds her arms across her chest and waits on the sofa as he finishes his last conversation. She was the one who made it all possible. She was the one who got Georgio, the biggest investor, to sign the check. Presently, Alphonso is about to destroy River Bank to complete his dream.

Alphonso turns to Margot and waves her over. "Come say good-bye to Martine!"

She gets up and moves to the front door, where both men are waiting. Alphonso grandly gestures with his hands. "She's my right-hand woman and the one I'll put in charge of all the extracurricular activities at the new resort," he says to the man.

The man looks at Margot. "Can I get a taste?"

"A taste of what?" Margot asks, pretending ignorance.

"The specials."

"Martine wants to sample the goods we'll be offering at the new property," Alphonso says with a grin. He turns to the man. "Trust me, yuh haven't had good sex till you try one of these girls. At the new hotel, all of them will be hired as workers there, from maids to bartenders to clerks to lifeguards to massage therapists."

Margot knows what's at stake, so she obliges. "I'll give you a sample tomorrow."

"How about tonight?"

Alphonso nods, but Margot refuses to play this game. "Will you excuse us?" she says to the man. "Alphonso and I need to talk."

"Be my guest! I can wait all night for you."

Once she and Alphonso are out of earshot by the palm trees, she says, "You got what you want, so what about what I want?"

"What is this in reference to?"

"The new hotel. You promised."

He cups her face gently. "Why not focus on what you're really good at? You're excellent with the girls."

She pulls her face away. "You think I want to spend the rest of my life doing this?"

Alphonso chuckles. "Oh, Margot, yuh nevah fail to amaze me. I give you an opportunity to shine and you complain."

"I want a promotion."

"You don't have what it takes, Margot."

"What does it take?" Margot doesn't suppress the slight tremor erupting inside her. "You promised me."

"But Margot, it doesn't work like that. You know the criticism I get for running the hotel differently from my father. I want to build my reputation back. You know people will inquire about your training and experience. I can't let that happen, that's why I brought Novia on. Not only because she's brilliant, but she brought people. She's Jamaica's first real ambassador."

"An ambassador who sleep wid underage girls."

Alphonso pauses and closes his eyes for a brief second. "I know Novia. She and my wife are best friends."

Margot snorts at this and rolls her eyes. "That explains it."

"She's a good person. Her indiscretions can be forgiven."

"Now yuh sound like a damn politician, or a priest."

"It's business."

"I showed you the plans. I fed you ideas. And now yuh saying I don't have what it takes to run a resort?"

"Margot, you are missing my point."

"Yuh made it loud and clear. I have news for you. You hire anyone else and I'm going to the authorities about the prostitution ring. Not only that, I have pictures to give to the press of yuh beloved ambassador fucking a prostitute. A female prostitute." She hurls this like a stone. Alphonso blinks. His mouth opens and closes before the words come out.

"You wouldn't dare."

"Watch me."

"You're a coldhearted bitch."

"You made me that way."

"Margot, don't do this."

"Don't do what? Let people see yuh fall from glory? Let dem see how yuh drag di Wellington dynasty down di gutter? Ha! You were always the incompetent one, Alphonso. A fool who depends on the brilliance of others."

"I never trusted you."

"Makes two of us. You either keep yuh promise or get yuh name dirty in di press."

"You're a nutcase if you think it's that easy."

"A nutcase who yuh continue to fuck. Time to pay up. You know I'm not fah free."

"I paid your sister's tuition. You seem to have forgotten."

"Still not enough."

Alphonso steps closer to her with his fists clenched. "You are a power-hungry whore who would fuck anything, Margot. I was surprised that it wasn't you they found with Novia in bed that morning, though I think my wife has given her better pussy."

Margot slaps him across the face. She slaps him so hard that the sound echoes, unexpected like a gunshot. But he only stands there, a smirk on his face.

"I think you should go," he finally says, holding his left cheek.

"You have one day to think about what I said," Margot says.

"I won't budge."

"Then I'll send it out tonight. It's that simple."

"All right, all right." He holds up both hands. "I'll announce your promotion as hotel general manager for the new hotel on Monday morning, eight o' clock sharp. Now see yuhself out."

Although she's standing, Margot feels like she's on her knees. She gathers her things and leaves in the cool darkness of the night. Martine is no longer in sight. The taste of victory is bitter on her tongue and reminds her of the day she gave her Uncle Winston the six hundred dollars that Delores received from the stranger at Falmouth Market. She handed the money to him, thinking he would leave her alone. The victory was short-lived, because Delores only got meaner, hungrier, subjecting Margot to more strangers to make up for the money she lost. Margot realized too late that when she gave Uncle Winston the money, she was giving away herself.

PART III
Here Comes the Sun

21

OUTSIDE, THE HUMID AIR HANGS LOW LIKE THE MANGOES ON the trees. It's June, the tail end of mango season. So the little breeze, if any, carries the sweet, battered smell of rotting mangoes. The school compound is empty, since classes have begun. The sun plays on the well-manicured lawn that is surrounded by quaint two-story buildings built by the British founders of the school. The walkways are lined with manicured hedges of bright red and pink hibiscuses, all leading to the Victorian architecture of the adminis-trative office—a place where Thandi imagines girls with pale skin wearing broad hats used to sip afternoon tea back in the day before black girls were admitted. She is finding it difficult to focus on her studies the way she should, dawdling between classes.

"Young lady, why are you not in class?"

Thandi turns around and sees Sister Benjamin, a wiry-thin nun whose pointed nose resembles a beak. She's the school nurse. "Uhm ... ah ... I was sent to ... I feel sick," Thandi blurts out, surprised at her ability to manufacture such a lie on the spot while staring straight into the eyes of a nun.

"Come with me," Sister Benjamin says with authority. Thandi follows behind her into a more shaded area by the physical education building—a newer building with a gymnasium and a swimming pool—where Sister Benjamin's office is located. Once inside the nurse's office, Thandi sits ladylike, back straight and legs crossed at the ankles, in the cold metal chair by the desk. There are plastic molds of human anatomy on the shelves inside the office—various parts like the eyes with squiggly blue veins drawn on the cornea, the intestines that zigzag all the way to the mannequin's bottom half, and the womb that is shaped like the horns of a ram. The air-conditioning in the office feels like opening Mr. Levy's deep freeze, revealing the bottles of soft drinks inside. These white nuns would never survive in Jamaica without air-conditioning. Thandi imagines that they would melt like candle wax.

Sister Benjamin stands over Thandi. She presses a cool pinkish hand to Thandi's neck. As if unsatisfied with what she feels, she retrieves her thermometer and tells Thandi to open her mouth. When she takes it out and looks at it, she nods to herself. "When did the sickness start?" she asks.

Thandi clears her throat. "Last month, miss." It's true that she hasn't been feeling like herself lately. Her drive to do schoolwork has diminished, though she still makes good grades. Maybe it's because the exams are only days away and she's ready to get them over with.

"Last month?" Sister Benjamin raises an eyebrow. "Have you been experiencing any headaches, nausea, vomiting?" Sister Benjamin asks Thandi.

Thandi nods, relieved that she can get away with the lie. She swallows, comforted by the recollection of the dizzying hot flashes she had been getting due to the plastic and sweatshirt she had been wearing since February. "How about fatigue?" Sister Benjamin asks. "Have you been feeling very tired lately?" Thandi nods again, thinking about the creeping wave of exhaustion that overwhelms her out of nowhere.

"Have you missed any periods?"

Thandi clears her throat and lowers her eyes.

"It'll be all right, dear," Sister Benjamin says, leaning again to touch Thandi on the arm. "You can talk to me."

Thandi tenses. She takes a deep breath to steady herself.

"How did it happen, love?" Sister Benjamin asks.

"I'm not pregnant." Thandi says. "I've never . . ."

"You've never had sexual relations with anyone? Is that what you're saying?"

"No . . . I mean, yes . . . I mean, no . . . I—I didn't do anything."

If she tells Sister Benjamin what really happened all those years ago, it would mean that her pain would no longer be hers. She shakes her head, her eyes downcast. "I'm not pregnant."

"Then what have you been hiding under that sweatshirt? It's been a hundred degrees outside."

Thandi's face grows warm. Sister Benjamin would never understand. How can she ever explain that she wanted to be fair—like the Virgin Mary or the nuns and girls at school who take their lightness for granted? Thandi doesn't know what's worse in the eyes of this woman of God—the discovery that she could be correcting God's mistake and even blasphemously suggesting that he made one; or the assumption that she has fornicated and gotten pregnant. Thandi's eyes catch on a poster on the wall. In bold letters it declares: YOU ARE MADE IN THE IMAGE OF GOD. Below the words, a frail girl who looks like the Virgin Mary is piously bowing her covered head, her milky white skin glowing in a light that appears to be descending from heaven. Thandi averts her eyes.

"Let us pray," Sister Benjamin says, reaching for Thandi's hand across the table. Thandi sits back down and puts her hands inside Sister Benjamin's. The woman's hands are tight around hers, her eyes closed. "Repeat after me. Oh, my God, I am heartfully sorry for having offended thee, and I detest all my sins because of Thy just punishment . . ."

When Thandi opens her eyes, Sister Benjamin is smiling. "Thank you, Sister Benjamin," Thandi chokes, unable to look her in the eyes. She feels Sister Benjamin watching her as she gets up from the chair and moves to the door.

"Concentrate on your education. A girl like you can't afford not to. Believe me, you wouldn't want to throw all this away just for your indiscretions. Or someone else's." A shadow briefly descends over her face like a veil. When Thandi blinks, it's gone, replaced by a cool stamp of disapproval.

Thandi makes a beeline to Charles's house, her backpack bouncing behind her. She will apologize to him for their last encounter, tell him that she wasn't herself; that something came over her and made her do what she did, embarrassing them both. She flings the gate open and hurries to his shack. Cain and Abel trail behind her. They recognize her now, jumping up to greet her, their tails wagging and tongues hanging. She knocks on Charles's door. When she knocks again and no one answers, she peers through the window. He's not there. She looks around the yard, wondering where he could be, given that he was not by the river. Neither was he by his father's boat. She contemplates the main shack, where the front door swings open in the light breeze. She never thought to look there. Never thought to go inside, for it is known in River Bank that Miss Violet does not take visitors. Thandi goes to the main house anyway and pushes the door open.

The house reeks of sinkle bible and boiled tamarind leaves. Thandi shudders from the stench, which reminds her of sickness. But it is the more potent mixture of piss, feces, and something else that makes her swallow the box lunch she ate at school earlier. The darkness doesn't permit Thandi to see much farther than the doorway. She considers turning and going back outside, but her feet remain grounded as though the floor is made of wet cement. Someone coughs. This is followed by a soft coo, like a baby bird or something more fragile. Thandi steps inside, her feet aggravating the wooden floorboards. She puts her backpack over both shoulders so that her hands are free to feel around. A sliver of daylight enters through the small tear in the curtain by the only window. The curtain, Thandi notices, is just an old sheet. This faint light allows her to see the small table with a couple of chairs, some cardboard boxes, a stack of old newspapers, and a barrel. Now that she's inside, outside seems like a foreign country. There's no concept of time and place. The date—though currently June 1, 1994—is still August 7, 1988, according to the water-stained calendar hanging on a wall.

Inside this house, Hurricane Gilbert has not yet come and devastated the island, flooding out some residents of River Bank. Inside this house, Edward Seaga is still Prime Minister of Jamaica, a yellowing picture of him pasted next to the calendar. Inside this house, a fisherman name Asafa still brings home lobster for his family. When Thandi approaches the bedroom (the partitioned area where the cooing gets louder, sounding like a wounded animal as opposed to the soft, fragile thing that Thandi had pictured earlier) a frail woman's voice calls out. "Asafa? Ah you dat?" But it's not the assumption that throws Thandi off guard; it's the sound of the woman's voice—gravellike and strained, as though she has been weeping for hours, days, weeks, months, years. Nearly a decade. "Asafa?"

Thandi pauses. Though she's barely breathed since entering the house, she gasps for the little air remaining.

"No, Mama, is jus' me. Yuh imagining t'ings again." It's Charles. Thandi tiptoes to the side of the partition, a red, velvety upholstery material that she's used to seeing on chairs in Mr. Farrow's furniture place. She spies Charles squeezing a piece of washcloth from a basin. Thandi hears the water swooshing around. His mother is sitting up on a narrow bed, naked, looking like a big doll. Her dark hair is wild, flanked with powdery grays. Her eyes are sunken and wide, the bags under them like dark pouches. It's hard for Thandi to recognize Miss Violet with all that wrinkled flesh. Her face seems to have crumpled under many years of disappointment, worry, sadness, and longing. This is Jullette's mother. A woman Thandi once thought to be the most beautiful, loving, and caring mother compared to hers. Miss Violet would give Jullette peanuts even when she didn't ask. She gave her perms too, something Thandi envied because it made Jullette seem grown. And when Jullette's hair started falling out, Miss Violet had her get those extension braids. They talked like friends, giggling and smiling at each other all the time. There was never any beating or shaming. As the only girl in her family of boys, Jullette did anything she wanted without living in fear of a domineering mother. Miss Violet used to sell peanuts, tamarind balls, and peppered shrimp outside the gate of their primary school. She was always ready for Thandi with a pretty smile, though she had only a few teeth left in her mouth then. "*Aye, coolie girl.*"

Currently the woman looks like she has aged fifty years, her eyes glazed with nostalgia. "Yuh rememba Irby an' Georgie?" she asks her son, pronouncing "*Georgie*" as "*Jaaaji.*" Her pink tongue wallows in her gaping, toothless mouth like a whale.

"Yes, Mama," Charles replies, using the cloth to bathe his mother.

Miss Violet is indifferent to this. Indifferent to her grown son cleaning her this way, wiping the wet cloth over her sandy-brown breasts
that are full, heavy sacks on her chest.

"An' Premrose. Is wah become ah Premrose?" Miss Violet asks.
The water trickles down her pouched belly and settles in her concave navel. Her eyes glisten as she appears to search her memory
for a woman named Premrose. "Mi will do anyting fi har sorrel
now," she says, clucking her tongue. "Those was some good days."
Charles continues to wipe, his face neutral despite the downward
stroke between his mother's legs, where the black and gray hairs
match the ones on her head.

"She's dead now," Charles says, looking away from his task out
of politeness and respect. Thandi can't see the look on his face,
but his motion is a mechanical one—his mother's hands are busy
touching her hair as if to replace a wayward strand from an elegant
coif. All she says is, "Uhn," as though this news of Premrose's passing means nothing. She says it again when Charles finishes.

"Yuh should get out di house sometime," Charles says quietly.
"Look for work an' stop laying up in bed like dis. Yuh is not a ole
'ooman yet, an' yuh still got yuh strength."

Miss Violet looks at him. "Is bettah fah yuh to kill me. Tek me
outta dis misery. Premrose is in a bettah place now. It shoulda
been me."

Charles straightens and looks down at his mother. "Mama, me
can't continue fi do dis."

Miss Violet presses her lips to her gums and holds his hand,
bringing him back down. "Jus' do it. Me will be forevah grateful if
yuh end it fah me. Put a knife to me throat, ah icepick to me 'aart.
Anyt'ing. Jus' kill me, son-son. Please, please, me ah beg yuh!"
Then her voice becomes cold. "Yuh is a coward! A lessah man than
yuh father!" The cooing starts again.

Thandi backs away. Her footsteps trouble the floorboards again and this time the creaking brings Charles to the curtain. Their eyes meet—his, questioning, ashamed; hers, apologetic. He stands there in silence, the wet cloth dripping to the floor, his mother cooing in the background. Thandi trembles with the urge to hold him and the need for forgiveness as she witnesses the rage building in his eyes, eclipsing them like moons. She turns around and cuts through the stink, running until she's sure she has escaped it. But the smell, like the look in Charles's eyes, follows her all the way home.

22

ON THE DAY OF THE PARTY, THANDI IRONS A MODEST GREEN dress that falls below her knees. With a big white collar, white buttons, pleats and a bow in the back, it's a perfect cover for the daring dress she intends to change into once she gets to the restaurant. Grandma Merle had sewn the green dress for Delores when she was Thandi's size. Delores kept the dress so that it could be passed on to Margot, then Thandi. In the mirror above the vanity she spies her clear complexion; the lightness has come into her skin like a slow-moving mixture of condensed milk and Milo. Truth be told, she hasn't given much thought to the party, medical school, or her bleaching regimen since Charles. But after seeing Miss Violet, the ugliness of being black and poor remains like intaglio on her mind. It's the one thing that connects her to Miss Violet's sickness, Margot's restlessness, and Delores's intermittent wrath. After being inside Miss Violet's shack, she saw, with overwhelming dread, what might become of her. That day she rushed home to the shack, and there, before the mirror, rubbed her skin with the Queen of Pearl and Miss Ruby's concoction mixed with hydrogen peroxide until it was raw and tender. But no matter how hard and how frequently she rubs, the imprint of Charles's mother remains, for it's indelible.

Delores comes in from the outhouse and sees Thandi looking at herself in the mirror.

"Is where yuh going?" she asks, putting a roll of toilet paper on a small table.

"They having last minute extra lessons today at school, remembah I told you? Since the exam started this week." She returns to ironing the dress.

Delores nods. She's filling up a basket with souvenirs to sell at the market later. Delores is in high spirits today. A big ship is coming into Falmouth, though it's Saturday. Thandi looks at the rag dolls and the coasters and key chains and handcrafted jewelry that Delores delicately places inside the basket. How would visitors know the real stories behind the faces of the wooden masks they'd buy to hang on walls; the rag dolls they'd use to decorate unused furniture in their houses; the figurines they'd place on mantels that they can marvel at then quickly forget? The smell of something burning brings Thandi's attention from her mother's basket to the brown outline the iron has branded into the dress. Thandi quickly removes the iron, but pieces of the green fabric have attached themselves to the hot metal surface. She gasps, looking both ways for a solution, as though one would materialize out of the steam. Delores runs over to the board when she hears the hissing sound of the iron. "What yuh do to di dress?" she yells, surveying the damage—the burned spot, ruining the polyester fabric that had survived years of washing and drying in the sun, and the hems that had been stitched with the care and precision by Mama Merle's then-abled fingers. All gone.

"Sorry, Mama. Ah wasn't paying attention," Thandi says.

They haven't said much to each other since that night when Thandi showed her the drawing and told her that she wants to be an artist. When Thandi looks up again, Delores is regarding her closely. Thandi lowers the dress. "What?"

"Don't *what* me." Delores is stepping closer. "What is it yuh using on yuh face?"

"Nothing, Mama. I wash it wid soap. That's all."

"Yuh t'ink me is a eeediot?"

"No, Mama."

"Then be honest wid me, Thandi . . . how come yuh look like yuh a spar wid di dead?"

Thandi touches her face, pretending to not have noticed the change. Miss Ruby was right. Her skin has lightened to how she wanted it by today. Just in time for Dana's sweet sixteen party tonight. "It's how me skin stay," she says. "I've not been in the sun, since I've been studying so hard."

"Don't romp wid me, Thandi." Delores puts her hands on her hips, her chest swelling.

"I'm telling the truth."

"You been going to dat Miss Ruby?"

"No, Mama."

"Tell me di god truth!"

Thandi beholds her pale hands. She can actually see her veins. How green and expansive they are; the sight of them inflating her lungs. She wants to show off her new skin so she'll be like the others, the ones who don't have to sit patiently, looking forward to the Day of Judgment, expecting its sweet relief. For heaven is right here, in her lightened skin. See? See? She got what she wanted; and she doesn't have to wait until she gets to someplace in the sky.

"Why, Thandi?" Delores's hands drop to her sides. "Lawd Jesus have mercy pon me!" She whips around to face the shadows perched nearby in the early morning before the sun scatters them. Like little black birds that crowd the branches of the pawpaw trees by the foot of the river, the shadows seem to descend with Delores's presence. "Yuh see me dying trial?" she says to them. "Di chile bleaching har skin, tun white woman undah me roof!"

"Mama, ah can explain."

"Explain?" Delores pounces and grabs Thandi, knocking over the ironing board in the process. She drags her by the collar of her nightgown. With one hand Delores rips the flimsy nightgown off Thandi to bare her chest so that she can see her bleached body in its entirety—everywhere as light as the cedar planks that Clover uses to patch holes in the shack. Gone is Thandi's once-mahogany cocoa skin. Delores jumps back, her hands flying to her mouth as if a ghost—a duppy—snatched her breath, her eyes watering.

"Thandi, is whaddu yuh? How yuh pay for it?"

"Mama, I can explain," Thandi repeats.

"How?" Delores is shaking mightily, like a tree branch in a hurricane. "Who is filling up yuh head wid dis rubbish? Is it di girl dem at school? Is it dem?"

When Thandi doesn't answer, Delores comes after her again, and Thandi runs. "Aftah me bruk me back to send yuh go school to learn, this is what yuh come home wid?" She raises her hand to slap Thandi, but Thandi escapes again. "How yuh paying dat blasted 'ooman? Dat blasted, thievin' 'ooman who selling nuttin but lies!"

"Mama, it nuh cost much."

"Ah g'wan find out fi me self," Delores says. "Yuh not going nowhere looking like yuh jus' drop outta one casket. Ah g'wan guh kill dat Ruby!"

"But Mama, I have extra lessons."

"Yuh not going anywhere t'day. Yuh g'wan stay in that sun till yuh color come back."

"But Mama!" Thandi cries. "I don't want to be black any longer. Where's dat going to get me? Nowhere."

"But Jeezas have mercy!" Delores crouches with her head in her hand.

"Mama, I want to be somebody. I want to go places. You want that too—for me to be a doctor, leave River Bank."

"Nonsense!" Delores springs back up from her haunches. "Yuh see how me black an' stay? How yuh fi tun white wid a black mother, eh?"

"Is not about you, Mama. Is about me."

"Is dat why yuh shame ah me? Because me black? Is dat why yuh neva bring any ah yuh school friend dem around? Because yuh nuh want dem fi see yuh black mother an' fi know seh yuh live 'mongst black people? First yuh change yuh accent . . . can't even chat patwa no more. An' now yuh go all di way wid di bleaching t'ing. What yuh do wid me Thandi? Beg yuh bring har back, because me nuh like dis one."

Just then Margot comes in with bags of groceries she picked up at Mr. Levy's Wholesale. An overnight bag is strung over one shoulder. A wave of relief washes over Thandi when she sees her sister. She runs into Margot to get away from Delores, almost knocking Margot over. "What's going on here? Why yuh naked?" Margot asks, letting go of the bags, which drop with a loud thud, to hold on to Thandi.

"Is blind yuh blind?" Delores asks Margot. "Yuh sistah turning into a white 'ooman undah me roof! Is you put her up to dis?" Delores shouts, her body shaking as though aggravated by the words. Margot turns to look at Thandi, who is in her arms. "What she talking 'bout, Thandi?" Her eyes are scouring Thandi's face. "Thandi."

"I'm not turning white," Thandi sniffs, wiping her eyes. "I was just bringing up my color. A lot of girls do it. I am the darkest at school. People either make fun of me or they ignore me."

"So let them!" Delores shouts from where she stands. "Yuh g'wan be bettah than them wid what's up here." Delores taps her skull.

"But Mama, yuh always say—"

"Yuh should be concentrating on the CXC. Yuh was supposed to be the one to rise above dat stupidness wid yuh books."

Margot is quiet this whole time, watching Delores through narrowing slits. She drops her hands to her sides like she did the groceries. "Mama!" She holds up one hand. "Let me talk to her for a minute."

Delores backs away, her hands curled in tight fists. She has never surrendered her power before, but Margot doesn't seem afraid to silence their mother. Margot seems to be the one in charge. Something is different about her, Thandi thinks. Lately she has been busier and busier, her clothes nicer and nicer.

She told Thandi that she was preparing to move them somewhere else. "*Where would we get the money?*" Thandi had asked her sister a few days ago. And Margot had given her the biggest grin she had ever seen on her face. "*Ah jus' win di lotto an' buy land. Yuh looking on the new hotel general manager of Palm Star Resort!*" Thandi hugged her sister before she pulled back. "*Does Mama know?*" Margot shook her head. "*Don't say anyt'ing to her as yet. Right now dis is between me an' you.*"

In this very moment, this indomitable woman is standing in their living space like the sun itself. Delores retreats inside the kitchen, mumbling to herself, as Margot sits Thandi down on the sofa. Very gently she cups Thandi's face and caresses it with both hands. There are tears in her eyes too. Thandi isn't sure if they are sad tears or happy tears. Margot clutches Thandi's chin gently and parts her ruby-red lips as though to blow a kiss. "This is unnecessary if yuh look in the mirror an' see what I see in those eyes." Margot runs her hands through Thandi's hair, untwisting the single braid and letting her hair fall around her shoulders. "Once you believe you are beautiful, then people will believe it too."

"Is dat what they said at the hotel when they hired you as front desk clerk and then gave yuh dat promotion?" Thandi asks.

"What promotion?" Delores springs back into view.

Margot looks at Thandi in stunned silence. Without turning to Delores, she says, "I was recently promoted as hotel general manager."

"When? Why yuh didn't seh anyt'ing to me about it? How much dem paying yuh now?"

"Is dat all yuh care about?" Margot faces Delores. "How much I'm worth?" Delores is seething quietly in the shadows.

"What have you been telling Thandi, Mama?" Margot asks.

"What yuh mean, what ah been telling har? Is me yuh g'wan blame fah this?"

"A man like dat," Margot says quietly under her breath. At first Thandi doesn't hear her sister's words, until she repeats it over and over again like a litany. Margot's whisper becomes a laugh that rumbles in her belly and snaps her head back. "A man like dat is what I was to aspire to get, remembah, Delores?" Thandi watches this, instantly becoming a shadow, a bat perched in the dark recesses of the shack, listening. "Remember?" Margot says quietly. Just then Maxi comes to the gate and hollers for Delores:

"What tek'n suh long, Mama Delores? Ship 'bout to dock!"

And Margot's attitude changes. She breaks the staring match between her and Delores and fixes her blouse. She bends to pick up the bags of groceries that fell earlier. Delores's face is still twisted into a deep scowl.

"Yuh sister is different," she says to Margot as she lifts her own weight—the basket of souvenirs. "I tell yuh dat all the time. So get offah me back an' guh run yuh hotel. God mus' really work in mysterious ways. I guess him bless yuh overnight, huh?" Delores's voice has a sharp edge. "What position did you pray in, Margot? Were you on yuh knees or pon yuh back?"

Margot stiffens. She clutches Thandi's shoulders. "Did she evah tell you?" she asks. "Did she evah tell what she did?"

"Kibbah yuh mouth," Delores says. "Don't bring yuh sistah in yuh mess."

Margot's tone raises the hairs on Thandi's arms. "No matter what yuh do to yuhself, it not g'wan change a t'ing," Margot says to Thandi. "Believe me, it won't change yuh place in society or how they look at you."

"Let me go!" she says to Margot, who still clutches Thandi as though Thandi is about to fall into some kind of an abyss that only Margot can see. Thandi stumbles backward when her sister releases her.

Thandi feels sorry for hurting her this way. She shouldn't have shouted at Margot like that. But she thought Margot would've understood her and taken her side. Can't she see that Thandi wants more than this life in River Bank? More than what Margot can ever give her? Margot waits until Delores leaves before she gets up and goes outside through the back door. Thandi watches her walk past the outhouse and the tire swing where Little Richie hides. Like a divi-divi tree thrashing in the wind, she walks with her head bent forward, storming through, parting banana leaves and trampling tall grass. Thandi slips into the fuchsia dress—snug at the hips with slits on both sides—which she bought last week for the birthday party. Might as well, since no one is there to see her wear it.

Thandi stands alone on the pier that evening, watching her classmates on the dance floor. She fights away thoughts of Charles, but no one asks her to dance. No one directs her to the table with snacks and soda. A feeling of alienation creeps up on her, cold like the night air. She fidgets with a piece of napkin folded in her damp hands, standing knock-kneed in the shadows. The other girls walk right by her as though they don't know her. Dance-hall music soars in the open air and Thandi adjusts her dress, hoping someone will ask her to dance. All the pretty brown boys have found all the pretty brown girls. The boys stir with excitement and jump on the girls' behinds, riding them to the rhythm of the music on the dance floor and against the rails. The girls don't seem to mind. They're oblivious to moist foreheads, smudged makeup, and damp collarbones where sweat sparkles like glitter. The more self-conscious ones fan and dab themselves with tissue, pretending not to be concerned or flattered by the looks from other boys, lining up and waiting their turn. Their smiles and skin glow under the disco lights.

Laughter takes everyone's minds off the awkwardness of trying to impress each other. The music changes to Dennis Brown and there's an unspoken acknowledgment that each person should find a partner. There is one boy left standing in a corner like Thandi. Their eyes meet. His dimples are visible from her vantage point. She moves from her corner and slips between the bodies on the dance floor. The boy stands up straight. Thandi tucks her hair behind her ears, confident that he can see her lighter, brighter face. She has dreamed of this moment, approaching a fair-skinned boy as though it is her birthright. The boy holds Thandi's stare. With a slight drop of his head, he looks her up and down as she gets closer and closer to him. As Dennis Brown's voice hits a high note, soaring into the star-filled indigo sky, the boy's dimples disappear and he wrinkles his nose and walks away. Thandi has been acknowledged and dismissed in the time it takes to get to the other side of the dance floor. The belly-skip of possible love with a cream-skinned mulatto is nothing compared to the vile liquid that presently shoots through her veins. Her hope wilts on its stem before it can bloom into promise. Miss Ruby was wrong. Bleaching her skin doesn't make them see her as beautiful.

Thandi walks to the restroom with pieces of her heart cradled to her chest. On her way, she spots a familiar face. She squints to see if her eyes are playing tricks on her. Jullette is sitting with a man at the bar—a foreigner who looks more than twice her age. He's a deeply tanned white man with silver hair, casually dressed in a white polo shirt and khaki shorts. He has one hand on Jullette's exposed brown thigh, the other around a drink. Such an unlikely couple they are, sitting there. The man leans in and whispers something in Jullette's ear. She laughs out loud above the music, cupping her hand over her mouth. Her face is a colorful mask of violets, greens, and reds. She playfully taps the man on the shoulder, and he drains her drink for her.

"Jullette?" Thandi calls from the end of the bar where she stands. When Jullette hears her name, she turns. The beam fades from Jullette's face. Her eyes, which are a startling hazel from the contacts she wears, widen. She quickly looks the other way.

"Jullette!" Thandi calls again, strangely happy to see her old friend since they had fallen out. The people at the bar glance at Thandi as though she has lost her mind, with her shouting to get Jullette's attention. But Jullette buries her face in the crook of the man's neck and whispers something. Soon they both get up and vanish from the bar.

23

THE PANTRY IS EMPTY. THE OPEN CUPBOARDS BARE THEIR skeletal insides filled with nothing but a can of chicken noodle soup. No crackers to moisten with tea. No tea bags. The refrigerator hums, its cold breath on Verdene's face. No eggs for breakfast either. She has no choice but to go to the market. She counts the last of the insurance money her mother left her. It's enough to sustain her, for the time being. Very slowly, she puts on her market dress. She zips the side and watches the dress fall over her knees, covering up everything. An attempt to gain respectability like the other women. She picks up her basket, the one her mother used to carry.

Outside, the sun is bright yellow like the yolk of an egg. Its one eye holds Verdene in place. For a second she ponders starving to death, renouncing her life within the safe confines of the house. Her body will rot, and when they find her she would be unrecognizable. She imagines the community people linking hands with their children to dance around her property, singing, "*Ding-dong! The witch is dead!*"

She makes her way down the road, hoping to be as inconspicuous as possible under her white sun hat. A man and a woman cross over to the other side of the road when they see her coming. A group of boys sitting on the branch of a mango tree throw mango seeds in her path. Two little girls jumping rope in a yard stop and hold the tails of their dirty dresses closed. The mothers of the girls standing nearby in the yard gasp. They don't say then, *You see that lady's fair skin? See how pretty? Yuh g'wan stay black an' ugly if you stay playing in the sun.* Instead, they look the other way, the sides of their eyes holding Verdene in place as they grab their daughters. "Oonuh come out the way! Mek the witch pass!" And when Verdene gets to the bar by Mr. Levy's, the men playing dominoes outside regard her closely, until she passes near enough to hear one of them, Clover, say to his friends, "All she need is a good cocky."

But Verdene doesn't falter. She holds her head high, knowing they probably won't touch her due to her foreign privilege. Had they wanted to harm her, they would've done so already. It's that crisp British accent, its stroke of precision sharp like a razor's edge. "Is there a problem, gentlemen?" Verdene asks, trying not to let her voice quaver. The men shrink under her view. They are seemingly embarrassed by her propriety. Clover takes a swig of rum from a flask, wiping his mouth with the back of his hand. He says nothing, only grabs his crotch and holds it. Verdene stares him down until he releases himself and drops his leer.

At the market Verdene barely sees or smells anything. She picks up fruits and vegetables and puts them in her basket. They all look bad, given that it has not rained in months. She wishes she could test their texture and smell them like her mother used to do. Verdene's mother could do this in her sleep. She always got the best price for everything she bought. But Verdene doesn't have that luxury. One look at her and the market vendors know she's a foreigner, a prodigal daughter who has still not assimilated back into the culture. It must be her clipped accent and mannerisms; her willingness to wait her turn to speak when they're speaking; the way she walks with caution, unable to be led by her hips like most Jamaican women, and always looking over her shoulder like the tourists who wander from the hotels. And in her face, the vendors from River Bank see her mother, Miss Ella, and they remember the old woman who died alone in that nice pink house on the hill. They remember the daughter who disgraced her. They remember the sin she committed. They whisper to the other vendors. *"Nuh Miss Ella dawta dat?"* And their words spread like the stench of raw fish, battered fruit, and gutter water that permeates the humid air. Some fan her away like the flies that pitch all over their produce, while others pause, their hands on their hips as though waiting for a confrontation. Verdene feels like one of the soldiers that march through the area with long rifles, her presence leaving a trail of silence and apprehensive looks. The vendors quote the highest price, stating it between clenched teeth, their eyes communicating to her that their price is final. That they would rather do without her money and have their children eat cornmeal porridge again for dinner. When she agrees to buy their produce, unwilling to fight, they grudgingly take her money. Verdene notices that they touch the bills with only the tips of their fingers.

Verdene fills her basket and walks to the end of the row. She has never gone this far into the arcade, but today something is propelling her. Delores is on her haunches, taking out green peas from their pods. Her expert fingers open them up quickly to let the seeds fall into a basket. Though she's getting a lot accomplished, her mind is elsewhere. Verdene can tell, for Delores doesn't notice her standing there watching her. "Hello, Delores." Verdene moves inside the stall and stands over the crouched woman, who appears smaller than Verdene remembered her to be. Delores regards her face as though trying to place her. Her large eyes widen and her eyebrows touch her hairline like she has seen a ghost. "You!" Delores says. This comes out as a whisper. Verdene takes a step back to disarm her, but Delores is already struggling to her feet, her gasp turning into a body-shivering cough. Verdene wants to step forward and hit Delores's back in order to help, but she's afraid someone might come and think she's trying to assault her. Delores's cough quiets. She breathes slowly, with her fist to her mouth just in case she might have another fit. "What yuh want from me?" Delores asks when she calms down, her voice hoarse.

"I was in the area. Just came to say hello."

Delores grimaces. "Who told you we're on any level for dat kind of thing?"

"You never used to mind me."

"Well, that was before I knew yuh was the devil."

Verdene wonders if she can risk asking Delores about Margot.

"How are you?" Verdene asks.

"Why is it any of your business?" Delores retorts.

"And how is Margot? I haven't seen her in years," Verdene lies. She tries to sound as casual as possible, though her heart is racing. Delores makes two fists and places them on her hips.

"Yuh asking after my daughter?" Delores asks. The weight of her suspicion is heavy, like the basket of fruits and vegetables in Verdene's hand.

"How dare yuh come here wid my dawta's name in yuh mouth!" Delores's eyes are flashing.

She wants to explain, but then thinks against it. "It's not like you treated her like your daughter. You never cared about her. You never loved her. Not like—"

"You have no business coming in here, telling what kinda mother yuh t'ink I am," Delores snaps. "She's not like you. She has a man. A moneyman who own a hotel. So if is come yuh come to see about Margot, then yuh bettah turn back around an' walk di other way."

"I didn't say—"

"I know exactly what yuh didn't say," Delores says through clenched teeth.

Verdene opens and closes her mouth. Delores sees through her. She knows. Has always known. It's obvious in the way she looks at Verdene, her nostrils flared and eyes ablaze. A sneer creeps up Delores's black ugly face.

"Margot has a moneyman," Delores says. "A man who can provide for her. So g'weh wid yuh foreign accent an' yuh inheritance. G'weh wid yuh nastiness! She's not like you!"

Verdene backs away from Delores's stall.

"She's not like you! She's not like you! She's not like you!"

The woman's screams get louder and louder the farther Verdene runs. The other vendors peer from their stalls to see the commotion. They see Delores screaming, Verdene hurrying away, bumping into things and people. *She's not like you! She's not like you! She's not like you! She's not like you! She's not like you! She's not like you! She's not like you! She's not like you! She's not like you! She's not like you! She's not like you!*

She runs into a young Rasta fellow who is holding a box of carved birds. She has seen him selling them on the corner. The box falls, the birds crashing to the ground, breaking. The Rasta man raises his hands to his head, his eyes wild. "Yuh bruk me t'ings dem!" He catches Verdene by the arm, his grasp tight. Her basket falls and the fruits burst open on the pavement. The overripe breadfruit, when it hits the ground, sounds like a fist punching the soft, fleshy part of a body.

"Yuh haffi pay fah di birds!" the Rasta man says, glaring at Verdene.

"Let. Me. Go," Verdene says through clenched teeth. Her chest heaves painfully as her heart presses against her rib cage. "I said let me go!"

But the Rasta refuses. "Gimme di money fah di birds."

"Hol' on pon har, John-John," says one of the other vendors. "She was messing wid Delores earlier too. Come talk ah 'bout how she love Margot."

"What yuh do to Mama Delores?" the man asks Verdene. "What yuh do to my Margot?"

His Margot? Verdene looks into his yellow eyes. "Who are you? You let go of me, or else."

"Or else wah?" The man draws back his fist. Behind him, the vendors chant, "Do it! Do it! Do it! Punch di sodomite in har face!"

"Only a coward hits a woman," Verdene says in a low voice that only he can hear. "*My* Margot would never want you."

The Rasta man pulls Verdene's face to his fist or his fist to her face. Verdene—who used to block fights between her parents, and who once felt the hard knuckles of her father's hand in her left jaw to prevent it from fracturing another bone in her mother's petite body—has perfected a self-defense maneuver that enables her to block the man's fist and twist his arm behind his back. He grits his teeth as she holds his hand in place.

"When a woman says to let her go, you let her go!"

These words come from someone else. Must be from someone who is standing in the crowd, watching this taking place. For Verdene no longer recognizes her own voice.

"You heard me?" the woman—that other woman—says.

The Rasta man lets Verdene go, his eyes wide with fear. He watches Verdene pick up her basket, which is empty. He says nothing. Neither does the crowd that has gathered. Verdene suppresses the urge to cry. Not in public for all of these people to see how humiliated she really is. One by one she gathers the contents of her basket, knowing she will never return to buy produce from these people again. When she thinks she's done, someone hands her an apple. Verdene looks up, from the clawlike fingers with blackened nails clutching the apple to the face of the woman.

"I believe this belongs to you," the woman says; her face is a web of lines as though someone had taken off her skin, crumpled it like paper between fists, then put it back on.

Verdene hesitates before taking the apple, meeting the woman's cataract-blue eyes. Miss Gracie grins with all her rotting teeth.

"Yuh mek Eve bite di apple," Miss Gracie says, the accusation like the jab of a needle. "Now tek it back! Tek it back an' go to hell weh yuh come from, yuh serpent!" She flings the apple at Verdene, hitting her in the head. Verdene drops her basket and runs, aware of the crowd stirring again with victory. "Yes, Mama Gracie, show har who run t'ings! Lick har backside! Buss har head!"

The Rasta man, who has suddenly regained his voice, shouts, "Next time me see yuh, you g'wan pay!"

Verdene hurries out of the market, realizing for the first time that Delores had been standing there in the crowd, her eyes red like the devil. It's as though she had orchestrated the whole thing.

"G'long, yuh blasted sodomite! An' nuh come back!" Delores says.

Delores's final words hit Verdene like a rock in the back. Verdene picks up her pace and runs.

24

ELORES WATCHES THE WOMAN FLEE. THE EVIL THE SODOMITE has brought to the arcade makes her shudder. Of all the days, Verdene picked today to come to harass her.

"But what is it yuh want from me, Lawd Jesus?" Delores asks, her head tilted to the steel-blue sky. It must be a sign. An omen. Miss Ella's daughter has never been up to any good. She poisoned Margot all those years ago, made her sick in the head for months. Margot was never the same after she became friends with that Verdene girl.

Margot was ten years old when Delores came home from work one day and saw her beaming. Immediately the muscles in Delores's chest tightened at the sight of white teeth peering through brown flesh. Something seemed odd about it. For some reason, the joy and innocence in her daughter only infuriated her. Had Margot known what life could become for girls like her, she would never grin like that. And the wider the little girl grinned, the more Delores's muscles contracted within the cavity of her chest.

"*What is it yuh so happy 'bout?*" Delores asked the little girl the day she saw her in the yard, putting a red hibiscus behind her ear.

"*She said I'm pretty,*" Margot responded.

"*Who said so?*"

"*Verdene.*"

"*Verdene who?*"

"*Miss Ella's dawta,*" Margot said, pointing in the direction of the bright pink house.

When Margot was born, she cried and cried and cried, as though she had inherited Delores's wails from childbirth. The baby was a burden, a living proof of something stolen, mangled, and destroyed. The man who was Margot's father had called Delores pretty too. Had pinched her fat as a young girl who was barely thirteen and told her one day to sit on his lap. When she didn't, he made her. He pinched and pinched and pinched her fat until Delores couldn't take it. The final pinch was one so deep that Margot came wailing from it nine months later. And Delores wanted to silence it. Even the baby's gentle breaths as she played or fed or snored were loud, and Delores fought the urge many times to stop her breathing with a pillow over her head.

When she saw Margot smiling that day, Delores wanted to crush the thing she saw in her daughter's eyes: that new thing that sparkled and shone like that ungodly sun Delores yearned to rip from the sky. She clenched her fists. "*Tek off yuh dirty clothes,*" she told the little girl. Delores watched the light disappear from her daughter's face; but not even that eased the pain inside Delores. "*Me say tek off yuh clothes, gyal!*"

The little girl did as she was told. Her little arms moved slowly as she undressed. She stood naked in the backyard as Delores filled a basin with water.

"*Get in,*" she said. Margot's obedience irritated Delores more. She felt the girl was silently mocking her. How vindictive could this child be, pretending to be so well behaved? Even when she was a toddler, waking up numerous times to catch Delores holding a pillow over her head, trembling, she batted her lashes at Delores as though Delores were God himself. She still trusted her. This had to be a trick. A plan to kill Delores with tenderness.

What Delores did next made the girl scream. She wanted to teach her a lesson. Delores held Margot down in the water and pinched and pinched. The little girl wailed under Delores's thumb and index fingers all over her body. Delores made sure to warn her.

"*Neva tek compliments from anyone else, yuh hear?*" Delores said. "*Especially not from another 'ooman! That's sodomite ways!*"

"*Yes, Mamaaa!*" The little girl's screams only egged Delores on. She wanted to tell her daughter that people only say these things to take advantage of her. Like her father took advantage.

Later that year when the news broke about Verdene messing with some girl at the university, Delores wondered if Verdene had indeed taken advantage of Margot. "*Don't let me see yuh going over there again!*" Delores said to Margot. This time she put Margot inside a basin to wash the evil out of her. Miss Gracie had suggested using Guinea bush to cure the girl, but it didn't help. Margot still ran away to Miss Ella's yard and hid from Delores. She latched on to the other woman and her sodomite daughter as though they were her family. Delores washed Margot every day. "*Yuh is neva going to be like her, yuh hear?*" Delores said. But still, when Verdene was sent away, most days Margot curled up like a fetus and wept for her. She fell mute for a while. The teachers thought something was wrong with her. All she did was run around the track. She ran and ran like something was chasing her. They put her on the track team and she won every race. Made it all the way to National Stadium. Delores tried everything to make her normal. Then the stranger came. When he offered Delores the money, she not only saw her redemption, but her daughter's too.

"Mama Delores, yuh all right?" John-John interrupts Delores's thoughts, the worry in his face pulling her venom, sucking the poisonous anger that nearly paralyzes her. Delores nods. She can't find her voice just yet. The exchange with Verdene has made her sick. A wave of nausea washes over her, twisting her stomach, and she searches for her bench to sit back down, her heart a big, solid mass pounding in her chest.

"Let me get yuh some wata, Mama Delores. Yuh nuh look too good."

John-John bounces out of her stall. Delores touches her right breast with her hand and feels the hardness there. It's bigger, spreading under her arm. She still hasn't taken herself to the doctor to have it looked at. What would they say? That she needs an operation? She can always drink more of the Guinea bush tea with soursop leaf.

John-John returns with a plastic cup filled with warm water.

"Donovan gimme this," he says, referring to the old shoemaker inside the shop across the street from the arcade. He hands the cup to Delores. "Him say if yuh want ice, Miss Bernice 'ave some. But she too far, mah."

Delores drinks the water in one thirsty gulp. She belches loudly and hands the cup back to John-John. "God bless yuh," she says. "Now help me wid this basket," she says to John-John. John-John eagerly picks up the basket off the floor and puts it on the table where Delores keeps the other sale items. Today is her produce day, but it doesn't seem to be selling. She only had one customer this morning. The ships won't dock in Falmouth again until next week, so she spends her off days here with no success. "Mi going home. Coming out here is a waste of time," she says, getting up again.

"Yuh all right, Mama Delores?" John-John asks, this time regarding her face closely. "Yuh sweating bad bad. Dat woman ... why she affect yuh like dat? Mavis seh yuh run har from yuh stall."

"Hush yuh mouth 'bout Mavis. What dat Mavis know? Is nothin' of concern to she nor you."

Delores fans herself with an old Courts Furniture Store calendar as she packs her things. John-John watches her pack. It's still early. Almost two o' clock in the afternoon. For Delores, this is usually the high time. Usually when she sees the other vendors leaving so early she chastises them, clucking her tongue at them. *"Oonuh lazy-like! Yuh don't see we have plenty more hours lef in a day? Stay an' work, man!"*

But today she's tired.

At home, Merle is sitting on the veranda staring out at the sky, a peaceful look on her face. Delores goes inside and puts down her things. The place feels small, no longer able to contain her. She looks around at the shabbiness and thinks she should have hidden that money better. With that money, she could've bought herself a ticket to America. But no. Winston took everything. She goes back outside to the veranda and stands in front of her mother, blocking her view.

"Him not coming back!" she yells to the old woman. Merle doesn't blink. She doesn't even stir. "Ah said, yuh ole neagger son not coming back!" Delores yells again. When her mother doesn't say or do anything, Delores grabs her by the arm and shakes her. "Yuh hear me?" The old woman cries out. Delores squeezes harder, her nails sinking into the old woman's flesh. It's soft to the touch, like tender meat on a chicken bone. Delores feels her mother's slight bones underneath. How fragile they seem under her powerful grip. Merle's cry turns into a whimper.

Delores picks up her mother from her chair on the veranda and takes her inside the house. She shoves her onto the couch. "No more looking at the sky. Him gone! Him not coming back!"

Merle whines louder, holding herself. She rocks back and forth, her whines becoming guttural like those of a tormented swine. Delores leans closer so that she can look into the eyes of the woman who used to tell her she was nothing, the woman who sent her brother (and not her) to school simply because he was the boy. The man of the house. The woman who knew about the pinching and blamed Delores for it.

"What? Yuh t'ink him g'wan save yuh now?" Delores asks her mother. "Yuh see it's not him taking care ah yuh. It's me. It's me! Him forget 'bout you! Him tek me money. Didn't you say everything used to belong to him? Didn't you say it was him who was g'wan mek it? But yuh see? How him gone an' lef' yuh like you is a pile ah shit pon me doorstep!"

Delores wheels around. She can no longer bear looking at the pain in her mother's eyes. A pain that isn't caused by Delores's abuse, but by the absence of her beloved son.

25

THE DAY THANDI FINISHES HER FINAL ROUND OF CXC EXAMS and sees Charles waiting by the school gate in his cutoff trousers, open shirt, and dusty old shoes, she nearly ditches him. She has been avoiding him since the day she walked in on him cleaning his mother. Since her miserable failure at the party, her focus has been on studying. Delores has always said that her education is the only thing she has going for her anyway—the only thing that will set her worlds apart from the people in River Bank. Charles sees her and waves, a grin slowly lighting up his face, as though against his will. But no amount of waving can get Thandi to lift her free hand and wave back. Already the stares of her schoolmates have bound her hand to her side. It dangles helplessly, her fingers twitching. Charles waits for her to cross the street to where he stands. Thandi greets him, managing a smile that she hopes will look to onlookers like a polite one—the kind given to beggars and unsolicited admirers. She walks a few steps ahead, aware of his shadow, his ripe pawpaw scent, and the distance between them.

"How it feel to be done wid all yuh exam dem?" he asks.

"Fine."

"Jus' fine? A heavy weight mus' lif' off ah yuh shoulders. Don't?"

When she doesn't respond, he says, "Yuh want me to hol' yuh bag?"

Thandi shakes her head and caresses the strap on her shoulder. "I can carry it."

"How about dat umbrella?" he asks, pointing to the black umbrella that Thandi keeps above her head so that she won't get dark. With all the skin-lightening creams she still allows Miss Ruby to rub on her body despite Delores's threat, just a few minutes of the sun could scald Thandi's delicate flesh.

"I can hold it too," she says.

"Yuh want a mango?" Charles digs inside his pocket and presents a Julie mango. Thandi looks over her shoulders. She's still in the square where anyone can see her accepting a mango from a street boy. She walks quicker, but he matches her pace. "Why yuh speeding? Yuh late fah something?" Charles asks, trying to catch up.

"Yes, I have to meet someone in Ironshore."

"Oh."

"I have to hurry an' get a taxi."

"Who yuh 'ave up dere?"

"None of your business."

She expects him to leave her alone, to back away and tell her that he'll see her later, then. But he doesn't. He continues to stand there, next to her in broad daylight, in a crowded Sam Sharpe

Square in Montego Bay while she's wearing her Saint Emmanuel High uniform. She hates him for making her feel so ashamed. She hates his naïveté—or is it arrogance? Can't he see that she wants nothing to do with him at this time? Not when she has every intention of going to the hotels, starting with the one where Margot works, to look for a summer job. With the CXCs over, how else will she occupy her time?

"Are you ashamed of me? Because of what you saw at my house?" Charles asks out of the blue.

"Ashamed?" Thandi asks, pretending to be shocked and hurt by this assumption, which is very well true. "I'm in a hurry, that's all."

Charles observes her. Thandi, who is used to convincing people she is somebody other than herself, immediately works hard to change his mind. "If ah was ashamed of you, then why would I be talking to you now?"

Charles shrugs. "You tell me."

"I'm not ashamed of you," she says again, this time hoping to believe this herself.

"Thandi, jus' tell me di truth. If it did mek you uncomfortable to see my mother dat way, I understand."

"I, well, yuh know, it reminded me of . . ." She pauses, trying to find the right words. "I don't want to end up like dat."

"It's not contagious."

"That's not what I mean."

"Then say what yuh mean."

"I don't want to depend on anyone else for my happiness. I always used to hate my mother for not letting me mix wid certain people. But after seeing fah myself what hopelessness really looks like, I realize why. She was trying to save me."

Charles is very quiet, so quiet Thandi thinks she can hear her own heartbeat. "All right, then. Ah get it."

"Charles. I'm sorry."

"No apologies necessary. Ah can't blame yuh. I'm nothin' but a *hopeless* street yout'. It's funny, because ah kinda know dat one day you'd come to yuh senses. Ah fool myself into thinking yuh was a different type of girl, dat you'd be above dem t'ings an' jus' follow yuh heart." He's shaking his head and peering at his dusty old shoes where she can see his big toe. Thandi begins to wish that she never said anything. He's not looking at her anymore. His shoulders are rounded and his eyes are trained on the small pebble he kicks with one foot.

"Well, ah hope dem people deh worth mixing wid," he says.

The disgust that she sees on his face when he turns to leave fills her with disgust too. It's disgust from trying so hard to fit in with everyone else. Where has it gotten her? She likes herself when she's with him. With him she doesn't fumble over herself to be someone she's not. She remembers the day on the beach when he risked his own life to save her; the times afterward, when he told her that she's beautiful.

Charles is several feet away, his head still down as he walks in the direction of the hill. "Charles!" she hears herself shout. Saint Emmanuel girls are warned against raising their voices in public. The world should see them as quiet vessels of God. But Thandi throws all this away when she runs after him. "Charles!" As she jogs, her bookbag slaps her back with its heavy weight. She lowers her umbrella; the sun is in her face, but she doesn't care. She's aware of the people watching, some stopping to let her pass. "Charles!" she calls in a panic. He continues to walk through the crowd. Only the back of his head is visible. Thandi picks up speed, knowing deep down that if she doesn't reach him, something inside her will crumble. "Charles!" Her voice is shrill, naked, broken. He stops. When he turns, she runs right into him. Her face is pressed to his chest, and she allows herself to be held by him, inhaling his ripe pawpaw smell. She imagines how it looks for her to be carrying on this way in public, but doesn't care. She's too tired to care.

"Thought yuh was in a hurry to get somewhere," he whispers quietly into the top of her head.

He takes her to his zinc shed. They pass the main shack, where his mother is probably staring at the ceiling, debilitated by the one thing Thandi now knows intimately—yearning. Charles takes off her clothes. He's gentle. The panic and desperation she felt earlier makes her willing to take him as he is—uncultivated, uneducated, unkempt, hard.

"Let me put it in, jus' a likkle," he whispers in her ear. She lies down on his bed, her back on the cool, rumpled sheet in complete surrender to this boy—the type of boy she was sheltered from. She opens up for him, but Clover appears in her mind. It's his breathing she hears; his rough kisses that she feels down her neck; his touch that makes her muscles clench like a tight fist. And that pulling and tugging and grunting to get inside, all of that his. She writhes with this memory, thrashing her limbs, her nails digging inside flesh, her teeth pressing into an earlobe. There's a sharp yelp. Clover is restraining her. Thandi spits in his face and screams until she's weak and exhausted.

When she opens her eyes a few minutes later, Charles has moved away from her to the other side of the bed, his naked body perched on the edge like a gargoyle in repose, his penis flaccid between his legs. He's staring at her, his pupils holding in them so many things that she cannot read, mostly questions. Pieces of his skin are under her nails, the moisture of his blood fresh on their tips. *What has she done?* In the silence he rolls a spliff and smokes it. He doesn't bother to tell her to get dressed, though she lies there naked, trembling, and covered in sweat. There's a cut over one of his eyebrows. Another one on his right cheek. A couple scratches on his arms and, she's sure, on his back. She reaches to touch him, but he flinches.

He lights the wick of the small kerosene lamp by the bed with a flick of his lighter. The lamp glows inside the shed. Thandi rests her head in the crook of her elbow and studies him in this light. A single tear runs across the bridge of her nose. "I'm sorry," she says finally.

But he only shrugs. "It's all right, is yuh first time. Ah shoulda been more gentle."

His face is obscured in the cloud of smoke he puffs. She reaches for him again. She doesn't want to go home. She doesn't want to see Delores. Or Margot. He doesn't pull away. Thandi gets up from the bed and stands before him. He lowers his spliff and tilts his head up at her. She bends to give him a kiss on his mouth, then on his throat. With his free hand he holds the back of her head to keep her face close to his. Their noses touch and she closes her eyes. "Yuh can stay as long as yuh want," he whispers. Thandi lowers herself onto his lap and buries her face in the crook of his neck.

26

WHEN MARGOT ENTERS THE HOUSE, DELORES IS THERE, HER elbows on the dining table, her head resting in her hands. Grandma Merle is rocking back and forth on a chair next to the bed. Delores straightens up when she sees her daughter.

"She's with you?" Delores asks.

"Who?"

"Yuh sistah! Is she with you?"

Margot shakes her head. "No, she's not."

Delores runs her hands over the purple hair-scarf she uses to cover her thinning braids. "But Jesus 'ave mercy. Where could she be?" It's eleven o'clock at night. "Weh she could deh dis late?"

"Did you ask the neighbors?" Margot asks her mother, feeling a little woozy from the wine she drank at the hotel. She had sat in a room by herself and poured herself glass after glass. She missed Verdene terribly, but every time she picked up the telephone to dial her number, she lost the courage the wine had given her and hung up.

"Maybe she's studying late somewhere . . ." Margot plops down on the bed and kicks off her shoes. She leans forward, resting her elbows on her knees and rubbing her temples with her hands, eyes closed. Her mother's talking in her ears, her voice rising.

"Which neighbor?" Delores asks. "Thandi don't talk to nobody in dis blasted community. She only go to school an' come home."

"You know dat for sure?" Margot asks her mother.

"Yuh sistah is not like you. She's a good girl."

"Mama, she's a teenager. She's not a likkle girl."

Delores is rocking back and forth like Grandma Merle. "Oh, lawd, what am I going to do?" She sniffs and uses the hem of her blouse to wipe her face. "Yuh see wah me haffi deal wid, Mama?" Delores asks Grandma Merle, who is silent. Margot notices the bruises on her grandmother's arms.

"Did you ask Grandma?" Margot asks, looking at the old woman, her eyes narrowing. "Maybe she saw something. She sees everything."

"Yuh don't see dat yuh grandmother is not a sane s'maddy?" Delores snaps.

"She's sitting right there. Ask her. You ask her what she sees. Ask her how many things she lets happen an' say nothing." Margot sits up on the edge of the bed. In reams of memories, she remembers her grandmother's knowing gazes. Margot used to like watching her make clothes, the concentration creasing her face. Back then, before her features became indistinguishable, she had high slanted cheekbones, a flared nose, and thick lips between which she held safety pins or threads. Margot kept Grandma Merle company as she hovered over the Singer, feeling they were in an intimate circle, joined together in the humming of the machine that made beauty from scraps.

"You is the mad one," Delores says. "You don't see yuh granny mute from yuh was fourteen? You did this to her. Ah have a feelin' dat is you give di money to Winston an' mek him run. Yuh mek him tek har heart wid him, leaving jus' a empty shell of a 'ooman. You! You mek t'ings haa'd fi people."

"Mama, I don't know what yuh talkin' about." Margot picks up Thandi's nightgown off the bed and holds it against herself.

"Yuh think me is a idiot?" Delores puts her hands on her hips, her shoulders squared, giving her upper body more proportion. "Because ah you, Winston run 'way. Ovah an' ovah me t'ink 'bout it. Me 'membah seh you did see where me hide di money! You was di only one who know 'bout dat money. You! Yuh lying snake. You is di livin' devil in flesh!"

Margot meets Delores's glare. "And what does that make you?"

"Now yuh sistah is missing and it's your fault!"

"So everything is my fault?"

"Yes. Yuh is nothing but a disgrace."

Margot steps back a little, afraid that her mother might pounce on her, hold her down and give her those pinches again.

"If anyone is to blame for Thandi acting out, it's you," Delores says. "Yuh brainwash har. The same how dat woman brainwash you . . ." Delores says this in a voice Margot could've mistaken for tenderness had her mother been a different person. "That was why I had to fix yuh."

Margot stumbles backward, as far away from her mother as possible. She bumps into the vanity. The mirror crashes down and breaks, the splinters scattering across the floor. Margot holds on to the edges of the vanity, helpless in her ability to defend herself from the memories. The black seeps into her, masking any sentiments, mangling any desire to forgive, hardening the weak pulp of a muscle beating inside her chest.

"You did more harm to me than anyone else," she says to her mother.

But Delores is defiant, her mouth drawn like a zealot's, convinced of the good of her actions. "It was the only way," Delores says. "The only way dat ah could save yuh from yuh ways."

Margot's rage finally breaks and she bounds toward her mother like a wildcat. She grabs Delores by the neck and backs her into the peeling wall next to where Grandma Merle sits rocking. Delores fights Margot off her, her hands clamping on Margot's wrists, Margot's hands around her neck like brass shackles. Margot doesn't give up.

"Go ahead an' kill me," Delores says. "Yuh might as well save me from this blasted life. Yuh is nothing but a low-down, dirty whore! A *nasty*, dirty, sodomite whore. And now yuh g'wan add murderer to yuh list. So kill me, yuh blasted fool!"

Margot loosens her grip around her mother's neck, but her hands don't fall. "Yuh have yuh place in hell," Delores growls.

Margot stands there with her hands around her mother's neck; but the evil look in her mother's bulging eyes is not enough to make her do what she thought she could. She wants desperately to press her face into the bosom of the woman she wishes had loved her, would hold her, rock her gently, stroke her hair. But Delores only spits in Margot's face, the slime running down Margot's right cheek, a thick and slow-moving tear.

27

VERDENE APPEARS ON THE VERANDA, FLOATING LIKE A GHOST in her nightgown. She doesn't move to open the grille to let Margot inside. They look at each other for what seems to Margot like an eternity. The chirping of the crickets grows around them. Verdene parts her lips like she's about to say something. The shadow of the moon, big and round, cuts her face in half. Her eyes fall to Margot's overnight bag. Margot tilts her head to the side, her eyes moist with all the words she wants to say. They weigh heavily, pressed like a rock against her rib cage. If only Verdene would let her inside. "Please?" she asks her lover. But Verdene lifts her head to the ceiling, sucking her quivering lip. When she lowers her head, Margot sees tears in her eyes too.

"Who do you think you are?" she asks.

Her voice is the scratch of a nail, a small cut that burns; it pierces the blackness around them.

"Just let me in, please?" she asks.

"How dare you, Margot? How dare you abandon me when I needed you? And now you come back begging me to let you in?"

"Please?"

Margot watches her move to open the grille, each click of the bolt loosening something inside her, this simple act of mercy.

Inside, the house is immaculate. With her back to Margot, Verdene picks up one of the pillows from the sofa, fluffs it, and puts it back. Margot watches Verdene's back, the boniness of it. She has gotten down to just skin and bones, the way her vertebrae stick out—round, protruding marbles in the back of her neck, visible through the sheer nightgown she wears. Margot suppresses the urge to wrap her arms around Verdene from behind. When Verdene turns around and peers at her out of a pair of hollow dark circles, Margot's hand finds the base of her own throat.

"You may have the couch," Verdene says. "I'm going to bed."

She walks off, leaving Margot alone in the living room. Miss Ella's pictures are back, staring at her from each frame as though reprimanding her: *Why have you hurt my daughter this way?* She goes to Verdene's room and peers through the crack of the door, watching Verdene remove her nightgown in front of the full-length mirror. Her body is leaner than Margot remembers. Her frailty more pronounced, like she can be broken into many pieces. A slow suicide is what it looks like. Margot pushes the door open, and Verdene drops her hands to her sides. She catches Margot's frown in the mirror. She doesn't move to cover herself. Margot walks toward her, and very gently clutches Verdene's bony shoulders. Her hands travel the length of Verdene's arms; and Verdene begins to weep softly. Margot turns her around and hugs her. "I'm sorry," she whispers.

She lowers her lips to Verdene's, but Verdene pushes Margot away. "Don't touch me," she hisses.

Margot disobeys her. Even as Verdene hits her, pounding her back lightly with her fists, then slapping her with big, open-handed slaps, Margot bears it. There are no screams, no shouts, just the sound of Verdene's slaps on Margot's back. Verdene fights and fights while Margot continues to cling to her. Margot closes her eyes as Verdene's blows pour down, for in this very moment she finally feels something more intense than she has ever felt. She feels alive, fighting for the one thing she thought was not meant for her. This feeling grips her, bringing tears and a deep sense of relief. The overhead light blinks as though all Verdene's rage has been transmitted to the fixture. The slaps begin to weaken, until they stop for good.

28

O N HER WAY HOME, THANDI TELLS CHARLES WHAT CLOVER did to her when she was nine. Charles is silent as she talks. Thandi is not sure if he's brooding or listening. He's still holding her hand, but she feels him stray somewhere in the dark. Peenie wallies swoop around them, dotting their path with glowing orange lights. It sounds strange to hear herself speaking to anyone about this. Delores would tell her never to wash dirty clothes in a public river. *"Dese people are human beings like you an' me,"* Delores said, referring to the priests in the confessionals at school. *"Dey hear yuh secret an' judge yuh jus' di same."* But Charles is different. Thandi feels at ease talking to him. Each word that leaves her mouth surprises her, dares her to tell more, and relieves her of a burden. Charles stops walking and turns to face her. He cups her chin with both his hands. Through the dark she makes out the glistening in his eyes, the ferocity of his voice when he speaks. "Him will haffi pay fah what he did," he says. His words are urgent.

"Charles, I'm fine," she says. "It happened long ago."

"If yuh was fine, yuh wouldn't have fight me like dat earlier." He's shaking his head, swatting away the peenie wallies that linger between them. Thandi can see a sense of purpose come into him—a gleam in his eyes—which might have washed down onto his cheeks had he not balled his hands into tight fists. It's a gleam she has seen in the past when he used to come over to the shack to collect Delores's leftovers. A shame that shaped his childhood and has now been projected onto her—stale, discarded, tainted goods. Frantically she searches his face for any hint of this, but finds it shut, inscrutable. "No, him mus' learn him lesson," he insists. "What he did was a crime."

"What will you do to him?"

"Don't worry 'bout dat."

"Don't do anything that will cost you. Yuh know he's a drunk. He can do anything."

Charles pulls away from her. A scowl transforms his face and twists it so that he talks from the side of his mouth. He walks a few steps ahead, his shoulders mounting like hills. Thandi runs to catch up with him. She tugs at his shirt. "What yuh going to do?" But he doesn't answer. He turns to her, just short of her gate. Mr. Melon is untying his goat. He's walking in their direction. When he approaches the both of them, he tips his hat. "Howdy." Charles and Thandi mumble a greeting to the older man. After he passes, Charles says, "Don't worry about what ah g'wan do. I'll take care of everything." He kisses Thandi and leaves her standing at her gate, panicked.

...

The next afternoon a crowd is gathered outside of Dino's Bar to watch Charles and Clover roll on the dusty ground like two lizards. Macka, the bartender, is trying to pry them off each other, but he stumbles backward when Charles pushes him off, the man falling over a group of small schoolchildren squatting nearby. The children scatter like mice, then return when Macka gets up and brushes himself off. "Fight! Fight! Fight!" the little boys yell. This brings more people to the scene—mothers who are just walking from the river with buckets on their heads. The women stop and lower their buckets to scoop their children close. This is not surprising to them, since the normal meanness that the heat and the sun brings is compounded by the drought, which provokes fits of rage. They set their eyes too on the young girl madly screaming, clamping both hands to her face, a woman in despair. "Stop it! Stop it!" This sets off mild whispers among the women, for they have only heard her speak just a decibel above a whisper. Always proper.

"What a sing t'ing!" they cluck, shaking their heads.

But Thandi ignores them. Her cries are uncontrollable. She stands away from the fight like the other spectators outside of Dino's. She had hoped Charles had forgotten his vengeance. He doesn't seem to care what might happen to him if he kills Clover. He's acting like a wild beast, a man with nothing to lose. Saliva fills her mouth as the urge to vomit rises.

Clover is weak and bloodied, but insists on fighting Charles, who is younger, more virile. Charles holds him down with his weight, wildly punching him. Clover pulls a knife. Charles struggles to pry it out of Clover's hand. "Somebody, please help!" Thandi screams, her blood running cold. But Charles wrestles the knife out Clover's hand, and in one swift motion Clover's shirt is ripped, a horizontal red gash printed on his shirt. Charles springs to his feet and Clover struggles to stand up. For a moment both men dance around each other, Charles with his shirt open and the knife in his hand, and Clover with his fists clenched and renewed strength and a dangerous look in his eyes. "C'mon, yuh pussyclaat, good-fah-nottin' bwoy . . ." he spits. "Yuh eat from people plate all yuh life, an' now dat yuh discover pussy yuh t'ink you is a man now." Charles drops the knife and lurches forward. Both of them are on the ground again.

"Oh, lawd 'ave mercy!" Miss Gracie shouts. She's stumbling out of the bar and into the street, a little tipsy, with the blind faith of a toddler walking into traffic. Miss Gracie is using all her strength to pull Charles off Clover, grabbing him by the end of his shirt as he punches Clover like a sack of rice. A few men—the types Thandi has seen hovering over pecking roosters with wild eyes filled with money and dust and sometimes tears of defeat—jump in to help Miss Gracie pull Charles away. Charles fights them off, but they outnumber him, pulling his hands behind him. Clover sits there in the middle of the road looking dizzy. He clutches his chest as if he's trying to locate a lizard slithering its way under his armpit. A few women stoop next to Clover to give him something to drink. They ignore Charles, who is busy snatching his arms from the men and then stooping to catch his breath.

The women around Clover start to scream. Clover is woozy, faint, bleeding from his nose and lip. "S'maddy help him!" Miss Louise shouts, untying her head scarf to dab Clover's forehead.

Someone yells for Macka to call an ambulance. But Macka doesn't have a phone, so he runs to Mr. Levy next door. Mr. Levy, who has long ago resigned himself to the shenanigans of the drunks next door, simply flips his newspaper and shakes his head. But Macka bangs on the mesh door. "A man is bleeding in di street, Missah Chin! How yuh stay suh? Have a likkle mercy an' call di ambulance!" Finally Mr. Levy picks up the phone and dials 119. It takes a long time for the ambulance and the police to come. Meanwhile, people are pointing at Charles. "*Is dat big-head bwoy do it!*" Thandi is able to catch Charles before he leaves the scene.

"What have you done?" She's pulling him, hitting him with both hands, demanding an answer. He just looks at her, his mouth down-turned. "Him get what him deserve," is all he says before he flees.

Clover is mounted on a stretcher and two policemen question residents, to discover the identity of the man who started the fight. They say that they have to make an arrest. Holding the knife—which was Clover's—as evidence, they say that only a dangerous criminal would attempt to kill a man cold-blooded in the street for no reason at all. Absolutely no good reason at all. But no one knows where Charles went. The news comes back later that night that Clover had a heart attack and died on the way to the hospital. But the people believe that it was Charles who killed him.

29

WHEN VERDENE SEES THE SHAKING BOY ON THE STEPS OF her veranda, she lowers the flashlight and opens the grille for him. He's bloodied and clutching himself as though trying to stop the shaking. Without asking any questions, Verdene wrestles one of his hands free from its grasp on his upper arm and leads him inside. JPS took the electricity again, so she lights a kerosene lamp to see. Charles sits still, resting his hands on the dining table where he once sat the first time she let him inside the house. Verdene regards the blood on his shirt. "Are you hurt?" she asks. Charles doesn't raise his head.

"Ah didn't know where else to go weh dey wouldn't look fah me," he finally says.

"What happened? Why are you running?" Verdene begins to wonder if she has made a mistake letting him inside before asking this question. She's suddenly fearful, but because she doesn't want the boy to think she is nervous around him, she busies herself with an internal script—the role her mother would have played.

"Let me at least get you cleaned up."

She gets up with the flashlight and goes inside the bathroom for a basin and washcloth. She also grabs a University of Cambridge T-shirt, which she inherited from her husband, out of her drawer. When she returns to the dining room, Charles still hasn't moved. He doesn't even seem to be breathing. The quiet roars in Verdene's ears as she holds the wet rag over his eyebrows. Slowly she wipes his forehead, the area above his mouth, and his hands. He winces when the damp cloth touches his upper arm where there's a gash. Verdene gets her first-aid kit and dresses it. "Calm down and just breathe," she hears her mother's voice say to him in a whisper. It must have been all the boy needed to hear, because as soon as Verdene says this, he breaks down. His body jerks with loud sobs, his hands covering his face. "What happened, Charles?" she asks, trying hard to keep her voice steady.

"Ah kill someone," he says. "Ah hear dat police aftah me now. Mama Gracie warn me."

Verdene regards him closely. His frame appears small and wilted in the light of the kerosene lamp. He doesn't look like a murderer, though his confession looms large inside the house, moving and shifting things. Something in the house braces. After a second or two, Verdene grabs a chair. "You what?" she asks.

"Ah kill someone," he repeats. "Him rape my girlfriend."

This time Verdene lets his statement fall inside the quiet like a single hair landing on the wooden floors. Not since she knelt by her father's stiff body on the kitchen floor after she watched him suffer a heart attack has she felt so paralyzed by ambivalence. She peers at Charles through the cloud of this memory, thinking how she had hurt with guilt for days, and how there were no remedies to quell the agonizing pain that she never expected to feel for the person who she thought deserved it. Verdene gets up and kneels in front of Charles. Her instinct is to grab him and comfort him, but instead she says, "Do you know for sure that he's dead?"

Charles nods. "Yes."

"Maybe you didn't kill him. Maybe he's just hurt."

"Ah know for ah fact dat him dead. Dat me kill him." His jawbone clenches. "When me look pon him face an' see him smiling like di devil himself, knowing dat him rape my girl, all ah wanted to do was to kill him. But ah didn't know when or how dat force tek ovah me. Next t'ing me know, me see Mama Gracie an' she tell me how dey pronounce him dead at di hospital."

"Oh, Charles . . ."

"Me neva mean fi kill him."

"I know you didn't mean to."

Charles looks at her. His face is colorless. Verdene has a feeling that if this man is really dead, then so is Charles. Not because of how the police treat criminals, but because of the guilt she senses has already begun to wear him down. Verdene wants desperately to ease his anxiety, so she decides on logic. "If you can prove that he raped your girlfriend, then maybe you can argue that you did it in defense."

Charles shakes his head and covers his face again. "There's no proof. It 'appen years ago." Verdene rubs his back, feels his muscles tense up again. "I can't stay here," he says suddenly. "I can't stay in Rivah Bank. Ah must get going." Verdene silently agrees, though she would never think of saying this out loud. She would have offered him a hiding place, but then she would have to explain to Margot when she drops by after her shift at the hotel and sees a boy—an alleged killer—inside the house. And besides, Margot can never be seen here by anyone. So Charles must go.

"At least change off first and eat something before you go," Verdene tells him.

"Ah can't eat anyt'ing." He takes off his bloody shirt and puts on the one Verdene gives him. "Thank you for this," he says, smoothing the fabric over his chest, his fingers trailing the University of Cambridge letters. He folds his soiled shirt, and Verdene offers to bury it outside, next to the dead dogs. She thinks of things to say to convince him that justice might still be on his side, but cannot come up with anything. "You must really love her. That girl?" she says as he heads toward the door. He pauses with his hand on the handle. The darkness is thick outside, since it's overcast and there are no stars or a moon tonight. One would think it might finally rain; but Verdene won't hold her breath. "Yes. I do," Charles replies.

"I would've done the same thing," she says.

Charles lets go of the knob. He leans against the doorpost and looks Verdene right in the eye. "Yuh know, ah used to be afraid ah witches."

With that, he leaves her in the dark. She looks around the house. Not since she returned to it, wanting to be closer to her mother, has she felt so alone. How repelled she is tonight by the floors, the walls, the curtains, the burglar bars by the windows through which most days she can barely see the wide expanse of the sky.

30

ALPHONSO CALLS MARGOT TO THE VILLA, WHICH HAS BECOME their meeting place. Sweetness is with her, because she happens to be on the schedule for tonight's soiree. But when they get there, the developers are frenzied. Alphonso is pacing, blowing cigarette smoke through his nostrils.

"What's going on?" Margot asks Alphonso as soon as she enters.

"The fucking police."

"Why are they involved?"

"A murder happened in the development area. They decided to shut down the whole fucking project until they find the killer. They think the activity from the construction could give the guy cover."

"What?"

"We're losing money, Margot. The longer the police make us wait as they investigate this crime, the more we suffer. Tourists aren't going to want to come to a high-crime area. The investors are shitting themselves as we speak! I got a call from Virgil. He's threatening to pull out."

"Calm down, I can fix this."

"How?" he almost shouts.

"Let me think."

An idea, which was really a thought uttered too loudly, too prematurely, surfaces from Margot's mouth; materializes into sound waves that halt the developers in the room, bringing them closer to the table where Margot sits. Alphonso too listens, his arms folded across his chest, visibly amused. "Where would we get the money to pay the reward?"

"We're flush with cash, Alphonso, and you know it," Margot says. "Sweetness alone is bringing in seven thousand a week. The other girls are just as profitable. We can do this."

"So ten grand and we solve everything?" one of the developers asks.

"Yes, ten grand," Margot replies. "I suggest we tell the constable about it so that he can relax his force. This money will have the residents of River Bank scouring every nook an' cranny for the criminal. In the meantime, we send Sweetness to the police station."

"Sweetness?" Alphonso asks. "Why Sweetness?"

"Because if you're going to take over a quarter of the island, then you should at least be smart about it. Be nice to the police. They can be your biggest allies or worst enemies. Like women, they love it when you bring them gifts."

The men in the room laugh. Alphonso laughs too.

"Margot, you're brilliant," he says.

...

Again people gather at Dino's. There's a search warrant for Charles and a prize of $10,000 in U.S. currency offered by the police department for the person who turns him over.

Word about the reward money spreads. No one knows why there's such a high price to find a scrawny boy who killed a drunk in a bar fight. Macka thinks the money has to do with the development in the area. "Those developers don't want no killah roaming 'bout di place. They want di worthy guests of dey hotel to be safe."

Some men have already paid a visit to Miss Violet's shack. They ransacked the place looking for Charles. The fact that they came in on a helpless woman means nothing to them; they were looking to fill pants pockets that only knew lint and loose change. They were already imagining the insides of airplanes and the promise of America. So when Miss Violet told them that she didn't know where her son was, they grabbed her by the throat and pulled her hair. One drew a knife and the other one a rope. Her screams were heard only by Miss Ruby, who ran from her shack to find the woman tied up in her bed with cuts on her face.

Thandi is paralyzed with regret. She lies on the bed, curled up under the covers. She clutches the towel she never returned to Charles and sniffs it, trying to inhale the memory of him.

"But is what is dis?" Delores asks, standing over Thandi. "Me leave an' yuh in bed. Me come back an' yuh still in bed. Ah wah do yuh?"

Thandi shifts under the cover, quickly wiping away her tears. "Jus' tired," she says.

"Tyad? Somebody can tyad so long? Yuh don't have nothing to do now the exams are finished? Get up!" Delores pulls the covers off Thandi. But Thandi doesn't move. "If ah count to tree an' yuh still lay dung, me will geet to yuh. Yuh know how much ah clock ah strike? Yuh have graduation rehearsal tomorrow, don't?"

Delores starts to move around in the kitchen to prepare dinner. Thandi sits up in the bed.

"Bwoy, me ah tell yuh 'bout dem yout' wid no ambition," Delores says as she slices open the skin of a green banana and drops the skinned banana into the pot. "Membah Violet boy, Charles? Di ole brute who used to come 'roun here fah food? Him deh pon di wanted list now. Ten thousand U.S. dollah." She whips around from the boiling pot to see if Thandi is listening. "Yuh hear? Ten thousand dollah! Yuh know wah dat can do?" She pauses as though Thandi is obligated to speak. When Thandi doesn't reply, Delores answers her own question. "It can buy we nuff t'ings!" She returns to skinning bananas. "But ah feel so sorry fah Violet now. Di poor woman lose everyt'ing 'cluding all di screws in har head. But I can tell yuh one t'ing, though. If she tell di police where her son is, she will get di money an' have a bettah life. True, true! She will be a rich woman if she send him to prison. Fah all di pain dat boy cause har. But dese hooligans 'roun here so hungry dat dem will t'ief it. Suh she should leave town an' not tell ah soul. See how dey do har wah day? T'ink she would tell dem where him hiding?" Delores peers at Thandi when she whips around again. Her eyes narrow. "I know 'bout you two. John-John saw di both of 'oonuh in Sam Sharpe Square hugging up like lovers. Yuh t'ink me nuh 'ave eyes 'roun here? If yuh know where he is, yuh should call it in. Do it fah all ah we. Yuh know how long ah could use a break? Every single day me bruk me back wid dese damn baskets."

Her mother is standing still by the stove, harping as if to the shadows that are perched nearby. "If yuh guh pick up wid a street boy, then yuh mus' at least get something out of it. Because what can a dutty, wingworm, gully bwoy who don't even own a pair of shoes do fah you, eh?"

"He's more than just a street boy," Thandi says when she regains her ability to speak.

Delores whips around. "Oh, suh yuh know where he is." This is a statement, not a question. Thandi doesn't like what she sees in her mother's eyes. It's a look she has seen before when asked about school and her grades—the image of herself crouched at the table with her books under the glare of the kerosene lamp mounting and mounting in her mother's pupils—a mammoth creature of her mother's lofty goals and dreams. It fills her mother's eyes, expanding the blackness and roundness that reminds Thandi of the look Miss Gracie gets when she experiences one of her holy visions.

"I didn't say that," Thandi replies.

"Di way yuh talkin' mek it seem suspicious. Yuh talkin' like yuh know where him is. For all I know, yuh coulda see him yesterday an' nuh tell a soul." Delores's voice is loaded with accusation. "I didn't sacrifice to send yuh to school fi guh pick up wid those types. You become di people you associate yuhself wid—" She pauses, her head shaking and her pointer finger wagging as though to make up for half of what she's thinking. Then the words appear—not the ones she seemed to search for, but new ones generated from somewhere as dark as the shadows from which she seeks counsel. Thandi can almost see them forming, rising from that place of darkness like soot from the inner workings of her mother's mind. Thandi is looking straight up into Delores's face, right up into her nostrils. "Do it fah all ah we, Thandi." She gestures to Grandma Merle, who is silently resting on her bed. Grandma Merle, who has long been a shadow except for the subtle rise and fall of her chest.

"I have a mind of my own," Thandi says.

"Yuh know where he is?"

"No, Mama."

"Yuh know wah ten thousand U.S. dollah can get we?"

"Yes, but I feel responsible."

"Responsible fah wah?" Delores stands up straight, no longer hovering over Thandi. She puts her hands on her hips. "What yuh sayin' to me?"

"He did it because of me."

"Wah?"

"Charles fought Clover because of me. I told him that Clover raped me years ago."

"Clover?"

"Yes."

"My Clover?" Thandi cringes at the possessiveness in her mother's voice. "Di Clover who used to come 'roun here an' help we wid t'ings 'roun di house? Clover who used to fix up di roof, mek sure seh we nuh get wet when it rain? Clover who guard di place when yuh wutless Uncle Winston lef'?"

"Yes," Thandi says.

"When was dis?" Delores asks.

"Six years ago. I was walking home from school, an' . . ."

Delores is quiet. She feels for a chair by the kitchen table and sits. The shadows flee back to their corners and crouch, waiting. Delores puts her hands on her head and slowly rocks herself the way Grandma Merle does in her chair. A sound erupts from her belly. It rises up as though through her air pipes, settling deep inside her throat, and stays. "Yuh turning into yuh sistah more an' more every day," she says in a low, raspy voice. "Jus' like har, yuh becoming a wench, a manipulative, trifling wench!" Delores stands up.

"Mama, Charles was only defending me."

"Why him need fi defend yuh now if it happen years ago?"

"Because it still affect me."

Delores comes close to Thandi, her arms open as if to embrace her. Thandi is prepared to rest her head against her mother's big breasts. She's ready to drop her shoulders and let her mother rub them, tell her that it will be all right. That Clover got what he deserved. The embrace is a sweet one—one Thandi had forgotten until now. Her mother's love is as vicious and domineering as her personality. Once it's felt, there is none other like it. Thandi relaxes in Delores's embrace, allowing herself to be rocked back and forth like a baby. But then it's cut short. Slowly, Delores pries Thandi off her and holds her at arm's length. "I want you to come to yuh senses an' turn dat boy in. Everything 'appen for a reason, an' dat was it," Delores says. "Do it fah all ah we, Thandi."

"He was defending me."

"Di devil is a liad. Him kick yuh dung, but it don't mean yuh can't get back up an' use the tool him fling give yuh. What Clover did is history. Something long gaan. So put it behind yuh an' do the right t'ing."

"Him is a brute, Mama."

"Shush! Yuh g'wan pay for cursing di dead." Delores pulls Thandi closer again and rocks her in her bosom. She smells like the green banana she sliced up. She runs her fingers through Thandi's hair as she speaks. "You an' dat bwoy Charles shouldn't mix in di first place. As me say, if yuh guh pick up wid a street boy, then yuh mus' at least get something out of it. Forget 'bout what Clover did. Dat won't set yuh free. Nuff people it happen to an' it didn't kill them. What will set yuh free is money. Don't say me neva teach yuh dat. I send you to school fah good reasons, yes. But is also for you to learn common sense. Yuh t'ink because Charles say him love yuh dat yuh worth something? Yuh t'ink because him say him want yuh dat him mean it? That is not one t'ing him aftah, an' when him get it, him run? What is dis love, eh? You don't know nuttin' 'bout no love. Love is foolish. Yuh eva see love put running wata inna pipe? Yuh eva see love build a roof ovah we head? Yuh eva see love give free education to those children whose parents can't afford school fee? Yuh eva see love full up we cupboard? Yuh eva see love hand we visa so we can go anyweh, far from dis rat hole? What can love do fah you, eh? How yuh g'wan love a stranger when yuh don't even know what love is? Him will jus' tek advantage of yuh an' walk away. Yuh haffi get yuh return in dollahs, not cents. An' besides, who g'wan want a naïve girl like you, eh?

"Suppose him did really want yuh. Could you really love some-body who is an absolute fool when it come on to these t'ings? Some-body who green? Yuh wouldn't want dat, an' neither would he. Yuh giving him everything fah free. Boys like chupid girls like dat. Dey tek one look at yuh black face an' know yuh desperate enough fi spread yuh legs at di first compliment. Dey see yuh true color before yuh tell dem yuh name. Dey know dey can tell yuh anyt'ing an' yuh black self believe it an' accept it, 'caw we so use to getting di left-overs. Who yuh know really love a black girl for more than what's between her legs? Yuh is a pretty black girl, but is my duty as yuh mother to teach yuh dese t'ings. Put somet'ing in yuh head. Chile, yuh know how much yuh coulda get? Ten thousand U.S. dollahs! Dat can tek yuh from here to eternity, pay fah yuh education an' everyt'ing. Use yuh head, chile. Yuh can't place more value on dis boy an' his foolish love over money. If it mean so likkle to you, then you'll lose everyt'ing. 'Membah dis, nobody love a black girl. Not even harself. Now get up an' guh get yuh pay."

31

THANDI GOES OUT TO THE BEACH, WHERE THE BOATS ARE tied. Asafa's boat is the brightest one, painted in red, yellow, and green. Over the years it has suffered some wear and tear, rusting on the sides. The letter *A* is missing from Asafa's name. Thandi makes her way to the boat and climbs inside. She sits on the rear wooden seat. By her foot is a white pail that she imagines Asafa used to store the lobsters he caught. From where she sits Thandi looks out at the ocean glistening in the sunset. This must be what Charles sees when he's out here alone. The waves are gentle, rising and falling like breath moving through a living body. The sea is liquid gold as the sun dips on the horizon. One by one the nocturnal insects hidden in trees inside the cove start to sing. The waves get louder in the presence of the new moon. They crash to the shore, their urgency driven by an invisible force. Thandi lies on her back inside the boat and listens to them. They speak to something stirring within her, something raging within her. The water rises and rises until it blurs her vision of the dotted stars above. It trembles at the corners of her eyes, then rolls down her cheeks.

"What color is di sky now?"

Thandi jumps when she hears his voice. She wonders if she's imagining it. But when she blinks, he's still there. She leaps up from the boat and into his arms, breathing in the familiar pawpaw musk mixed with smells of weed and sweat. His face is pressed into her neck. And Thandi thinks she feels something warm and wet. When she pulls back, she wipes his face with her fingers. "If yuh t'ink it blue, look again," he says. But Thandi is not interested in looking anywhere but at him. She flings her arms around his neck and kisses him. Charles climbs into the boat and they lie together between the seats.

"Yuh came out here to look fah me?" Charles asks.

"I missed you. They're looking for you everywhere."

"I leave for Kingston in a couple days. I'm only here to say goodbye to all this." He inhales deeply as if to take in all the air.

"Who yuh staying wid now?"

"Jullette."

"Jus' be careful."

"I didn't mean fi kill him."

"We don't really know if is you cause it. It could be anything. Don't be so hard on yuhself."

He cups her chin. "It was my fault. I'll accept di responsibility."

"I want to come with you."

"Yuh can't come wid me."

"How will we stay in touch?"

"I will find a way."

Thandi relaxes into him. She meets his passion with equal fervor, allowing this heat to take over, spread throughout her limbs, her core. The night forms a protective cloak around them. Their bodies move inside the boat like seals trapped inside a net, fighting to free themselves. The agony, the terror, the surrender.

Charles helps her out of the boat. He kisses her one last time before he departs. Thandi holds on to his hand. "I want to come with you," she says again.

"Not now. I'll let you know when. Right now it's not safe."

"What about Miss Violet?"

"Jullette will tek care of her. She moving wid har to St. Elizabeth."

Thandi wonders if he knows what Jullette does to make money. That moving out of Montego Bay wouldn't be good for the type of business she does.

She grips his arms. "Jus' take care of yuhself."

He kisses her goodbye and leaves her to the sound of the waves crashing.

32

MARGOT LEANS BACK IN HER NEW OFFICE. SHE KICKS OFF HER shoes and inhales. Through the partially open louver windows on her left she can see into the hotel lobby, though no one can see her. Right behind her are the beachfront suites where visitors lie flat on their backs and bellies in the bright sun while maids dash in and out of rooms with mops and linens. The walls in the office are decorated with accolades the hotel has won over the years, most of which were acquired during Reginald Senior's tenure. She's in charge in the interim as Alphonso still scrambles to replace Miss Novia Scott-Henry. It's up to her to prove she can do the job, which will also give her practice for the new hotel. She runs her hands along the wide mahogany table where all the paperwork sits in an orderly fashion, stacked and awaiting her signature. Pens and pencils are kept inside a steel cylindrical holder. Important folders are stacked solemnly inside a drawer at her feet. Margot brings her cheek to the surface of the table.

She breathes, carefully exhaling into the open room, afraid to disturb the silence. Her lipstick leaves a mark that she quickly wipes clean. She swirls around in her adjustable chair a few times, glad that no one can see her. Happiness feels like an office with good air-conditioning, a chair that adjusts to her back as though it is made for her, a mahogany desk with her name on it, a better view of the beach, the ability to slip out of her shoes and wiggle her toes, and a door she can keep locked. She can't believe that Miss Novia Scott-Henry had all this to herself yet chose to leave the door wide open. Margot will only respond to visitors who call in first through Kensington.

So when Sweetness barges in unannounced, Margot nearly falls out of her chair. She scrambles to slide her feet back inside her shoes and sit up straight. "Who let you in?" Margot asks the girl.

"It doesn't mattah now. Yuh secretary out there reading har Bible."

Margot fights the urge to ask the girl to retrace her steps so that she can be announced the right way, but stops herself. Sweetness's eyes are red. Margot hasn't seen or heard from her since last week. There were clients who refused to be paired with other girls when Margot told them that Sweetness was unavailable. She has become a client favorite. Margot should be furious with this unannounced visit; but she has never been so happy to see the girl. Though Sweetness looks disheveled, like she has not washed in days. Her hair is matted on her head and she wears no makeup to hide the blemishes on her cheeks. Her blouse and skirt are mismatched, as if she got dressed in the dark.

Margot leans back in her chair and clasps her hands in front of her.

"Yuh look like Satan drag yuh through hell," Margot says to the girl. "Please sit."

"Is okay, ah won't be long," Sweetness says.

"We've been losing money because of you," Margot says. "This meeting won't be determined by you. Sit."

"I'm sorry," Sweetness says, still standing.

"Sorry?" Margot looks up at her. "Yuh know how much money we coulda mek dis week alone if you were here? 'Membah we have more responsibilities now"

"I know."

"So what's yuh excuse?"

"Excuse?"

"Why haven't you been to work?"

"Work?"

"Sweetness, what's di mattah wid yuh?"

"I can't do dis anymore."

"What?"

Margot gets up from her chair.

"I can't work fah yuh no more, boss lady."

For the first time since the business started, Margot has never felt so dependent on a girl. Like the men that Sweetness leaves begging for more, Margot is tempted to throw money at the girl. She would throw herself if she has to. What will she do without Sweetness? "What yuh mean, yuh don't want to work anymore? Why?"

"Ah have to go, boss lady," Sweetness says, holding her head down and clutching the raggedy leather purse on her shoulder. "Ah not coming back." She heads toward the door.

"Sweetness!"

The girl stops. Margot hurries around the desk toward her. The girl stands still, trembling. Margot cups her chin. "You know I care about you. You know I'll do anyt'ing for you." She draws her face close to Sweetness, who closes her eyes and parts her lips, her sweet, eager breath hot on Margot's face. She exhales slowly through her mouth, which Margot grazes with her own. "Jus' stay wid me till the end," Margot whispers. "You're my number one girl."

She strokes Sweetness's arm. But Sweetness pulls away.

"Yuh only care 'bout dat other hotel. You don't care 'bout me. If yuh did care, you woulda tell Alphonso to call off di reward or I will—"

"You know di reason why I had to," Margot says, cutting her off. "Don't pretend you don't know."

"Unlike you, is blood dat pump through me vein. Not greed."

"Sweetness!" Margot reaches for her arm again.

"Nuh touch me! Either yuh tell Alphonso to change him mind, or I will mek sure to let him know how yuh scheme fi get dis office."

Margot folds her arms across her chest. "Yuh t'ink because yuh give good pussy dat you have a voice? Dat yuh is worthy of an opinion? Yuh is nothing but a tar-black country girl wid not even a high school education. A girl wid nothing going for her but har long legs an' big behind. Yuh t'ink anyone want to hear what yuh have to say? You'll never talk to di Alphonsos of dis world without being laughed at. To them, you're a servant. And will always be a servant."

"So be it, then," Sweetness hisses. She walks out of the executive office and slams the door behind her. Margot whips around and with all her might hits the cylindrical pen-and-pencil holder off the desk. It crashes to the floor and rolls out of sight, all the pens and pencils scattered on the immaculate floor.

33

THE BULLDOZERS APPEAR OVERNIGHT. THEY STAND IN PLACE like resting mammoths, their blades like curved tusks. It's as though they landed from the sky or were washed ashore. One by one they begin to knock down trees in the cove and along the river. They also take a chunk of the hill, cutting down the trees that cradle the limestone, which they chip away. Their big engines grind two-thousand-year-old tree trunks—trees the ancestors once hid behind, crouching in search of freedom. The workmen, imported from overseas, gather the fishing boats and load them on a truck. The men fold the earth in ways Thandi would have thought impossible. Bits and pieces of rock scatter as trees are uprooted. When they collapse, the earth shakes. A huge silence follows. Thandi always knew that the sky would fall. The clouds gather together, and the sun stands still and watches her world crumble. People begin to snatch their things from their shacks, forced into the unknown, leaving just the John-crows that brood like hunchbacked witches sniffing death under their armpits. The men rope off the fishing village, right where you go when heading to Miss Ruby's or Charles's shacks. Those shacks are marked to be destroyed. But Thandi has an inkling that her side of the river might be next.

Rumor has it that Miss Ruby, interrupted from rubbing cream on her face one morning, stood outside her shack and cussed the men. "*Ovah me dead body! Oonuh tek everyt'ing else, but not me house! This is mine!*" The men must have taken one look at Miss Ruby's white face and decided she was an obeah woman wielding spells with her wild hand gestures and that strange language that she spoke. All of a sudden the earth started to shake. The shaking was harder and longer than the tremble of the falling trees. The men clutched their helmets and searched for safety. They ran for cover, diving behind bushes and under sheets of zinc. After the shaking stopped, they came out slowly, cautiously, and surveyed the damage around them. They then looked at the white-faced black woman, who appeared just as stunned as them. Later it was reported that what they had experienced was an earthquake. They decided to halt the construction until a later date. They left the bulldozers where they were, the engines baring their teeth like a threat, leaving the residents of River Bank to wait for whatever will come next.

Currently there is yellow tape all over town. The warning is as clear as the sun. In a matter of weeks, River Bank will be no more. Everyone gathers to meet at Dino's at night to discuss the development. They talk and talk, the men pounding fists on tables or countertops and the women shaking or holding their heads. Macka offers them hard liquor, like he offered the farmers when their crops had started to die, and they take gulps, not sips, throwing their heads back and wiping sweat from ridged foreheads. Little children play hide-and-seek under the tables and chairs, avoiding the grown-ups, who are beside themselves in panic. Even if they block River Bank Road in protest, the developers will still proceed. Look what happened to Little Bay. They have already erected hotel resorts on top of people's homes, and they will do it again and again.

In the midst of their chatter, Verdene Moore appears in the doorway. A hush falls over the bar. Even the children stop playing to look. She glides inside Dino's without a pause, as though she has always belonged. As though she hasn't noticed the women shifting to avoid touching her, the mothers hissing for their little girls to move away, and the men clutching their bottles like a neck they want to strangle. Thandi, who is seated beside Delores, watches her with curiosity. Verdene smiles at Thandi and she almost smiles back before remembering not to. Verdene sits next to her. "Hello, Thandi," she says, her voice laced with familiarity. An agitated Delores grabs a slipper as if to hit Verdene. "Get behind me, Satan!" Delores shouts.

"I'm not going to let you run me off again," Verdene says calmly. She doesn't move away from Delores and her slipper. "My mother didn't raise a coward. This is my community too. I was born and raised here just like you." She glances around the room. "Just like all of you."

One by one people take their hands from their jaws or lolling heads to look. They become animated in their disapproval again, Verdene's presence seeming to revitalize their spirit. "Yuh crazy?" Macka asks Verdene. "Why yuh t'ink yuh can come in here an' stan' up like yuh own di place?"

"This problem concerns me too."

"It might do yuh more good to leave." Macka moves closer to her like he's about to do something.

"I'm not the one to blame," Verdene says. "Why don't you focus your energy on those who are responsible?"

"You're a bigger devil," Delores says. "Worse than the devil driving us out of our country." The room quiets, its occupants waiting to see which way the conflict will go. Verdene walks up to the bar and stays, her body stiff with determination. Realizing she's undeterred by their bullying, and sick with their own troubles, everyone returns to clutching their bottles of liquor to wet their parched mouths and throats, completely drained and powerless as they were before.

Thandi stares out into the darkness as Margot brushes her hair. Like old times, she's sitting between her sister's legs absorbing the comfort of the gentle strokes, the mild scrape of the bristles on her forehead as she bends her head back, the *sheesh-sheesh* sound of hairs being pulled from the roots and tickling the back of her neck soothing. Thandi is sitting with her knees pressed to her chest and her arms encircled around them. It's dark except for the kerosene lamp that Margot uses to see what she's doing, and the wood fire that burns nearby, the flames crackling in the cool night air. Margot is humming a song Thandi doesn't recognize. Earlier Thandi had heard her mother and her sister whispering about her, their hissing fight stirring from the back of the house. She knows it has to do with her being withdrawn over the last few days. Delores went out to get more eucalyptus leaves from people who have the trees in their yards, to boil for Thandi's bath. They want her back to her old self as graduation approaches, but her ache is deeper than any she has ever felt. It's deeper than her bones. A soul ache that rattles her already fragile body so great that it knocks her down and yanks her under the throes of a restless sleep. When she's awake, all she can do is try to recall those dreams that were swept away by the turbulent waves. In her waking moments the water closes quickly over the place where Charles disappears, though Thandi can still feel him—the pressure of his body on hers.

Margot gently parts Thandi's hair into sections and applies Blue Magic on her scalp like a balm. Thandi inhales the familiar scent, which mixes with her sister's. She closes her eyes and just feels Margot's fingers massaging her scalp.

"You told me dat yuh didn't have a boyfriend," Margot says gently.

"What does that have to do with anything?"

"We agreed."

Margot begins to massage Thandi's scalp again with the oil. "Now look at all the pain he caused you, when this is supposed to be the happiest time of yuh life." Her voice is as soft as the hair on Thandi's shoulders. "I've never seen you like this. Thandi, yuh have to snap out of it. He's not coming back. This is the kind of thing that mek women go mad, yuh see all those mad people in di streets wid their hair like thundahclouds an' privates exposed? They get like that because they expected too much. Nothing lasts forever, Thandi." She picks up the comb and resumes her languid strokes. "Delores used to give me baths." Margot's voice cracks. "I was sick too. Sick wid the same t'ing. Over a girl who told me I was pretty." Margot chuckles at this. "Ached all ovah my body. Ah couldn't explain what was happening to me. Nothing Delores did could get me back to myself. I didn't know what it was then that made me so . . ." She pauses when Thandi turns around to look at her, flame dancing in her eyes. "I was young. And naïve," she says. "But I knew something was inside me. Felt it here." She puts her hand to her belly. "It was like a ball of fire. Delores thought the baths would heal the sickness. She thought all sorta things. Even took me to ah obeah woman to get rub down wid oil an' black magic concoction. Di woman gave me goat blood to drink in a soup an' I ran. But there was nothing that coulda get my mind off her."

"What yuh saying, Margot?"

"I neva thought of myself as di devil," she says.

Thandi gets up from between her sister's legs, and stands in the dark.

Margot looks up at Thandi from where she sits, the red dress she wears between her legs. "I mean, I was a child. What did I know? Maybe I thought it was something special because I was shown love an' affection that I never got from my own mother." Margot shrugs. "Delores made sure I came to my senses."

"How did she do that?" Thandi asks, the questions swirling inside her head. She makes out Margot's face in the light from the flames and the kerosene lamp next to her.

Margot shrugs, avoiding Thandi's eyes. "She put me in situations where I . . ." Margot's voice trails off as though the words are stuck in her throat. "I met new people—men—who offered me a lot more. Delores introduced me an' they liked me."

"But you were—"

"Young. The cure. That's what Delores said. Di first one was a man who gave her six hundred dollars an' in return she gave me to him. It only made me sicker. But dis sickness was different than the first—the first had to do wid losing someone I cared for and who cared for me. The second had to do wid losing myself. But it worked. Because I couldn't hurt no more. I could no longer feel. It's been easier that way."

Thandi stares at her sister in confusion, Margot's eyes rimed with the charcoal, her blood red lips, the red dress, the overnight bag she packs that sits nearby. "Ah don't get it," Thandi says, shaking her head. "All of dis is not making any sense."

"The only person I ever loved was you, Thandi. You asked for nothing, so I gave you everything. An' I work hard suh dat Delores neva feel she can use you di way she used me."

"Clover hurt me and you weren't there to protect me." Thandi blurts this out to Margot. "All Charles was doing was protecting me. He doesn't deserve to be punished for it."

Margot drops the comb that she has been holding all this time. "When?"

"In primary school."

Margot mutters something under her breath. She doesn't say anything else for a while. Thandi is looking at her sister, who is clutching both hands so tight that the bones of her knuckles are visible against the skin, even in the dim lighting. She just squats there. Her eyes, from what Thandi sees in the light of the crackling flames, are still like glass.

Margot awaits Delores's return in the stillness of the dark veranda. Thandi and Grandma Merle are asleep inside; and the whole place is quiet except for the songs of the crickets that are hidden in the bushes and Pregnant Heidi thrashing about under the full moon. Flashlights blink in the dark like the illuminated bodies of peenie wallies as the search for Charles continues. When the gate opens and closes and Delores's form appears in the doorway, Margot stands. The wooden chair creaks, relieved of her weight.

"Who dat?" Delores asks. Margot imagines her mother squinting in the direction of the sound. She walks slowly toward Delores like a bride approaching a groom, the dark veil lifting halfway up her face.

"Why yuh sitting in dark like dat?" Delores asks when she sees Margot. "Is me yuh waiting for?" Her perplexed face peers at Margot, who offers no answer.

"You know what he did?" Margot asks. A vein throbs fiercely at the base of her neck.

"Who?" Delores says.

"Clover," Margot hisses, bitterness rising from her gut, coating her tongue.

At the utterance of the dead man's name, the crease disappears from Delores's face and she remains motionless in the moonlight. Margot steps closer and Delores steps back in panic, as though Margot is everything she has ever feared. As though she were death itself, here to claim her too. "Why yuh questioning me about di dead?" Delores whispers.

"Answer me!"

"You is nevah around."

"Why didn't you tell me?" Margot demands.

"What was I supposed to do? Go up to dat palace dat yuh work at an' announce it? She jus' tell me 'bout it last week."

"Yuh could have told me!" A choked scream comes from Margot's throat. The sounds of the crickets and Pregnant Heidi's scream grow louder.

"An' what would you have done about it, eh?" Delores asks. Margot's grip tightens on the overnight bag over her shoulder. For once her mother is right. What could she have done? All her life Margot thought she could shield her sister, protect her; but Clover has proven to her at last the futility of her effort. Margot whispers, more to herself than to Delores, "We let him in our house."

Delores's hands drop, and with them the defense she usually puts up when she's around Margot. "People g'wan disappoint in life. Is jus' so it guh." She gives Margot an apologetic look, but Margot is wary; she sees a dark satisfaction under its mute plea for forgiveness. "At di end ah di day, dis is we life. Look around yuh, gyal. Look where yuh is. Dis piece ah ground worth more than we. Yuh see dis air we breathing? Is debt we owing."

The air is stale, the dust-yellow lights piercing the night, looking for Charles, as clear as the moon that follows men with machetes all over town. Pregnant Heidi's screams rush in to fill the silence on the veranda of the shack, impurities of the past dredging from the bottom. Standing before her mother in the glare of the moonlight, Margot refuses to hum the same tune of grief. She begins to walk down the steps when her mother stops her. "Yuh sistah is a smart girl," she says. "Ah tell har to do di right t'ing an' turn in dat boy fah di money. Ten thousand dollars is a whole lotta sorry."

Giving Delores a final bitter glance, Margot leaves.

34

MARGOT TAKES A SHORTCUT TO VERDENE'S HOUSE. THOUGH she's aware of the danger in going to Verdene's during the active search for Charles, she needs to clear her head. Put things back into perspective. She cuts across Miss Gracie's yard, perhaps trampling the already dead cayenne peppers as she makes her way to the back of the pink house. She lets herself inside through the back door, careful not to make the bolt on the grille squeak when she lifts it. The house is quiet as usual, but from the orange glow inside the bedroom, Margot can tell that Verdene is still awake. She slips out of her shoes and drops her bag on the floor. She heads to the bedroom and pushes the door open. Verdene is sitting up in bed with her reading glasses, sheets of paperwork scattered around her.

She's sexy this way. Margot bends and kisses Verdene deeply. "I'm home," she whispers. She steps away and unzips her dress, letting it fall.

Verdene takes off her glasses and places them carefully on the nightstand. As Margot searches for a nightshirt in the dresser, she pauses and puts her head back, inhaling the patchouli incense Verdene lights to keep the mosquitoes away. Margot wasn't prepared for what Thandi had told her, but all that is in the past. Soon she will celebrate Thandi's future and move them from this godforsaken place. And from Delores. She and Verdene haven't made love in a week with all the late-night shifts managing the girls. Plus Verdene is selling the house, and the paperwork has been keeping Verdene occupied. Margot doesn't know what's taking her so long, and quite frankly, it's making her a little nervous. Maybe this is her fault, since she discouraged Verdene from hiring a lawyer. All Verdene has to do is sign the contract, which was drafted by a subsidiary group under the Wellington Estate. Alphonso did not want his or Wellington name on the contract, and Verdene is the last property owner in River Bank who has not signed yet.

"Come here." Verdene gets up off the bed to pull Margot close. She lowers herself just a little and puts her head under Margot's chin, slipping her arms around Margot's waist.

Margot cups her face. "We're about to build this new life together, might as well we celebrate that." Verdene nods in agreement and kisses Margot on the chin, then on the lips.

"Wait till you see the design of the sunroom," Margot says, thinking of the sketch of the dream villa in Lagoons that the architect showed her at the office today. She was finally able to put down money for it with her raise. "Everything will be made of glass."

"I'm excited," Verdene replies. "But first things first. I still have a couple pages to read." She steps away slightly and assumes a mannerism Margot imagines she adopted from her days as an editor.

She has never seen the business side of Verdene. Had not counted on it to interfere with the progress of the new development. "I have to read every word carefully before I sign on the dotted line. I don't trust these—"

Margot puts her finger on Verdene's lips. She slips her right hand down Verdene's pajama pants, for she would not be able to tolerate another excuse. Not tonight. It seems as though Verdene, despite her resistance, cannot wait either, because they collapse onto the pile of papers beneath them, some of which sail off the bed, loose and free.

35

MORNING CARRIES THE SOUND OF A ROOSTER AND THE BIRDS and, if you listen closely, the waves in the sea too. Morning also carries with it the residues of a sleepless night. Margot had left with her overnight bag slung over her shoulder after awkwardly kissing Thandi on the forehead. At breakfast Thandi plays around with her food, using her spoon to stir her cornmeal porridge. Delores watches her from across the table. She's waiting on Maxi to take her to the market. Margot hasn't returned.

"Ah wondah where yuh sistah could be," Delores says. Thandi doesn't respond. She can't. Neither can she look at her mother. "Ah tell yuh 'bout dat Margot. She see dat yuh sick an' can't even tek time fi stay wid yuh. She know me haffi go work. Unlike she, ah can't get no time off." Delores fidgets with the two bags of eucalyptus leaves on the kitchen table that she got last night. She gets up to put them on the kitchen counter, then walks over to feel Thandi's neck to see if she has a fever. Thandi flinches. "Is wha do yuh?" Delores asks.

"You sold Margot," Thandi blurts this out, unable to keep it in any longer. She still cannot look at her mother.

"Is dat what she tell yuh?" Delores asks.

"How could you do such a thing, Mama?" Thandi turns to face Delores.

"Watch how yuh talk to me. Me is yuh mother."

"She was young."

"An' sick." Delores lowers herself into a chair. "Yuh sistah was sick. Possessed. Did she tell yuh 'bout dat? Ah bet she neva mention dat. Ask har 'bout Verdene Moore. She was di cause ah har sickness. Dat Verdene did something to dat chile. Put di devil in har. Mek she tell 'bout dat."

So it's true after all. All of it. And Verdene Moore is a part of this? Margot never mentioned the girl's name. Thandi pushes her bowl away. It repulses her to look at it. She fed out of Delores's hands, licking the lifelines in her dirtied palms. Thandi breathes calmly, hoping that this will appease her unsettled stomach.

"Yuh sistah did need straightening out. She did need fixing. So I fix har."

"But why?" Thandi hears her voice come out small, like a baby chicken hatching out of an egg.

"Me was sixteen years old when ah had Margot. I was a young girl who neva know me lef' foot from me right. Margot father was a man who all di children in di community used to call Uncle. Him took special interest in me. Maybe because me was fat. I was big for a young girl an' him did like dat. When me get pregnant, my mother ask me is who'fa pickney. I tell her dat di pickney belongs to Uncle.

She get so mad dat she beat me terrible. Everyt'ing aftah dat hurt. Margot come, an' jus' di sight of har hurt. Then yuh father came along. A good-looking coolie man wid hair down to him shoulders. Him did come to visit him cousin who was living in River Bank at di time. Nice, nice man. Me an' him was together for a couple months. An' two months lata ah was pregnant. When him found out about it, him neva like it. I neva like how him look at Margot either. She was fifteen at di time. Is she him did want. Ah couldn't do nuttin' 'bout dat. Him was helping me a likkle wid money. But it wasn't much. As long as him could have Margot. One day ah come home an' see yuh father gone. All him t'ings dem pack up an' gone. Ah ask Margot where him gone an' she tell me dat she refuse him, an' him neva like dat. So him disappear. Raising two children on yuh own is not easy. Yuh hear wha' me tellin' you? Not easy a'tall, a'tall."

Thandi wraps her arms around herself, because suddenly she is cold. She thinks of the man with the oblong face—the beautiful man she imagines as her father. He never wanted her. He wanted her sister. "It was him putting food in di cupboard dem," Delores says. "Margot already did owe me fah everyt'ing ah went through wid har. Di least she could do was—"

There's a knock on the door. Delores moves to open it. A man dressed in a white shirt and black pants greets her when she goes out on the veranda where Grandma Merle sits. Thandi can see his silhouette through the curtain. She can also see the silhouettes of the other men that accompany him. They hold narrow cylindrical tubes across their shoulders. As the main man talks, the other men survey the yard and the field where Mr. Melon ties his goat. The main man is American. Thandi can tell. "Good day, miss. We're giving these out to all the residents who don't own property here, but are renting. We've gotten the green light from the property owners." He hands Delores a letter, then leaves. The other men go with him to the next shack.

Delores hands the letter to Thandi for her to read it out loud. Thandi looks at the piece of paper before taking it.

Dear Resident,

We are officially informing you of the development of a brand-new hotel resort on this property and hope that you will cooperate with us. We kindly ask that you vacate your premises by **August 1ˢᵗ**. The owner of this property, Mr. Donovan Sterling, has sold us the right to build our hotel resort here. Failure to vacate by the requested date will result in forceful evacuation. Thank you for your cooperation.

"But Jesus, lawd 'ave mercy, Missah Sterlin' sell we out. Weh we aggo go?" Delores snatches the letter from Thandi and reads it herself, her eyes moving swiftly over the page. When she finishes, she blindly searches for a chair to sit down on and stares at the ceiling. Delores then lowers her head and looks at Thandi. "Is dis is punishment fah what I did? I'm not a bad mother," she says, mostly to herself.

36

EVERY DAY THANDI FEELS THE FUTURE SLIPPING AWAY FROM her. Having light skin and going to medical school seem distant dreams, and even the results of her exams promise little in the way of hope. Her family is falling apart. She needs Charles. He is the one person who won't fail her. She packs a few things in her bookbag— clothes, her sketchpad, Charles's towel. It's barely dawn, before the rooster crows. Delores and Grandma Merle are asleep. Margot is still gone. Thandi slips out the front door of the shack. She walks briskly down the path that leads farther away from the hill. She walks in the opposite direction of the women who saunter to the river with pails on their heads—women who march together to the river that is miles from where they live, only to see that it's blocked off by cement and working tools. They return to their towns, each one with her neck held straight to balance her pail and what appears to be the weight of the world on her head.

The sun is peering above the hill, just the cap of its head rising. The sky is a clear violet blue sprinkled with leftover stars and half of a moon. Thandi quickens her pace. She has to get across the Y-shaped river to where Charles's mother lives. She might be lucky enough to get Miss Violet to tell her where Jullette lives. She opens the gate despite the yellow tape. Mary and Joseph are no longer in the pen. Someone must have taken them to sell. Or killed them. The four dogs roam the yard, their bones more visible, protruding through their skin like ridges of broken sticks. They follow Thandi, sniffing up her skirt. "Shoo! Shoo!" She waves them off. She bypasses Charles's zinc shed and goes directly to the main shack, where she knocks. There's no answer. No sound. The familiar foul smell hits Thandi when she pushes the door open. This time there are no cooing sounds to guide her as she makes her way farther inside, feeling around in the dark shack. She pauses when she gets to the upholstery curtain that shields off the bedroom. Thandi pushes it aside, looking for the woman lumped on the bed. But when she parts the curtain there is no sign of Miss Violet. Just the soiled rumpled sheets. She has already left.

Thandi backs away, nearly stumbling this time over a footstool. She goes next door to Miss Ruby's shack. Before she knocks, she sees an eviction note posted on the door. By the faded look of the paper, it seems to have been there for weeks. Thandi bangs on the door, her heart somersaulting in her chest. Her dream of finding Charles seems further away with Miss Violet gone. Miss Ruby might know something. When Miss Ruby opens the door, Thandi is surprised to see the woman's face. It appears bruised all over with purple blemishes on her cheeks. Gone is the clear salmon-colored hue she bragged about just months before. Presently she appears to have aged, her skin paper-thin, wrinkled, and blotchy like a days-old navel orange. When Miss Ruby sees Thandi staring, she fumbles with her house-dress, bringing the collar up to her mouth. "What is it yuh want so early in di mawnin'?" Miss Ruby asks.

Thandi tries her best not to appear troubled by Miss Ruby's appearance. "Do you know where Miss Violet went?" she asks.

A deep scowl transforms Miss Ruby's face. "Why yuh askin' me dat fah? Me look like me keep tabs pon people? I survive by min'ing my own business."

"Do you at least know where Jullette lives? I have to find her. I have to find Charles."

"Where have you been? Yuh so locked into yuh books dat yuh not even know what time it is. Everybody want to know where Charles is. Him is a wanted man. Anyone who know where him is, is a rich s'maddy. Rich enough to buy a house and not be treated like shit. If I did know where dat brute was, me woulda move out long time. Suh why would you ask me such a stupid question? Now get away from me front door an' nuh come back unless yuh have money for my service." She looks at Thandi's face. "From where ah standing, it look like yuh need more rubbing."

"No, thank you," Thandi says.

"Yuh sure 'bout dat? Didn't I tell you? Didn't I tell yuh dat God nuh like ugly? Look what's happening to us."

But Thandi turns and walks out of Miss Ruby's yard without looking back.

She hurries toward the square before the sun rises entirely. She passes Miss Gracie's house and stops by the mango tree where she once spotted Charles and his gang stealing and devouring mangoes. Thandi reaches toward the lowest branch and picks one. But when she lowers the mango, she sees that it is rotting, the inside carved out by worms. She tosses it and keeps moving. When she gets to the pink house, she slows her pace. The French shutter windows are closed, but leaving the house in this early morning hour is her sister. Margot stops in her tracks when she sees Thandi. And Thandi halts too, her breath drawn so sharply that it hurts her lungs.

"Thandi, wait!" Margot says. She's opening the latch on the gate.

"You didn't have to lie to me," Thandi says as soon as her sister approaches.

"Ah didn't think you'd understand."

"You could have told me that it was *her.*" Thandi has this odd feeling that they are being watched from a window inside the pink house.

Margot touches Thandi on the arm. "I'm sorry—"

Thandi pulls away. She starts to run, ignoring Margot's plea for her to come back. She cuts through a grassy area, wiping away tears from her face. Her feet pound the ground, stirring up dust. She has to find Charles. Her bookbag slaps against her back the way it did that day when she chased him through the streets. When she reaches Sam Sharpe Square, she turns and turns, unsure where to look first. She doesn't know where Jullette is hiding Charles. Who could she talk to? Where can she go? She sits outside and observes the gradual chaos of the shoppers, hoping Jullette will appear. Thandi waits the whole day, until sundown and the sky becomes a stunning shade of violet and fuchsia.

On the street she spots two women in short tube dresses. One of them has rail-thin limbs. The rest of her looks like parts belonging to another woman—a high, round ass upon which one could rest an elbow, and sizable breasts that squeeze together inside the dress like two breadfruits, the way grocers display them in the square. The other woman is big all around—her voluptuous frame snug in the little elastic dress that looks like it's about to bust open when she heaves and sighs from the fitful coughs caused by the smoke from her cigarette. The women are standing together behind the veils of smoke, their eyes alert on the pedestrians. The skinny one digs into her purse for a small compact mirror. She grins to check for lipstick stains on her teeth and pats her short black wig. But really it seems as though she's trying to check out the man who just passed them by—as if to gauge if he's looking back at her. Her fat friend shakes her head when she turns and sees that the man is walking straight ahead, not even giving them a backward glance. The skinny one puts the mirror back inside her purse and rolls her eyes. Thandi approaches them.

"Can we help you?" the fat woman asks. Up close she looks a lot older than she dresses, the skin on her face ashy and drooping as though all the elasticity has been worn.

"Yes, I think so," Thandi says, uncertain.

The two women glance at each other before they look at Thandi. "How much?" the skinny woman asks. She's wearing a lot more makeup, complete with fake eyelashes and a drawn-on mole on her upper lip.

"I—uh." Thandi is speechless.

The women burst out laughing. "Lawd, Doreen, yuh laugh like a damn hyena! No wondah why no man nuh want yuh!"

"Shut yuh claat, gyal. Yuh laugh like faa'ting donkey."

The fat woman taps her friend on the forehead and her friend fans her off, the way one fans off a person they're used to joking with. She turns back to Thandi. "What is it dat yuh need help wid, baby?"

"I need help finding someone. A girl name Jullette."

"Why not look har up in di directory? What's her last name?"

"Rose."

That's when the fat woman slaps her hand on her forehead, nearly knocking off her red wig. "Oh, Sweetness!" She hits her friend on the shoulder. "Doreen, she ah talk 'bout Sweetness!"

Doreen's eyes light up. "Oh, Sweetness! Yes, yes, me know who she is!" She turns to Thandi. Then to her friend she says, "Annette, yuh t'ink we should—"

"Big boss would know," Annette offers, cutting off Doreen. She lights another cigarette.

"Who?" Thandi asks.

"Big boss. She come aroun' dese parts an' recruit girls. Di younger ones."

"She?"

"Yeah, man. Is a woman who's in charge ah dese girls. We call har boss lady or big boss," Doreen says. "She oversee everything, from how much di girls get pay to when dem get lay. Me an' Annette is we own boss. We sleep wid who we please, when we please. An' di money we earn is ours to keep."

"How can I find her?" Thandi asks.

"Trus' me. Yuh g'wan haffi be careful. She might convince yuh to work fah har. Dat woman, from what I hear, is a snake. A vicious one."

"So can you help me?"

The women glance at each other. Then Annette waves Thandi to follow her. She stuffs the pack of cigarettes inside her brassiere and lifts her breasts so that they stand up. She walks with a slight limp.

37

VERDENE FEELS AS THOUGH SHE IS PLANNING A WEDDING— or rather, is already at the reception, where she's tipsy with wine, drunk off merriment and hope. But something nags at her. She can't put her finger on it, but it's always there, lurking like a bad odor trapped inside the walls, seeming to strangle her in her sleep. During these sleepless nights she's cuddled next to Margot, comforted by her presence. It's nice to think about Margot's sweet dreams and avoid the inkling that has been nagging her. She hopes Margot's dreams will become hers, relieving her of any doubt.

Verdene's suspicions began with Margot's argument against hiring a lawyer. At first she didn't think anything of it, since Margot kept on harping about her big promotion and the new prop-

erty. That all Verdene has to do is sign, since she holds their future
in her hands. But Verdene cannot shake the guilt of selling the
house for less than what her parents had put down for the property back in 1968. Why would the property be so devalued now?
She's kept it quiet from Margot, but Verdene has been spending
her days scanning each page of the contract, noticing more and
more flaws—like the fact that the company identifies itself as
a subsidiary group without mentioning its affiliate. After Margot left for work this morning, Verdene dialed Mr. Reynolds—
the lawyer who did the paperwork for her mother's will, which
granted her ownership of the house and property.

"Did they come by yet?" Mr. Reynolds asks Verdene over the
telephone.

"They're supposed to be here soon." She looks over her shoulder
to see if the developers are at her gate. She runs her fingers through
her hair and pulls slightly to alleviate the mild headache forming.
"The bastards owe me money," she says. "I should be getting qua-
druple what they quote here."

"Don't do anything until I read the contract," Mr. Reynolds
says in his raspy smoker's voice. He's about seventy and has been
practicing law for years—first in Britain, where he was a Rhodes
Scholar who became friends with Aunt Gertrude and her husband.
The last Verdene saw him was after her mother's funeral. He still
has height, for his age—about six feet—with a shock of white hair
and skin the color of night. A proud Maroon from Accompong, St.
Elizabeth.

"Can you fax me the contract?" Mr. Reynolds asks. "I leave
Montego Bay this evening for a business trip until next week, but
ah can look at it when ah come back."

Verdene closes her eyes. What will she tell Margot? That she has
to delay until her lawyer looks it over? Margot already thinks that
she's stalling. As though Mr. Reynolds is reading her mind over the

telephone, he says, "Don't let them bully you, Verdene. Why didn't you contact me earlier?"

"I—I thought I could handle it on my own," Verdene says, feeling like a child again who has been caught stealing Scotch Bonnet peppers. She remembers the promise she made to Margot and how drunk she was with happiness for their shared future.

"Yuh know who the company is?" Mr. Reynolds asks. "Maybe I can do some research on them through my contacts at NEPA."

"Doesn't say on here. Just the subsidiary group."

Mr. Reynolds lets out a long whistle over the telephone—not the melodious whistle Verdene hears the farmers blowing on their way to the fields, a stark contrast to their silhouettes limp with defeat against the dull brown of the drought. Mr. Reynolds's whistle is the tuneless, drawn-out alarm of fire trucks in London that cut corners on wet, slippery roads whose sheen reflects the bright red lights of their sirens. "Either you wait until I get back to Mobay, or risk losing your inheritance," Mr. Reynolds says.

After the telephone call, Verdene fills a pot with water to boil some cerassee leaves to get rid of her headache. As soon as she turns on the stove, she hears knocking at her gate. Two men dressed in white shirts, dark pants, and blue hard hats are standing there, waiting for the sealed envelope with the signed contract. Verdene goes out to greet them on her veranda.

"I'm not signing this," she tells them through the grille. She won't give them the satisfaction of robbing her this way. Uprooting people from their homes like this and having the nerve to pay them less than what their property is worth.

"Ma'am, we need your signature," the shorter one says to Verdene. "We gave you time. We are behind on construction. You're the only property owner who hasn't signed."

"What do you want me to do about that?" she asks the man,

who looks to be in his twenties. Perhaps a new university graduate convinced that he's making a difference.

"Comply."

"What for? You think I'm stupid like the rest?"

"Ma'am, you seem like the most reasonable one around here." The taller one gestures to her frame behind the burglar bars, leaving off words Verdene knows he's thinking when he sees her lighter skin and hears her British accent. "Legally, we cannot do anything without your signature."

"Legally?" Verdene laughs, throwing her head back. "Did you read this?" She holds up the paper and rattles it for emphasis. "This is illegal! Your bosses are sending you out here to do their dirty work. This house belonged to my mother. I'm not signing this without a lawyer."

The two men glance at each other.

"May I ask who's in charge? I'd like to take this up with them."

"Ma'am?"

"Who's in charge?" she repeats. "And stop calling me ma'am!"

"It's Sutton and Company," the taller man says.

"I want the name of the parent company. It says here that you're a subsidiary group, but there's no information about your affiliate."

"Wellington Estate, ma—I mean, miss."

"Wellington? Like the rum and coffee plantation?"

"They also own properties on the coast. Alphonso Wellington is the one in charge."

Alphonso. The one Margot works for? The one who promoted her to general manager for his new hotel? Somewhere remote and off the beaten path, according to Margot. Verdene covers her mouth with one hand as everything takes shape in her mind. How many nights has Margot been with her, knowing that this would happen? Verdene reaches for the doorknob.

"I—I have something on the stove, if you don't mind," she says. "Let your boss know that my lawyer will be in touch."

"Miss, we can't—"

But Verdene stops listening as the door closes behind her. She takes slow, careful steps toward the kitchen, seeing but unseeing. She sits at the table and cradles her pounding head in her hands. Margot knew how much this house meant to her. Not once did she let on that she was aware of the details of this development. The night when Verdene returned to the house shaking with relief from surviving the meeting at Dino's, Margot gave her a bath. She had climbed inside the tub with her and gently cooed in her ear that it's a sign for them to leave River Bank. *"You, me, and Thandi can live together in the house I bought. For us."*

"I'm not letting them destroy my mother's house."

"You're a property owner. You'll get your money's worth."

"I need a lawyer before I make any decisions."

"Why go through all that trouble to hire a lawyer and drain the life insurance money Miss Ella left you? For what? For them to read a couple pages that you can read yourself? All I'm asking is for you to trust that I can take care of you. Consider my offer. The new house is in a gated community where no one will bother us. You don't have to suffer like you suffered here. This house might be your mother's legacy, but our new house is ours."

"I need some time to think."

"Verdene, jus' give it a rest." Margot pulled her back into the tub. *"Jus' trust me."*

Verdene begins to chuckle, clutching the edges of the table as her body gives way to trembling. Her eyes fill with tears. She had been fooled. Tricked into being vulnerable. By the type of woman who gave her the urge to sing along to the radio, feeling light and heavy at the same time. The type of woman who makes her think of rain-soaked October days in the midst of a drought. The type of woman who brought her to the kitchen—once on all fours—to lovingly cook her meals. And when they make love, the type of woman who cries as though Verdene has given her the best gift in the world. And yes, Verdene gave her everything—her whole self—and wanted for nothing. She thought that being with Margot would make up for lost years. She had begun to look forward. Verdene wipes her face. She feels old. Worn out and old. She smells something burning and remembers the pot of water for the cerassee tea. It was her mother's favorite pot. One she has kept and cared for over the years. Verdene moves quickly to the kitchen to turn off the stove. She stands over it for a long time, peering inside the blackened interior where the water has evaporated.

38

WHEN JULLETTE LOOKS UP AND SEES THANDI, HER EYE-
brows furrow and her mouth twists to the side. She's hovered over a pail, catching water from a pipe. Her face is wiped clean
of the makeup Thandi saw on her at the restaurant. Once again she
looks like a teenage girl, Thandi's age. Her hair is parted in a straight
line in the center and twisted into two French braids. Her loose-
fitting dress billows in the wind like a parachute filling up with air,
revealing a pair of long skinny legs and white cotton underwear. She
holds the dress down with one hand while the other remains fixed
on the standpipe. She probably made the dress herself. Thandi can
tell by the slightly uneven stitching along the hem, though it is near-
perfect. Jullette has been making her own clothes since Thandi can

remember. She used to sketch dresses, blouses, and skirts, which she would then attempt to make from fabric given to her by Miss Priscilla, the fabric vendor (who is also Mr. Melon's common-law wife). Miss Priscilla and Miss Violet were good friends, and when Miss Violet took sick, Miss Priscilla gave the little girl anything she asked for—even if they were just scraps of material.

"What is it yuh want?" Jullette asks. Thandi holds out her hands. It's a humble gesture, she hopes. She needs her friend's forgiveness before she can ask for her brother. But something about Jullette's face lets Thandi know this might not be possible. She cuts to the chase: "I came to look for Charles. He told me that he's staying with you."

"Chucky?" Jullette claps her hands together and laughs out loud. "God mus' ah come!" Jullette says, laughing. "What in Jeezaz' name can Thandi want wid me brother? My pickey-pickey head, dry-foot, old, crusty brother?" Jullette puts her hands on her narrow hips. They jut forward as she rests most of her weight on the enhanced parenthesis of her bowlegs. "If ah remembah correctly, he isn't your type. So if is come yuh come fi carry him to di police station, then forget it. He's not here."

"Where is he? I need to find him."

"Fah what? Yuh own selfish needs?"

"We're together, did he tell you?"

"Him nevah mention yuh name. An' I'm sure up until dis point, yuh neva mention his to yuh uppity friends either."

One of the many secrets they had shared as girls was what they'd want their future husbands to look like. Thandi never wanted a boy as dark as her to be her husband. Neither did Jullette. Thandi looks down. There is nowhere else to look, and meeting the mockery in Jullette's eyes isn't an option.

"Jus' leave us alone," Jullette says very calmly. "You wanted nothing to do wid us, an' now yuh coming aroun', expecting me to trust yuh? I know what yuh really want. Money. Well, ah have news fah yuh. Charles not here. Him gone long time." Thandi stands there with her feet planted firmly on the ground, her toes digging into the soles of her shoes. Inside, Thandi's heart bangs against her rib cage. Charles cannot be gone. This cannot be true. Can it?

"So yuh g'wan leave now?" Jullette puts both hands on her hips again. Thandi notices that her nails are painted red. "Likkle Miss Perfect. Yuh expec' everyt'ing to be handed to you. Yuh nuh know struggle, don't?" Jullette asks.

"I'm not perfect," Thandi responds. "And what yuh mean, I don't know struggle? We grew up in River Bank together."

"Me an' you was different from day one, Thandi. Two different peas. Yes, we was friends, but yuh mother neva like yuh 'roun me a'tall. She did always want you to have a special-type of friends, ones who neva have to beg fah food." Jullette taps her pale wrist to indicate the lighter shade. "Dat was di first difference between me an' you. Yuh was trained to be di opportunist, an' me was suppose to be yuh doormat. Di one who would always come to yuh rescue when those children used to bully you pon di playground. Is like yuh always did need me there, but neva return no favah as a friend. An' then yuh stop talking to me right aftah yuh pass yuh exam fah dat school. Yuh wear yuh white uniform wid nuff pride, suh much pride dat it blind yuh. Yuh walk pass me like me neva exist."

"Jullette, I'm sorry."

"Listen to you. Dat twanging yuh do. Yuh can't even talk patwa no more. Yuh soun' like a foreigner. As soon as yuh become ah Saint Emmanuel girl yuh mind twist."

"I can't believe after all these years you still have me up for getting into Saint Emmanuel."

"It's not dat, Thandi."

"Then what is it? If it's not jealousy, then what is it?"

"I'm not jealous, Thandi. Ah can't be jealous if it's clear dat yuh neva learn ah t'ing in school anyway. Yuh come out more confused than evah. Look at yuh skin!"

Thandi touches her face. She hasn't been using the creams in a while, but traces of its results linger.

"Why yuh so upset, Jullette? A mistake is a mistake. It happened long ago. Let it go. Yuh acting like it happened yesterday."

"Yuh is a fraud. A lizard wah change color anywhere it go. Yuh don't know yuhself. Yuh don't have no roots, no grounding. Yuh don't even have a mind of yuh own. Yuh is a puppet, Thandi. Delores use yuh. Margot use yuh. Even if you an' Charles did have something, I woulda mek sure to not mek it happen. Him is too good fah you." The scowl deepens in Jullette's face. "So keep on moving. Di sky is dat way. We don't want yuh 'roun here."

Thandi burns with rage, her face twitching from the hard slap of Jullette's words. She thinks of Jullette parading around with that man in high heels and a skirt too short. Thandi was sure Jullette had seen her too. "You acted like yuh neva saw me at Sea Breeze when you were with that man, yuh client."

"Whatever, Thandi," Jullette says. "Who are you for me to waste my time wid? I learn to mek money to survive. Is long time me an' me brothers surviving on our own. But you wouldn't know dem t'ings. If it was you, yuh woulda end up dead. So don't yuh dare judge me."

Thandi hisses like a rattlesnake: "I might be sheltered, but at least I'm not a *whore*." It's a stone thrown too far. Thandi claps her hands over her mouth as soon as she says it.

"Yuh think yuh betta than me?" Jullette asks Thandi, her voice still measured but quieter now. Her eyes reveal something nasty and reptilian. "Well, ah have news for yuh. Look in di damn mirror. No apple nuh fall too far from di tree."

"What yuh mean by that?" Thandi asks.

"Tell me where yuh get money fah yuh schoolbooks an' fah yuh school fee. Yuh suh wrapped up in yuh own world dat yuh believe anyt'ing people tell yuh. Yuh probably believe dat di likkle scrap Delores an' Margot mek can put togethah to sen' yuh to dat school. Yuh really t'ink likkle chicken-feed money can afford dat deh school, Thandi?"

"I got a scholarship."

"Ha!" Jullette laughs. "Yuh neva realize dat a scholarship is for a year? Ministry of Education nuh dat generous, m'dear. Is di empire dat fund yuh precious scholarship."

"What yuh talking about?" Thandi asks.

"Yuh sistah, Margot, eva tell yuh what she do fi mek ends meet?" she asks Thandi instead.

The last person Thandi wants to talk about is Margot. "She works at Palm Star Resort. Has been there for eleven years," Thandi says, swallowing.

"Jus' ask har again," Jullette says, narrowing her eyes. "Ask her where she get extra money from fah yuh school fee, the nice clothes she wear, the money she just put down on the villa in Lagoons."

"She just got promoted as hotel general manager," Thandi says through her teeth. Jullette doesn't know what she's talking about.

"Next time yuh see Margot, ask her *who* help her to get dat promotion," Jullette says, with that nasty reptile look in her eyes. "Bettah yet, ask her how many of those *big-money* man she sleep wid. Ask 'bout her empire. Ask har about the girls she owns. Yuh sistah, Margot, is more of a whore than I will ever be. She's the biggest pimp on di North Coast. Yuh sistah sell out River Bank. She's di one who g'wan manage dat hotel dey destroying River Bank to build."

Jullette sneers when she sees Thandi slump as though physically wounded. "Ask yuh sista, she'll tell yuh. An' yuh know what she tell the girls weh work fah har? Girls like me? Yuh know what she tell anyone who would listen? She tell dem seh it's all fah her sister, who g'wan be a doctor. Her precious, perfect Thandi, who can do no wrong. Her dainty, stuck-up Thandi, who, in my opinion, will one day kick dirt in har face as soon as she reach somewhere, because she wouldn't want to associate wid har own color."

"Enough!" Thandi clamps her hands over her ears. She stoops down, resting on her haunches as though cowering from the sun. She cannot let Jullette see the shame that reddens her face. "What yuh get from telling me this?" Thandi asks Jullette, raising her head to meet her eyes. "How much bettah yuh feel from letting all this off yuh chest?" Jullette seems taken aback by this question. Thandi sees a glint of her former friend—the one who stood up for her on the playground when they were girls in primary school. Jullette is breathing heavily from the exchange, her chest rising and falling under her loose dress, as though she's struggling to maintain her hardness. Very slowly her shoulders lower as though melting in the sun. In a soft voice she says, "Thandi, some people run. Some people mek up fantasy to deny or forget. While some people stan' up an' face di storm, whicheva direction it blow. Ah was hoping dat yuh would come outta yuh fantasy one day. I neva mean to say it like dat."

"You meant every word."

"Forget ah said anyt'ing. Jus' do what's best, Thandi, an' leave us alone. Yuh done cost my brother a lot already."

"I love him."

Jullette says nothing at first, allowing Thandi's professed love for Charles to linger like the smell of breadfruit roasting in the yard. The dark soot carries in the breeze and thickens the air. Jullette cocks her head to the side. "Then ah want yuh to do something fah me."

"Whatever you want."

"I want you to jus' let him be. Is fah di bettah. Yuh only going to lead him on an' destroy him."

Jullette walks off and heads toward the house. Thandi follows her, but stops when Jullette slams the mesh door in her face.

"Is he here? Charles! Charles!" Thandi calls out.

"He's not here. Jus' leave us alone."

Thandi begins to bang on the door. "Please, I won't leave until you tell me where he is." The neighbors are looking at her, but she doesn't care. She wants Charles to remind her that she has the capacity to love and be loved despite where or what she comes from. They can run away together and make a new life. The familiar ache dissipates and in its place is a violent instinct to throw herself against the door until it breaks. She takes gulps of breath between sobs. She bangs and bangs, feeling as though she's in a dream where she's screaming without making a sound, or like she's moving but is really stuck to the ground. She's Thandi, the one who would make it. The scholarship girl who would make everything better for her family. As graceful as a skirt tail blowing in the wind. Now here she is, banging down the door of a boarded-up house of a prostitute in search of a street boy.

Thandi thinks of Margot and her secrets and the legacy Thandi's inherited, how she'll carry it now like the bucket of goat blood that Miss Gracie and Delores carried under the light of the full moon. They balanced the bucket between them to Verdene Moore's house. Thandi had caught them one night, afraid and giddy as the women dipped paintbrushes in the animal's blood and wrote across the pink house: *The blood of Jesus is upon you.* They said they had seen Verdene kill those dogs. Delores continued to go with Miss Gracie many nights after that, but Thandi grew sickened by it. Especially after witnessing Verdene Moore bent down on all fours one day, scrubbing the blood off her walkway. Thandi looked at the bending woman, her back hunched. Verdene dipped a coconut husk in a bucketful of water and scrubbed. She paused every once in a while to look up at the sky. Her movement was methodic, humble, graceful. Thandi thought of the rumors, stale and old, yet so indelible. She saw sorrow and regret in Verdene Moore's decorum, and felt her weariness.

She gives up on the door and crouches on the ground, her head on her knees, her arms wrapped around them. She can almost smell him there with her, that ripe pawpaw scent. She inhales it as she folds into herself, tired and defeated. She doesn't hear the door open or the coming footsteps. Thandi jumps with fright when Charles, as quick as lightning, pulls her inside and into his arms.

Charles and Thandi embrace inside Jullette's living room. When she raises her face to his, he wipes the tears off her cheeks with his thumb. They remain like this, with Jullette fading in the background. His face is leaner, his eyes alert like an animal used to being hunted. Thandi runs her hand over the hair stubble on his face. When he pulls away, it's clear Charles is aware of his haunted look too, because he refuses to meet her eyes. When she reaches for him again, he takes one step back. "It's better to end it," he says. Choked by all the questions and pleading that rise in her throat, Thandi cannot respond. "We only foolin' ourselves, Thandi," Charles says. "Dey g'wan catch me an' throw me in prison. What good would I be to you in jail?"

"You don't have to go to jail. We can run, we can hide someplace where they won't find you."

"Thandi, where would we hide? Yuh not t'inking 'bout anything right now. Yuh too emotional."

"You can hide in another parish, grow a beard."

"Yuh don't undahstand, I'm a walking jackpot fah di people dem who believe ah can get dem ten thousan' dollahs. Yuh t'ink that's a good position to be in? Always looking ovah yuh shouldah . . . at yuh own family membahs?" He glances at Jullette, who is silently listening to them with a hand stroking her chin and legs apart like a bodyguard. Charles sits down on the red velvet sofa and Thandi throws herself in front of him.

"I can talk to Margot. Jullette told me everything. Charles, yuh listening to me?" She's tugging his shirt, but he only holds his head in his hands. Thandi stands up and looks down on him. From this vantage point Charles appears shrunken, hopeless. Like a fisherman with an empty net. Thandi exchanges glances with Jullette. "Yuh not going to just let him give up hope like this, are you?" she asks Jullette.

"We might have more options. Right now I need to get dressed. I have to be somewhere. Mama already staying here wid we. You can't stay." She doesn't look at Thandi.

"Please," Thandi says, standing up. "I have nowhere else to go."

"I don't think you can be trusted," Jullette says.

Charles raises his head. "Jus' cool it, Jullette. She's my girl." Thandi looks into his face. She takes his hand in hers and turns to Jullette. Jullette is regarding her with the same meanness Thandi saw earlier. "Okay. I'll be back soon," Jullette says.

When she returns two hours later, she's carrying two shopping bags full of clothing items. She throws a dress at Thandi and tells her to get dressed. "If you love Chucky as much as you say, then this should be easy."

39

THE TAXI PULLS UP TO THE VILLA, ITS LARGE BLACK AND GOLD gate, the manicured hedges and the waving palm trees in the front yard poised like hula dancers welcoming them. The place sits like a castle overlooking Montego Bay and seemingly the entire island. Thandi turns to Jullette. "What is this place?"

"The headquarters." Jullette pays the taxi driver.

Once they set foot on the property, the lights come on in the yard. Jullette knocks on the oak door, lightly at first. Then harder. A woman finally opens the door and peers at them. "Can I help you?"

"We here fah Alphonso," Jullette says to the woman, whose brown neck and chest are covered with talcum powder. She has

on a long denim skirt and a red top. A simple black leather bag
is slung over one shoulder. In one hand she carries a maid's uniform on a hanger, covered by a garment bag. In her other hand
is a black plastic bag that she holds delicately at her side. The
smell of some kind of a stew—maybe oxtail or red pea soup with
pig's feet—follows her. Her shift must be over. Her face con-
torts with a smugness that communicates to Thandi the fact that
they are unlikely guests. She lays eyes on Thandi. Thandi tries
to straighten herself, since she's propped up like a rag doll with
her right arm around Jullette's neck, unable to walk in heels.
"Don't I know you?" the woman asks Thandi. Thandi is surprised. She has never seen this woman before. She might be
younger than she looks. Maybe not a day older than Delores. But
she appears tired. Not so much in a physical sense; it's a fatigue
Thandi knows too well, for she herself has felt it. The woman's
blackened lips don't curve upward into a smile to match Thandi's
uncertain one. Thandi can't tell if the woman is wearing black
lipstick or if that's her real lip color. A pair of large hoop earrings
soften an otherwise hard, chiseled face.

"I don't think we ever met," Thandi responds.

"Hm." The woman regards Thandi. "I'm good wid faces. That
is one t'ing me pride me self on. I remembah t'ings you'd normally forget. Like di clothes ah person was wearing, dem shoes,
di color ah dem socks, whether dem slip was showing, what dem
request di first time me serve dem. But ah remembah mostly
faces. Me mind tek pitcha like camera an' store dem," she says
to Thandi.

But Thandi cannot remember her. She turns to Jullette, who
says to the woman, "You've seen har sistah."

Though Thandi knows why she's here, the thought of Margot
makes her want to turn back. Jullette kept telling her to wait and
see. That Margot has no idea about their plan. Thandi imagines

a string being pulled from her, unspooling every ounce of life left in her. She feels sick all of a sudden, the imaginary thread that reels from inside her taut.

"So di both ah oonuh is nothin' but misguided girls like all di res'," the woman says to them. "These girls who would do anyt'ing fah money. Yuh mother know yuh out here in di street, doing dese t'ings?"

"If she knew, she would ask for her cut," Thandi says.

"It's sad and disrespectful to speak of yuh own mother that way."

"Clearly, yuh never met mine."

Thandi thinks she sees a veil of sadness descend over the woman's face. She fidgets with the black plastic bag containing the food, adjusting it, then readjusting it. Finally, as though finding the right words, she says, "Go home. Di both ah you. If oonuh know what's good fah oonuh self, go home."

Jullette holds the door, her movement swift. "Not before we see Alphonso. Him expecting we."

Just then a shiny silver Mercedes pulls up, crunching stones under its wheels on the driveway. The woman closes the door behind her and walks toward the car. She lowers her things onto the paved walkway, her handbag, uniform, and plastic bag with food abandoned. Thandi watches her bend to the driver's side, furiously knocking on the window with her knuckles. The driver rolls down his window as she gesticulates widely with her hands, pointing at Jullette and Thandi. "Dey claim dey looking fah you, sah!"

There is something magnificent in her movement. Thandi could watch her all night. The light from the car has become a stage light. In different circumstances she would have tried to capture the wild strokes of this woman's arms in her sketchpad, the impassioned annoyance and disbelief that shake her body like a mighty wind shakes a tree. "Look at har," Jullette says next to Thandi, staring straight ahead with a stricken look on her face. "Actin' like she own di place. Is like she nuh know seh she'll pass through dis godfahsaken life without a donkey hair to har name. She spen' har whole life cooking, cleaning, an' protecting dese people, t'inking what belongs to dem is hers too. But is bare crumbs she scrape from dem dinnah table fi build di pride wah she 'ave. A pride weh hide di truth dat she will always deh pon har black knee, scraping."

Two white men get out of the car. One is wearing shades even though it's night. The silver-haired one is dressed in an army-green general's uniform, complete with epaulets.

"You're sure that Margot won't be involved in this?" Thandi says to Jullette in a whisper between clenched teeth while observing the people in the driveway.

"She's not," Jullette says with a smirk. "Dis is your show."

"No need to worry, I'll handle it, Peaches," the man wearing the shades is saying to the maid. "You can go home now." The woman gives Thandi and Jullette a final glance before picking up her things and hobbling toward the front gate like a bird, her neck long as if to match her annoyance. Thandi could have sworn that she was looking up into the woman's flared nostrils earlier at the door; but her fading, small, off-kilter frame makes her seem less intimidating. Once she steps through the gate, Thandi lets out a breath. The two men make their way from the driveway toward the front door. The man wearing the shades jingles his keys in his pocket. Right behind him, the general takes stiff, measured steps.

"You're early," the man wearing shades says to Jullette, his tone as casual as his gait. "And I see you've brought a friend."

"Yes." Jullette gives the man a toothy grin. Here she doesn't seem like Thandi's friend at all, but someone who came to do business. Her demureness is a tool. "My friend is new. I'm here wid har to mek har feel comfortable," Jullette says. Thandi cringes at Jullette's inability to switch from backward patois to standard English in the presence of these men. Its cadence clashes with the beauty and elegance of the setting. Like two Dutch pots banging into one another. Thandi imagines the smirks on their faces when they turn away. But Jullette doesn't seem to care about the way she sounds. She seems confident, like she owns some part of them. They laugh with her, not at her. Thandi doesn't get the joke.

"What is your friend's name?" the man wearing the shades asks Jullette. Thandi senses him looking at her, though he doesn't address her directly.

"Thandi," Jullette answers.

The man lifts his hand to shake hers. A gesture that surprises Thandi, since she has never shaken anyone's hand before in greeting.

"Alphonso," he says.

"Nice to meet you, sir."

"Sir?" The man guffaws. "Just call me Alphonso."

Embarrassed, she apologizes. She cannot see his eyes behind his dark sunglasses, though she feels him studying her, the revelation denting a comma at the sides of his mouth. It forces her to pull her hand away. But he holds on to it.

"You're quite stunning," he says. "Are you a model?" He's still holding on to Thandi's hand.

"No, I'm—"

He puts a finger to Thandi's lips. This catches her off guard. His touch is gentle, like a soft kiss. The same intrusion by someone else would have annoyed her, made her slap the finger away. But she does nothing. "You should learn to take a compliment," he says, removing his finger.

Thandi feels perspiration trickling down her sides. God forbid if it soaks the skintight dress. "Uhm, where is the bathroom?" she asks.

"Come. I'll gladly show you." Alphonso gently pushes the front door with his shoulder. As soon as it opens into the well-lit living space, Thandi notices the paintings. "Follow me." He bends slightly like a portly butler, one hand behind his back, the other gesturing for her to step farther inside. There are paintings and sculptures everywhere. Thandi resists the urge to turn and turn like the bamboo ceiling fan spinning above their heads. Alphonso must have noticed her noticing everything, because he slows to her pace.

"You like?"

"It's like a museum," she says.

"I'm a collector."

"You live here?"

"Sometimes."

"I really like your place."

"I'm glad. My goal is to make everyone who walks through those doors feel like they belong here. You can stay as long as you want." He says it so quietly that it feels like an intimate confession. He stops short when he gets to the guest bathroom door and holds it open for her. For a second Thandi wonders if he'll move to let her pass. "How old are you, Thandi?" he asks.

"Fifteen. I'll be sixteen at the end of this month."

"Hmm. Fifteen."

His tilts his glasses on the bridge of his nose, his pale eyes appraising her.

"You have a nice figure for fifteen. A body like yours could make men do anything."

She walks quickly past him, aware of the tension in her neck and the rodlike sensation in her back. She locks the door. Instead of sitting on the toilet, she bends over it. She feels sick again. She can hear Alphonso and the general talking to Jullette in the living room.

Before they left the house, Charles had sulked on the sofa as Jullette gushed over how much Thandi was transformed with makeup and skintight clothes. Thandi noticed him staring as though seeing her for the first time. It made her uncomfortable, yet aware of what she possessed—a power she once thought only her sister had. Charles pulled back when Thandi came close. Something came over his face like a five o'clock shadow. *"Yuh can't go, looking like dat,"* he spat, a renewed fervor in his eyes that Thandi recognized as contempt. Or fear. Charles turned to his sister. *"This is not a good idea."*

"Charles, you agreed," Jullette argued, lowering her voice to a hiss so as not to wake Miss Violet, whom Charles had put to bed just an hour before. But Charles wasn't having it. *"Take it off,"* he said to Thandi, ignoring Jullette's plea. Thandi froze, caught between Charles's disapproval and her desperation to free him. *"Yuh hear me?"* Charles said. Thandi had never seen this scowl on his face before. He repeated himself as though she hadn't comprehended the first time: *"Ah say yuh mus' tek it off. Or else don't come back here to me."* It was an ultimatum that almost knocked the air out of Thandi's lungs. The anger in Charles's eyes dared her, convicted her, softened her.

"I'm doing it for you," she heard herself say, stroking his arm. *"You'll thank me later."* But he pushed her hand away, his face screwed into a tight fist, as though he could already smell the other man on her fingers. *"Charles, you know I'm doing this for you,"* Thandi said, pleading. But he turned away from her, standing like a wilted tree in the middle of the living room. A small tug from Jullette took Thandi away from the scene and into the chilly night.

...

When Thandi returns from the bathroom, Jullette is already sitting next to the general like she has known him intimately. They are blowing smoke into air diffused by the spinning bamboo fan above their heads. Warm light glows from a sculpted lamp in the room, gilding the paintings on the coral walls. The general taps the empty space next to him on the green couch for Thandi to sit too. On the glass coffee table is a *Gleaner*. And on the front page Alphonso is shaking hands with a government official. The headline reads "HOTELIER CHANGING JAMAICA FOR BETTER." Thandi sits just so she can read more of the article, but the general mistakes her willingness as obedience. The general places his hand on Thandi's thigh. She doesn't move. Jullette gives her a smirk and waits a couple of seconds too long before pulling the man toward her, relieving Thandi. Alphonso is on the telephone. Thandi watches him pace the tiled floor, where she can see his reflection.

When he finishes his private conversation he walks in the direction of the bar and pours himself a drink. He stops short when he catches Thandi staring. "How about a shot of brandy for the lady in pink?" Alphonso says, winking at Thandi. Jullette had explained to her earlier that if a man offers a drink, accept it and make sure to display the acrobatics of the tongue while working the straw. *"But what if they don't give you a straw?"* Thandi asked. *"Then yuh mus' use di ice to wet yuh lips,"* Jullette quipped.

Thandi watches Alphonso pour brandy in two mini-glasses that look like they belong in a dollhouse. No ice or straw. He hands the glass to her and lifts his own. "Cheers to a memorable night!"

Thandi feebly clinks her glass with his and watches him throw his head back. She drinks too, squinting at the burning sensation of the alcohol in her throat. He pulls out a cigar from his left breast pocket and lights it. "I would like us to play a game of show-and-tell. I couldn't help but notice your fascination with the artwork. So how about you show me your favorite artwork and I show you mine?" He turns his head to blow smoke the other way. He's studying her again.

"All right." She glances at the walls, not knowing where to begin. She points to an abstract painting with geometric shapes and vibrant colors. This elevates a slow, uneven smirk on Alphonso's face behind the veil of smoke. The orange ash glows like the inside of an oven. "You have good taste." He takes her by the hand. "Let me borrow you for a minute. You haven't seen anything yet."

She glances over at Jullette, who is already tonguing the general, whose free hand is clamped firmly, possessively, on her bottom. "*Yuh don't have to do whateva dey ask of you*," Jullette told Thandi when they waited on a taxi in the square. "*But yuh get as much as yuh give. 'Membah dat.*"

Thandi follows Alphonso. He takes the brandy bottle with him and leads her through the backyard like they are going on a picnic. The lights along the cobblestone walkway shine brightly, bringing into view a gazebo, a swimming pool, and a Jacuzzi. The space could hold a wedding with a hundred people. On the other side of the yard is a small cottage. It looks like it might be the maid's quarters. Outside the cottage are palm trees with lights strung up and down their trunks like ivy. The dark sea roars nearby. Thandi can hear the waves nudging their way onto the pristine white sand.

Alphonso opens the door to the cottage and leads her to a couch. A gentle breeze floats inside from the open window as he busies himself in the small kitchenette area, searching for two more glasses. Thandi tries to distract herself with the canvases that are leaned against the green walls.

"I store stuff here when I don't know where to hang them," Alphonso says, handing her another glass of the brown liquor. "I don't allow many people in here. So consider yourself special."

He hauls plastic cover after plastic cover from large frames. Each time he uncovers a painting, Thandi is taken aback, unable to believe one man could own so much beauty. She's aware of him watching her as she marvels at his collection.

"Go ahead," he says gently. "You can touch."

Thandi touches the frames. There's one painting in particular that she's drawn to. She likes how the artist captures the essence of the naked woman with chiney-bump knots in her hair—the way mothers style their daughters' hair after washing it in the river, taking their time to part, oil, then wind the kinks into corkscrews with their fingers all over the girls' heads. But this woman is grown, though she poses demurely on a red couch—similar to the one in this room under the window. She smiles with her eyes, not her mouth, one arm slung over the back of the couch, while the other hand rests comfortably across her small potbelly. Her soft brown flesh seems palpable even in the painting, and her breasts are perfectly round. One leg is propped seductively on the couch, while one foot rests flatly on the floor, the separation revealing the dark triangular patch between them. But it's the chipped red nail polish on the woman's big toe that gives the painting a personal touch—a vulnerability that makes Thandi feel like she's both violating the woman's privacy and getting to know her. "She's beautiful," Thandi says.

"So are you. And I know you have a lot more to show me." Alphonso sets down his glass on the counter. She senses that he knows why she's here. He's in front of her, holding her hand in his, his grip firm. He gets down on one knee as though he's proposing. He nearly loses his balance but quickly steadies himself. He reaches out and touches her face. She flinches. He doesn't seem to notice. She does what Jullette told her to do and remains calm. His hand is trailing her left cheek. "Why are you here, Thandi?" he asks. "Clearly you know I can do something for you. Something special." His hand is coarse against her skin. Her mouth opens and closes. She has no ownership of anything. Not the scholarship. Not herself. And certainly not Charles. She exists merely as a debt to be paid.

Thandi closes her eyes as Alphonso undresses her. When she opens them, she focuses on the covered paintings in the room, their worth already established. It's Charles who comes to mind at this very moment as Alphonso tilts his head to study something on her face. It's the possibility of strolling with him along the river that releases Thandi's mind from the slow pull of the zipper, the cool, damp air that washes her back from the open window, which clutches her shoulders and grazes her nipples like a baby's teeth. "Beautiful," Alphonso says. His hands are cold on her thighs. She remains focused on the paintings. Frames and frames of them he has collected. He's easing off her under-wear. He's pulling her onto the floor. Charles's face begins to transform into a watercolor painting. Soon he begins to fade, his eyes becoming the same bluish glazed color of a dead fish. Thandi gasps. She realizes that she has been crying. And when she blinks through her tears, she's surprised at the sight of her brown flesh. Alphonso is on top of her. "Don't be nervous, it won't hurt." He's unbuckling his belt.

Just then there's a rattle at the door. Alphonso stops what he's doing. "You stay right here," he commands in a whisper. He goes to the door, adjusting his pants. Meanwhile, Thandi looks around for a hiding place. But before she can find one, Alphonso opens the door and a woman's voice enters like a breeze. "Sweet-ness sent me in here. Told me you have a surprise for me. I've been trying to get in touch with you. I thought you wanted me to bring the package. Yuh have me waiting in the villa with dat prick of a sergeant. Who or what on earth could you be doing that is more important than—" Margot stops short when she sees Thandi trying to pull up her dress. She looks from Thandi to Alphonso, then back at Thandi again.

"What's going on?" She turns to Alphonso. Thandi fumbles with the zipper in the back of her dress. "What is my sister doing here?" Margot says; her voice is a high-pitched screech. "You bastard!" Margot shouts. "How could you?" She hits Alphonso on the arm and he grabs her and turns her around, her back pressed into him.

"Calm down. You know exactly why she's here. I thought you sent her here with Sweetness, since you owe me," he says.

"We've talked about this! I helped you with the police!"

"She came of her own free will."

"Am I supposed to believe you?"

"Why don't you ask her?"

Margot narrows her eyes at Thandi. "Why are you here? Delores and I were looking everywhere for you! And here you are, taking off yuh clothes for ah man? What di hell is wrong wid you?"

Thandi has lost her ability to speak under her sister's smothering rage. She wonders if the alcohol has gotten to her brain too, for she has forgotten the reason why she's here.

"Thandi, answer me."

"Margot, you're interrupting us," Alphonso says. He holds on to Margot's hand, but she pushes him away.

"Fuck you! This was not the plan!" she says, whipping around to face him again and pointing her finger at him as if he were a child. "My role in this was to help you so that you can help me. *Why her?* Why my sister?" she screams at him.

But his answer is a grin. A chuckle that becomes a boisterous laugh. "You people," he says with a laugh, shaking his head. "You people with your drama just continue to amaze me. Margot, you have a business, a responsibility. You work for me. So you're the last person I expect to be telling me who I should and shouldn't have. I hired you to do what you do because you're the only person without a conscience. Then you have the nerve to blackmail me with it." His eyes turn from jovial musing to stone. "Your sister, as far as I am concerned, is fair game."

For a second Thandi thinks she sees Margot lose her ground, but when she turns to Thandi, her eyes are steady. "Everything I do is for you. You are the reason why I work hard, you ungrateful—"

"So that I can pay you back tenfold, right?" Thandi asks, cutting her off. "Isn't that what you always say? That one day I will pay you back tenfold? Now I know it's because you owe him! My scholarship? That was his money!" She gestures to Alphonso with her hand. "You use me to justify your dirty work. That's all I've ever been to you and Delores, a way out. Your own conscience won't do it for you, so you pull me into it."

Margot raises her hand to slap Thandi, but it stops midair when Thandi says, "Go ahead." Thandi knows she has spoken the truth. She sees her words wrap themselves lovingly around her sister's neck. She steps closer to Margot. They are the same height. Thandi always thought her sister was a few inches taller. That too was an illusion.

Margot shudders. She loves nothing in this world except Thandi. She wants her to be successful, but she has wanted so much more for herself too. Now she feels as though she's been emptied. "*No compassion, no conscience, no heart.*" That's what Verdene said to her when Margot confessed that she knew her precious pink house would be worth nothing, that River Bank would be sacrificed. Verdene's love turned to ash before Margot's eyes. Margot looks at Thandi now, all that's left. "You owe me. For all I have done for you, sacrificed for you. You. Owe. Me."

Thandi, whom she clothed, sheltered, fed, gave every bit of herself to. With her body she shielded her sister from Delores's wrath. Gave her an opportunity to get away. To be better than them so she wouldn't have to sacrifice anything. But instead of gratitude in Thandi's eyes, Margot sees the looming resentment.

"You don't even know yuhself. My childhood was spent like a hundred-dollar bill on you. Everything you needed was put on me. If yuh needed formula, I had to sleep wid yuh father to get it. If yuh cry fah hunger, I had to feed you. If yuh wanted a special toy, I had to get down on my knees an' do more than play. I had to play wid yuh daddy too. "

Thandi doesn't say a word. Her eyes are a pair of dark round circles, empty of understanding, struggle.

"When yuh got into that school, I had to work overtime so that you could go. But not even that was helping, so I asked Alphonso to write that check. You talk about being used? Walk a day in my shoes an' you'll know what dat mean. I stayed in dat shack when I could have moved on with my life, because I was afraid Delores would have done to you what she did to me. So where yuh get the right to judge me? Now tell me, Thandi, once and for all: if it's not to be the doctor we prayed you were going to be, then, What. Do. You. Want?" Margot stretches this question between her teeth.

Thandi glances over at Alphonso as though seeking his permission.

"I want Charles to be free. I want the charges dropped against him, and the reward. I want us to be together."

Margot chuckles at this. "Really? Is that it?" A lump of pity rises in Margot's throat, seeing her sister's rounded shoulders, her young, pretty face bleached and sullied with confusion and defeat. How many girls has Margot seen this way? How many girls has she told to work for what they want? Girls her sister's age and younger. "*Mek me proud*," she tells them. They bring business to the island that shuns them, lumps them like logs to be eaten away by the elements. Or rather, leaves them to sink at sea. Margot collects them one by one and gives them a new life. A new way to claim the freedom they were denied. Terrified of what the experience might bring, these girls cling to Margot for guidance. And very methodically, she turns them out, daring them to either sink or swim. Never in a million years had she thought it possible to let go of Thandi this way. She thought she would always be the ship on which Thandi sails. The buoy that keeps her afloat. But it occurs to her that maybe her sister will only learn how to swim when she, like Margot, is pushed into the deepest parts of the ocean—that she'll be able to manage out of sheer will for survival. Not even Pregnant Heidi's waves will be able to deter her. So Margot leans in and kisses her sister gently on the forehead for what will be the last time. And, very gently, she pushes her toward Alphonso. "Mek me proud."

40

MARGOT WAKES UP IN THE BEACHFRONT VILLA—HER VILLA— surrounded by damp, rumpled sheets. She sweated through the sheets again, though the overhead fan spins and spins above her king-sized canopy bed with its dark wood frame and its white netting. She cannot remember her dream, not even the tail end of it that still wraps itself around her neck and chokes her. It's the fourth time in a row this week that this has happened. She looks around the large bedroom, where daylight has crept through the shutters, and touches her neck. Earlier she had clawed at hands that were not there. Her skin is raw, bruised.

"Desrine?" she calls after her house girl. But then she remembers that Desrine, entering through the back door from her cottage, doesn't come until eight, which is around the time Margot leaves for work in the black Range Rover parked in the driveway. If Desrine were already here, Margot would have heard the *slap-slap* sounds of her slippers echoing on the marble tiles. All she hears now is the *tap-tap* of raindrops on the windowsill and on the upper veranda that her master bedroom door opens on to. It has been raining for days, as if to make up for last year's drought.

Margot throws off the bedcover, rises up from the sturdy mattress, parts the netting, and moves from the bedroom, padding lightly, as though the marble tiles might crack with her footsteps. She walks from room to room, opening and closing the arched French doors, her long silk robe sweeping the floor behind her, as she searches for . . . what? She doesn't know. Each of the three guest bedrooms, painted the color of the sky—not the gray that it has been these last few days, but blue—are empty, almost austere, like well-dressed strangers. She wraps herself in her robe and makes her way to the sunroom—the only place in her home where she feels like herself. Whatever that means. Each detail took months to perfect— the exposed wooden beams in the arched ceilings, the dark rattan furniture and white cushions, the brightly colored walls that she painted herself, experimenting with hibiscus-pink, Valencia-orange, and sunset-red, before deciding upon clean, clear white.

If Delores could see me now, she thinks, rubbing her neck where the gashes have turned to welts. Last Margot heard of her mother, Delores moved one parish over to Trelawny with Grandma Merle to be closer to the dock. She heard Delores has lost a lot of weight, her skin sagging on bare bones. It was Maxi who relayed the message. Margot had gone into town to deposit money in the bank—an errand she doesn't trust Desrine with—when she bumped into him. His eyes examined her new clothes, her Italian-leather pumps, her Chanel handbag, the Range Rover keys dangling from her manicured fingers. He nodded his head slowly, though no one asked him anything. "*Tek good care ah yuhself, Margot,*" he eventually said. He spoke more formally—no jokes, no sexual innuendos, and no Rasta-man philosophy. And worse, it sounded final. Like a good-bye. When she turned away to go inside the bank, she almost lost her balance.

Margot sits on one of the wicker sofas in the sunroom and gazes at the panoramic view of the sea. It's a wonder to look at from up here. The view is more beautiful in the sunlight that usually streams in through the glass in enchanted beams. But lately the sky has emptied itself of everything, including stars. Like the ocean, it's deep and brooding, roaring over the city as if God has played a trick on mankind, the sea and sky switching places. It threatens to swallow Margot.

She pictures Verdene on every surface, their bodies pressed together as they listen to the sound of water hitting the glass exterior. Margot imagines them looking out at the lush green of the landscaped garden surrounded by rosebushes, hibiscus, bougainvillea, and manicured hedges. A garden that Verdene would've certainly taken pride in maintaining. Margot had built this room so that they could watch the sunrises and the sunsets together. But she has hired people to populate her property; people whose presence has kept her afloat—Cudjoe, an older man who used to be a farmer but turned yardman after his crops died in the drought, and Desrine. They both show up for work on time in the mornings—Cudjoe tending to the property and Desrine to the house. Though, whenever they are there, the house is still quiet—too quiet: the lull of the ocean, the intermittent billowing of curtains by the breeze. In River Bank she was used to hearing the crowing of roosters. But here, in Lagoons, when she wakes up, there is silence, as though the day has held its breath. Desrine and Cudjoe speak in whispers to each other or make no sound at all after their initial, "*Howdy, Miss Margot.*" It's this frozen formality that sparks an occasional burst of fire inside Margot's chest that makes her snap at them for no reason. *"Desrine, didn't I tell you to stop using that blasted cleaning liquid? It affect my sinus. What yuh want to do? Kill me?"* or *"Cudjoe, what am I paying you for? To sit under dat tree? Don't t'ink ah not watching! There's plenty more people like you in Montego Bay. Half ah dem need a job."*

This, she hopes, would force them into a conversation, or even a protest. But that never happens. They simply nod in agreement and apologize profusely. *"Sarry, Miss Margot. Sarry. It won't 'appen again."*

From time to time, strangers enter and leave—people she meets at the new hotel she manages. Most times it's one or two of the girls she hires—the ones more willing to work extra for a bonus. Tired of pining over Verdene, Margot lives from one orgasm to the next, trying to fill her loneliness with other bodies before kicking them out under the awestruck gaze of the night stars. Never mind if Desrine sees them from her cottage in the back. The girl has been trained to see and unsee. To hear and unhear. When Margot hired her, she had hoped for the closeness she once shared with her sister. Desrine is young, with dark velvet skin and a gaze that flutters away quickly like a skittish bird.

The welts on Margot's neck sting as though aggravated by the nightmare. Since the hotel opened last October, tourists have fallen victim to Pregnant Heidi's waves. One woman disappeared when she went for a swim in the deep part of the sea, and a little boy almost drowned when a wave reached for his leg and pulled him under as it receded from the shore. It's costing the hotel millions to install breakwaters and settle lawsuits, which inevitably have forced Alphonso to cut back on other expenses—like salaries.

When the rain finally lets up, Margot makes her way to the other side of the villa, walking through the house. Along the way, she passes the kitchen with the stone countertops, the living room that opens onto the pool terrace. The grass glistens with rain, and the bright green leaves of the mango, palm, and banana trees shudder under the weight of water. There's a small fountain by the pool, where a naked female statue pours water into a base that is shaped like an oyster—an inspiration Margot took from one of Thandi's drawings. She had kept it, though Thandi, like Verdene, has faded from her life as if she were never there. The last Margot heard of her sister, she had moved to Kingston. Maybe she'll make something great of her life, Margot thinks, examining the statue, which was carved to perfection by a young Rasta fellow Margot found on the street. "*Will I be paying for all this water?*" she once asked the landscaper she hired to install the fountain. The man had looked at Margot with his one good eye like she spoke another language. "*Is from di sea, miss. Unless di sea disappear, di wata won't stop pour. Seawata free.*"

As Margot stands on the pool terrace, the sun, which hasn't shown itself in days, makes its way from behind the soft, dove-gray clouds, bright and unflinching. The rectangular pool shimmers before Margot. Everything glitters in the new sunlight, just like Margot had always thought it would. Except for her lone, grainy figure on the water's surface, dark in the face of the sun.

Acknowledgments

It is with great honor that I express my overwhelming gratitude to those who made this book possible—those who provided me with advice, wisdom, encouragement, support, mentorship, instruction, and opportunities. Without you, *Here Comes the Sun* would not have been the book that it has shaped up to be.

Many thanks to my amazing agent and reader, Julie Barer, who believed in this book; my wonderful editor, Katie Henderson Adams, for loving this book and going above and beyond for it; Cordelia, Peter, Philip, Bill, and the entire W. W. Norton/Liveright team; Michael Taekens, for loving the book and opting to work for it; my mentor, Marita Golden, for her unwavering, unmatched support and encouragement from the get-go; David Haynes, for your vision and insight; Janae Galyn Hoffler, for being my dedicated, phenomenal reader; Erica Vital-Lazare and the *Red Rock Review* team, for publishing my very first story; Laura Pegram, Juliet P. Howard, and Ron Kavanaugh, for nurturing me and other writers in search of community and an outlet.

I am grateful for the MacDowell Colony and the Hedgebrook Residency, for providing me with the space and time to write; the Barbara Deming Fund, for the gift that enabled me to create; and Sewanee Writers' Conference, Kimbilio, Lambda Literary, and Hurston/Wright, for providing fellowship.

Special thanks to the staff of Silver Sands Villas in Duncans, Trelawny, especially Tanesha, Kimesha, Miss Claudette, and Tracy-Ann, for your loving support and insight as I wrote this story; and also for the opportunity to be a part of a family. My heartfelt thanks always to the following cast of phenomenal people in alphabetical order: Alistair Scott, Brian Morton, Cheryl Head, Dahlia Campbell, Daniel Townsend, David Hollander, Dennis E. Norris II, Diana P. Miller, Diana Veiga, Dionne Jackson-Miller, Dolen Perkins-Valdez, Donovan Rodriques, Joan Silber, Jessica Deliazard, June Frances Coleman, Karenn Cohen Jordan, Kate Schmier, Kathleen Hill, Keisha Phipps, Krystal Brown, Laura Diamond, Lorraine Correlley, Mary Morris, Melesia Senior, Michael A. Fanteboa, Michelle Y. Talbert, Nancy Diamond, Natalie Wittlin, Nelly Reifler, Patrick Wilson, Rafael Flores, Romaine McNeil, Sadeqa Johnson, Sanderia Faye, Sharon Gordon, Shayaa Muhammad, Sheri-Ann Cowie, Soraya Jean-Louis McElroy, Stephen O'Connor, Timothy Veit Jones, Tracy Chiles McGhee, and ZZ Packer.

Also, I will forever be grateful for Professor Duane Esposito, for you knowing my destiny before me. Tina Whyte, for being the first real writer that I know and who inspired me to write my own stories! Verdene Lee, Ken Glover, and the Wari House girls, for enriching my experience at Cornell University; the University of

Michigan, Ann Arbor, where I wrote many a first draft and buried them; the Sarah Lawrence College MFA Program, for asylum. R. Erica Doyle, OyaBisi Id, Julia Fierro, and the Sackett Street Writers' Workshop, for the courage to venture back into writing; and my Stuyvesant Writing Workshop students for being great teachers. Also, to the greats, Toni Morrison, Paule Marshall, Edwidge Danticat, Zora Neale Hurston, and Marlon James, who gave me permission.

I am grateful to my parents—Sharon Tucker-Gordon and Danville Dennis—who have instilled in me the importance of hard work; and to the rest of my family: Lewis "Louie" Benn, Juliet Jeter, Eugenia "Cooky" Benn, Joe Murray, David Watkins, Carol Horton, and Charles "Turkey" Benn, for your understanding and support.

And of course, my gratitude goes out to my beloved homeland, Jamaica, my muse and home of my grandmother Rowena "Merna" Hunter and my great-grandmother Addy—the woman who gave me the courage and freedom to write and live freely.

Finally, much gratitude to my amazing wife, reader, editor, listener, Emma Benn. Without you and your unconditional love, all this would not have been possible. Thank you so much for your patience and for putting up with me.

ABOUT THE AUTHOR

NICOLE DENNIS-BENN has received fellowships from Hedgebrook, MacDowell, Lambda and the Sewanee Writers Conference. Born and raised in Kingston, Jamaica, she lives with her wife in Brooklyn, New York, where she teaches writing. *Here Comes the Sun* is her first novel.

www.nicoledennisbenn.com